Everlasting

Also by Nancy Thayer
in Thorndike Large Print

My Dearest Friend
Spirit Lost
Morning

Everlasting

Nancy Thayer

THORNDIKE~MAGNA
Thorndike, Maine U.S.A.
North Yorkshire, England

Library of Congress Cataloging in Publication Data:
Thayer, Nancy, 1943-
    Everlasting / Nancy Thayer.
        p.   cm.
ISBN 1-56054-181-4 (alk. paper : lg. print)
1. Large type books. I. Title.
[PS3570.H3475E9   1991b]   91-15593
813'.54—dc20   CIP

British Library Cataloging in Publication Data:

A catalogue record for this book is available from the
British Library.
ISBN 0-75050-263-0

Thorndike Press Large Print edition published in 1991
by arrangement with Viking Penguin, a division of
Penguin Books USA Inc.

Large Print edition available in the British Common-
by arrangement with Macdonald & Co., Ltd.

Cover design by Tom Odle.

The tree indicium is a trademark of Thorndike Press.

This book is printed on acid-free, high opacity paper. ∞

*This book is dedicated
to the memory of my brother
William S. Wright II*

I WOULD LIKE TO THANK

Mark Hagopian, florist at the Ritz-Carlton in Boston, for generously giving me information, anecdotes, and insights;

Rhon Logan, florist at For Any Occasion in New York, for showing me around New York's flower district at five-thirty one March morning and for sharing his wealth of information; and especially

Harrie Wagtenveld, florist at Grass Roots in Nantucket, who was endlessly knowledgeable, patient, creative, instructive, and kind.

The florists mentioned above are good-humored, generous-spirited, charming, and highly ethical. Any negative qualities possesssed by the florist in this novel are absolutely her own.

CHAPTER 1

Everly
Christmas Night 1960

Home is where you go for Christmas, Catherine thought, but she wondered what "home" meant. If home was a building, then this expansive old Victorian folly of her grandmother's stuck out in East Hampton was her home. It certainly wasn't her parents' gloomy apartment on Park Avenue. Her brother thought Everly was boring; her sister thought it was creepy; but Catherine had loved this labyrinthine house with its tangled gardens all of her life.

At Miss Brill's, where she'd been at boarding school for the past five years, there was a girl whose parents were diplomats; they lived in a different country every year. For her, home was her parents; she was at home when she was with them. It wasn't that way for Catherine. She was her parents' oldest child, but not their favorite, and in fact the amazing thing was that she seemed to have nothing in common with them at all. The older she grew, the more different she felt. She did love her brother and sister, though; they were younger than she was, still children, and they had no idea of the secrets in her heart. Yet it was when she was with them that she felt truly at home.

Downstairs, they were preparing for the party. Christmas Eve the family exchanged presents, and Christmas morning Santa came, but Christmas night was for the adults. It was 1960, and the routine had remained unchanged since just after the war, when her grandmother first began her now famous Christmas parties. A formal cocktail hour began the evening, followed by a lavish buffet dinner, to which the children were allowed to come if they behaved with impeccable manners.

The third floor of Everly was the nursery floor, with bedrooms for each of the three children, a large playroom, and extra bedrooms for visiting friends. Shelly and his friend George Collier were in Shelly's room building a complicated structure from electric Tinkertoys. Ann was being dressed by Miss Smith.

Catherine was sewing.

She'd been sewing since this morning, when Miss Smith presented the three Eliot children

10

with their Christmas clothes. Catherine and
Ann were given dresses made out of rustling
taffeta in a bright red, green, black, and
gold Christmas plaid, and Shelly was given
a matching vest to wear under his camel
hair blazer. Catherine and Ann had gone to
Catherine's room together to try on their
dresses, which had been cut exactly the same
way: a sexless little-girl style, full, long-
sleeved, the material falling straight from the
shoulders to the floor in a wide A. The
collars and cuffs were of intricate white lace.
The dresses were beautiful, and ten-year-old
Ann, with her blond hair and blue eyes,
looked like a Christmas angel, but Catherine
felt like Alice in Wonderland once she had
eaten too much cake and grown up so fast
that she hadn't had time to change her clothes.

Catherine had stared at herself in the mirror, her mouth tightening in resolve. She'd
slipped out of her dress and into a robe.

"Don't you like it?" Ann had asked nervously.

Catherine had knelt, put her hands on her
sister's arms, and smiled.

"Ann. How old are you? You've just turned
ten. Shelly's almost twelve. But I'm almost
eighteen. Your dress looks perfect on you.
But my dress makes me look like a giant
circus baby! You know it does."

11

"I think Mother wants us to look like children."

"Yes. That's what she wants. But that's not what she's going to get. I'm not a child anymore."

"Oh, Catherine. What are you going to do now?"

Catherine had hugged Ann against her. "Don't you worry about that. I've got a plan. Go on now, find Miss Smith."

As soon as Ann had headed reluctantly to her own room, Catherine swooped down on the horrid Christmas dress. She turned it inside out, studied it, then with great care began to rip it apart at the seams. All Christmas Day, while the adults slept off their Christmas Eve indulgences and Shelly and his friend George ran screaming through the gardens, falling into the shrubbery with hair-raising shrieks, while Ann played dress-up with her porcelain doll, Catherine had cut and fitted and sewed. She used an old swimming suit top as a pattern. When she was through, she had constructed a dress from the Christmas material that had a full skirt but a tight and strapless bodice. She would wear no jewelry. At seventeen Catherine had the slender, wraith-like waist and hips her mother torturously dieted for and the swelling full bosom that her mother lost whenever she succeeded in her dieting.

Now she clipped the thread that closed the last seam, shook out the dress, and laid it across her bed. Looking down at it, she smiled. "There," she said, satisfied.

She stretched to relieve the ache in her neck and shoulders, then rose and stretched again. The room was stuffy. She went over to kneel on the cushioned window seat and cranked open the casement window. Cold December air blew in. It was not snowing, but the shrubbery and trees were iced with a frost that glittered like the laughter drifting up the stairs from the party below.

Catherine took a deep breath of the bracing air, then closed the window. It was time to get dressed.

She bathed, then carefully daubed herself with her grandmother's light perfume. There had been enough taffeta left over to make a wide headband, and now she twisted and tied it around her head so that it held back her abundant curly dark hair. Catherine's mother despaired of Catherine's hair. She thought it made her daughter look "ethnic." Marjorie also thought her daughter's hazel eyes were "boring." Only now was Catherine beginning to find another vision of herself, like a person turning from a clouded mirror to a clear one, yet caught between, unsure which reflection was the truth.

How many times Catherine had been summoned to her mother's room dressed for some occasion, how many times had she stood, head bent obediently as her mother labored over her hair — how many times had her mother, attempting to pull that dark, willful, untamable hair into pigtails or a braid, collapsed, sobbing, head on crossed arms, at her vanity table, knocking perfume bottles sideways, the Wedgwood dish of hairpins upended, scattering its contents across the carpet, as Marjorie cried in frustration?

Catherine was a disappointment to Marjorie, who wore her thick bronze hair in an elegant French twist, who spent every day of her life making herself beautiful. In the early years, this had been the supreme fact of Catherine's life. When, at twelve, she was sent to Miss Brill's School for Girls in Fairington, Connecticut, she was shy and frightened. Now she was about to graduate, and it had taken all these years for her to learn that her mother's criticisms of her had more to do with what her mother thought than with the way Catherine looked. Catherine's best friend and roommate, Leslie Dunham, one of those easily self-confident bossy girls, was mostly responsible for changing Catherine's opinion of herself. One spring Leslie had come down to New York with Catherine to stay with her at the Eliots' Park Avenue apartment. They were attending a graduation party for Kimberly Weyland's older brother. It was a big, elegant event, and they were almost hyperventilating with nervousness. Marjorie had come into Catherine's room while the girls were dressing. She was wearing her hair up in its usual French twist, and because this was one of her overweight phases, she was wearing black, which was slimming, and lots of jewelry to distract.

"Lovely dress, Leslie," Marjorie had said, leaning against the door, a cigarette in one hand, a whisky sour in the other. "Pretty color on you. But Catherine, darling, should you be wearing that shade of green? Don't you think it's a bit too Carmen Miranda? I mean, it makes me want to put bananas in your hair."

Catherine had shrugged. She only wanted her mother to go away and let her dress in peace. Marjorie had sighed and left to freshen her drink.

The moment Marjorie had gone, Leslie said, "What a bitch your mother is! Who talks that way to her daughter? Your mother's crazy! You never told me. Listen to me, Catherine, you look great in that dress."

"No, I don't. I don't look good in any

15

formals. My bones are too big and my boobs are too big and my coloring is too flagrant." Catherine was perfectly matter-of-fact. This was the truth as she knew it, as she had heard it stated over and over to dressmakers and saleswomen in department stores when her mother asked for help in making her daughter look presentable.

"Your coloring is too 'flagrant'? What does that mean? Catherine, you're sexy. I think your mother's nuts. I really do."

"Oh, well, you know how mothers are," Catherine said tactlessly, because Leslie's mother was dead, but quickly caught herself: "Sorry."

"But I *do* know how mothers are!" Leslie protested. "I've stayed with my aunt, I've summered with the Weylands, I know how mothers are — they love their children."

Catherine had shrugged again. She was amazed and grateful for this news flash from Leslie, but she was also on guard, protective of her mother, in spite of everything. It was one thing for her to think her mother was horrible, but for anyone else to say so . . . well, it was confusing, to say the least.

That night she had received so much attention from the boys at the dance that Leslie had forced giddy Catherine to admit that *perhaps,* even *probably,* her own mother might be wrong about her daughter. So like sunlight flashing over a dark horizon, the bright light of Leslie's vision beckoned at Catherine, urging her toward a new consideration of herself.

What Catherine could not articulate to Leslie or even to herself was the sense that although she wanted her mother to be wrong, she also, just as strongly, wanted her mother to be right. If her mother's judgment about her looks was wrong, then what else in life could Marjorie be wrong about? If Marjorie's standards were not the right ones, then whose were? For Marjorie was famous for her beauty, or as famous as any New York socialite could be. With her husband, Drew Eliot, by her side, she was caught in camera flash at the openings of everything her world considered important: operas, ballets, theater, museums, exhibitions, charity galas. Catherine read about her mother in the society section of newspapers and in *WWD* and the women's magazines, and everything she read confirmed Marjorie's sense of beauty and style.

But there was something deeper, too, a private sense of indignation Catherine felt at having her mother criticized. She didn't exactly know why, but Leslie's criticism of Marjorie wounded not Marjorie, but Catherine.

Yet Catherine knew she couldn't explain all this to Leslie, who had the least complicated life of anyone they knew. Leslie's mother was dead, and her father, a charming and brilliant man who dealt in antiques from the Orient, adored Leslie unequivocably. She was his only child, and they were a happy couple in their own way. Leslie's father let her have everything she needed, and when he was away — and he almost always was — there were friends who welcomed Leslie into their homes for Christmas or summer vacation. For Leslie, family life was simple, two people holding each end of one rope, but for Catherine there were so many people with so many complications that the lines of her family life were in a tangle, like a ball of yarn, and she felt caught in the middle.

Catherine had always longed for her mother's approval, but she had always been afraid to ask for it.

Yet on this Christmas night, she was asking — demanding. Scrutinizing herself carefully in the full-length mirror, Catherine found herself smiling. She felt something very like triumph. Her mother was right. She did not look like the rest of the family, with their healthy cool Anglo-Saxon faces. Catherine's skin was pale, but it was tinged with olive. When she was younger, after studying their bodies in detail, she and Shelly had decided that his blood must be blue and hers green.

18

Shelly's eyes were her father's green; Ann's were her mother's clear blue. But Catherine's eyes were a changeable hazel. Odd eyes. All this, topped with that dark curly hair, made Catherine look like no one else in the Eliot clan. She looked like a gypsy, or a witch, or some medieval European peasant/queen. Nothing looked more inappropriate on her than the navy plaid pleated skirt, navy V-neck sweater, and white blouse that was the school uniform.

The bold red plaid of the Christmas formal, however, looked good on Catherine. It gave her a Scottish look, and there was Scottish blood in the family. The headband, holding back her hair, tamed that hair a bit, and now she pulled on three-quarter-length white gloves for formality's sake. Her bosom was more exposed than she had intended, but she didn't think she looked immodest, only very feminine.

She went to find her brother and sister, in the nursery. "Wow! You look great!" Shelly yelled, surprised, while his friend George grinned and goggled and stared at her breasts.

"Oh, Cathy, you look like a princess, you look *amazing*," Ann said rapturously.

Even Miss Smith, their reserved governess, expressed her admiration. "You're turning

19

into quite a beautiful young lady, Catherine," she said, and Catherine's face went warm. Someone had called her beautiful — even if it was only unbeautiful Miss Smith.

So perhaps this dress would work a charm.

Catherine descended the stairs with high hopes, Ann and the boisterous boys behind her like an attending court, holding her gown in one hand, the other hand on the banister so she wouldn't trip, ready to make the entrance of her life.

A majestic Christmas tree, glorious with colored lights and brilliant glass ornaments, towered in the grand entrance hall. Catherine could have leaned over the banister to touch the golden star that topped the tree. For a moment she lost her self-consciousness and let herself be carried away in the beauty of it all. It was Christmas, and Grandmother Kathryn, usually so preoccupied and solitary, had once again transformed her home into a magic palace and thrown it open to her family and friends.

Catherine's grandfather, Drew Eliot, had built this house in the early 1920s, when he was famous and when his new British bride was homesick for her country estate. Back then, houses like this — replicas of English "country houses" — were still being built. Drew and Kathryn had named their home Everly, after Kathryn's British home, and they had spent a few good years in it before their divorce. Since then, Kathryn had lived in the enormous place alone, except for the occasional visit from her son when he was on school holiday. In those early years she had been thought eccentric, a single woman living in that vast house in East Hampton all year round, but in fact Kathryn *was* eccentric and didn't care what others thought. She was a devoted gardener, happy working in her garden when the weather was right, happy reading and planning her garden during the winter months. Now she was a grandmother, and her son and his wife and their children spent every Christmas at Everly, and each year they held a gala dinner and dance on Christmas night.

Kathryn didn't mind all this fuss and bother. After all, it happened only once a year. In her best moods she said it was good for the old house to get opened up and really used now and then; it reminded her of her British childhood. In her worst moods she said — to anyone in the family who'd listen — that perhaps all this folderol would satisfy her son and his family enough to make them leave her alone for a year. It wasn't such a bad trade. Her son, Andrew, and his wife, Marjorie, came out from Manhattan, and the three children came to Everly from their boarding schools, often bringing friends, and the adult Eliots invited their guests to stay the night, because the party always lasted until morning. Every room in the house was full of guests. Kathryn brought in extra help from the town to cook and serve. Children raced through the house, adults danced and quarreled and met for secret love affairs, everyone feasted and celebrated. Kathryn was satisfied that a year's worth of life went on in her house during those twenty-four hours.

And tonight even Kathryn, who tended to be absentminded and uninterested in people, actually had guests of her own, P. J. and Evienne Willington. It had just been announced that the Willingtons were bequeathing their staggeringly expansive East Hampton residence, a Gothic mansion and one hundred acres of gardens, to the state of New York, to become a museum and public garden upon their death. Their children didn't mind, the Willingtons confessed, for they would be receiving all the money and wouldn't have to be burdened with the upkeep of the estate. And the Willingtons were young, only sixty, so they had many years ahead in which to luxuriate in the gratitude of the state.

Catherine, Ann, Shelly, George, and Miss Smith stood at the door to the library, gazing at the beautiful room, the shining people. Grandmother Kathryn had had this room and the dining room splendidly decorated, with laurel roping looped over all the oil paintings and mistletoe tied with red ribbon to the chandeliers. Crystal bowls of hard red and green candies were set on every surface. The room was fragrant with evergreen and expensive perfume. The guests were gathering here for predinner cocktails.

The elderly Willingtons were seated with Kathryn, sipping sherry, discussing the newest breeds of Dutch tulips. Marjorie and Drew Eliot were laughing in the center of a group of friends, the men elegant in tuxes, the women's gowns swaying, as colorful as a field of flowers.

Tonight, as on other Christmas nights, Marjorie had adorned her gown with a bit of the same material used for her children's clothing. Her dress was full-skirted and full-sleeved, made of a vibrant rich gold satin that made the accompanying gold lights in her high-swept hair glisten. Around her waist was the matching red plaid material, tied in an enormous plump bow in the back. Her earrings were dangling, heavy and ornate, unusual for Marjorie, who usually preferred more sedate jewelry.

Catherine knew her mother looked magnificent. She could tell by the lift of her mother's head that Marjorie knew it and was glowing from the compliments of others. But she knew she looked beautiful, too.

It seemed to Catherine that all eyes in the room turned on the four of them as they entered. She saw her father's eyes widen as he looked at her. He excused himself from his group and approached Catherine and the others, his face beaming with happiness.

"Merry Christmas, darlings," Drew said to his children, approaching them and kissing the girls formally on each cheek, then shaking hands with his son and his son's friend. "You all look wonderful. Come in and join us. Tonight, a special occasion, you can all have champagne. George, I don't think your parents will object, do you? Catherine, how grown-up you look. It's too bad there aren't some young men here for you to dazzle."

Their father was leading them into the room when Marjorie came sweeping toward them, glittering but, Catherine realized with a cold shock of dismay, smiling her public smile. Marjorie's blue eyes were cold. Fear caught in Catherine's throat like a hard thing she could not swallow.

"Hello, everyone," Marjorie said smoothly.

"Shelly, dear, take George over and get him something to drink. Drew" — this was to her husband, and as she spoke she touched each person lightly on the shoulder, directing — "take Ann in and show her to your mother and the Willingtons. They'll be pleased to see such a pretty, *innocent* girl." Marjorie took her younger daughter's chin in her hand a moment and tilted Ann's face so that Ann could see the affectionate approval in her mother's eyes.

Now Catherine hoped for one dreamy instant that Marjorie, having dismissed the others, would link arms with her in the smug, snug way Marjorie had of making one feel chosen, and the two of them would walk into the room, two beautiful Eliot women together.

Marjorie bent close to Catherine and spoke directly into her face so that Catherine had to read her mother's lips as much as hear her words.

"Catherine," Marjorie said, "what have you done to that dress? You look like a *fool*. Go to your room and stay there. I don't want to see you again tonight."

Marjorie turned her back on Catherine then and swept regally back into the crowded room.

Catherine stood for a moment, stupefied with shame. But no one else was looking at her. She turned and, with what dignity she had left, slowly walked back through the entrance hall, past the towering, glittering Christmas tree, and up the wide curving stairway, away from the party, to the solitary third floor.

She shut herself in her room. Stunned, she sat on her bed, looking at her hands, waiting for her heart to stop thudding. It was lonely on the third floor, for even Miss Smith was down in the library. It was quiet, for the huge old house was well insulated by the thickness of its walls and floors; the party might have been a thousand miles away.

She hugged herself; she tried to keep from crying, but the painful sobs broke forth, hurting her chest. It had happened again. It always happened. She should not have pretended she could change it. She did not belong here, she was wrong here, always wrong. Catherine wept, hating herself and her family and her life.

She knew she had to escape, change, leave — but she didn't know where to go, or how.

If she didn't belong with the family she had been born to, then where did she belong?

The next day her father summoned her to the library. It was a little after noon, and the adults were just rising. Even Shelly,

George, and Ann were still asleep. The Christmas night revelry had lasted late into the night, as had Catherine's tears.

This morning Catherine thought her father looked old and tired, but handsome as always. He had a Bloody Mary, his typical morning drink, in his hand. He sat on a leather chair near the fireplace, but there was no fire lit this morning, only dead ashes as deep as the grate. Perhaps the worst and most British quality about Everly was that some rooms were impossible to heat. Catherine, in wool slacks and sweater, shivered.

"So, Pudding, sorry you couldn't be with us last night," her father said casually.

Catherine shrugged. She and her brother and sister knew that their father loved their mother with a slavish devotion that would prevent him from ever crossing her in the smallest thing. He would not protect his children, if it meant defying his wife.

"Your mother's been a bit miffed with you lately, Cathy," he went on. "This college thing, you know. You're really going to have to do something."

Catherine stared at her father. Many times she had heard her mother say to her father that he had inherited all of his famous father's charm and good looks but none of his intelligence or common sense, and Catherine knew her mother was right about this, as she was about so many other things. Now she knew that her father would have nothing helpful or surprising to say about the matter of her college applications — or rather, her lack of them. She was not planning to apply to college. In fact, she was not planning to go to college. If she didn't go, she'd be the only Miss Brill's girl in the history of that school not to attend college. The school guidance counselor and the headmistress were furious with Catherine.

It was not from rebelliousness that Catherine was not looking at colleges, but rather from apathy. As each year of her life progressed, she had less enthusiasm for it and its routines. Studying and taking tests bored her. She wanted action.

"It's simple," her father went on, "you *have* to go to college. People like us just don't not go to college."

"Maybe I don't want to be like you," Catherine said. She was speaking truthfully, for she knew she didn't want to be like her mother and father and their friends. The problem was that she had no idea in the world what she wanted to be instead.

"Oh, I don't think we have such bad lives," Drew Eliot, Jr., said complacently, looking around him at the luxurious room.

Catherine thought of pointing out to him that this house was his mother's house, built by his father, that he had never built a house himself; and that as far as she knew he didn't work at all, at anything. But she had been taught that it was vulgar to discuss money, and she had no idea what kind of money her parents had. Still, it seemed to her that the inherited prerogative to sit in a room of beautiful furniture was not sufficient justification for a well-lived life.

But Catherine remained silent. Shelly argued like a bull ox when confronted by his parents, and Ann either went into pathetic orphaned-child tears or into full-blown floor-kicking tantrums, but Catherine tried to hold her tongue. She knew this irritated her parents, but she found it too difficult to break into speech. Her most eloquent pleas had never helped her before.

"Your mother has asked me to pass on an ultimatum to you, Catherine," her father said now, drawing himself up on his chair and trying not to look hung over. "If you apply and get into a college, any college, we will continue to support you in every way. If, however, you choose to continue this bizarre path of rebellion, we have no choice but to tell you that we will not support you. Not in any way. Once you turn eighteen, you'll be on your own. We won't allow you to live in the Park Avenue apartment or to summer with us on the Vineyard. You'll have to find your own living accommodations — everything."

"What about money?" Catherine said. Terror made her bold. She certainly couldn't stay at school after this May when she graduated. If she couldn't live at her home in New York, where would she live?

"What do you mean?"

"I mean — don't I — isn't there some kind of trust set up for me? Don't I have some money of my own?"

"What money there was left for you went to pay your tuition all these years, and to buy your clothes and traveling expenses, and so on. You've had an expensive childhood, Catherine."

"But Grandfather — "

"All of my father's money is in this house. And that belongs to my mother, to do with as she wishes."

"But if I don't go to college, couldn't I have the tuition money?"

"No."

"But why not? If you don't have to pay tuition, why couldn't you give me the money instead — "

"To do what with? To throw away? Why

30

should we give any money to an uneducated, disobedient daughter? It's out of the question, Catherine."

Catherine and her father sat staring at each other then, antagonists.

Finally her father, weary, rose. "Well, I've said what I have to say. You've got the rest of the semester to think about it. I'm sure Mrs. Plaice will help you find some college that will admit you in spite of your grades. I don't understand you, Catherine, nor does your mother. Testing indicates that you have superior intelligence, but your grades have been abysmal, as you know. You just have not applied yourself. We have tried to help you, and repeatedly you've met us with a brick wall. Quite frankly, we're tired of battling with you. We've given you everything a girl could want, and in return you give us ingratitude and insubordination. If you don't go to college, I'll tell you in all honesty, we'll just wash our hands of you."

In any other place, Catherine would have risen now, too, and gone off with these last words from her father. But the library at Everly was a comfortable place in spite of its grandeur. Perhaps it was the presence of her grandmother's cats and the cat hair that no amount of dusting could completely remove, or the worn spots on the sofas and chairs where people had curled, reading, and that had been rubbed by countless children's hands as they had crouched behind the furniture, playing hide-and-seek. Perhaps it was the books themselves, which reminded her of different worlds beyond her own.

"Well, Dad, where do you think I should apply?" Catherine asked. She caught her father's look — he was on guard, expecting some smart-aleck reply from her. But now she pitched her voice as perfectly as she could to the register of civility — even servility. "There are so many colleges. It's confusing. And I don't know what to major in. I don't know how to choose."

"Isn't that what Mrs. Plaice is there for? Isn't she supposed to help you choose colleges?"

"Yes. But I want to know what you think."

She could feel her father's impatience with her. He ran his hand over his forehead.

"I've got a cracking headache," he said. "If you need to talk more, let's do it later."

"Well — all right, Dad." Vaguely disappointed, Catherine left her father, shutting the door carefully so as not to aggravate his headache. She climbed the stairs to the second floor. The house was still quiet. Without thinking she went down the long carpeted hall to the left wing, where her parents had their bedrooms. She knocked on her mother's door. When there was no answer, she turned the knob quietly. The door was unlocked. She stepped inside.

"Mom?" she called. Then, remembering how her mother hated being called "Mom," she said, "Mother?"

A wicker bed tray sat on the floor with a silver pot of coffee and several stacks of emptied plates. The bedclothes were rumpled, and the room was overheated — how had her mother managed so much warmth in any one room at Everly? The heavy brocade drapes had been pulled shut against the winter cold and light, and the room was dim. Conflicting aromas hung drowsily in the warm room like a fog: her mother's expensive perfume, the morning's coffee and bacon and eggs, the sharp tang of alcohol, cigarette smoke.

The bathroom door opened, and before her mother could appear another smell drifted out: the pungent, thin, familiar reek of vomit.

The loud rush of water in the flushed toilet died down, and in the following silence, Marjorie Montgomery Eliot entered her bedroom. Her bronze hair hung around her head, released from its twist but still shaped by it, the thick ends of her hair curling up. Marjorie's skin was pale and puffy, so puffy that the skin above her eyes and beneath her eyelids stood out in balloonlike ledges. Marjorie was holding the silk wrapper of her gown closed, one hand pressed against her stomach, as if she were holding her stomach in. She walked with caution to the chaise and gingerly settled her body on it.

"What are you looking at?" she said to her daughter. "I'm just hung over."

Now Catherine could see the other signs — the golden edge of a large gift box of gourmet nuts and candied fruits protruding from under the chaise, the wastebasket brimming with crumpled emptied sacks of smuggled-in potato chips and pretzels, the serving tray from the kitchen set on the dresser, the silver dome hiding whatever remained of Marjorie's late night or early morning snack. Old memories of similar smells and gagging sounds, of the sight of her mother's head hanging into the toilet, her sun-streaked hair dank with sticky vomit, lurched through Catherine's mind.

Catherine shrugged. "Dad was telling me about your ultimatum," she said. "About colleges. I thought I should talk it over with you."

Marjorie, with great effort, waved her hand, as if swiping at a fly. "Not now. Later. Go away." She covered her eyes with a trembling hand.

Catherine turned and left the room. She

34

climbed the stairs back to the nursery. Her parents would leave for their apartment in the city today, but Miss Smith and the three Eliot children would remain here one more night, before going on up to Vermont to a lodge for a ski trip . . . one of their parents' Christmas presents to them and yet another way of keeping their children away.

Catherine walked up and down the long hallway, peering into the rooms. Shelly and George had already gone outside. Miss Smith was playing a heated game of Sorry with Ann on Ann's bedroom floor. Catherine went into her room and sank down on her bed.

If only Leslie were here. If only she were Leslie. She envied her friend because Leslie had what Catherine didn't — Leslie had talent. Leslie wanted to be an important painter, and that mattered to her more than anything else in the world. Even better, the art teachers assured Leslie that she had talent as well. Leslie knew exactly what she wanted to do when she graduated: she was going to study at a famous art school in Paris. She would live in a garret on the Left Bank, where she would paint and have lots of artistic love affairs.

Catherine had tried painting, but although she had some skill, she had no real aptitude for it. She had tried piano and flute lessons and for a while, when she was younger, had dreamed of being a prima ballerina, until her ballet teacher sympathetically pointed out that no matter how strenuously Catherine dieted, she would always have a bust that was, well, inappropriate for a dancer. She was no good at sports, because they bored her.

Over and over again during chapel, the girls were reminded of their good fortune in life, their *exceptional* good fortune at being Miss Brill's girls, at the quality of their education, and at the duty this imposed on them to hold the standard high when they went out into the world. But no one had anything specific to suggest to Catherine. When she asked them what should she do with her life, the teachers and counselors grew impatient: why, she could do *anything,* she didn't have to earn a living, she was well educated, she could go where her fancy took her. "Try volunteer work," was as specific as they got, but Catherine had the example of her mother, that famous volunteer, before her, and she knew that was not the choice for her.

"Bored people are boring people," Mrs. Plaice, the counselor, often said, and if so, then God knew Catherine was boring. Now she twisted on her bed, healthy, well fed, energetic, lost. She didn't want to go skiing with her siblings and Miss Smith, and she didn't want to go to college, but what did she want to do?

Restless, angry with herself, she rose, straightened her clothes, and went back downstairs. The guests were up and around now in the dining room, laughing at the long mahogany table, having coffee and a late breakfast. Now and then a car would start up with a roar and someone would leave, rolling down the long white pebble driveway until it disappeared around a bend of evergreens.

No one was in the library now, but someone had made a fire that glowed and flared, warming the room. Catherine pulled her favorite old leather photograph albums from the shelf and curled up on a leather chair. The present faded as she lost herself in pictures of the past. Here was her grandfather, Andrew Matson Eliot, in a full-length beaver coat, top hat, and red mittens, waving at the camera from a group of friends, looking as if he were having more fun than any man had a right to have. He was wickedly handsome. Catherine had heard stories about him. She knew he'd been a cad and was probably responsible at least in part for her grandmother's retreat from all others. Still, he always looked so exuberant. Catherine smiled every time she saw his face. She wished he'd lived long enough for her to know him.

Here were the pictures of Kathryn's childhood home, the original Everly in England. Most of the photographs were blurry and curling with age, showing the house sprawling in a grand and formal dilapidation.

In contrast, the Boxworthy family, who now owned the British Everly, looked young, robust, infinitely attractive. Years ago, when Kathryn's dissipated brother, Clifford, sold the estate to the Thorpes who then sold it to Dr. Boxworthy and his wife, Madeline Boxworthy had written to Kathryn Paxton Eliot. She wanted to revive the gardens and asked for any helpful advice Kathryn might have about how to go about it. This had resulted in a hearty correspondence between the two women, including eventually the arrival of photographs of the three Boxworthy children: splendid Ned, the eldest, and the sisters, Elizabeth and Hortense. Ned was Catherine's age, the girls were a few years younger. They had always been Catherine's dream family. They always looked so carefree, so jolly, as if caught in a bit of mischief. She wanted to *be* them. Or at least, someday, she wanted to meet them.

Suddenly restless, Catherine laid the albums aside and went off to search for her grandmother. Perhaps Kathryn would be in a sociable mood.

Catherine found her grandmother in the conservatory. This was a room Catherine was not fond of, for she found the plants that wintered here — the monstera and philodendron, schefflera and dracaena, the rubber plants and all the hanging plants whose tendrils brushed against her face or caught in her hair — slightly menacing, with their gnarled woody stems and far-reaching, beseeching leaves. Her grandmother's joy was an enormous jade tree, as fat and glossy in its huge Chinese pot as a Buddha. She had been growing the thing for years.

Kathryn was watering her African violets. First she stuck her finger under each fuzzy leaf, testing the moistness of the dirt, her lips moving as she mumbled instructions about the plants to herself. At sixty-three she was still as ethereal in her beauty as an angel, and just about as approachable.

Every person in her family was a mystery to Catherine. Because her father favored daring, incorrigible Shelly, and her mother doted on baby-sweet beautiful Ann, the only living adult left to Catherine was her grandmother. She had after all been named after her.

But Kathryn was the most mysterious of all. At least Marjorie made it clear that Catherine was the embarrassment and Ann the embellishment of her life. Obviously Drew would feel closer to his male child. But Kathryn was an ambiguous woman, cool and vague, who made only one thing clear: that she preferred the company of flowers to that of people.

Catherine knew from the albums and newspaper clippings in the Everly library that her grandmother had been exquisitely beautiful as a young woman, with a delicate figure, blue eyes, blond hair, and serene, elegant manners. It was no wonder that Andrew Matson Eliot, a brash egotistical New York journalist, fell in love with her during World War I and brought her home to live with him. It was no wonder she fell in love with him — he was handsome, charismatic, infinitely charming. But he loved society and could never get enough of people, while his wife found people exhausting and became increasingly obsessed with her plants and gardens. Before the Depression — and before their divorce — he had bought her this house and the surrounding six acres. The rest of her life she had spent transforming the place into her garden, which was really several different sorts of gardens: an open meadow, which she had sprinkled with wildflowers and bulbs, the forest, the formal garden with its paths and fountains and steps down to the lily pond, the kitchen garden, the cutting garden. Kathryn had stopped pining for her English country home. She had been happy at this Everly — so happy that she hadn't needed anything or anyone else.

Kathryn seldom left Everly, but she always kept it open to members of her family. Catherine knew that if she chose, she could just move into the big old house. Her grandmother's maid, Clara, would feed her and shelter her, and her grandmother would never ask when she was planning to leave or why she didn't go to college or do something with her life. She could disappear from life here.

But the last thing in the world Catherine wanted to do was to disappear.

"Good afternoon, Cathy," her grandmother said now, and presented a powdery white cheek for a kiss.

"I was in the library. Looking at the albums. I thought you might — "

"Look," her grandmother said as if Catherine had not been speaking. Kathryn indicated with their eyes what Catherine should see.

Through the open conservatory doorway, Catherine and her grandmother watched as a lady, one of their guests, pointed up at the mistletoe which was tied by a red ribbon to the living room chandelier. A man smiled, took the woman in his arms, and kissed her.

"Mistletoe," Kathryn began.

Catherine knew at once by the tone of her grandmother's voice that the older woman was about to launch into one of her lecturing spells. Sometimes she and Shelly and Ann enjoyed these, for their grandmother was full of unusual and often amusing information. The grandchildren had gone into giggling fits at the news that dandelion had powerful diuretic qualities and was known in Europe as "piss-en-lit," or piss-a-bed or pittle-bed.

But often Kathryn's speeches about her beloved flowers were rambling and incomprehensible, full of Latin and scientific terms. Today, because Catherine was bored, and because she needed someone in her family to pay attention to her, she tried to look interested.

"We treat it so frivolously," Kathryn said. "Yet mistletoe has a fascinating history. It used to be thought sacred; it used to be worshiped!"

Kathryn sat down on her enormous high-backed wicker chair, which rose above her and around like a throne. Catherine sank onto a wicker stool.

"Mistletoe is a parasite, you know. It has no roots. Think of that. No roots. Then how does it grow? It belongs to Santalales, the sandalwood order of flowering plants who live off of other plants. In primitive times all these plants were considered sacred because of their ability to survive without roots.

"You see, mistletoe grows best in oak trees, which have long been considered sacred. In the winter, when the oak tree leaves have fallen, the mistletoe remains fresh and green. So mistletoe, which does not grow in the ground, but appears high in the sky, came to mean in many cultures 'life everlasting.' There are numerous superstitions about it, and it used to be thought the cure for all sorts of diseases."

Suddenly the older woman turned and looked directly at Catherine with her pale, magic blue eyes.

"Something to ponder, don't you think? That a living thing without roots, without a home, without nurturing and care, can still flourish, and more than flourish, thrive, and be useful, and even magical. Even if the host on which it begins has turned brown and hopeless, the mistletoe remains green and living. It can move on."

The old woman shifted on her wicker chair. She shook her head and rubbed her arthritic hands, as if smoothing the bones. "My back hurts. You're my favorite grandchild, Catherine. Sometimes I think you're the only one in my family who has any understanding of how important flowers and plants really are. But I must excuse myself. I must go lie down. I'm not as young as I once was. No, no, don't get up. I can manage to get my old body to my room alone."

Catherine watched as her grandmother, erect as always, but painfully erect, the straight carriage purchased by pain, rose and walked over the flagstones and out of the conservatory. She remained on her wicker stool, looking around her at the plants growing or hanging, green stalagmites or stalactites; it was as if she were inside a breathing, humid cave. She thought that her grandmother was probably a little crazy, but was *she* crazy to think her grandmother had been trying to tell her something? Did her grandmother think that she, Catherine, was a parasite on a dying tree? Did her grandmother see her own son so clearly?

Through the open French doors, Catherine could see the mistletoe hanging from the doorway. She crossed to it and, standing on tiptoe, reached up her arms and broke off a sprig. She didn't want to stick it in her hair — someone might think she wanted to be kissed — so she found a pin and fastened it on her sweater, just over her heart.

CHAPTER 2

When Catherine returned to Miss Brill's after Christmas break, she told Leslie about her parents' threats.

"They're bluffing," Leslie said flatly.

But the year unrolled into spring and early summer, and Catherine became the first Miss Brill's graduate to have "Unknown" printed in the spot in the school newspaper where other students had printed the name of the college they'd attend. Catherine received two warning letters and one warning phone call from her parents, then nothing. Silence. Over spring break in April, her parents took Shelly and Ann to Bermuda but didn't even contact Catherine about their plans. It was as if, for them, she'd stopped existing.

Luckily she was invited to Kimberly Weyland's home for some of the two-week vacation. The last few days of spring break she spent at Everly. Her grandmother was engrossed in the gardens already and was glad to have Catherine's help. Catherine worked at Kathryn's side, pruning the forsythia and other flowering shrubs, mulching around the rhododendrons, azaleas, and mountain laurel, preparing the ground for the cutting gardens, sowing the cornflower, sweet alyssum, larkspur, snapdragon, poppy, and sweet pea seeds. She enjoyed the physical, repetitive, meticulous work, the sun warm on her back, the air fragrant with lilac and hyacinth blooms, the only sounds bird-songs or the click clack of clippers and shears.

One night as she sat dining with her grandmother, she said shyly, "I like working here, Grandmother. Perhaps you should hire me as one of your gardeners."

Kathryn contemplated this suggestion, then shook her head. "I don't think so, dear. It wouldn't be good for my gardens or for you. You're too inexperienced. And you're too young to spend your life shut away out here."

Catherine was never certain just how far she could go with her grandmother into discussions of real life. "I guess you know I'm not going to college. Mother and Father have said I'm completely on my own when I graduate from Miss Brill's."

"Yes. I know. They told me."

Catherine waited for words of sympathy, wisdom, advice. Kathryn was silent. The whole room was silent except for the clink of Catherine's silver fork against the china plate.

"I don't know what I'm going to do, Grandmother." She was ashamed of the slight quaver in her voice. Kathryn had always disdained sniveling.

"No. Of course you don't. But it will come to you, Catherine." She looked directly at Catherine, her gaze intense, the blue as fiery as the dancing tip of a flame. "It will come to you."

Catherine's breath caught in her throat. Entranced, she waited.

Kathryn looked away. The moment passed. Pushing back her chair, Kathryn rose. "Shall we take our coffee in the den? There's a nature show on PBS I don't want to miss."

Catherine went back to Miss Brill's for the final two months of the term in even more of a fog than before. Now the season was heady with celebration and romance; every weekend there was a party or a dance to attend. Catherine had plenty of dates, but there was no one boy she loved; she thought if there had been, she would have married him, simply to have something definite to do with her life. It was not too late, the school counselor advised her, even now, to apply to a college. But Catherine held firm. That was not what she wanted.

Her family did not attend her graduation ceremony because they were embarrassed by her. They sent no graduation present. Marjorie called to tell Catherine that as soon as she moved out from her dorm, she was to stop by the Park Avenue apartment to collect her belongings.

"Do you know where you'll be living?" Marjorie asked.

"Not yet," Catherine said.

"You are an obstinate little fool," Marjorie told her.

"I know," Catherine agreed.

As she packed in her dorm room, she repeated her grandmother's words like a charm. "It will come to you."

Leslie's father flew all the way from Japan to watch his only child graduate. Afterward he drove Leslie and Catherine into New York, then took them for a celebratory dinner at the Rainbow Room. An odd, remote, utterly civilized man, Mr. Dunham remained a puzzle to Catherine. She'd met him many times. He was polite, but vague. "He's always off in the Orient, one way or another," Leslie said of him fondly, and it was true that when he wasn't actually in the East on his extended buying trips, he was remembering the Orient or planning his next trip there. But at their graduation dinner Mr. Dunham urged the girls to order whatever they wanted and made an obvious effort to take part in their conversation, for the one and only thing he loved more than the Orient was his daughter.

"Daddy," Leslie said over their baked Alaska, "Catherine's parents have sort of kicked her out since she refuses to go to college. So! *I* thought since I'm going to be in Paris for a few years, Catherine should stay at our place."

Catherine was so surprised, she nearly dropped her fork. Leslie hadn't said a word about this to her.

Mr. Dunham took a sip of wine. "Leslie, dear, I'm not sure — "

"It would actually be a great help to us, Dad!" Leslie interrupted her father in her enthusiasm. "You know our housekeeper wants to visit her son in Florida when we're not there, and you've said you don't like leaving the apartment empty. You're always traveling. I'll be in Paris. It makes perfect sense for Catherine to live in my rooms!"

Mr. Dunham smiled at his daughter. "Well . . ."

"Come on, Dad!" Leslie cajoled, stroking his hand. "Please?"

"All right. Yes. Of course. Catherine, please feel free to live at our place."

Leslie grinned triumphantly across the table at Catherine, then followed up her grin with a swift sharp conspiratorial kick on Catherine's shin. So easily, it was settled. It had come to her! Catherine thought, smiling.

The day after her graduation, Catherine stepped off the elevator into a small marble-floored foyer. She knocked on the door to Leslie's apartment.

Immediately the door opened and there was Leslie, hugging Catherine, grabbing at her suitcases, and pulling her inside all at once.

"Come in, come in! You're really here! This is wonderful! You look awful. Was it awful?"

Catherine shrugged. "Not really. I mean, no one was home when I went to collect my things. They're all on the Vineyard. I felt a bit odd, but all the drama was over long ago."

"Good! God, they're such creeps. Let's take your stuff to *your* room. Dad flew back to Japan yesterday."

Catherine followed Leslie down the long hallway. It was unusually hot for early June, but Catherine was strangely chilled. Walking down the windowless hallway, she shivered. For a few days now everything had seemed a little unreal, or rather she had seemed a little unreal. After the extreme routine and

50

protection of boarding school, the knowledge that she was out on her own was stunning. Things were moving so fast, she felt dizzy.

This was her new home. She'd been here often before, visiting Leslie, but now she looked at it with a different eye. Just off East Eighty-sixth, the apartment was huge, elegant, even glamorous, full of space and light and Oriental antiques. Leslie's father's rooms were at the opposite end. Mrs. Venito's quarters were off the kitchen. Leslie's end of the apartment had a suite of rooms, a bedroom and bath, and a large sunny room that had been her studio but that Catherine decided as she looked around she'd make into her private living room so she wouldn't muck up the Dunhams' elaborately pristine living room. She'd use the kitchen to cook her own meals.

"There!" Leslie said, plunking down Catherine's suitcases. "Time for lunch. Oh, Catherine, our last lunch together for who knows how long! I can't *wait* to get on that plane to Paris!"

Dutifully Catherine tagged along after Leslie that day, trying not to be a bore to her generous, spirited friend. She'd never envied Leslie more. Leslie was full of plans, hope, movement, color. In contrast, Catherine felt as white and paralyzed as a person in a coma.

The next morning Catherine went down to the street with Leslie to see her into the taxi that would drive her to the airport and her flight to Paris. Leslie was wearing huge hoop earrings and a dress that looked like an ensemble of flowing black rags. On Leslie the outfit looked artistic, but Catherine knew that if she put on anything like that, people would expect her to tell their fortunes. Leslie was Catherine's age, only eighteen. How had Leslie found her style so soon, her place in life? How would Catherine ever find hers?

The girls kissed and hugged good-bye. Catherine forced herself to keep smiling until Leslie's taxi had disappeared from sight. Then she let her smile fade. Her shoulders drooped. She went back into Leslie's apartment, back down the long hallway to her rooms, and lay down on the bed. She didn't move. She felt as flat and lifeless as a paper doll.

For a week Catherine stayed in her new room, a vegetable girl, waiting inertly for something to happen, for the rest of her grandmother's prediction to come true. "It will come to you," Kathryn had said. But nothing came, except Mrs. Venito knocking nervously at the door on the seventh day.

Catherine had to rise and move across the room to open the door. The housekeeper, nervously twisting a dazzlingly white apron in her hands, peered in.

"You are sick? You are well? You are all right? You need a doctor?"

"No, no, I'm fine, Mrs. Venito, thank you, just fine."

"It's just you are so quiet. You don't go nowhere. For a young girl you are so quiet. I worry."

"Don't worry. I'm fine. It's all right. I'm — making plans."

"Ah. Good girl. I see. Good girl."

Catherine stomped into the bathroom the moment Mrs. Venito went away, in order to curse without the housekeeper hearing her. "Old busybody!" she hissed. "Nosy old troublemaker! Why can't she leave me alone!" Then she saw her reflection in the mirror. She was wearing her terrycloth bathrobe. It was just after noon. She hadn't combed her hair. In fact, she hadn't washed her hair for the past week.

In a helpless fury at herself, at life in general, Catherine showered, set her hair, and dressed. She grabbed up her purse and stormed out of the apartment.

It was a perfect June day, but as she walked along she hated the day and she hated herself. Turning off onto Seventy-second Street, she caught sight of her reflection in a plate-glass window. She stopped, stared, and hated herself even more. There she was in her lavender *linen* dress with *shell* earrings, for heaven's sake, so *original* of her. When would she ever have any style of her own?

At first hazily, then with more clarity, as she stared at her reflection in the glass, masses of flowers appeared. Spring flowers: periwinkle and pink hyacinths, sunny daffodils, creamy and flame-red tulips, buckets and buckets of them. The flowers made her think of Everly.

Without another thought, she walked into the shop. She had only a little money left from her grandmother's Christmas check, but she had to buy some flowers to cheer herself up.

The bell on the door tinkled. A tiny old lady, rather a trollish-looking lady, came rushing up to Catherine. Clapping her hands together, she said, "Youf come about de shob!"

Catherine stared. The little woman was short and plump. Her hair was pulled back in a bun so untidy that most of it flew out around her head in a halo. Her eyes were bird-bright, dark as chocolate.

"I haf been nearly out of my mind, but now here you are!" the little bird-woman said.

"Excuse me?"

"You are here about de shob?"

"The job? I didn't — " The fragrance of flowers entranced her. A job! With flowers! "But I suppose — "

A short fat man in red suspenders and a red bow tie stormed in from behind the curtain that separated the front from the back of the shop. He glared at Catherine.

"Jan!" the little woman cried out. "She's come about the shob!"

Now the little man looked suspicious. He rolled onto the heels of his foot, tucked his thumbs into his suspenders, and squinted.

"So! You want a job. Where are your references? Do you have any experience?"

The little troll wife turned back to Catherine, looking worried, encouraging, and hopeful all at once.

Catherine took a deep breath. Then, in her best boarding school manner, she said, "My name is Catherine Eliot, and I've just graduated from Miss Brill's School for Girls. I have no retail experience. But I have spent many hours helping my grandmother and her gardeners in her garden in East Hampton, which is quite extensive, several acres, actually, so I know quite a bit about flowers and houseplants as well. As for references, I have none with me, but I would be glad to give you a list of names."

The little troll man looked surprised

55

enough to explode right out of his suspenders.

"*Gut!*" he yelled at Catherine. He turned to his wife. "Henny, find her the forms. I am late for the church." He bustled off behind the curtain.

My God! I've got a job in a flower shop! Catherine thought. She wanted to run home to write Leslie, to call her grandmother.

The bell tinkled. Behind Catherine, the door from the street opened. A distinguished-looking man in a gray suit entered.

"Good afternoon, Mrs. Vanderveld. Do you have a dozen nice red roses for me?"

"For you, I have sublime red roses!"

Smiling, head bobbing, Mrs. Vanderveld led the man over to a large glass refrigerated display case full of flowers in buckets.

At that moment the phone rang.

"Could you, dear?" Mrs. Vanderveld asked Catherine, her arms full of roses.

"Could I . . . ?" For a moment Catherine didn't understand. Then, her face flushed with embarrassment at her dimness, she raced for the phone. "Hello?"

There was a long silence on the other end.

"Hello?" she said again.

"Is this Vanderveld Flowers?" The voice was disdainful. At once Catherine's euphoria dissolved. She had begun all wrong. She should have answered the phone with the name of the shop. How could she think she could hold a job! She didn't even *know* anyone who worked, except for Patsy Wells, the scholarship girl at school.

Mrs. Vanderveld took the telephone, holding it to her ear with her shoulder while boxing the roses for the man. He paid and left. Mrs. Vanderveld hung up the phone. Catherine waited to be reprimanded.

"Oh, dear, oh, dear, I never can find a pen around here, and I must leave a message for Jan!" Mrs. Vanderveld cried.

A chance to redeem herself. Catherine looked down at the counter and the space underneath. It was a wooden warren of cubbyholes stuffed with papers, ribbons, scissors, little cards and envelopes, magazines, cloths, receipt pads, order pads, scribbled-on notepads, and a jumble of pens and pencils. Everything was on the verge of falling out onto the floor — which was already littered with stems, leaves, and bits of ribbon and paper.

Catherine found a pen, tested it on a scrap of paper, and turned to hand it to Mrs. Vanderveld, who had disappeared. Catherine stepped behind the curtain. The shop extended in a long and narrow rectangle to wide double doors at the far end. Two long tables stretched almost the entire length of the shop. They were covered, as were the shelves along one wall, with huge spools of ribbon, piles of tissue paper, cardboard to be folded into boxes, and sheets of bright foil. Here, too, the floor was carpeted with stem ends, leaves, flower petals, bright paper, and ribbon snippets.

Well, it's colorful, Catherine thought.

Mrs. Vanderveld was at the far end of the shop, next to an even larger walk-in cooler full of lustrous glowing flowers.

"Here's a pen, Mrs. Vanderveld," Catherine said.

"A what? What for? Oh, yes. I had to write a message for Jan. Now what was it?"

"Something about a phone call you just had — "

"Oh, yes, yes, of course — "

Catherine followed the little woman to the front of the shop, but the richness of all the colors at the back of the shop beckoned to her.

"Would you like me to do some flower arrangements?" she asked.

"Oh, no!" little Mrs. Vanderveld cried. "*You* can't do the flowers! Only Mr. Vanderveld does the flowers! Unless he's not here — and someone wants cut flowers in a box, or one of the arrangements Mr. Vanderveld has already made up. I can do that, sell his arrangements or wrap the cut flowers. But only Mr. Vanderveld makes the arrangements." The little woman smiled to soften her words. Leaning forward toward Catherine, she said confidingly, "He's an artist, you see. He's really an *artist* with flowers. I just assist him at sales, and of course I do all the bookkeeping. That's my talent."

Catherine, puzzled, asked, "Well, if I won't be arranging flowers, what will I be doing?"

"Why, sweeping up, of course. You can see how messy it's gotten, and helping Mr. Vanderveld by bringing him what he needs when he's designing his arrangements. We will teach you how to unpack and clean the flowers when they arrive. That's extremely important. We need you to run errands, go out for our lunch, deliver the flowers sometimes — you'll enjoy that. People are always so pleased. Many of our customers are in this area, so you can walk. You'll collect the used containers — "

The phone rang again. This time Mrs. Vanderveld took it while Catherine stood, stunned, watching. *She* was supposed to run errands and *sweep?* She had never swept anything in her life except for the summer she was at that stupid camp where all the kids had lists of chores. She was supposed to sweep the cabin but had traded with a girl

59

who was afraid to unsaddle the horses.

"Oh, dear," Mrs. Vanderveld said despondently, hanging up the phone. "I haven't paid the ribbon bill. That's the second time they've called me. I really must get my books organized. You go on back and get started, dear" — she waved her hand vaguely toward the curtain — "I'll be fine out here with the phone." She began digging through the cubbyholes and pulled out a black checkbook. "No, no, that's the wrong one," she muttered to herself, putting it back and searching again.

Catherine stepped through the curtain to the back of the shop. She looked at her watch. She had been here less than half an hour. It had been fun and would be a good caper to write Leslie about, but enough was enough. She wasn't about to spend her life with a broom in her hand.

Still, there was something challenging about the chaos of the back room. It reminded her of the child's playhouse, complete with furniture and window boxes filled with pink geraniums and trailing ivy, which Grandmother had had built on the back lawn of Everly for Catherine and Shelly and Ann. One summer after they'd all been abroad, they had returned to find the playhouse in a shambles. Raccoons had gotten in, tipping over furniture, pulling down the curtains, prying lids off the cookie tins, chewing on the legs of the chairs. Putting it back in order had been fun and even satisfying. They had played *Little House on the Prairie* — since that was what Catherine had been reading that summer — and she insisted she was the mother, Shelly the father, and Ann Laura. By the end of the day they had reclaimed the little playhouse for their own. In a way it was really more their own after they had saved it, cleaned it, and rearranged it to suit their fancies.

Really, at least she could roll up the ribbons on the spools before they got into an even more hopeless tangle. Catherine reached for the ribbons, which were the colors of sherbets, shining, satiny to the touch. But instantly she stepped on the end of a small branch — apple, she thought — which flipped up and sliced her leg, tearing a run in her hose.

"All right," she said to the floor. "We'll do you first."

After a search, she found the broom, dustpan, and trash sacks at the back of the store, next to the card table, which held a hot plate, a pot of water, some crusty jars of instant coffee, sugar, and a jar of fake cream. Little bits of chicken wire were scattered on the floor, with dust, leaves, petals, and paper stuck to it. The wire caught on the edge of the dustpan and refused to slide in without a fight. Catherine swore under her breath, but she was not about to give up yet. She found two perfectly good folding knives hidden in the mess on the floor and a pair of wire cutters under the table.

Catherine washed off the shelves and tables. She stacked and rearranged things: cardboard boxes and tissue paper, vases and bowls and containers, sheets of foil, ribbons, chicken wire. All the tools, knives and scissors and shears, their edges wiped clean and closed up, together.

Finished, she looked around at her work, quite satisfied. She felt like a child with a very pretty dollhouse.

"Oh, my dear! How nice! He'll be so pleased!"

Mrs. Vanderveld stepped behind the curtain and clapped her hands like a child.

"You are just heaven-sent!" she said. To Catherine's surprise, she grabbed Catherine in a hug.

Catherine couldn't remember the last time anyone had hugged her. Well, of course she could, Leslie had hugged her good-bye before she got into the taxi. But that hug had been over almost before it began, it was little more than a flurry of promises and perfume — "Write, take care, I'll send you postcards from

Paris" — before Leslie had hurried into the cab, all her black layers fluttering in her rush.

This hug was a real embrace. Catherine was surprised at the little woman's strength. She could feel Mrs. Vanderveld's plump arms through the gray cloth of her dress. She was so tall and Mrs. Vanderveld so short that the older woman's head came only to her shoulder. When Mrs. Vanderveld hugged her, a floral scent wafted up from the older woman's hair and dress and body. For just a few seconds Catherine was enclosed in the smell of summer.

The phone was ringing. Wanting to please, to show her competence, Catherine rushed to the front to answer it.

"Vanderveld Flowers," she said, this time feeling very much in control.

A woman with an arctic voice wanted to make an order. Catherine scrounged around in the cubbyholes, at last closing her hand on a pen and a blank piece of paper. At first she intended to write down everything the person told her so she wouldn't lose any information. But the woman on the phone seemed intent on telling her not only what kind of flowers she wanted, but what the occasion was (a dinner party) and where the flowers were to be (on the dining room table, which was twelve feet long, and on the dining room buffet) and what colors she'd prefer (pink, red, white, yellow, purple, but not blue, blue depressed her) and what time she would be home tomorrow to accept delivery of the flowers (four-thirty in the afternoon and not a moment earlier: she had a hairdresser's appointment).

"This is an important dinner party. Everything should be perfect," the woman said sniffily. She reminded Catherine of her mother.

"In that case," Catherine replied in her snootiest Miss Brill's voice, "shouldn't you have a corresponding arrangement in your entrance hall? And perhaps one or two in your living room or library, wherever you'll be having cocktails?"

From the other end of the line came a gasp of surprise. But Catherine's mother and grandmother always had every room filled with appropriate flowers when they gave parties.

Catherine noticed that the little woman was looking at her with dismay, shaking her head wildly, so that the strands that had escaped from her bun waved back and forth like antennae.

"Yes, actually, you're quite right, what a good idea," the woman said, her voice slightly less chilly.

64

"A large one for your entrance hall and two or three smaller arrangements to be set around your living room?" Catherine's voice was proportionately more haughty. She knew what was right. That was the way Catherine's mother always had it done.

"Yes, fine, perfect," the woman said, now almost friendly.

Catherine double-checked the woman's name, phone number, and address before hanging up. She smiled at Mrs. Vanderveld, who was now looking back at her, nearly trembling.

"Oh, dear, did she cancel her order?"

"Oh, no, she agreed she needed more flowers," Catherine said.

"Oh, my. Well, that's good, that's all right, then," the little woman said.

Catherine was surprised at how worried Mrs. Vanderveld looked when the phone conversation had gone so well. There had been something quite satisfying about telling the haughty woman on the phone what to do, even if it was only with her flowers. She was beginning to think she would like working here.

"But I don't want you to answer the phone any more, please," Mrs. Vanderveld said firmly. Seeing Catherine's expression, she continued hurriedly: "You did beautifully, yes, it's obvious that you know a lot about what flowers people like for their dinner parties. But you don't know what flowers we have available, or which flowers we will be able to get for which days — and still make a profit. So you see talking on the phone with a customer is not just a matter of helping him decide what he wants, but helping him decide that *he wants what we can give him,* what we have available or know we can get, and for a reasonable price to him and yet making some little money for us."

"Oh," Catherine said. "I see. There's so much I don't know." She felt her good spirits evaporate.

"You will learn, my dear. You are a smart girl, I can tell you will learn very quickly. Now I am exhausted, all this talking! Why don't you go to the back and make us a cup of coffee? It is getting close to five o'clock. Often we have a rush then, people leaving for work, on their way to dinner parties, wanting to pick up a little something. I always try to have a little sit-down and a cup of coffee around now."

Catherine looked at her watch. It was already four o'clock. Mrs. Vanderveld climbed onto a high cushioned stool behind the counter. Catherine pushed aside the curtain and went into the now clean, garden-scented back room toward the hot plate.

The back doors flew open and a slender, dark young man entered, his arms full of bags of potting soil. Grunting, he bent to set them on the floor, then straightened and looked at Catherine.

"Hello," he said formally. His face was terrifyingly beautiful, classic, exotic, as if carved in high relief.

"Hello," Catherine said, equally formal. Her legs had gone weak.

"I'm Piet Vanderveld," the man said, holding out his hand.

"Oh," said Catherine, taking it. His hand was warm and hard and callused. "I'm Catherine Eliot. I'm . . . I guess I'm . . ." She didn't know what she was. A salesgirl?

"The new help," Piet said. "Good. We can use you. I've got another shipment to bring in. Could you hold the doors open?"

"Oh, of course," Catherine said, moving quickly, thinking: The *help?* Her mother would *die. Good.*

She could not stop staring at Piet Vanderveld as he passed in front of her, carrying bags from a van in the alleyway. He was wearing jeans, a white button-down shirt with the sleeves rolled up, and a dark narrow tie. Nothing unusual there. But *he* was unusual, that was obvious. He was so . . .

foreign. He was slender, with black tulip eyes and sleek black hair. His face was long and narrow, his eyes slanted slightly, his eyebrows arched up like a devil's. He had a deep cleft in his chin. His looks were exotic; he would have looked perfect naked, frozen into marble, a wreath of flowers on his head, a chalice of wine in one hand, a cluster of pearly grapes in the other. His beauty was excessive, satyric. When he passed by her, she thought she smelled sweat, and immediately she sensed him on the back of a horse, or part of a horse, a centaur, slathered with sweat from the rider's legs. . . .

Piet set down the last box. "I'm Dutch," he said as if answering a question. "I'm the Vandervelds' nephew." He was panting slightly. "I help them, sometimes here, sometimes from Amsterdam."

"Oh," Catherine said, embarrassed but caught in her intoxication. She wanted only to stand staring, even sniffing, like an animal trying to place a scent. Finally her old school manners saved her. "This is all just so new," she said as if that would explain why she was staring, dumbfounded. "This is my first day. I have a lot to learn."

"I'm sure you'll do well," he said, smiling. His teeth were very white and even.

"Catherine? Dear? Have you started the

coffee?" Mrs. Vanderveld called from the front.

"Oh! I'm doing it right now!" Catherine called back.

She moved quickly to the hot plate. But she was spellbound, and for a few minutes more she could only stand, watching the rings turn from dull black to glowing red as heat rushed through the coils.

The afternoon rushed by. Catherine brought Mrs. Vanderveld her coffee and drank a cup herself as she filled out the employment forms. She held the door for Piet as he carried arrangements to be delivered out to the van. She didn't see Mr. Vanderveld again that day. She promised Mrs. Vanderveld she'd be at work at nine on the dot the next morning.

Stepping out onto the street that evening, she felt buoyant. It was still light, and the June sun gleamed off taxi bumpers, store windows, and doorknobs like golden blasts from heavenly trumpets. It had come to her! She had a job; she had a home; she had a future. She was starving. Stopping by a bakery, she bought a sandwich and, in her glee, an apple pie for herself and Mrs. Venito.

Back at the apartment, she ate ravenously. She wrote Leslie, words racing from her pen as fast as her hand would go. Before she went to bed, she spent an hour deciding just what to wear the next day. The linen sheath she had worn today now had to be dry-cleaned, and she knew she'd never save any of her salary if it all went to cleaners' bills.

The next morning, dressed in a washable blue-and-white-checked cotton shirtwaist dress, Catherine arrived at Vanderveld Flowers exactly at nine o'clock.

Already the shop was in chaos. Catherine was shocked, almost offended. All her hard work!

Mr. Vanderveld was working with robot speed at the long work table, stabbing a mixture of flowers into small round clear glass bowls that were already filled with green pittosporum, or pit as Mr. V called it. Flash, flash! in went two white carnations, two yellow daisies, two day lilies, and in the middle, two tight-budded yellow daffodils. Flash, flash! Mr. V slid the bowl aside and did another one. Sloshed water, discarded leaves, and sliced stems flew over the table to the floor.

Without preamble, without so much as a "good morning," Mr. Vanderveld barked at Catherine: "Take these. Five flats, twenty-four bowls on each flat, they slide into the van. You know where the Gold Room is on Fifth Avenue? Go to the service entrance in the alley. Take them in, collect the other bowls. Be sure they have all one hundred twenty. They owe me if they break a bowl. They always try to cheat me."

Catherine did as instructed. Driver's ed at Miss Brill's had not prepared her for maneuvering a wide van through the city's narrow back alleys, but after a few days she became expert and enjoyed the driving. She found it especially fun to carry in the trays of cheery bobbing spring flowers.

The return trip, however, was not fun. She was presented with five flats of twenty-four stinking, streaked, disgusting glass bowls full of dead flowers and decaying leaves. When she had parked back in the alley, Mrs. V quickly told her what to do, then hurried back to the front, leaving Catherine to work alone.

Catherine had to empty the fetid refuse into the huge green metal dumpster in the alley. People had put cigarettes out in the bowls; had stuck gum inside. Clumps of stubborn slime stuck to the bottom and sides. She had no choice but to stick her hand in — a tight squeeze — and scrape or scoop out the stuff. The smell was rank. Overwhelming odors of garbage from the restaurant two stores down floated by with its accompanying swarm of flies. She slapped the flies away from her face, getting green gunk in her hair.

Then she had to carry the flats of bowls down the creaking, sagging, wooden steps into the basement, where two huge soapstone sinks stood waiting. She hated the basement on sight. It was cement and brick and cracked stone, with bare light bulbs that hung from pull chains barely illuminating the dim, low-ceilinged room. Shelves of containers and tools lined one wall. Enormous sacks of potting soil, moss, and clay sagged against the walls like drunken men who might at any time begin to move toward her. A rusty water heater burped, a circulating fan pumped dully from the ceiling, and a dehumidifier gurgled. It was like being in the engine room of a sluggish boat on the river Styx, Catherine thought.

She had been told to scrub out the glass bowls with hot water and ammonia. It was essential, both the V's stressed, that the bowls be perfectly clean, for any slight residue of dead flowers would hold with it bacteria that would cause the new flowers in the bowl to rot quickly. For hours Catherine scrubbed. When she emerged from the basement, hot and sweaty, her dress spotted where the putrid greens had splashed, Mr. V growled,

"Why did that take you so long? You must work faster. We don't have all day."

For a split second Catherine thought she would quit. It would have been so easy simply to walk out the door. She had never intended to spend her life scrubbing bowls in a basement.

But Mr. V's, "Here. Prep these. Pound the stems on the lilacs. Slice the roses diagonally," made her think again.

Mr. Vanderveld steered her to the table where buckets of flowers fresh from the flower market stood awaiting her preparation. The sweet fragrance from the masses of lilacs and roses, so many roses, hundreds of long-stemmed roses in pink and red and buttery yellow, drifted up around her like a spell. She prepared the flowers. This she could do well and fast, for she had learned to do this for her grandmother at Everly. When she was through, Mr. V raised one eyebrow and nodded brusquely. "That's *gut*," he said.

She went home that second day with her hands stained and her clothing dappled green. The next day on her lunch hour she bought a long-sleeved smock and comfortable flat shoes. From that day on, only when she was sent off delivering or asked to take charge of the front for a while when Mrs. V had errands did she remove her smock and put on dress shoes or comb her hair and freshen her lipstick.

Clearly in this job her appearance was not of primary importance. Still, as the weeks went by, Catherine worried about her hands. Even though she had learned to protect her clothing, her hands still got stained. The skin under and around her nails was rimmed with green. Her hands were in water so much of the time that the natural oils were washed away, and her skin became chapped and brittle. Holly or boxwood or thorned flowers sliced at her hands, and she developed an allergy to the sappy film from the eucalyptus. At night she constantly washed her hands with Lestoil and Borax, then coated them with Vaseline.

For the first time in her life, Catherine was busy. All day long she worked hard, and by evening she was tired. Tired, and yet not settled, not finished. By late August she'd come to realize how imprecisely she understood some of the phrases Mr. Vanderveld tossed at her with urgent carelessness. What was the difference between art deco and Louis Quinze? Between teak and walnut? Between a wedding for two young people and for two widowers? She studied catalogs from the various colleges and trade schools, and that fall she began to take evening courses in interior design and art history.

She kept up with the activities of her old Miss Brill's classmates — who were in college, going to dances, skiing, traveling to Europe, getting engaged. Catherine might deliver corsages to the homes of friends for dances or help set up floral displays for their parents' holiday parties, but she handed the corsages to the maids who answered the door and worked with the families' secretaries or housekeepers, and so she seldom saw her friends. That didn't matter. None of the past seemed to matter. She was engrossed in her current life. There was so much she wanted to learn. Suddenly there were never enough hours in the day.

Perhaps, she thought, she had caught some of her passion for work from the Vandervelds. Certainly they were an energetic, even frenzied pair. Mr. V was always in a hurry, always late, always frantic, and clearly he considered his work of crucial significance in the world. With his red suspenders, red bow tie, and flushed face, his nose and cheeks bouquets of broken capillaries, he resembled a cardinal, twittering, fluttering, thrashing through his life. Mrs. V was the perfect cardinal's wife. She hopped around the shop, bustling and chirping, pecking at her receipts and bills, rustling things into shape. When

Catherine was in the shop with the Vandervelds, she felt intense, alive, and dramatic.

In contrast, Piet Vanderveld contained a quality of stillness that both attracted and frightened Catherine. The older Vandervelds hustled and flurried. Their nephew moved calmly, wasting not one movement. They babbled. He listened, nodded, acted. As the months passed, Mrs. Vanderveld told Catherine about her past, about her early life in Amsterdam, meeting Mr. V, starting the store, their desire for children, their sorrow at having none, the success of the store burgeoning beyond their early dreams. Piet told Catherine nothing about himself. Sometimes women phoned him, but he never confided his interest in them by so much as a smile. He didn't ask Catherine about herself. He didn't flirt with her.

But he was darkly and sensually attractive. He was like a coiled snake sunning on a rock, so still, yet so beautiful, that Catherine longed to reach out to him. Piet was magnetic. She always felt his pull. As time passed he began to fill her dreams, and in defense, during the days, she avoided him as much as possible.

She continued to live in Leslie's apartment and in time came to think of it as *her* apartment. It was within walking distance to

Vanderveld Flowers, to her parents' apartment to visit her brother and sister, an easy subway ride to her evening courses. The shops, the parks, even some of the neighbors' and doormen's faces and names, became as familiar to her as the faculty and students at Miss Brill's. She was beginning to feel at home.

Leslie's father came to the apartment about twice a year. Ceremoniously, he took Catherine to dinner at the current fashionable restaurant, pleased to have an elegant and attractive dinner companion who could understand his tales of discoveries in the Orient. Except for the two or three nights a year when Catherine went to dinner with him, she knew she didn't impinge upon Mr. Dunham's life at all, not even when he was in his apartment.

Leslie wrote her often from Paris about her escapades in art and conquests in love. Her letters ended with the same advice: "Get out and live a little! Your life sounds so *dull!*" Catherine would smile. She'd fold the letter, put it in the paisley box where she kept all her letters, muse on the pleasure of Leslie's friendship for a while . . . then turn back to her book on dried flower arrangements, or houseplants, or primitive and contemporary religious symbols and ornaments.

Her holiday and vacation time she spent

at Everly. Kathryn was fascinated by Catherine's work. She quizzed her granddaughter about every detail, now and then mumbling to herself when something Mr. Vanderveld did sounded particularly brilliant or foolish. She never praised Catherine for choosing this work; Kathryn was not the kind to praise. But her attention to Catherine, her interest, her enjoyment and obvious curiosity, were all the accolade Catherine needed. The days she spent at Everly flew by with the same happy speed as her days working in the flower shop.

It was different the few times she visited her parents, on Easter or Ann's or Shelly's birthday. Catherine knew she would always have to maintain a delicate balance when she saw her father and mother. She had to be pleasant in the face of their scorn — to them, she'd become working class. She didn't attend any of the right balls or coming-out parties or dances; she hadn't chosen to attend the right college; she didn't date the right people — as far as they were concerned, she was doing nothing right, and they had no interest in her. She was a disgrace. Worse, she was boring.

Catherine remained stoically pleasant in the face of their disapproval because she wanted to see her brother and sister. Shelly was bright, but too bold. At thirteen he had been suspended from boarding school for smoking in his dorm room. At fourteen he was expelled from his school for drinking whiskey and vomiting in the library. Drew considered his son's escapades amusing and promptly found a new school for him. When Shelly wanted to, he could make A's and charm his teachers. He was a great jock, a good-natured guy; people liked being around him. But he got bored easily, especially when Catherine tried to talk to him seriously.

As if in reparation for her older sister's desertion and her brother's troublemaking, Ann was busy being the perfect child. At ten, eleven, and twelve, she spent more time with her mother than with her own friends. Not yet at boarding school, she was free to spend her afternoons with Marjorie. Pattering after her mother in her black patent-leather shoes and white socks, her white-gloved hands holding her little handbag, Ann followed her mother everywhere. "That dress looks divine on you, Mother!" she said.

"Call me Marjorie," her mother told her one day. "It sounds better."

Catherine watched and listened, grateful at least to see her brother and sister growing up, though she could hardly influence the direction their lives took. She pitied them. Whenever she left her parents' home, she felt like a prisoner escaping. Their life was so superficial. She wanted to rescue Ann and Shelly but didn't know how. But she at least had won her own freedom, and there was never a day in her life when she worked at the shop that she doubted her choice. The flower business had overcome her. She was possessed by her love for her work. She was lost in it. She was found.

CHAPTER 3

Catherine had a hard, sensible plan that she now and then let soften into a buoyant fantasy. While her friends hoped for Prince Charmings and engagement rings, Catherine played with numbers in a small black account book. In June of 1964 she'd been working at Vanderveld Flowers for three years. By now even cranky old Mr. Vanderveld had come to trust her and, more important, to rely on her. Every year the Vandervelds had given her a raise, and since she didn't have to pay rent to the Dunhams, she was able to save a large portion of her paycheck. Someday, she hoped, she'd be able to buy into the Vandervelds' business. Become a partner. Have a voice in the future of the shop.

Someday, perhaps, but not soon. No matter how much she scrimped on clothes and food, she still seemed to be accumulating so little money, so slowly. She was toying with the thought of asking her parents for a loan. Every time she envisioned asking them, her stomach cramped, but really she could think of no other way to get enough money to buy part of the shop before she was old and gray.

Kathryn had given Catherine a substantial check for Christmas, which Catherine had eagerly added to her savings account. Then she received the invitation to Kimberly Weyland's wedding. Kimberly, one of Catherine's and Leslie's best friends at Miss Brill's, was marrying Philippe Croce, the son of one of France's wealthiest financiers, and the wedding was to be held at the Croces' country estate outside Paris.

"You *have* to come!" Leslie wrote. "I'll *die* if you don't!"

It would be a treat to see Leslie, Catherine thought, and in an odd way didn't she owe it to Leslie, since Leslie was giving her a free place to live? Also, this particular wedding party would be crammed with wealthy people, especially young people her age, planning more weddings. It would be a great way to make contacts for the flower shop.

And besides, Catherine wanted to go. She'd been working hard for a long time, and the thought of staying in a château in the French countryside was too tempting to resist. Catherine took her grandmother's Christmas money from her savings account and bought a round-trip ticket to Paris.

Catherine had asked for so little over the past three years that the Vandervelds couldn't refuse her the time off even during the busy month of June. Piet surprised her by offering to drive her to the airport in the delivery van. She accepted, partly because she wanted him to see her transformed by her pale green silk suit, gold jewelry, and high heels and partly to save the cab fare. It was delicious to dress up, as if slipping into a new, resplendent self, and as she stepped out into the bright June evening, she wondered if Piet would be moved to compliment her. If he did, she thought, it would mean that a new chapter of her life was opening. At the very moment she had the thought, she knew it was foolish, yet it was so sweet to indulge in such illusions!

But she might as well have been a pig in an apron for all Piet noticed. He talked shop talk all the way to the airport.

Then he surprised her. At the terminal Piet handed her bags to the porter, then fixed Catherine in his gaze.

"You look beautiful, Catherine. Be sure to come home."

Without warning he kissed her on her cheek, close to her mouth.

"Oh," she said.

"Have a safe trip," he said.

Piet was the one to turn away first. Catherine stood wavering in her high heels, transfixed, until he got into the van. Behind her, the porter cleared his throat. Stunned, jubilant, Catherine trotted to the airline counter and then to the gate. It had been only a kindness, she told herself, to send her on her way full of self-confidence. Still, she smiled.

While waiting to board the jet, she discovered three other classmates also going to Kimberly's wedding. Their squeals of delight at seeing Catherine made her feel young again. She was aware of the other passengers noticing them: four pretty girls in pastels full of high spirits, on their way to a wedding. It was like drinking champagne, inhaling perfume, to be so lucky, so lovely. With earnest, profuse professions of gratitude, the girls charmed other passengers into trading seats so they could all sit together, and the flight was passed in an orgy of gossip, memories, and laughter. Hours later the four women arrived in France sleepy and silly.

A stoic chauffeur met them. It was his task to deliver them to the Croces' country house two hours from Paris. In the privacy and quiet of the smooth, luxurious limousine, the young women fell asleep and missed seeing the change in the landscape as the city gave way to small stony towns and sun-dappled green fields.

They awoke to find the limo entering high, wrought-iron gates that led to the grounds of the Croce estate. The massive, honey-colored stone château was set formally in the middle of manicured gardens, symmetrical paths, and graveled drives. After the long flight and the brief nap, Catherine felt as if she were moving inside a dream as she walked up the wide stone steps and through the great doors into the château.

Inside, the vaulted, tapestry-hung entrance hall echoed as the Miss Brill's girls were all reunited. Leslie came running down the long curving staircase, arms wide, chattering and laughing. Her father, who was a friend of Monsieur Croce, greeted Catherine more decorously. While their luggage was taken to their rooms, the four new arrivals were led into a small salon for refreshments. Leslie ate heartily of the hot anchovy canapés and tiny crepes filled with chicken liver and mushrooms, but Catherine felt stuporous. It was all she could do to remember enough French to converse with the bridegroom and his parents. Finally, after a polite hour of the requisite courtesies, the four travelers were shown to their rooms to rest. There would be a banquet and ball that evening; the wedding was the next day.

Leslie took Catherine to the room she had arranged for them to share.

"We're up on the third floor," Leslie whispered, her arm linked through Catherine's. "Family members, the maid of honor, and the bridesmaids get the posh rooms on the second floor. You'll have to come down later and see Kimberly's room — it looks like a brothel!"

Their room was small and sparsely furnished, with white plaster walls, a shining oak floor, two narrow beds, and an enormous, ornately carved armoire with mirrors on the doors. The large open window looked out onto the long reflecting pool and the statue-adorned paths through the gardens.

"Don't you love all this?" Leslie babbled. "Decadence. Yum. But do you know what? There are only two toilets and two bathtubs on this floor. We'll have to share with everyone else. There's no shower anywhere I can see. I don't know how I'll wash my hair. You look exhausted. How was the flight? I promise I won't talk forever. You have to get some sleep so you can be ready for tonight. It's going to be an amazing party."

"The flight was fine," Catherine said. "It was fun talking to Anne and Robin and Melonie, but you know, Leslie, it's just like when we were at school — they're still as interchangeable as ever. They dress the same way, they study the same stuff at college, they think the same way. I think they could marry each other's fiancés and the men wouldn't even notice."

"You're so wicked and critical." Leslie laughed. "And I'm so glad! Never mind them, tell me about you! Did you bring pictures?"

"Umm," Catherine said. She jumped off the bed, dug through her luggage, and came over to sit next to Leslie with her packet. "Here," she said. "This is it."

She handed Leslie the first photograph: a picture of a small shop with a pink-and-white-striped awning and, in gold script on the door, the words *Vanderveld Flowers*.

"It's pretty, Catherine. Smaller than I thought from all you'd written me."

Catherine laughed. She looked lovingly at the photograph.

"Yes, I'm sure of that. It's changed my life so much it should be as big as a church or a university . . . but even as a flower shop it's too small. Far too small. Unfortunately the Vandervelds don't have the money for expansion . . ." Her voice trailed off as she remembered all the financial problems the Vandervelds were facing, problems that might change her future.

"Look at all those daffodils!" Leslie said, taking the next photo, which was a closer shot of the shop window. "And the tulips. I love tulips."

"Mmm," Catherine agreed. "You know, I didn't realize it when I took it last month, but the window in this photo looks just like it did when I first saw the store. This is Mr. and Mrs. Vanderveld. They look like trolls, don't they?"

"Who's *this?*" Leslie interrupted. "You didn't tell me about him."

Catherine looked at the photograph, which was supposed to show Leslie what the back of the shop looked like but in which Catherine had inadvertently included a dark young man with his arms full of cardboard box flats.

"Oh, that's Piet. Their nephew."

"Ye-es. Go on."

"That's all."

"That's all? You work with a man who looks like that, and you tell me that's all? Catherine, come on. I don't believe that for a minute."

Catherine pushed herself off Leslie's bed and threw herself across her own. "Oh, give me a break, Leslie. God, I'm bushed. It's five o'clock in the morning my time. I've got to go to sleep."

"You're trying to get out of telling me

something! That's not fair! I gave you my apartment, Catherine — you owe me."

"Owe you what?"

"Everything. Your soul. At least all your secrets. So tell."

Catherine opened her eyes. "I swear I'm not involved with him. Leslie, I've been working so hard now, at the shop in the day and classes at night, I haven't had time for men at all. I promise. Don't look that way. I'm not lying. Listen, let me sleep and I'll tell you everything when I wake up."

"Everything?" Leslie said threateningly, squinching up her eyes.

"Everything. And believe me, it will take about five seconds."

"All right," Leslie said sulkily. "I'm going on down to see who else is here. I'll wake you in time to get ready for the party."

Catherine closed her eyes and pulled the covers up to her neck. Her brain seemed filled with fuzz. Her body was disoriented after the transatlantic flight and the excitement of seeing old friends again. She wanted to sleep and to rush around seeing everyone, not missing a second, all at the same time.

It was so odd being with Leslie again, feeling young again — feeling rich. She tossed and turned on the soft, duvet-covered bed, suddenly sinking into an ocean of sleep. In this

French country house, far away from New York and the Vandervelds, Catherine dreamed of Piet. Her body filled with warmth, a delicious blood-red-rose warmth that relaxed her, and yet a dizzying warmth, like Burgundy wine drunk before a winter fire.

All her life, Catherine thought, she had lived by grasping at anything that caught her eye, because she didn't know where to go. Piet was different. He knew exactly what he wanted. He was centered, his mind, body, and desires so powerfully contained and compressed that they formed a dark axis, a black pole around which his world turned. She always resisted the power of that magnetism, because she was afraid.

She twisted on the bed, toward him, away, moaning.

"Catherine! Wake up!"

Catherine opened her eyes. Leslie was seated on the bed next to her with a tray in her hands.

"Sorry, honey, but we've got to get you awake. I know how hard it is to wake up after an ocean crossing. But you've had five hours of sleep, and it's the first few minutes that are the hardest. Here, I brought you some coffee and bread, butter, and strawberry confiture. Touch the bread. It's still hot. Smell it. And the coffee — yum! Milk? Sugar?"

As Leslie spoke, Catherine pulled herself up into a sitting position, propped herself against some pillows, and let Leslie busy around with the tray. Her head was still filled with fuzz, her body with a voluptuous heaviness.

"I have to have a bath," she said after sipping some of the rich café au lait from a cup the size of a soup bowl.

"Good luck. Everyone's using the bathtubs. I doubt if there'll be enough hot water, but never mind, the cold will wake you up. Eat something first and drink your coffee — Oh! You have to tell me which dress you want to wear tonight. The maids are coming around to collect things that need ironing. Which one — this? Well, la-de-da, Miss Catherine, how swanky. Where did you get it? I thought you were pinching pennies."

Catherine grinned and stretched. "I stole it. From my mother's closet. She'll never know."

"You stole it! Good Lord, I didn't know you had it in you! I'm so proud of you, my dear. The beginnings of a life of crime. How did you manage it?"

"Easily. They invited me home to the Park Avenue apartment for Ann's birthday party. I came in with a huge satchel full of presents, and left with the same satchel stuffed with the dress — and some suitable jewelry. Oh, don't look at me that way. You know Mother will never miss it. It wasn't even in the closet in her room. It was back in the closet in the storage room. She'll never fit into this again anyway, it's sizes and sizes too small. Besides, if she does miss it, she'll just think she ruined it in one of her drunken moments. Believe me, she won't want to embarrass herself by asking. God, I feel like I've been poached in these clothes. I've got to bathe."

Grabbing up her robe and bath things, Catherine headed down the hall in the direction Leslie had pointed. She hated the French system of putting the toilet and sink in their own little room and the bathtub in another. Fortunately the bathtub was free, and she hurriedly bathed off the flight and her exhaustion and returned to her room refreshed.

"All right," Leslie said the moment Catherine entered the room. "I've been patient. So tell."

"About what?" Catherine sat on the edge of her bed and hungrily wolfed down her café au lait and bread, liberally slathered with strawberry jam.

"Your love life! You can start with that Arabian knight, or Russian prince, or whatever he is. The dark stranger in the photo."

"He's Dutch. I've told you. Piet Vanderveld. He works with the Vandervelds, sometimes in Amsterdam, sometimes in New York, wherever they need him. He's very helpful because he's multilingual. . . ."

"Catherine! I swear I will not be your friend one second longer if you don't stop fooling around and tell me."

Catherine looked at Leslie.

Leslie stared back at Catherine. "Well, it's only fair! I've told you everything. You know every single detail about every man I've slept with, all my broken hearts . . . Come on, Catherine. Aren't I your best friend anymore?"

Catherine bent her head. She tore off a piece of baguette and rolled it between her fingers. "It's just that I'm embarrassed," she said quietly. "You probably won't believe me. Leslie" — she was now sculpting the warm bread into a work of art — "I'm still a virgin."

Leslie whooped. "I *don't* believe it! My God. Catherine! Why? Or do I mean why not?"

Catherine played with the bread in silence. Finally she tossed it onto the plate and looked up at her friend. "I'm not apologizing," she said. "I'm not ashamed of it. I'm not like you."

"I know you're not. That's one of the

reasons we've been best friends for so long. I'm not making fun of you. But Catherine, you are twenty-one."

"I know. I'm twenty-one and I know what I want in life and it's *not* to be swept off my feet by love! I just don't have time for love now, Leslie — or romance, or sex, or any of that. I have to make my own way."

"Oh, Catherine. You're so hopeless. You take everything too seriously. You can fall in love with someone, go to bed with a man, without changing your entire life! I do it all the time! Where are your hormones? Don't tell me you haven't wanted to go to bed with that Dutch nephew! *I* want to go to bed with him, and I've only seen him in a photograph!"

Catherine grinned. "I suppose I do want to go to bed with him, Leslie, in my own way. But . . . first of all, I have to work with him, and I can't afford to offend the Vandervelds. Besides, Piet's not around all that much. He's in Europe for months at a time. Also . . ." She hesitated. "I don't know how to say this. I *am* attracted to Piet. Very attracted. I . . . I dream of him. But something about him scares me."

Leslie studied Catherine. "Baby," she said at last, sympathetically. Then, with a rush of enthusiasm, she jumped up from her bed.

"Oh, well, it's not the end of the world. Now you're in France, maybe you'll get lucky. There are absolutely mobs of gorgeous men downstairs. Come on, let's get beautiful. Maybe we'll both get lucky tonight."

"I feel like Grace Kelly at the least," Leslie whispered to Catherine as they descended the winding stairs to the ground floor of the château.

"I feel like Eliza Doolittle," Catherine whispered back.

The last time she had been so dressed up had been at a friend's graduation party in Newport. Tonight she had real jewels on and a turquoise gown that must have cost her mother more than several months' worth of Catherine's salary. After three years of working in the flower shop, she had forgotten how expansive the world of the wealthy could be, making time itself relax and drape and lounge and linger.

"Yeah, you're a real poverty-stricken flower girl!" Leslie said.

Catherine grinned. She wished Leslie could see how she looked during any normal working day.

Her work gave a depth to everything she experienced that made her both proud and irritated. She knew the basement side of the world, the alley and back room side, the harsh smelly frantic side where leaves were savagely ripped from stems so the blooms would have all the water and nourishment. She was glad that she had learned all that. She prided herself on knowing secrets. At the same time, she wished she could forget it all and drift in the same dreamy world her friends inhabited — just for this one night.

"It's gorgeous!" Leslie said, linking arms with Catherine and pulling her close.

They were entering the grand salon, where cocktails and hors d'oeuvres were being served to a glittering assembly of elegant people in formal dress. Various languages — French, Spanish, German, Dutch — flickered around them like colorful butterflies. Silks and satins and taffetas rustled, perfumes and laughter drifted through the air, and Leslie and Catherine took flutes of champagne from a silver tray.

Catherine looked at the room. It was much grander even than Everly. The marble fireplace was intricately carved with garlands and figures and flowers. Along the melon silk walls hung vast oil paintings of former Croces playfully dressed as shepherds or nymphs. Enormous faience vases lushly packed with roses, lilies, delphiniums, stock, and greens were set about on antique tables inlaid with mother-of-pearl and ebony and rosewood.

"Don't you dare rearrange those flowers!" Leslie whispered in Catherine's ear, making her laugh.

"I wasn't planning to! I was just toting up the cost in my head."

"How vulgar you've gotten, my dear!" Leslie said in her best Miss Brill's voice. "Really, darling, can't you let it drop for one night?"

"All right, I will. I promise. I know I should. It's been a long time since I've just enjoyed myself."

"Drink your champagne," Leslie ordered. "I'm putting a spell on you. The past three years have been erased from your life. The only thing you know how to do is be beautiful and charming at parties."

"I think I can manage that."

They joined a group of American friends. Lifted away into a mist of pleasure by their chatter and the bubbling champagne, Catherine relaxed. She let go. *Now, tonight,* was all that mattered, a world complete in itself, glittering, golden, dreamy, as free from the real world as a balloon cut free from its tie to the earth, to drift above spires, mountains, clouds.

The Croce family and the Weyland family

and those in the wedding party dined in the formal dining room. The others ate in the library, at tables for eight covered with elaborately embroidered white tablecloths and set with the family's gold-rimmed white china, platinum-rimmed crystal, and heavy elaborate silver.

Catherine was so taken with the food, she could scarcely concentrate on the conversation. The first course was a fresh whole salmon with an elaborate herb sauce for each table; next a galantine of duck, an elaborate dish of cold ground pressed duck, pork, truffles, pistachio nuts, and ham, decorated with truffles and sparkling cubes of golden aspic; then a saddle of lamb with vegetables that had been shaped and sculpted into miniature works of art; then a leafy green salad. Each course was served with the appropriate wine, and finally, with the château's own champagne, came the *pêches cardinal,* poached peaches coated with thick raspberry sauce and whipped cream, decorated with fresh whole raspberries.

Satiated, Catherine sat back in her chair, looking at the gold-embossed spines of the books behind the glass doors of the library. Surely she was incapable of doing anything else for the rest of the night, or perhaps for the rest of her life. She felt as though she'd never eaten so much before. But courtesy demanded that she respond when the pleasant French gentleman who had been seated next to her asked if he could escort her into the ballroom, so she rose and took his arm.

Four sets of high wooden doors had been pulled open at the end of the grand salon to reveal the ballroom, which had been decorated especially for the wedding festivities. The ceiling, which arched three stories above the dancers, was painted in mythical Greek scenes of love, hunting, and feasting. Like the long French windows that opened onto the terrace, and the high mirrors on the opposite walls, the ceiling gleamed with gilt.

At one end of the ballroom a band was playing Strauss waltzes. At the other end stretched a long table with drinks of every kind and more champagne than Catherine had ever seen in her life. The room was lined with striped love seats and chairs for those who wanted to sit and watch, but most of the guests were dancing, compelled by the delicious music. The French doors had been flung open to the early summer night. Outside, steps led down to the formal garden, at the center of which was an oblong pool surrounded by small fat flickering candles.

A man asked Catherine to dance. Then

another. And another.

Soon her head was light from jet lag, dancing, and champagne. Her mother's strapless turquoise gown, with a tight waist and a flowing skirt whose chiffon fluttered out in a sea of rippling pleats, flattered Catherine, and she knew it. She held back her dark curls with rhinestone-studded combs, but her earrings, large drops of Persian turquoise surrounded by small diamonds, were real. She loved the feeling of them swinging against her neck as she danced or laughed. She was introduced to so many men and women, she finally gave up even attempting to remember their names.

Catherine's French was passable — one thing she *had* learned from Miss Brill's — and most of the French guests spoke excellent English, so everyone mixed and mingled, until Catherine was certain she had danced with all of the forty or so young men in the room. They all seemed equally tall and handsome, courtly and clever, an entire team of beaming Prince Charmings. She forgot her real life and surrendered to the intoxication of the night and the music — and the champagne.

"May I?"

Catherine was released from the arms of her current partner into the presence of a new man, an American, with a pleasant face . . . a really likable face. . . .

She leaned back a little as they began to dance, to get a better look at him. He was tall and handsome, in a kind, easy way. There was nothing smug or insolent in these good looks. He looked gentle, with a thatch of blond hair and lushly lashed, almost amber eyes.

Now here was a man she could go to bed with! she thought, and promptly stumbled and stepped on his foot.

"You look like a golden retriever," Catherine babbled to cover her embarrassment.

"Do I?" the man replied. His hands were firm and warm as he steadied her easily. "I'm Kit Bemish," he said.

"I'm Catherine Eliot," she replied.

The band was playing a waltz, and Kit Bemish waltzed beautifully. Catherine's gown breezed and belled around her as they danced. He led her with such ease that her own body felt light and graceful.

"I think I'm getting a little silly," she confessed sotto voce. "All the champagne."

"We'll get you some water," he responded solemnly. "If you drink a glass of water for every glass of champagne, you won't get a hangover."

"I never knew that!" Catherine said. Suddenly, that seemed like great wisdom.

Kit grinned. "One of the more useful things I learned at Harvard."

When the dance ended, Kit escorted her off the dance floor. He got them each a tall glass of sparkling water, then took Catherine's arm and led her out the long doors onto the terrace. The night air was fresh and mild after the warmth of the ballroom.

"You're a friend of Kimberly's?" he asked.

"Yes. We were together at Miss Brill's School for Girls. God, that sounds so insipid, doesn't it? It was a million years ago. And you?"

"I've known Philippe Croce since we were about ten. We spent several summers on international sailing expeditions that were also supposed to be floating summer schools." Kit laughed. "We sailed and swam all day and spent perhaps five minutes on lessons at night. At least Philippe learned English and I learned passable French. We haven't sailed together for years, though." Kit sighed.

"That must have been wonderful fun."

"It was. And it was a great way to see the world. One year we sailed the Mediterranean, another year we were off the coast of Newfoundland, another year down in the Caribbean. It was rather unreal, though. Just men, wearing only swimming suits, no schedules, lots and lots of days when we never looked at a watch and the hours just drifted by. . . ."

"Sounds like you'd like to be there right now."

"I wouldn't mind a week or two of it. I could use some unreality. I'm in law school at Harvard. My life is divided into tight little segments. Oh, I like it, it's what I want to do. It's just that being with Philippe again brings back memories. . . ."

They walked in silence to the end of the long reflecting pool. Candlelight streaked the still water.

"I like remembering my school days, too, but not as much as you seem to," Catherine said. "I was always so confused. I didn't have any idea what I wanted to do when I grew up."

"I've always known."

"You have! That's amazing!"

"Maybe only predictable. My father's a lawyer, my grandfather was a lawyer and a judge. I always knew I'd go into law. But not to please them. They didn't pressure me, and they certainly always showed me there were other options in life. I think my mother kept sending me on the summer sailing school in hopes that I'd develop an interest in diplomacy. She loves traveling. My father hates it. I think at the back of her mind she hoped I'd grow up and live abroad so she could come visit me."

"Instead you're going to become a lawyer."

"Yes."

"And then? Do you want to be a judge?"

Kit hesitated. He looked down at Catherine, and she felt his scrutiny, his caution. "No. I want to go into government. Politics."

Catherine returned Kit's gaze. In the candlelit night, his face was gentle. "You don't seem the type to be interested in power."

"I'm not." He hesitated again. "I don't talk about it much. I always end up sounding like some sanctimonious drip. It's just — in my family, there's a tradition. 'Not for self alone.' I know I'm fortunate, extraordinarily lucky, but I also know this world is in a bad state and getting into a worse one. I want to change that." Kit looked at her. "I want to change a lot of things. I want — " Kit stopped. "Sorry. I'm boring you."

"No!" Catherine objected, putting her hand on Kit's arm. He looked down at her. "I know what you mean, how you feel, at least a little, I think. That's why I like what I'm doing now, working in a flower shop. It sounds pretty insignificant, doesn't it? But few things can claim to be as *good* as flowers are. There's nothing soiled or evil or degraded about them. They make people feel loved, and cheerful, or consoled, they brighten our spirits, our day, our thoughts of the future — " She caught herself and laughed. "So you see? I do understand. I mean, it's not the same level, and it's much less complicated, but — " She paused, unsure of just what she meant. "But I do understand," she said finally.

She realized she was still holding on to his arm. All this eager understanding plus this lover's clutch — what would he think? She started to pull away.

But Kit said softly, "Hey." He slid his hand down to hold hers. His skin was warm and electric.

They walked around the pool and gardens, talking in a companionable way. For Catherine, it was a new and delicious sensation to feel both safe and excited at the same time. She had forgotten how charming a well-educated man could be. After a while they went back into the ballroom for another mineral water, and realizing they were hungry again, they took plates of smoked salmon, cheese and raspberries and bread, and sat on the terrace, eating. They talked. They had friends in common. New York and Boston were not so far apart. They had much in common, a similar sense of humor, of perspective.

They danced again. By now the tone of the party was changing. The quieter couples danced in solitary worlds of their own, drawing closer and closer to each other with each dance. The rest of the party was getting silly and boisterous and outrageous, performing stunts on the dance floor, spilling champagne. Catherine had lost track of time and was glad to let it flow.

She liked Kit's voice. It was low and even and calm. He was not glib or flirtatious; he didn't pepper each sentence with a compliment or a sexual innuendo. Still, as she listened to him, as his body grew more familiar to her as they danced, she felt sexual desire rising within her as if each of his gentle words were rain, wetting and nourishing something hiding deep inside her, something so fragile it would not respond to harsh light, a bright sun, or a torrent of seductive speech. Something within her lifted, responding to him.

From time to time, when she pulled her head back a bit as they danced so that she could look into his eyes, she realized that for once she was not afraid. Once, after she had looked at him as they danced, searching his eyes for a clue to the nature of this man, he gently brought his hand up and pressed her head against his shoulder, as if she were a child. He stroked her hair. He let his hand linger on her head, so gently it brought tears to her eyes. It felt like the times when she had been a child with a nanny who had touched her so fondly, and she remembered being loved.

The next time she drew her head back to look in his eyes and smile at him, he bent and kissed her, lightly, on the lips.

Suddenly she was impatient. She brought her hand up to press his neck. They wrapped their arms around each other and kissed as they danced. When they stopped kissing, she was breathless, eager, greedy. She wanted the people around her to disappear. She wanted to kiss him again, she wanted to undo the studs of his tuxedo shirt to see his chest, his belly. And more. At last.

"Do you want to come to my room?" Kit asked.

"Yes," she said.

Taking her hand, he led her out of the ballroom onto the terrace. She started to object, but quickly she realized that he was taking her the long way around the large house so no one would suspect where they were heading. He *was* a gentleman.

Fortunately he was not sharing a room. It was tiny and spare, with only a narrow single bed, but that was enough.

He didn't turn on the light when they

entered. Enough moonlight came in through the two open windows to paint their bodies and the bed in a silver sheen. Kit kissed her mouth, her face, her neck, and stroked her arms and back. He was being courteous, going slowly, gently, but Catherine was ravenous, almost ill with desire. She needed to go through with it before her courage failed. It occurred to her at one point to tell him that she was a virgin, but quickly she decided against it. She knew enough about him already to know that if she did, he might have second thoughts. He might tell her she should save herself for a husband or some such nonsense. And she did not want to ruin this.

"Do I need to use something?" he asked.

At first she didn't understand the question. When she did, she grew hot with shame. If she said yes, he would know she wasn't on the Pill like every other sophisticated female her age. If she said no, and he didn't "use something," she could get pregnant. Tears of frustration sprang to her eyes.

"It's all right," he said, pulling her against him. She still had not managed to reply. "I'll take care."

They undressed each other. Their clothes fell in silky piles around the floor. They stood together, naked in the moonlight, warm and aching, aching and soothing at once, like invalids with a fever that was lightened by a cool cloth. Everywhere they touched, the heat grew more intense, but that touch soothed the ache.

He brought her to the narrow bed with its coarse white sheets and lay next to her, kissing her, stroking her, touching her. Finally he entered her. At once her desire abated as pain took over. It made her angry. She had to keep herself from crying out. At the same time the pain sobered her enough so that her natural curiosity took over and she thought: So this is what a man looks like, acts like, sounds like, when he is making love. She watched him. He looked as if he were in as much pain as she was. She had never heard that sex hurt men. His suffering looked so private. Suddenly he arched away from her, his chest rising up and back. He groaned and fell against her. She was suffused with a great boiling sense of triumph. *Triumph?!* She felt utterly smug about it. Gently she stroked his back and head, as if he had done something wonderful.

"Do you want me to move?" he asked, murmuring, his voice so low she could scarcely hear him even though his mouth was next to her ear.

"No," she whispered. She luxuriated under

the heaviness of his body against hers. As she turned, smiling, she saw through the window that day was dawning. The sky was filled with a golden-white light that glimmered and deepened as if reflecting the way she felt now inside her skin: warm, and shining, and infinitely full of beauty.

Kit slept, then made love to her again. This time he went more slowly. He watched her face and seemed to be listening to her body, as if trying to lead her on whichever path pleased her most. When they finished making love again, she knew she had not experienced the wild ecstasy she'd always read about, but still she felt satisfied, pleased right to the bone. Somehow, curled against each other on that narrow bed, they managed to sleep.

When she awoke, it was full day. Catherine had no idea what time it was, but the sun was mercilessly bright. For the first time she was embarrassed. She was naked in bed with this man. No doubt her mascara was smeared, and she couldn't even imagine what her hair looked like. When she looked down at her body, she was surprised: it was as if overnight she had been coated with a rosy bloom, for her breasts seemed fuller, the nipples fat and swollen with heat, her skin flushed.

She looked at the man lying next to her. He was firm and muscular, with golden furlike hair on his chest and belly. He was so tanned that he seemed to be wearing a white swimming suit around his pelvis, except for the dark golden nest of pubic hair and the penis curled in it. She touched the hair on his thighs. It felt like spun gold, like the delicate silk of a milkweed pod.

He opened his eyes and saw her looking at him and smiled. He pulled her to him for a kiss.

"God, I'm hungry," he said. "I'd sell my soul for a cup of coffee and a glass of orange juice," he went on, sitting up. "That champagne . . . God, we're going to have to get dressed in order to get breakfast." He rose and stretched, seemingly without any self-consciousness about his nakedness in front of her.

Catherine sat up, pulling the sheet around her. She wasn't sure what to do now. Was she supposed to just leave? Maybe now that he saw her in daylight he didn't like her. Maybe she hadn't been "good in bed." Perhaps she had cheapened herself by going to bed with him so quickly. She looked at the swirl of turquoise chiffon abandoned on the floor.

"Where's your room?" he asked.

"Down the hall. The one next to the corner. I'm sharing with a friend."

"Well, look," he said, grinning, "put this on." He took a white long-sleeved shirt from the cupboard and draped it over her shoulders. "It's not great, but it'll cover you, I think. Stand up. Good. If you don't mind, I'll keep my robe — I need to get to the bathroom, and that shirt covers a lot more of you than it does of me."

Catherine stood and busied herself with the shirt. She felt the white cotton falling to just below her bottom. She wasn't nearly as concerned with what others would think, seeing her wandering down the hallway in a shirt, as she was about the fact that he was lending it to her. He had to see her again, if only to get his shirt back.

"Give me a few minutes to get cleaned up and shaved. Then I'll come get you and we'll go have breakfast together." He looked down at his watch. "Perhaps I should say lunch."

Catherine smiled. "All right." She gathered up her evening's dancing shoes and jewelry and dress and went to the door. Kit opened it for her. He kissed her lightly before she went out.

No one saw her as she hurried along, her feet chilled against the cool floorboards. Leslie

112

was in their room, sleeping deeply in her bed, alone. Catherine gathered up her bath things and went out. When she came back a while later, dressed in a lilac summer frock, fresh and glowing, Leslie opened her eyes and said, "What? What are you doing? Where did you spend the night?"

"With a man." Catherine was unable to keep the jubilation out of her voice. "With a gorgeous, wonderful, sexy man."

"Oh, God, my head is throbbing. Why did I drink so much? I think I'm going to die."

"Shall I bring you some water? Or orange juice? Or coffee?"

"Oh, God, oh, God, not yet, give me a few more days to sleep. This is gruesome. Who is he?"

"Kit Bemish. He's from Boston. He's finishing at Harvard Law School. He's — "

"Oh, God, if I had the energy, I'd laugh. My dear Catherine, how perfect for you to have a Bostonian lawyer for your first lover. Truth, justice, and the American way, right? Clark Kent. Does he wear glasses?"

"You're just jealous. Or you would be if you met him. He's really wonderful, Leslie. He's handsome, and kind, and fascinating, and ambitious in an altruistic way, he's not just greedy, and — "

"Do me a favor," Leslie interrupted. "I'm glad you met this paragon, but try to remember that you don't have to fall in love with a man just because you slept with him. This is a party, Catherine. Don't make a one-night stand into the love of a lifetime."

"I don't think I like you when you're hung over," Catherine said.

Leslie groaned. "I, on the other hand, adore myself when I'm hung over. I think I'm going to throw up. Oh, God."

At that moment Kit knocked on the door. Catherine slid out quickly, gladly leaving Leslie to her miserable self. But as they walked down the stairs and into the enormous dining room, where servants were serving various groups breakfast and lunch, Catherine reminded herself that Leslie was right to warn her not to take it all too seriously. Perhaps underneath Kit's charmingly trustworthy exterior was a wild playboy, a cad. Perhaps tonight he'd find another woman to enchant. Well, then, she'd find another man to be enchanted by. She looked around the room — there were certainly a lot of handsome men here.

But none of them compared with Kit. She knew it couldn't be true, but he looked like the handsomest human being she'd ever set eyes on, as handsome as a god. His hands, with their long, sturdy, thick fingers, seemed not like mere hands, but perfectly shaped, sexy, sensitive, tender, knowing. His eyes. Had she noticed last night what unusual eyes he had, like topazes, so reddish and striking set against his pale skin and blond hair? When he looked at her, she felt nearly ill with lust. Sitting next to him, she felt the strangest thing: a kind of *homesickness* for him, a terrible pulling melancholy that wouldn't be satisfied until she was back in bed with him, naked, with his penis inside her and his breath against her face.

"What are you thinking?" he asked.

Catherine grinned. "You'd be very smug if I told you."

He took her hand and held it on top of the table. This gesture, so public, made her breath stop. Surely he wouldn't do this with others watching if he meant to abandon her tonight. And she could not see or think or plan or desire any further than tonight. Tomorrow she would be driven back to the airport with her three silly friends. Then she'd fly back to the States. The most she could hope for was that he would be on the same plane. But that was tomorrow. Like a child, she didn't want to see past tonight.

"What are you thinking?" she asked him.

He was looking at her hand and gently

stroking her skin with his thumb. He looked up and met her eyes. "I was wondering if I could convince you to stay in France for a few more days. I don't have to get back to the States for a while. I think it would be very nice if you and I could spend some time together in Paris."

Catherine would always remember that moment, how it spread around her, opening up the world, as if with his words he had cracked her open. Open sesame: from within her heart light came pouring out. Light flooded out in waves, it illuminated the world. She smiled back at Kit, too stunned with joy to speak, feeling golden, glowing, a perfect thing in the universe, joy splitting her open to reveal a heart of dazzling light.

Kimberly Weyland was married that day in the ancient stone Catholic church, which was so small that the guests were crowded against one another and many had to stand. It was a splendid day for a wedding, which was fortunate, since according to custom the bride and bridegroom and wedding party had to walk to the church and back to the house. On the lawn blue-and-white-striped tents had been set up. There were tables of food on the lawn and the terrace as well as throughout the house. The Croces had invited everyone in the village to the wedding feast.

Some of the party looked dimmed by the night before, with deep circles under their eyes, exhaustion making their faces slack. But Catherine — and, she fancied, Kit — looked better than they ever had in their lives, perfect, splendid, and shining. She wore a pale pink silk dress to the wedding, a dress the color of the maiden blush rose, but she didn't wear it for very long. After the wedding and the toasts and feasts and laughter, when the dancing began again, she and Kit went up to his room. They spent the rest of the night there, sleeping and waking to make love.

The next morning she hurried to her room to organize her clothing and pack for the trip to Paris. Kit had rented a car, a little white Renault, and he was packing, too. The bride and groom had left the night before for their honeymoon. The party was winding down. Leslie wasn't in her room when Catherine came in, and she hadn't returned by the time Catherine was through packing, so Catherine carried her luggage down to the first floor and went to look for her.

Leslie was in the front living room with a group of friends, drinking coffee and yawning.

"Leslie, come here for just a moment."

Giving Catherine a quizzical look, Leslie excused herself from the group.

In a low voice Catherine said, "Look, I'm not going back with Anne and Robin and Melonie — I've got to find them and tell them. I'm going into Paris to spend a few days with Kit."

"Oh, my God, how romantic! He's yummy, Catherine. Good for you. Well, give me a call before you leave for home, okay? I want to hear every detail!"

"I will!" Catherine kissed her friend on both cheeks.

In a flurry she found the girls and told them her news, much to their squealing delight. Then a servant carried Kit's and her luggage out to the Renault. They climbed into the red leather interior and rolled away from the wedding house, toward Paris.

Catherine and Kit stayed at the Crillon for three days and three nights. Now and then they forced themselves out of the room to walk onto the Place de la Concorde and up and down the Champs-Elysées, or to attend a symphony concert at the Petit Palais, or to walk through the Louvre. One night they ate at La Tour d'Argent. But they had both seen Paris before, when they were younger. The only sights they really wanted to see were each other.

They talked. They talked about important things. Catherine felt even closer to him when he told her about the side of his family he didn't like — their complacency, their terrible restraint, which was often interpreted as snobbishness. In return, Catherine was able to talk honestly about her family for the first time since she had talked to Leslie about them years ago at school. He didn't dislike her for her bitter feelings about her family. He told Catherine that in spite of his family's faults, they were committed to helping him in a political career.

"I thought all politicians were slightly crooked by definition," Catherine said once.

"I think you're right. But maybe I can change that," Kit said. "Perhaps I'm being idealistic, but I'd like to try."

His ambitions, his aspirations, made her slightly in awe of him. Humming along in the back of her mind was the question of what all this meant for her, about *them*. Oh, she knew she was getting ahead of herself, but how would she fit in? Could she be a political wife? She didn't think she was the type to smile and shake hands with a thousand strangers. But she knew she would do anything to be with him, even that. But what if she wasn't the right person to be the wife of an ambitious politician? What if he thought he should marry someone with real wealth or a more helpful political background? . . . She spoke none of these thoughts aloud, but they were always there, murmuring their self-centered queries in her ear.

Mostly, though, they didn't talk, or walk, or sightsee, or eat. Mostly they made love. It was crazy. They were obsessed. If they were doing anything else, they were thinking about how soon they could stop doing it so they could return to the hotel. Catherine felt that she was taking the sustenance of life from Kit. When she wasn't attached to him, skin to skin, she felt as if she were dying, she could hardly breathe, she panicked, even though he was sitting right next to her.

The odd thing was that she knew she hadn't yet experienced the ultimate pleasure of lovemaking, and she thought Kit probably knew it, too. But that didn't matter. She still wanted — *needed* — to make love to him. But by the second day in Paris she could hardly walk, and sometimes when she sat up on the bed her knees trembled. She felt hot and swollen between her legs and felt relief only when taking a bath — or, strangely enough, when making love. It was insane. She had sometimes seen odd couples together, the man well over six feet tall, broad and burly, with a wife who was only five feet tall, bird-boned, her hips the width of her husband's thigh. How do they ever manage to make love? Catherine had wondered. Now she felt she knew, for although Kit wasn't huge and she wasn't tiny, it *felt* that way when he entered her. It felt primitive and bestial, even brutal. She would lie with her head turned to one side, eyes closed, whimpering, broken, in a glorious pain.

"Do you want me to stop?" Kit would whisper, soothing her, smoothing her sweaty hair away from her face.

"No, no, please don't," she would say.

So he went on and on, as if he needed to be there, inside her, fastened on to her, and so he labored, holding himself back, working hard, both frenzied and desperately calm. It was as if they were cursed to make love every second of the day, as if they would die if they stopped making love. As Kit worked against her, eyes closed, concentrating, grimacing, breathing heavily, exhausted, trembling, swollen, shuddering, she knew they were doing more than making love. It was as if they were making a vow with their bodies and sealing it with the glue of their sex.

Finally, of course, they had to stop. They

had to leave Paris, go home — and not together. The time came when they showered and dressed in respectable clothes. They packed their luggage and checked out of the hotel. They dropped off the little rented car, which they hadn't used.

Suddenly, too soon, it was over, and they were at the airport.

Kit was flying to Boston, Catherine to New York. Her plane left two hours before his, so he came with her to her terminal.

The hardest thing for Catherine during their Paris stay had been to keep herself from saying to Kit, "I love you." For she knew she loved him. Even though she had never loved a man before, except for schoolgirl crushes, she knew this absolutely. All her life, she'd had trouble finding out what she knew, what she wanted to do with her life, who she was, but when she met Kit she was certain at once. She was supremely confident. She wanted him, and the more she had him, the more she wanted him. For once in her life she had found the perfect thing.

She wanted him to know that. She hoped she'd told him with her body, but she wanted to tell him in words. So before leaving the hotel, while Kit was in the shower, she took a sheet of hotel stationery and wrote:

Dear Kit,

These days with you have been the most wonderful days of my life. Even if I never see you again, I want you to know that. I love you. I'm sure I'll love you the rest of my life.

Catherine

There was much more she wanted to say, but when she rehearsed it in her mind, the words seemed overblown and sentimental. This was simple and honest. She folded the note into an envelope, and just before she got on her plane back home, she handed it to Kit.

"Wait till I've gone to read it," she said.

"I'll call you when I get home," Kit replied.

They embraced tightly. She did not think she could pull away. But when her plane was called, she wrenched herself from him and walked through the gateway to the ramp.

It was afternoon when she arrived back in New York. She went right to the apartment, showered, then lay down on the bed to wait for Kit's call.

The next thing she knew, it was morning. She woke up, stunned. Had she slept so soundly that she'd missed hearing the phone ring? She was amazed at the power of her disappointment. She wanted to weep.

But she had to go to work, and once there she was able to relive the trip during coffee breaks, when she told Mrs. V about the wedding, the flowers, the château. Kit knew she worked during the day. He would call when she got home tonight.

But he didn't call that night, either, although she sat in an agony of suspense, waiting, eating her dinner right next to the phone so she wouldn't miss its ring. By midnight she was miserable. What had happened? Should she call him? She didn't know his number, but she could call directory assistance in Boston. . . . No, she wouldn't call. She wouldn't chase him. He would call tomorrow. She stretched out on her bed, pressing against the pillow, reliving her days and nights with Kit in Paris.

The next morning at eight o'clock Catherine let herself into the shop with her own key, then locked the door behind her. The shop wouldn't open for two hours, but this was when Piet and Mr. Vanderveld returned from the flower market on Sixth Avenue. As usual, they had been there since five-thirty, looking over the day's flowers and choosing the best ones at the best prices. Now Piet was carrying them in from his van to the cooler. Mr. Vanderveld was at a church consulting with a client about decorating the church and the adjoining hall for a wedding and reception. Mrs. Vanderveld was sitting at the counter at the front of the shop, muttering over her account and order books.

"Good morning, Catherine," she said. "I think Piet needs help in the back."

Catherine tossed her purse under the counter and went behind the curtain. Today the shop looked and smelled like a luscious jungle; they were preparing for several weddings. Buckets of Queen Anne's lace stood at the back of the shop, waiting to be used as fillers for the less hardy, more precious roses, gladioli, peonies, lilies, carnations, delphiniums, and iris that filled the large cooler at the back. Bags of potting soil leaned against the walls and table legs, waiting to be filled into vases and pots. As usual, utensils were everywhere.

Catherine put on her smock and tied her thick hair back up off her head. It was already hot inside and out today, and everything was swollen with heat.

Piet came through the opened double doors at the back of the shop, his arms loaded with a heavy cardboard box of flowers. Catherine hurried back to pull open the wooden cooler door for him. A rush of fresh sweet-scented air mixed with the sour, familiar odor of mildewed wood spilled over her, and she inhaled happily. Her eyes fell on the curve of Piet's back as he bent to put down the box. Already he had taken off his shirt, and his back gleamed bronze and smooth. She wanted to run her hand over his back in the way one instinctively reaches out to stroke a cat. She wanted to slide her fingers along the glistening sweat that slid over his skin.

She was grateful to her body for that, that small rush of lust. It told her she was not totally obsessed with Kit.

"You need to start cutting the roses," Piet said, straightening up. "And those damned frogs have to be unpacked."

A new fashion was sweeping the flower industry, a sort of minimalist movement that involved the exact placement of one or two or three flowers in an unusual container. Now the shop had to buy almost as many figurines and containers as flowers. One design that Mr. Vanderveld had come up with to satisfy his customers' desire for something modern was a piece of bark with a thimble-size container for water and one rose or lily, even a glad or iris with its stem cut off, surrounded by pebbles, stones, moss, shells, and a china frog or bird glued to the surface. Mr. Vanderveld hated these things, but his customers considered them works of art and bought them as fast as he could make them.

Quickly Catherine unpacked the horrid little mushrooms, water creatures, and leprechauns. She tossed the box out the back door into the dumpster. Already the alley reeked. She took up a bundle of long-stemmed roses, laid them on the table, and turned to get the knife to cut and split the stems. Just then Piet tried to pass her, his arms lifted high to protect a sheaf of lilies. They were caught facing each other in the narrow aisle, their hips nearly touching, and although they'd shared this kind of intimate instant many times over the past three years, this time Piet did not ignore it. He stood still, and he looked at Catherine.

With his arms lifted high, she was aware of the thick tufts of dark hair under his arms and the way the veins and tendons ran around the muscles of his arms like vines around a tree trunk. She felt that he was daring her.

"I need a knife," she said. She was surprised at how low her voice was. "No matter how much I clean and arrange this place, Mr. Vanderveld always manages to mess it up and lose everything."

Still Piet looked at her, arms high, not

moving, but now with a smile beginning on his wide mouth. She could feel the heat of his body.

"Piet," she said, caught in his heat, and stopped, confused.

"Catherine," a man said, but it was not Piet who spoke. Catherine looked toward the front to see Kit Bemish standing just inside the curtain.

"Kit!" For a moment Catherine was paralyzed with joy. He was wearing chinos, a pale blue shirt with the sleeves rolled up, and a striped tie, loosened at the collar in concession to the heat. How handsome — how *magnificent* — he was.

"Mrs. Vanderveld said I could come on back. I apologize for interrupting your work, but — "

"No! Oh, don't worry, it's fine, it's all right!" Now the wave of shock had passed, and Catherine could move. She rushed toward Kit, smiling, and threw her arms around him. "I'm so glad to see you! I can't believe it! Why didn't you call?"

He didn't put his arms around her. His reserve surprised her, and then she realized he would never embrace a woman passionately in front of another man. She dropped her arms, drew away. She heard Piet slam the back door.

She said quickly, "Let's go over to Nini's for coffee. There's really no room to talk here."

At the door she paused long enough to introduce Kit to Mrs. Vanderveld and promised she'd be back in fifteen minutes.

"Too bad I don't have a little more time," Catherine said, smiling smugly as they settled into a booth. "My apartment's so close. If we had even half an hour — "

"Two coffees, please. Is that what you'd like, Catherine?"

Catherine looked at the waitress impatiently. "Yes, fine. Kit. Now! Why didn't you call? How long can you stay?"

Kit had seated himself across from her. Now he reached out and took her hands in his.

"Catherine." He looked down and cleared his throat. His face was flushed, and Catherine's heart cartwheeled inside her.

"Catherine. I came here because I have to tell you something I couldn't tell you on the phone. Catherine — what happened in Paris . . . I didn't mean for it to happen. It shouldn't have happened. I'm almost engaged to someone else. Haley Hilton. I've had, this, um, understanding with her for two or three years now, that we'll get engaged and married when I've finished law school."

Catherine pulled her hands away.

The waitress put two white porcelain mugs on the table between them. Kit waited until she had scribbled the bill, dropped it next to his spoon, and left before speaking again. Then he kept his voice low.

"I've been going crazy the past few days, Catherine. What I had with you in France, what I felt for you . . . Catherine, I think I was falling in love with you."

"Then fall in love with me! Forget Haley Hilton," Catherine said, puzzled.

"It's not that easy. I mean, it's easy enough to fall in love with you, Jesus, Catherine, that's pretty obvious. But this thing with Haley goes back a long way. It's what our parents want."

"What your parents want? But what do *you* want, Kit?"

"Catherine, that hardly matters — I'm an only child. My mother almost died giving birth to me. I owe my parents a lot." He paused. "I want to be honest. I chose Haley, too. I thought I loved her. Until I met you." He smiled ruefully. "Catherine, what you and I had together in Paris was so — extreme. I'm not sure it would make a good marriage."

"I think it's exactly what marriage is all about," Catherine said quietly.

"Believe me, Catherine, I've agonized over this."

Catherine reached out her hand to take Kit's. When their palms touched, warm, naked, solid, she knew he felt the electricity between them — as strong as a shock.

Kit pulled his hand away. Glaring, he said, "It wasn't just that between us, Catherine. I don't want you to think it was. I like you. You made me laugh. I felt at home with you. If I could, I'd marry you, but I can't. That's what I came to say." He rose, tossed some money on the table, and turned to leave.

"Kit," Catherine said, rising, grabbing his arm. "Don't leave!"

"I shouldn't have come in the first place. I should have phoned." Kit looked at her. "Catherine, I've got to leave. Let go."

Catherine took her hand away and let him walk out the door. If she'd had any doubts about how they belonged together, how they were meant for each other, all those doubts had faded now. Kit loved her. It was plain on his face, in his voice, in his touch. "It will come to you," Kathryn had said three years ago, and Catherine repeated those words to herself now. Kit had come to her; he would come back. In spite of what he had just told her, she knew he would come back.

She waited at the table for half an hour. When he hadn't returned, she went back to the shop and worked furiously, ignoring Mrs. V's questioning looks. She was glad to work. It made time blur.

That night she waited by the phone. All the next week she waited for his call. She checked her mailbox as soon as she got home from work.

The shop was busy. She worked hard, doggedly. The end of June passed. July came. Slowly the days crawled by.

One night in the middle of July Catherine began to cry. She forced herself to face reality. Kit had told her he had to leave her, and he had. He had told her he was marrying a woman named Haley Hilton, and he would. And now her world of work, which once had been all-consuming, appeared drab, leached of color, and of life.

CHAPTER 4

August was Vanderveld Flowers' slowest month. The normal business and restaurant orders still came in, but society was out of town. People had escaped from the city's heat to Long Island or Maine or the Cape. The Vandervelds knew it happened every year, but they were short-tempered and grumbly anyway.

Catherine was miserable. She hadn't heard from Kit, and now she was trying to give up the hope that she ever would. She hated him for not wanting her, but she hated herself more for loving him so much, so easily. She had *known* he was the one for her, the love of her life. And she had been wrong. The realization that she'd erred instinctively about love made her doubt every decision she'd ever made and every new one she faced.

She was making the last delivery of the day, one only a few blocks from the shop.

She climbed the steps of the gracious old building on Sixty-second Street, took the elevator to the third floor, knocked listlessly on the door.

"Oh, it's you, honey, hi, come on in," Helen Norton said.

Catherine had no choice but to obey, since Helen had turned to walk back into her living room, leaving the door wide open. Catherine wasn't in the mood to socialize. Still, she knew she couldn't afford to insult Helen, whose "friend" was one of the shop's most regular and best-paying customers.

Catherine crossed the room behind Helen and set the long narrow box filled with a dozen red roses down on the coffee table.

Helen snatched the lid off.

"Any extra little goodies today?" she said. She shuffled through the flowers, then dropped the lid back in disappointment.

Sometimes Helen's admirer brought in a bauble from Tiffany's or Cartier's for Mrs. Vanderveld to arrange artistically in the sheaf of flowers, but today he had sent only the usual dozen luscious, fragrant, exquisitely tapered long-stems, which Helen treated like a snarl of poison ivy. This drove Catherine crazy.

"Shall I put these in water for you?" Catherine asked.

"Oh, would you do that for me, honey? You know where the vases are," Helen said. "And when you come back, I've got a treat for you."

Helen, wearing a skimpy fluttering ruffled robe, was preoccupied with about eighteen evening gowns draped over the backs of the chairs, the sofas, every piece of furniture in the room. Catherine carried the roses into the tiny kitchen, filled a glass vase with water, cut the stems, and arranged the flowers. It always surprised her how little Helen cared about the flowers she received. But then many things were surprising about Helen.

One day about four months ago, an elegant older man had entered the flower shop, requested that a dozen roses be sent to Mrs. Helen Norton, with a card enclosed, and insisted on paying in cash. Catherine had carried out his instructions with the bored face she had learned to wear while serving the upper-crust patrons of Vanderveld Flowers.

But as soon as the man walked out the door, Catherine had grabbed Mrs. V.

"I know who that is! That's P. J. Willington! I've seen him at my parents' parties! He's married. And his wife is certainly *not* named Helen Norton."

"Now, dear, why get so excited? You're old enough to understand this sort of thing," Mrs.

135

Vanderveld had said. "This isn't the first time it's happened, and it won't be the last, and if you want us to keep the gentleman's business, you'll continue to act with the discretion I just saw. You were very good, Catherine."

But even Mrs. Vanderveld smiled when they found out that "Mrs. Helen Norton," who lived in an elegant apartment house off Park Avenue, a bastion of respectability, had only months before been "the Exotic Eleena Mourzekian, Belly Dancer to Kings."

Catherine and Piet had been at the back of the shop one morning, unpacking a box of glads from Long Island. The long-stalked blooms were packed with newspapers to absorb the melting ice, and smiling up at her from a crumpled page of an old *Daily News* was the woman P. J. Willington sent flowers to, dressed in a belly-dancing costume that showed off her considerable charms. The advertisement said that she was appearing nightly at the Sheiks' Club, off Eighth Avenue between Twenty-seventh and Twenty-eighth streets. The newspaper was several months old. When Catherine checked the day's paper, she found the Exotic Eleena had been replaced by the Magnificent Mona. It was obvious to Catherine that P. J. Willington, scion of one of New York's finest families, had relocated the Exotic Eleena to a location more suited to one of his station.

Catherine liked Helen, who was not only about ten years older than she was, but much wiser in the ways of the world. Helen seemed tough and vulnerable at once and was always so solicitous of Catherine's attentions that it would have been rude for Catherine not to come into the apartment now and then.

In fact, the first time that Catherine knocked on the door with a narrow box of roses in her arms, Helen had opened the door, reached out, and actually pulled Catherine into the apartment.

"Thank God you're a girl, honey. Put that thing down and zip me up, would you?" Helen had said.

That day, Helen was wearing a silver lamé sheath, clearly an off-the-rack garment that hadn't been cut for true hourglass proportions like Helen's. Catherine came in, set the flowers on the coffee table, then struggled with the zipper. When she finally succeeded, Helen's full white breasts bulged over the top of the low-cut silver dress like meringues. She gave Catherine a huge tip and offered her some coffee, which Catherine refused.

As the months passed and Catherine continued to deliver the flowers, she grew fond of this enterprising young woman who had enough brains to realize she didn't have enough brains to get very far without using the gifts of the extraordinary body she'd been given. Helen's plans were to keep any of the jewelry and money P. J. Willington gave her until she had enough to go back to New Jersey and start her own beauty shop. Until then, she said, the old man was nice enough, even kind of touching in a way.

"Let me tell ya, honey, nobody likes to get old, not the poor, not the rich, not the powerful; nothing helps when you're getting old and facing the big blackout."

Today, when Catherine came out of the kitchenette carrying the vase of ruby-red roses, Helen pointed at the gowns tossed around the room and said, "Take one. Find one you think you could use, and keep it. I've gotta make some room in my closets."

"Oh," Catherine said, "I don't think" — she stopped to think of how to phrase it politely — "um, that I'll ever have any place to go in a gown like those."

"Nonsense!" Helen said. "Don't be so pessimistic, doll. You never know what will happen in life. You're not a bad-looking girl, and you're young, why, some nice young wealthy kid might come walking into your flower shop and see you and *bam!* True love, just like that! It happens every day. Then he'll want to take you dancing at El Morocco and you'll be all set. Go on, choose one!"

It was clear that Catherine couldn't leave without taking one of the flashy dresses unless she wanted to insult Helen. Privately Catherine thought Helen was a little bored with her life of clandestine luxury. Certainly she always welcomed the occasion to talk with Catherine, although she had never once spoken her friend's name aloud. Catherine searched through the glamorous gowns, with Helen providing a running account of where she'd bought each one, how much it had cost, and where she'd worn it and how many times. Finally Catherine found a fairly conservative emerald satin she could actually imagine herself wearing, although it took a stretch of imagination to consider ever dancing again in her life.

"I'd like this one," Catherine said. "If you're sure — "

"Oh, doll, you're doing me a favor, believe me. I've gotta get some new things, you know a man gets bored easily. Want some coffee?" She stuffed the shimmering gown into a Saks bag.

"No, really, I can't, I've got more deliveries to make," Catherine lied.

Back on the street, Catherine half wished she had stayed. She had no place else to go, no one to see. Helen would understand the furies that played beneath her skin, she thought. Helen would understand the grief that flashed high inside her whenever she thought of Kit Bemish.

Catherine could imagine Helen saying, "Aw, kid, the old, old story. I could have told you, never trust a man."

It was after five now, but the August brightness made the day seem still young and full of promise. Catherine walked down Sixty-second and turned up Park Avenue in the direction of Leslie's apartment, her shoulder bag on one arm and the rustling Saks bag with the gown on her other.

"Catherine!"

Catherine turned. Ann, fourteen beautiful years old, ran down the sidewalk to her sister, her blond ponytail bouncing from side to side. "I've been waiting outside your apartment for you and then I saw you coming down the street and I've been yelling your name for about two hours now, have you gone deaf?"

"I'm sorry, Annie," Catherine said, hugging her. "What in the world are you doing in New York?"

"Oh, Cathy, I'm so miserable!" Ann's enormous blue eyes filled with tears.

Catherine put her arm around her sister and pulled her against her as they walked. "Come on. Let's go get an ice cream. That will stop any misery for a while."

"Okay. I'm so glad to see you — I miss you so much! Mom and Dad are skunks. What's in that bag?"

"A used dress a friend gave me," Catherine said.

At an ice-cream parlor on Lexington they settled into a pink-and-white-striped booth and ordered hot-fudge sundaes.

"Now. Why aren't you on the Vineyard?" Catherine asked.

"I came into New York with Dad. He's got some appointments. I wanted to see you." Ann paused until the waitress had gone away. "Cathy, I can't stand it out there with Mom and Dad anymore. All they do is drink. And fight. They're driving me crazy."

"Well, get out of the house. Where are all your friends?"

"At camp. That's another thing. Mother won't send me to riding camp or tennis camp or anywhere this summer; she said they can't *afford* it this year, if you can *believe* she said that. I can't believe they expect me to just hang around the Vineyard the whole summer doing nothing."

"What's Shelly doing?"

"Drinking." Ann spooned a giant glob of syrup into her mouth.

"What?"

"Drinking. I'm serious. He's just like Mom and Dad, he goes out at night with his friends and comes home about dawn, puking all over the front porch and the bathroom floor. He sleeps all day. You really should come stay with us a few days, you wouldn't believe It. It smells like biology lab."

"Where's Genene?"

"Oh, she's still there. She's as crazy as the rest of them. Every day she cooks up these meals, Catherine, roast beef and mashed potatoes for lunch, lobster for dinner, corn on the cob, and she sets the table like the queen's coming, but no one ever eats the stuff. She's got roast beef on the table at noon while everyone in the house is stumbling around in a robe clutching a glass of Alka-Seltzer or a cup of coffee. I don't know why she does it, it's like she's been put on automatic and doesn't want to admit she sees what's going on." Ann spooned some ice cream into her mouth. "But she's so quiet, and she never talks to me, just 'Yes, miss,' 'No, miss' — I really hate that crap, you know — "

"It's not Genene's fault. Mother makes her say it."

"I know. Still. She's a spook. Catherine, I can't stay there anymore. I'll go crazy."

"What are you going to do, then?"

"I want to live with you."

Catherine, who had been toying with her sundae, stopped and looked at her sister. "Annie, you can't live with me. Mom and Dad wouldn't let you. Besides, you'd hate New York in the summer. It gets so hot here, and it's so boring. Where are Berry and Sandy? Aren't they on the island this summer?"

"Yes."

"Well, can't you enjoy being with them? You can swim and play tennis and go sailing. You'll have more fun there than you possibly could here. Mother and Dad will come out of it, they always do. It'll get better."

Ann put her spoon down next to the glass tulip sundae dish and bent her head. Tears shimmered in her eyes.

"I have an idea," Catherine said. "Tomorrow and Monday are my days off. Let's go out to Everly and visit Grandmother."

"Whoopee." Ann looked glum.

"Oh, Annie, don't be that way. At least it will be cooler out there."

The first Sunday in August, Catherine sat with her grandmother by the lily pond at Everly. Ann was lying on her stomach by the pond, pulling a stick through the water, watching the ripples and curls. It was a perfectly beautiful day. Birds flitted in and out of the fruit trees, iridescent dragonflies and damselflies skimmed the blue water of the pond. If Catherine closed her eyes slightly, the bank of purple-flowered rhododendrons and fuchsia azaleas, blue delphinium and pink geraniums, blurred into an Impressionist painting. The sun beat warmly onto her skin.

Kathryn was pouring tea. China cups, silver spoons, and the fat china pot were arranged on the white wicker table with plates of cake and cookies.

"Would you like some tea, Catherine?" her grandmother asked.

"Not now, thank you."

"It might do you good. You're looking peaked. So is Ann, for that matter."

Catherine was quiet. Always before, when she had tried to confide in her grandmother, Kathryn had reacted with boredom and even impatience. Finally she said, "Ann is having a hard time with Mother and Father. They're drinking."

"Yes. I can sympathize. My brother drank. My husband drank. Poor Ann."

Warmed by her grandmother's sympathy, Catherine felt bold enough to say, "And I've had a bad summer, too. I fell in love with someone. I thought it was serious. But he, ah, well, dumped me." She tried to keep her words and her voice from being too maudlin.

Grandmother bored quickly of self-pity.

Kathryn didn't respond. Catherine quickly looked at her grandmother. Kathryn was idly stirring her tea but looking off into the distance. Her marvelous blue eyes were untroubled, as if she were gazing at mountains. I've lost her, Catherine thought.

"I think I should take you two to Everly," Kathryn said. "I haven't been back there for a long time. You girls have never seen it. It might be just the thing to cheer you up."

"Oh, Grandmother!" Catherine cried. "I'd love to go to Everly! I'd love to go to England! I know the Vandervelds will let me go if I don't ask for pay! And Ann will love it!" She jumped from her chair and flew to hug her grandmother.

"Careful, Catherine," Kathryn said, shoulders stiff. "You'll spill my tea."

At first, to their surprise, Catherine and Ann hated the British Everly. It was so formal. Their first sight of the house was in a taxi from Heathrow through a curtain of rain that chilled the air and drained all color from the landscape. They were sleepy from the flight and dozed during the hour's drive, to be awakened by Kathryn as they approached the estate.

"Girls," she said. The quality of reverence

in her voice was enough to jolt them awake.

There it stood, a stern stone-and-brick Georgian giant, rising up out of the fog. Its massive bland symmetry was in sharp contrast with the whimsical, rambling hodgepodge of Kathryn's Victorian Everly. The taxi pulled to a stop on the circle drive, and the girls were hastened under umbrellas up the wide urn-bordered steps and into the main hall.

"Kathryn, my dear!"

"Madeline."

Catherine and Ann watched as their grandmother warmly embraced Madeline Boxworthy, Everly's new owner. Madeline was a beautiful woman, tall, with an erect, soldierly carriage, blazing blue eyes, and thick white hair swooped up off her forehead and face in a sort of Gibson-girl twist. She had that famous British skin, creamy and translucent as Haviland china. Her eyes, when she turned them on the Eliot girls, were coolly appraising.

"You must be Catherine. The florist. We'll have so much to talk about. And you're Ann. I know you must be tired, Kathryn, so I thought we'd wait until later to have your granddaughters meet my children. We will have to wait until this annoying rain stops to look at the garden."

"We *are* tired, Madeline. I think we all

146

will need a little rest before tea. But if you don't mind, I'd like to show the girls a bit of the house before we go to our rooms."

"Of course. Feel free to go anywhere downstairs. Upstairs, you know, are the guest bedrooms. We're full this week. I was lucky to be able to fit you in. I'll have your luggage taken to your rooms. When you're ready to go up, you'll find me in the kitchen."

"Thank you," Kathryn said. Putting a hand on each girl's shoulder, she steered them into the library. "Aah," she breathed, her voice filled with content. "It's still here." She led her granddaughters across the wide Turkish carpet and parquet floor to the one wall that wasn't covered with bookshelves. An ornate wood-and-glass display case of war medals stood against the wall, but what their grandmother wanted them to see was the photograph hanging above it.

"I was born in this house in 1897," Kathryn said. "I was christened Kathryn Patterson Paxton. Life was very different then. England was still England. My parents were alive, and young, and Clifford was at that first rather glamorous stage of alcoholism. Here we all are, just as I remember it."

Catherine and Ann stood in dutiful silence, peering at their grandmother and great-grandparents. They knew this photograph was slightly famous, reproduced in history books and books on English country houses, because it served to show the strict formal class structure of English society at the turn of the century. It was taken in 1914, in front of the massive building, where Kathryn's mother and father and their staff had organized on the front lawn to serve tea to the British troops stationed nearby. Twelve long tables were arranged in a long rectangle on the grass, covered with white damask tablecloths and silver, laden with pastries and crumpets and sliced hams and marmalades. The housemaids, gardeners, butlers, even the two gamekeepers, had been brought in to serve and also to be photographed for posterity. Kathryn's parents stood in front of the table, stiff, stony-faced, dignified to petrification. Kathryn's mother wore a long black dress and a hat with a shockingly frivolous plume. At a respectful distance behind them stood the ladies' maid, steward, and head housekeeper.

Adolescent Kathryn and her older brother, Clifford, stood between their parents, formally dressed, wooden-faced.

"My brother Clifford eventually inherited Everly," Kathryn told them. "Though by the time he reached majority it was obvious that he had no talent for anything except gambling, drinking, and partying in the fine old tradition of wealthy sons. Fortunately I met your grandfather, Andrew Eliot, three years after this picture was taken. I was twenty and he was twenty-five — a major in the American troops stationed at Everly. He was absolutely dashing. I married him and went to live with him in the United States. And thence came your father."

"Did Clifford have any children?" Ann asked.

"Ah, no. He drank himself into impotency, childlessness, and despondency. He died of a liver disease in the early fifties. Not, unfortunately, before enduring the disgrace of having to sell Everly. It had been in the Paxton family for eight generations." Kathryn sighed deeply. "A shame. A terrible shame."

More to release her grandmother from painful memories than out of true curiosity, Catherine asked, "Was it the Boxworthys who bought Everly from your brother?"

"No. It was the Thorpes. A good family, but unfortunately they found it too expensive to keep as a private home. They sold it to the Boxworthys in the early sixties. Mr. Boxworthy had been a surgeon, much loved and overworked. He died much too young, in his fifties, leaving Madeline to shoulder the financial burden of Everly herself. That's how Everly became a bed-and-breakfast, although I must say under Madeline's care it has more the atmosphere of a private club."

Kathryn's voice weakened then, and she sagged. "I'm tired, girls. I think we should go and sleep off some of this jet lag."

Catherine and Ann shared a lovely old high-ceilinged room with a fireplace and casement windows. Except for a few discreet notes about checkout time, tea time, and fire escapes printed on fine-quality bond paper and left on the desk under a vase of lusty red French roses, this could have been a room in any elegant private home. The twin beds were high and hard.

"We might as well be back home," Ann wailed, throwing herself on her bed. "I mean at least Grandmother is talking to us, but everyone here is a thousand years old and nothing fun's happening."

"Don't be a pill, Ann. You haven't met everyone here. Mrs. Boxworthy has three children, and I think one of the girls is your age."

"Yeah, and the boy is your age, lucky you. But it's so dark here — it's creepy!"

"Wait till the rain stops. And you're tired. Let's take a nap. I'm exhausted."

"Oh, there's something wrong with you. All you ever want to do is sleep," Ann said petulantly.

Catherine looked over at her sister. Ann

was fourteen. Of course she had boyfriends and crushes on boys, but she was still innocent and impressionable. If Catherine told Ann about Kit, it would make her sad, and that wasn't what they had come here for. Catherine slipped out of her clothes, which were wrinkled from traveling, let them fall on the floor, then climbed between the sheets. Burrowing her head in her pillow, she was surrounded by a faint sweet scent: lavender. She fell asleep.

She awakened thinking of Kit. Something about the state between deep sleep and consciousness, the slumberous fluidity of her body and mind, recalled vividly to her just how Kit had made her feel. Now always when awakening, and often when falling asleep, her body would bring up, like a blush on a plum, rosy memories of their time together. What she had shared with Kit had been as deep and possessive as sleep. Her body could not forget him. Her mind could not believe that he was gone.

The pain of losing him was still a sharpness, but the memories of their time together were strangely soothing. Because of Kit she knew sorrow, but he had taught her many other things, too. He had opened her up to an awareness of the world. So now she lay among the lavender-scented sheets, listening to the streaming rain, feeling very much alive and oddly desirous.

A tapping came at their door. Their grandmother looked in.

"Girls? Tea time. Get dressed and meet me in the library, will you?"

Ann grumbled at being awakened, then immediately said, "I'm starving. I hope at least the food's decent here."

They slipped into dresses and sweaters, for it was cool even though it was August, and hurried downstairs.

Wide doors had been opened between the library and the front drawing room. Both rooms were full of people and dogs. Catherine counted five gawky spotted hounds curled up on overstuffed chairs or patroling the room for dropped crumbs.

"Catherine. Ann." Their grandmother beckoned them to join her in a corner of the library. Madeline was seated on a long sofa next to Kathryn. As the Eliot girls approached, a young man unfolded his long legs and stood up politely.

"Hello. I'm Ned Boxworthy."

Ned Boxworthy was so gorgeous, Catherine had to keep herself from gawking, but fortunately his sisters jumped up to introduce themselves. All three Boxworthy children were good-looking, but Ned was thrillingly handsome in a sort of British World War I pilot way. Tall, slender, he had sleek black hair, violet-blue eyes, and a ravishing smile. He was exactly her age, Catherine remembered, sinking onto a chair next to him.

Mrs. Boxworthy handed her a cup of smoky Hu-Kwa tea in a tiny cup as fragile as an eggshell. On side tables were silver platters of tiny sandwiches filled with watercress or cucumber slivers, fish or foie gras paste, thin slices of ham or beef with mustard, crisp crackers and white breads with an assortment of cheeses, shortbreads, cheese biscuits, Dundee cake, and hot scones with strawberry jam and clotted cream. Catherine was famished and wanted to try everything; at the same time she wanted to appear slightly civilized in front of the marvelous Ned. She glanced sideways to see how Ann was faring. Her sister's plate was full, and her eyes were huge as she looked from the Boxworthy sisters to Ned and back down at all the wonderful food.

"This was Kathryn's home," Madeline was telling her children. "She grew up here. She hasn't visited Everly since we took it over. It will be interesting to see what she thinks of all the changes. And Catherine and Ann have never been here before."

"Well, I might as well warn you, it's the most boring place on God's earth," Hortense announced.

Catherine looked at Hortense, amused by her boldness. She was the youngest of the children, only fifteen, and Catherine could see Ann's expression light up as Hortense talked.

Hortense was still speaking. "Well, really, Mummy, it's true, you know. That's even part of its advertisable charm. People come here for the quiet. For the feeling of old England. It's old all right. *If* you're very good, Ann, we might persuade Ned to drive us into the nearest town for a movie, but other than that, nothing goes on around here."

"No movie tonight," Kathryn said. "We're all much too tired."

"Hortense is just whining because it's raining," Elizabeth said. She was nineteen, a pale, watercolor version of her older brother, with soft curling brown hair and gray-blue eyes. She was plump in a pleasant, feminine way and gracious, in sharp contrast with skinny Hortense, whose brown hair was clipped back carelessly with barrettes while her eyes were hidden behind thick glasses. "Hortense is our gardener. She knows people come here to see the gardens, and she's piqued because no one can go out today."

"All my children help here," Madeline

Boxworthy said. As she spoke she looked at each of them with an odd sort of pride glinting from her eyes, as if they were hounds or horses she had bred and trained especially well. "Hortense helps in the gardens, as Elizabeth says, and she is very capable. Elizabeth helps me with the baking. In fact, she's in charge of the kitchen and the daily girls who come in to help. And Ned keeps the books. I couldn't manage without them." Her gaze softened when it fell on her son.

"Mum, we've had tea, let me take Ann and show her the house."

"Darling, they'll be here all week. And perhaps Kathryn would prefer to give them the tour."

"Do you know where the old dogs are buried?" Hortense asked Kathryn. Before the older woman could answer, she rushed on, "Because I have a theory about where the spot is. Out by where the forest begins, right?"

Kathryn smiled. "The dogs loved the forest. Because of all the game they could chase, rabbits and so on. Yes. How clever of you. But really, Madeline," she said, turning to the other woman, "it's fine with me if Hortense takes Ann around. I won't want to move from this spot for hours. It's so comfortable by the fire."

Madeline nodded then, and Hortense

jumped from her chair, grabbing Ann by the hand.

What luck, Catherine thought. She noticed with surprise, however, that as Ann left the room she cast a long, rather covetous look at Ned. Catherine had to admit she was perfectly content to stay by the fire with the staid, boring adults. The Eliots and the Boxworthys talked late into the evening, about the American Everly, and Vanderveld Flowers, and the British Everly as Kathryn had known it.

When Catherine went to bed that night, she decided to make herself dream of Ned, but it was Kit's face, voice, body, that floated up to her. Her love for him had become part of her, and it would be a long time before she could release the thought of him from her heart's hold.

The first few days at Everly, Catherine watched her grandmother carefully. She thought it must be hard to see her childhood home so changed. But far from being distressed, Kathryn seemed quite happy. The gardens had been kept up; that was the most important thing, and as soon as she saw that, she settled in to enjoy her stay.

It rained most of the first week they were there. Every morning Catherine and Ann rose, dressed, and went down for breakfast in the dining room, one of the major events of the day. Guests were invited to help themselves from the silver platters and chafing dishes arranged on the mahogany sideboard. Catherine hovered greedily, plate in hand, over hot fat sausages, crisp bacon, salty ham, stewed prunes, creamed mushrooms, fresh tomatoes, a kedgeree of flaked smoked fish and rice, broiled kippers, and eggs scrambled and fried and hard-boiled. The toast, muffins, butter squares, jams, and marmalade were set on the table, along with the large silver urns of coffee and tea and the silver cream and sugar bowls. She filled her plate high.

So much food, and the weight of the Boxworthys' sterling silver, made breakfast a serious occasion. There were also all the guests, and the four Boxworthys who came and went, everyone smoothly sliding in and out of the conversation. It was easy to linger at the table, chatting over one more cup of coffee, and then another. For once in her life, Catherine was in no hurry. It was luxurious.

After breakfast she and her sister walked with Kathryn through the house or, if it wasn't pouring, out in the gardens. In the silvery mornings of that rainy week, Catherine and Ann followed their grandmother through the shadowy corridors and up and down the various stairs at Everly. Mrs. Boxworthy had given them carte blanche to roam. This British Everly was much larger, darker, and even colder than Kathryn's Everly at East Hampton, which at least had central heating. The attic rooms, which in the new Everly had been given over to a nursery and bedrooms for Catherine, Shelly, Ann, and their governesses, were here cheerfully wallpapered, decorated and turned into guest rooms. Kathryn could find no trace of any wallpaper from her childhood on the walls. But signs of her mother's reign were everywhere outside, in the wonderful gardens, which Kathryn's own mother had overseen.

By afternoon Hortense was free of her duties in the gardens. She'd take Ann off to some secret part of the house to play darts or cards or simply to talk. Kathryn and Catherine took naps in the afternoon. Catherine's body craved sleep. She fell eagerly into oblivion each afternoon and always struggled to awaken.

In the afternoons Catherine joined her grandmother and the others for high tea, which was served with the ceremonial cadence of ritual. In the evenings she read or played bridge with the guests. Fires were lit in all the downstairs rooms that first week to fight off the chill the rain brought. Catherine was content and glad Ann had Hortense to entertain her.

One night a couple arrived who had just been touring the Lake District. Somehow a discussion among the Boxworthy family about British poets erupted.

"Coleridge is the best," Hortense said. " 'Beware! Beware! His flashing eyes! His floating hair!' "

"Coleridge was a drug addict, my dear," said Ned.

"Coleridge was a genius," Elizabeth said.

"He was a drug addict and a sot and a lunatic. All that Lake District lot you're always mooning over were loony. Coleridge was so drunk at a dinner party that he thought his shirttail had come out of his trousers. He kept tucking it in and tucking it in. Really it was the gown of the woman seated next to him." Ned's laughter rolled through the room.

"That was Coleridge's father, I believe," Elizabeth said.

"What's the difference? It runs in the family. All these literary families you worship were nuts."

"The Wordsworths were wonderful gardeners," Mrs. Boxworthy said.

"Yes," Elizabeth agreed. "Dorothy used

to bring wild mosses home from the fells to plant around her house. She even transplanted wildflowers. I've always thought that such a lovely idea."

"Have you visited the Lake District?" Madeline asked Catherine. She shook her head.

"Oh, but you should!" Hortense said passionately.

"You'll become *drunk* with joy," Ned cried in a mincing falsetto.

Catherine watched and listened, entranced. She and Ann and Shelly could no more sit arguing about American poets' lives than fly to the moon. Had her family ever sat around conversing like this? The most similar occasions in her memory were holidays, Christmas or Easter, when circumstances forced them to be together. Even then her parents would have fortified themselves with a glass of liquor clutched in their hands. Why couldn't her family be as charming as the Boxworthys, full of clever conversation and literary gossip? She tried to envision her family taking over her grandmother's East Hampton Everly, working together to run it as a bed-and-breakfast. Impossible. Her parents would drink and sleep late, her brother would disappear with his rowdy friends, and Ann would complain bitterly that the work was too hard.

"Children," Madeline Boxworthy announced the fourth night the Eliots were at Everly, "I've heard the rain is going to continue for several more days. We've had some cancellations here because of it."

"Oh, bad luck, Mummy," Hortense said.

"No, good luck, I think, dear. I've decided it might be a good time for us all to go to London. With Kathryn and her granddaughters."

"Oh, smashing!" Hortense cried, and ran to hug her mother.

"I suppose Mrs. Frame can manage without us." Elizabeth looked worried.

"Of course she can! Come on, Elizabeth, a little jaunt will do you good!" Ned said.

Catherine watched with amazement and envy as charming Ned urged his serious, dutiful sister to join them. What a family this was! She wished it were hers.

In London Madeline and Kathryn went their way, leaving "the children" to go off on their own. During the day, Ned acted as their tour guide, rushing them through Trafalgar Square, St. Paul's, Westminster Abbey, Hyde Park. He and his sisters encouraged Catherine and Ann to buy bright-colored boots and Mary Quant clothes on Carnaby Street. The Boxworthys loved London, and as they rushed Catherine and Ann here and there, they seemed as proud and possessive as if they'd created it all themselves.

For Catherine, New York was a million miles away. New York was a dark dream. Kit and Piet, Shelly and her mother and father, Mr. and Mrs. Vanderveld, all were enclosed in a glistening balloon that Catherine tossed in the air and watched float away until it disappeared from sight. She was among clever new friends. She was relaxed. She was intoxicated by the Boxworthy family. She was almost happy.

It rained during the drive back to Everly. But the next day the sun came out blazing. At last the Eliot women could have a thorough, leisurely tour of the Everly gardens. Hortense had to get back to work weeding and picking fresh flowers and vegetables for the house, and for the pleasure of her company, Ann helped. Ned had to catch up on the paperwork and Madeline and Elizabeth on the baking, so Catherine and Kathryn meandered together through the formal boxed hedges down to the gurgling stream or sat on a marble bench next to a brick wall engulfed by plumy spills of wisteria.

The air was warm, the sky a rapturous blue. Delphiniums, phlox, daisies, hollyhocks, sunflowers, and roses dappled their vision, while birds chirped from fruit trees and made rustling raids on gooseberries and currants.

Which Everly do you love best, Grandmother? Catherine longed to ask, but never did. In the gardens of the British Everly, Kathryn was at her most aloof. Her very carriage declared: Stand back. Don't intrude. The American Everly was less formal, more inviting, Catherine decided, if only because of the rambling house and the wild superabundance of the gardens, which Kathryn didn't have the time or money to control. Upstarts at the American Everly, seeds that had drifted in on air currents or birds, often managed to take root and grow, causing startling and cheerful combinations.

One lovely day they went on the excursion Kathryn had been longing for — to Sissinghurst in Kent, to see the elaborate gardens Vita Sackville-West had designed. None of the Boxworthy women could go; they were too busy. But Ned came along, insisting on driving them in his father's old, immaculately cared for Bentley.

"It's good for the old thing to get some fresh air," he said, fondly stroking the silvered gray of the hood.

Catherine was surprised that Ann chose to join them rather than spending the day at Hortense's side. Then she noticed as the day passed how Ann's eyes brightened each time she looked at Ned. Ann had a crush on him, and Catherine didn't blame her. He was beautiful, and clever, and kind. Catherine left Ann to herself with Ned, a romantic afternoon young Ann would remember all her life, Catherine thought. She looped her arm through her grandmother's and strolled with her along a brick path, under an archway of white roses so abundant, they looked like a foaming cataract of blossom. They climbed the steep spiral staircase to the turret room where Vita Sackville-West used to write. At the top of the tower they stood looking down at the flowers, divided by hedges and glowing with color like stained-glass windows, surrounded by the rolling meadows of Kent.

That evening Catherine showered and dressed for tea. She had just stepped out into the dark upstairs hall when Ned appeared so suddenly that he startled her.

"I've got something for you!" he whispered. "Come up to my room a minute."

"The others — "

"Won't notice if we hurry!" he said.

She had never been to his attic room. It

was charming, entirely masculine, furnished in dark heavy oak and rough green plaids, the ceilings low and slanted, shadows striping the floor.

"Here," Ned said without preamble. "I brought you a present."

He handed her a package. She tore off the paper to find an exquisitely decorated book about the Sissinghurst gardens and the life of Vita Sackville-West.

"How lovely! Ned, thank you!" Catherine's face warmed with pleasure and surprise.

She was even more surprised when he pulled her against him and folded her in an embrace. At first she resisted, but his kiss was very pleasant. He smelled like summer grasses. His body against her was warm, animal-hard, masculine. His breath, tongue, teeth, and lips were as sweet and dazzling as strawberry jam and clotted cream.

"Come up here to me tonight," he whispered into her ear. "Please."

Catherine realized she was kissing him, pressing herself against him at the same time knowing she should push him away. "I don't know," she replied. "Oh, I don't know."

"I know," he said. "You should come."

Flustered, she moved away from his embrace and rushed down to her room to smooth her hair and fix her lipstick. What should she do? What did she want to do? She thought Ned immensely handsome, and she liked him, too, but something about him amused her. She was able to observe him from a distance, to remain separate from him, while with Kit she had instantly felt bonded, completely at home. Well, with Kit she had been tricked, by him and by herself. Perhaps Ned was the cure. It was obvious that Ned wanted only a fling with her, nothing more; that was what she wanted, too.

In the library, Madeline Boxworthy was working on a needlepoint cushion cover. Kathryn was looking through the books on the shelves. Various guests were playing bridge or just milling around. Catherine could not settle down to any one thing. They would be going home in two days, she and Ann and Kathryn, and perhaps that was why Ned had waited until now to invite her to his bed. That way, the offer clearly involved nothing more than enjoying themselves. Now Ned was gently teasing Elizabeth, who was reading a book of poetry. Suddenly Hortense said, "Ann, sleep in my room tonight, will you! We'll eat pastries in bed and stay up all night telling ghost stories." Ann agreed at once. Catherine stared at Ned. She could not tell if he had orchestrated Hortense's offer or not. But at least now she did not have to consider what to tell Ann if she wanted to slip out of their room.

What an odd summer this had been. After three years of grinding routine, she'd been to Paris in June and now to England in August. She'd made love for the first time in her life and fallen in love for the first time in her life. And had her heart broken for the first time, too. Damn Kit!

Perhaps she only thought she loved him because she had made love to him.

She would go to Ned's room, after all.

Ned had the courtesy to seem happily surprised when she knocked on his door at midnight.

"I was afraid you wouldn't come," he said, drawing her in.

"I don't know what I'm doing here," she began, suddenly confused, but then he wrapped himself around her and kissed her. He was still dressed in a soft white shirt and slacks, while she wore a light summer nightgown and robe. His hands moved down her body. When his mouth moved to hers, his kisses inspired a need in her, like a thirst. Together, they went to his bed. He turned off the bedside lamp.

She was pleasantly surprised by how playful Ned's lovemaking was. He wasn't intense as

Kit had been; he wasn't in need. Ned teased Catherine, tickling her with his tongue, tasting her, testing her to find her most sensitive, susceptible spots. He smiled; he chatted.

"Do you like this?" he asked her several times. The first time the question embarrassed her, but eventually his tenderness broke through her shyness.

At one point he took her hand and placed it around his erect penis. "Do that," he said, moving her hand. "Ah. Yes. John Thomas likes that a lot."

"What?" Catherine asked, puzzled. "Who?"

Ned laughed. "I guess you've never read *Lady Chatterly's Lover*. John Thomas is what the gamekeeper calls his penis."

"Good heavens, you're literary even when you're making love!" Catherine exclaimed, and Ned laughed again.

When he finally entered her, Catherine didn't feel the dreamy glow of first love that she'd felt with Kit, but she did feel pleasure. She enjoyed the slide of skin against skin. His breath, his sweat, his concentration . . . the intimate shock of connection. The sounds he made. The puppyish way he had nuzzled against her. It didn't matter that he hardly knew her and didn't love her. It was just so very pleasing to be touched.

This is good, Catherine told herself. Now

I'm not even thinking of Kit, and how he made love to me, and later I won't remember Kit's body, but Ned's. This is helping me forget Kit, she told herself as she moved against Ned's body in the dark.

Ned was driving Kathryn, Catherine, and Ann back to Heathrow. Ann was sitting on the front seat next to Ned, babbling nonstop. In the back, Catherine and her grandmother were quiet, looking out the window. The car rolled past fields of grass, corn, flax, and wheat, with occasional streams curling through, but Catherine was not really seeing the landscape. Nor was she thinking of how Ned had felt against her last night. Oddly, she was thinking of Vanderveld Flowers, and her heart was doing little drumrolls of anticipation. She had enjoyed this vacation, but she was glad it was over. She missed the fragrance and feel of all the cut flowers, the rainbow variety she casually worked with each day, the slither of wrapping paper, the festivity of ribbons, the sight and smell of so much sweet green. She even missed the Vandervelds, especially Piet. She had not learned to forget Kit, but she had learned that there were other things in life she wanted: right now she felt a raging desire to go home, and "home," she realized with a smile, meant the flower shop.

But first she had one final duty to perform. She'd promised Ann she'd go with her to the Eliots' Vineyard home to visit their parents. Maybe this time she could change things. Life at the British Everly had made her more optimistic about happiness in her own family.

Catherine hadn't been to the Vineyard for the past three years. When she arrived at her parents' house, she was shocked by how shabby it looked. The outside needed a new coat of paint, the roof needed reshingling, the garden was weedy and overgrown. Inside, the blond oak furniture and lightweight tables lacquered in Oriental reds and blacks — so modern in the fifties — looked dated. There were no fresh flowers, and the windows needed washing. Catherine's heart sank as she looked around. No wonder Ann had been upset.

Her father entered the living room. "Hi, Dad!" Ann cried, running to hug him. Formally, he shook hands with Catherine.

Catherine was pained by how old he looked. He was nattily dressed in patchwork cotton pants and a lime green linen blazer. He was well groomed; he would always be handsome. But he had lost weight, and his skin hung around his jawline. His eyes were sunken.

Nevertheless he smiled as he offered his daughters drinks.

Catherine almost cried out when Marjorie entered the living room, the change was so terrible. Her mother had gotten so fat that she looked absolutely porcine. Her beautiful blue eyes were hidden in a face so swollen with fat, it looked quilted. Her dainty feet and hands looked ridiculous attached to her gross body. In her vividly flowered muumuu, adorned and clanking with necklaces and bracelets and rings, she looked like some kind of costumed circus animal.

"Marjorie! You should have gone with us!" Ann cried, hugging her mother. "The British Everly is smashing! There, don't I sound British! I love the Boxworthys! They've got a daughter, Hortense, and . . ."

Under the cover of Ann's excitement, Catherine sipped her gin and tonic and wondered how, why, had her father allowed her mother to get in this state? Always before when her weight had gotten out of control, Marjorie had gone off to some posh beauty spa in Arizona and returned after a few weeks or months slimmer and calmer. Why hadn't he sent her off weeks, no months, ago?

Genene had cooked a perfect summer dinner: broiled swordfish, potato salad, corn on the cob. Drew and Marjorie toyed with their food and drank whiskey. Ann kept up a running burble of talk about Everly. Catherine wasn't hungry. How could she have considered her family in the same light as the Boxworthys?

Shelly stumbled in when dinner was almost over. He was with two older boys. His face broke into a delighted grin when he saw his older sister. "Catherine! Hey, babe! You're looking great! Hi, Annie-fanny. How'd you like the Brits?"

At sixteen Shelly was attractive in a dangerously adult way. Tanned and fit, his body radiated health and pleasure. His green eyes were as freshly innocent as Easter grass, his smile dazzling, boyish, but as he leaned over to hug Catherine, she smelled the alcohol, cloying and offensive, on his breath.

"How are you, Shelly?" He's growing up too fast, Catherine thought.

"Great! I need to change my shirt. There's a party at John's tonight. Don't wait up for me. Bye!"

He was out of the dining room in a flash, his two friends trailing him like the tail of a comet.

"That boy," Drew said proudly.

"Drew. I need another drink," Marjorie said, rattling the ice cubes in her glass.

Ann wanted Catherine to take her to a

movie after dinner. The movie, a Pink Panther comedy, hardly captured Catherine's attention. She needed to formulate a plan, a plan that would save them all. She had to talk to her father. But she couldn't think of a thing.

They returned from the movie to find Drew waiting up for them in the living room. He and Marjorie had gone to the club to meet some friends for a drink, and now, he told them, Marjorie was already in bed.

"It's your bedtime, too, honey," Drew said to his youngest daughter.

Always the good daughter, Ann kissed her father and sister good night. Drew led Catherine into the den, a large room with a pool table and a Ping-Pong table at one end and a nautically decorated bar along one wall. In the dark, it gave more an illusion of privacy and coziness than the other rooms of the house. Without asking, he poured a large whiskey for each of them, then sat down across from her on an overstuffed chair covered in blue sailcloth ornamented with white anchors and ropes.

"Catherine," her father began, then stopped. He cleared his throat. He could not seem to bring himself to meet her eyes. He busied himself with a cigarette and lighter, rattling the ice cube in his drink as he spoke.

"We've never been close, you and I. What I have to say is difficult, but you should know the truth."

"Dad. What's wrong?"

"Well. To be blunt, I've had a bit of . . . a financial setback. Quite a bit, actually. I made some bad investments. To be brief, we don't have any money." He sighed. He looked older with each word he spoke. "I'll be the first to admit I didn't always give significant attention to my portfolio. It's my fault, there's no doubt about it. But assigning fault doesn't help. We're going to have to sell the Park Avenue apartment."

"Daddy!"

Drew held up his hand to stop her. "There's no money for Shelly to finish at his prep school or for college. Nor for Ann at Miss Brill's. We've decided to remain on the Vineyard. There's a decent public high school here for Ann, and it seems more — whimsical — than anything else we could do. At least Shelly and Ann feel at home here."

"Can't Grandmother help?"

"She has helped. Is helping. She's tiding us over until the apartment sells. But she doesn't really have all that much free money, you know. What she does have will have to last her and a cook-housekeeper and a gardener for the rest of her life. She would never leave Everly. She should never have to leave Everly. But she can't keep it up by herself. She's not as strong as she used to be. Hell, none of us is."

Catherine shook her head, trying to imagine it all. "Shelly has to go to college, Dad," she said. "Shelly can't *not* go to college!"

Her father laughed. "This from you, my dear, who insisted on not going to college?"

"That was different. Shelly needs discipline. Oh, Dad, what are you going to do?"

"What am I going to do? Me, specifically? Well, I'm not without plans." Drew smiled and pulled himself up. "I'm going to do what one does when he looks and speaks well and has a lot of friends. I'm going to get my broker's license. I'm going to sell real estate."

They sat drinking in silence for a few minutes while Catherine tried to take it in.

"Poor Mother," she said at last. "No wonder she looks so awful."

"Yes," Drew agreed. "It's hard on your mother. We've had to sell a lot of her nicest jewelry. And some of the oils in the apartment."

"Oh, Dad. Oh, what will poor Annie do? Does she know?"

"No. Not yet. She knows we don't have the money we used to, but so far she's only found it an inconvenience. I haven't told her yet that she's not going back to Miss Brill's. I suppose I should tell her soon. We're getting on toward the end of the summer. I just keep putting it off."

Drew tossed back his head and downed his drink. He set the glass on the coffee table. He leaned forward and said quietly to Catherine, "We're going to have to let Genene go. We've kept her on, just for the summer, till our friends leave. Then it'll be just the four of us in the house. Imagine." He laughed, shaking his head, his eyes tearing up, his nose and cheeks turning red as the twiggy blood veins brightened.

"Well, I just thought you should know. You're still part of the family. I know you'll be a comfort to Ann."

"Yes. I'll try."

"At least you got to go to Miss Brill's. So you shouldn't feel so mistreated by your mother and myself after all."

"Oh, Dad. I — "

"I believe I'll go on to bed now," he said, rising. "I find I get tireder than I used to. No wonder, I suppose."

"Daddy," Catherine said, standing. "I'm sorry. I'm so sorry."

Her father didn't turn around. His shoulders were slanted forward, but his back was still elegant in the lime blazer. "I'm sorry, too, Catherine," he said. "I am sorry, too."

When he had left the room, Catherine crossed to flick off the light switch. She wanted to be alone in the darkness to think.

Shelly was energetic and cocky; he needed a strong hand. He'd been an adventurous, daredevil boy, the type of boy who with the right direction could grow up to be a hero. His father was not the best role model, and if he didn't continue at prep school and go on to college . . . Catherine couldn't imagine what would become of him. And poor Ann, who was only beginning the adolescence she'd been dreaming of, when she could start dating and going to dances and parties . . .

Catherine knew she had to *do* something.

But she could not come upon one wise thing to do, although she sat in the den until she was so tired, she simply stretched out on the couch and fell asleep in her clothes.

The next two days she spent with Ann. They swam and sailed, they played tennis, and Catherine laughed with Ann about her friends. But at every moment her father's words occupied her thoughts.

"It will come to you."

Kathryn had said that to her, and now Catherine wondered if that didn't mean responsibility would come, as well as gifts. She knew she could abandon her parents, but not Ann and Shelly. They mattered. To her. Even if they didn't realize it, they mattered to her, and that was something for her to hold on to. However mysterious and frustrating her grandmother, brother, and sister were, still their fates were connected with hers.

She was desperate to leave the Vineyard — it was too hard to keep pretending to Ann. Once she was alone, she knew she could come up with a plan. If she gave her parents her savings, would that be enough to pay for Shelly's tuition or Ann's? Her savings, her savings . . . her savings, the money she had pinched and hoarded these past three years while she lived for free at Leslie's place; her savings, in the face of what her family needed, was nothing. Even if she gave up all she'd worked so hard to accumulate, her family would squander it in the blink of an eye.

CHAPTER 5

The tamarisk shrubs, growing low and close to the brick building, were in bloom today, their feathery spikes of tiny pink flowers trembling fragilely against the evergreen leaves. The doorman nodded at Catherine as he opened the door for her.

"Oh, hi, honey, come on in," Helen said.

Catherine paused in the doorway. Today the roses had a gift from a Madison Avenue jewelers laced through it, a gold bracelet studded with diamonds. It was a pretty trinket, but not a terribly valuable one, certainly not valuable enough to make up for the bruises on Helen Norton's face.

"Please," Helen Norton said.

On this warm September day, Helen was wearing a heavy robe of green plaid flannel, not at all her usual flamboyant style. She huddled inside it as if it were a blanket. Her hair looked strange. As the Exotic Eleena, she had dyed her hair black, but she was really a blonde. Catherine had never seen a brunette with blond roots before.

"Sit down and have some coffee with me," Helen said.

Catherine hesitated. This was her last delivery of the day. All she had ahead of her was the walk back to Leslie's apartment, where she would sit worrying about her family. It was funny; she could have confided in any of her old school friends about all sorts of problems — if Shelly were homosexual, or Ann in love with an older man, or either of her parents having affairs with anyone — but she could never speak to any of them about money problems.

"Come on, kid, have a heart, sit down," Helen said.

"All right," Catherine replied, and sat.

"Would you rather have a drink?"

"No, coffee's fine."

"Iced coffee? How about iced coffee? It's so hot."

"Iced coffee would be great. Thanks."

Catherine looked around the room while Helen Norton clinked and clanked in the kitchenette. The florist's box of roses lay on the coffee table between them, but Catherine didn't take them into the kitchen for a vase of water. There wouldn't be room with Helen making coffee. Catherine would remind Helen to put them in water before she left. Or perhaps she'd tell Helen to open the box right away. The bracelet might cheer her up.

Helen returned with two tall glasses of iced coffee. At Catherine's suggestion she opened the box, took out the bracelet, and held it up, inspecting it.

"It's not much, is it?" she said dejectedly to Catherine. She let the bracelet fall back among the red flowers.

"Well," Catherine said, "I think it's very pretty. . . ."

"Yeah, well, do you think this is pretty?" Helen pointed to her swollen cheekbone and bruised jaw. The green plaid of her robe made her skin look especially sallow.

"I was wondering about those," Catherine admitted.

"He hit me. The old bugger." Anger flared in the woman's eyes so intensely that for a moment Catherine seemed to be looking at the Exotic Eleena instead. She could see how the woman's fiery disposition would appeal to men.

"That's awful," Catherine said. "What did you do?"

"Hah! What did I do? More like what I didn't do. Or won't." She sighed, sipped

181

her coffee, lay back among the sofa cushions. "I'll tell you, honey, I've gotta get out of this, and soon. I thought he was just a harmless old gent, but I should have known better. Men are men. They're all alike. No, rich men are worse. Take it from me. Rich men think they can buy anything they want. They think they deserve it."

Catherine was quiet. She wasn't sure she wanted to hear any more.

"He's getting kinky," Helen Norton said. "I should have seen it coming. God, am I blind or what? He wants to watch me do it with an animal. A dog. Can you believe that? Jesus H. Christ. I said I wasn't that kind of woman. He said, in that ice-up-the-asshole voice of his, 'I think we both know exactly what kind of woman you are.' The prick. So I called him a name. So he hit me. So I tried to kick him out. So he reminded me just whose apartment I was trying to kick him out of. So we compromised. No animals — yet. But I said he could bring in another woman."

Catherine's head hurt. She had to work hard to understand exactly what Helen Norton was talking about. It all sounded so tawdry.

Suddenly Helen Norton set her coffee on the table and put her face in her hands. Her shoulders were shaking.

"Sometimes you just think it's no use," she said. "Sometimes you think you've got a chance, you're gonna make it, after all, this is America, the land of the free and the home of the brave. Then something like this happens and you know you're nothing. Men like that have everything, and you'll never have anything no matter how hard you work."

Catherine set her coffee down on the table, too. Helen Norton's words moved her greatly, partly because Catherine realized that Helen could be speaking for Catherine as well. Catherine had no chance, no chance in hell, of getting her family out of the fix it was in. No matter how hard she had worked and saved over the past three years, it amounted to *nothing* compared with what her family needed. It was nothing compared with what she would need to buy her own flower shop. She had nothing. Helen Norton had nothing.

But P. J. Willington had more money than he could count — money he had inherited from grandparents and in-laws, more money than he could ever use in his lifetime.

"Helen," Catherine said, "I have an idea."

Helen raised her head and looked at Catherine.

"Listen," Catherine said. "I think I know a way for the two of us to get some money."

★ ★ ★

When Catherine finally left Helen's, it was evening, time for dinner, but she was not hungry. She wanted to walk. She needed to move. It was early September, so night closed down faster on the city, and the subtle fading of the sky, the luminous streaks of color as the sun sank low, were blocked and blurred here by all the skyscrapers. Already there was the false daylight from storefronts, marquees, and headlights. It was neither dark nor day. People rushed instead of strolling, even though the air was mild.

Catherine was remembering her conversation with Ned.

"Perhaps you'll come to the States someday and visit the American Everly," Catherine had said to him as they lay together, naked in each other's arms.

"Perhaps. Probably not."

"Why not?"

"We don't have money for traveling. Everly looks grand, but only because the four of us slave for it and put all our money into it."

"Do you resent that?"

"No. Not at all. On the contrary, I'm rather proud to be part of such a place, such a family. I'm the man of the house, you know. Everyone relies on me. It's up to me to take care of my sisters and my mother, and this house."

"That doesn't make you feel trapped?"

"Trapped? Oh, you Americans! Always ready to move. No. I feel that I'm exactly where I belong, and lucky to be here."

"What will happen when you fall in love?"

"Well, I'll have to fall in love with a woman who's willing to live here and get along with the rest of the family, won't I?"

"What if you fall in love with someone who doesn't want to live here?"

Ned had shrugged. "I won't."

For Ned, Catherine thought, it was all so clear. Family first. And he would be able to pull it off, she thought. Ned would be able to break off with a woman he loved if she wouldn't move to Everly, or not get involved with such a woman in the first place. Look at what Kit had done, breaking off with her in order to marry the woman his family had chosen.

It would be nice, Catherine thought as she strode down Park Avenue, the hard pavement hitting against her feet like a hammer pounding sense into her body, if she had an older brother. An older, protective brother, like Ned, who would take care of her. But she was the oldest in her family, and though she didn't even want to be part of that damned family, she didn't know how to escape. She could turn her back on her parents, but not on her brother, and especially not on Ann.

Catherine had always known her life would not be normal or easy. Her life hadn't come to her in a gentle unfolding of years, like the gradually opening petals of a rose. Her life came at her in waves. So much had happened this summer — meeting Kit and falling in love with him. Going to Everly. Sleeping with Ned. And now discovering that her family was on the edge of financial ruin.

For years the waves of life had just rolled in easily, then all at once they'd arisen, pounding down on her with a great and unfair blow. She had to fight against them, stand up to them, or surrender and be swept away.

Well, she would fight. She would always choose to fight.

The next morning Catherine spent a few minutes showing Mrs. V the pictures she'd taken of Everly's gardens. Then she went to look for Piet; she found him in the basement, unpacking a shipment of containers. It was cool down there, dim and cluttered. Scrolled wrought-iron pedestal stands lay on their sides among chicken wire and discarded boxes. Sweat from the summer humidity beaded and dripped from the overhead exposed pipes. The air smelled sour. An appropriate place, Catherine thought, for this particular conversation.

Piet was bent over a cardboard box with his switchblade in his hand.

"Piet. Could we talk for a moment?"

"Sure." Piet stood up, hitching up his jeans, which had slipped down his narrow hips.

Catherine moved closer to him, wanting him, and only him, to hear. She could feel the warmth of his body.

"There's something I'd like to discuss with you," she said. "But before I tell you what, I'd like you to promise that you won't tell anyone else. What I'm going to say has to be a secret, whether you agree to it or not."

"Such mystery." Piet smiled, but his black tulip eyes remained impenetrable.

"Will you promise?"

"I promise."

His solemnity was intense, and wasn't that what she wanted? Catherine shivered as she looked at Piet, as if she were the hunted with the hunter closing in. His black eyes, his leaf-dense skin, his smell of musky sweat, flowers, and some spice she couldn't quite place, all seemed to wrap around her like the cloak of a vampire or an angel. This was not a man ever to take lightly.

"It's about making some money. Quite a lot of money. Piet, it's illegal, it's immoral, but it's foolproof. My friend and I have it all planned out, but I need your help. For which, of course, you'd be paid." Her voice was quiet and blunt.

"Catherine." Piet grinned. "You surprise me."

His grin broke the spell. She moved away from him, toward the soapstone sinks. "To be honest, I surprise myself." Suddenly she felt ill-at-ease. "Look. I can't talk about the details here, when the Vandervelds could interrupt us at any moment. Can you meet me at the bar on the corner after work? If you're interested, that is."

"Oh, I'm interested."

The bar was crowded at six o'clock; Catherine was glad, because the laughter and chatter of the patrons made her certain no one could overhear them.

"What I want you to do is this," Catherine said, and explained her plan. He would get one-third of the money.

Piet smiled slowly as she spoke. And then he said yes. It didn't surprise her. What did surprise her was that he asked so few questions. For instance, "Why would a nice girl like you get herself involved in blackmail?"

The next day after work, she took a bus down to Forty-seventh Street. At a cut-rate shop on Forty-seventh and Sixth, she spent some of her savings on a small black Leica 35-millimeter camera, which, the salesman promised her, had the softest shutter in the business, and several rolls of 400 speed film. She took a bus back up town and hurried to Vanderveld Flowers. It was after seven now, and the older Vandervelds had gone home. The shop was dark. She went to the back door off the alley, where Piet was waiting. Once inside, she gave him the loaded camera.

"Good luck," she said.

"See you tomorrow," he replied. They left the shop together but parted at the cross street.

All Catherine could do now was wait. She sat in Leslie's apartment, a plate of fruit and cheese in front of her, a glass of wine in her hand. She drank the wine, and then another glass, but she was too nervous to eat. Helen had promised to call when it was over. Until then all Catherine could do was to imagine what was happening now, at Helen's place.

When he left Catherine, Piet would have headed to Helen's apartment, and Helen would have hidden him inside her bedroom closet. She had showed Catherine how easy it would be for someone to hide there; the closet was stuffed with filmy evening gowns, and the sliding doors were louvered.

Helen was planning to wear a flamboyant red-and-black negligee with see-through net and lots of makeup. Puritanical old P. J. Willington's cold blood always got hot with "Malaguena" and "Bolero" playing on the stereo. And the music would mask any sounds the camera shutter made. Fortunately P. J. liked the lights on, the better to see Helen.

Helen told Catherine that P. J. always arrived between nine and ten. At nine-thirty Catherine let herself imagine the next step. The old man would enter. He would drink some whiskey. Helen would put on music, then lead P. J. into the bedroom as she had so many times before. And all the while, Piet would be hidden away taking pictures that would cost Willington a fortune.

Helen had promised to call Catherine when it was all over. By ten-thirty the phone still hadn't rung. By eleven Catherine picked up the receiver to be sure the phone wasn't broken. When, at eleven-thirty, it rang, Catherine almost screamed.

"Hi, honey," Helen said. "It's all over. It went off perfectly."

Catherine began to shake. She couldn't speak.

"Your friend said he'll give you the camera tomorrow, and you'll take care of the rest. I'm going to start packing. The day you call him, I'm leaving this place. How long do you think it will take to get the photos developed?"

"Oh, just a few days," she said, hoping it was true. "I'll call you as soon as I've got them."

After that, oddly enough, she didn't worry. She went through her routines at work with impeccable, robotlike efficiency. At night she walked the streets of the Lower East Side, looking for the sleaziest photography store she could find. But even here the smirks and knowing eyes of the men seemed to penetrate the layers of anonymity the city afforded, until finally, on her day off, she went down to Chinatown. There, in a tiny shop that advertised passport photos done quickly, she had her precious film developed. The passive Chinese clerk took her film. A few hours later he handed back the roll of negatives and a manila envelope with ten glossy black-and-white eight-by-tens. Catherine couldn't wait. She opened the envelope and looked at the top photograph. It was perfect. She realized she was smiling.

"That's my husband," she said. "I want a

divorce. He's been — with another woman."

"Twenty dollar, please," the Chinese man said, his face expressionless.

That evening Catherine phoned Helen Norton. "I've got the pictures. I'm doing it next week on my day off. You'd better get ready to leave."

One of the useful bits of information Helen had given Catherine was that P. J. Willington liked to have lunch every day at "21," to which P. J. had never taken Helen, no matter how much she pleaded with him. He knew too many people there, he said.

On Wednesday, her day off, Catherine hung around 21 West Fifty-second until she saw the old man enter. She waited, then she knocked on the door and handed the doorman a manila envelope addressed to Mr. Willington. She asked the man to see that it was hand-delivered and pressed a five-dollar bill into his hand.

She walked over to Saks and found a bank of phone booths on the first floor. She took a deep breath, then phoned "21" and asked for Mr. Willington. When he answered, she could tell he was downstairs in the club bar. She'd gone there often with her father.

"I want one hundred thousand dollars in cash. In return, I will give you the rest of the photographs and all the negatives," she said.

The old man was silent. She imagined him in the dark bar, surrounded by silver-haired men in expensive three-piece suits, all hefting their Scotches, their expensive gold cuff links flashing. She prayed he wouldn't have a heart attack.

"All right," he said.

Catherine was surprised. She had expected some resistance, but what, after all, could he do, caught in a place where he couldn't argue without others hearing?

"There's a 'Back to School' sale at Macy's this Saturday morning. Be on the first floor next to the elevators at ten-thirty. Have a Macy's shopping bag with one hundred thousand dollars in cash in it in your hand. Someone will approach you. She'll say enough to let you know it's the right person, give you a Macy's shopping bag, and take yours. Then it will all be over."

"All right," P. J. Willington said.

Catherine was shocked. All right? That was all he had to say?

Then she realized how tightly she had trapped him, there at his favorite club, seated no doubt between friends, whose wives were friends of his wife. He was an old man who cared about his reputation. The pictures were clear and damning. To him a hundred thousand dollars was nothing. Certainly not worth risking the public tar and feathering that exposure would bring.

"Macy's. First floor. Ten-thirty," Catherine said, and hung up the phone.

Thursday and Friday passed quickly. Everyone was moving more briskly now that summer was gone and the rhythm of the New York autumn took over.

Saturday morning Catherine phoned the Vandervelds. She told them she had a bad headache but would take some aspirin, sleep some more, and try to come to work that afternoon. Then she collected the items she had bought at Woolworth's and at various Salvation Army shops, stuffed them into a duffel bag, and took the bus to Broadway and Thirty-fourth Street. By nine in the morning the sidewalk was filled with women shoving and pushing and clamoring to get through the doors to the sale. Catherine joined the throng.

Once inside, she went to the ladies' room on the sixth floor and entered a stall. When she came out she had on a gray crimped wig, a shapeless black felt hat, a shiny black dress with a cheap brooch at the neck, and the thick-lensed dark sunglasses of a blind person. Her legs were wrapped in flesh-colored support bandages. On her feet were scuffed black orthopedic shoes. She carried the duffel bag and a stout cane in one hand. In the other she carried a Macy's shopping bag full of photographs and negatives, neatly organized in manila envelopes.

Standing before the mirror, she reapplied her lipstick. Before she left the apartment, she had heavily applied cheap beige Pan-Cake makeup. As she dusted her face with old-ladyish beige powder, the powder sifted into the cracked makeup quite nicely. Her skin looked almost wrinkled. She went over and over her lips with the "Persian Melon" lipstick until she had achieved a shakily outlined mouth much larger than her own.

She shuffled out the door toward the elevators. She still had time to kill. She went down to the first floor and stood peering into the cases of gloves and lace handkerchiefs. She had practiced hunching forward and shuffling; she was doing a great job of being a little old lady. It was surprising how ruthless and rude all the other women were, shoving past her and not even bothering to say "Excuse me."

When the large clock high above the perfume counter announced that it was ten-thirty, she shuffled toward the elevators.

She could barely believe her eyes.

There he was, P. J. Willington himself,

with a Macy's bag in one hand. He was wearing a biscuit-colored summer suit that made him look more slender and firm than he was. Pretending to inspect some silk scarves, she watched to see if he was making eye contact with anyone. But he only stood, erect as a soldier, looking impatient, jaw held high.

Catherine shuffled up to him slowly. Other women were gathering to wait for the elevator, which was making a slow descent from the eighth floor.

The elevator arrow indicated that it was on the second floor.

Catherine bumbled over to P. J. Willington. In a quavery voice she said, "What you want is in here, sir. Give me your bag."

She held out her Macy's bag. She felt his eyes studying her, taking in every detail. It had been a few years since he'd seen her at Kathryn's Christmas party; would he connect the young girl she'd been then with the old woman standing before him? Or would he recognize her as the girl who had waited on him often at the flower shop? He'd never paid any attention to her then, but still she kept her head bent and tried not to meet his eyes.

The elevator had stopped on the first floor now, disgorging its load of babbling females, while more anxious women shoved toward the open doors.

"How do I know — " P. J. Willington began, but Catherine cut him off.

"Give it to me!" she hissed, honestly angry. If she didn't get on the elevator now, her escape would be cut off.

P. J. Willington blinked, flinched, but held out his bag. Catherine snatched it from him. At the same time she thrust her bag into his hand so quickly that they almost dropped it in the exchange. As she shuffled to the elevator, she peered into the bag. Whatever was in there was wrapped in white paper. She would have to trust him. She had kept some other pictures anyway, just in case he tried to cheat her. He would probably assume that only a man would think to protect himself that way.

The elevator doors clacked toward each other, almost stranding her there with P. J. Willington. Desperate, Catherine stuck her rubber-tipped cane between them. The elevator operator looked at her, sighed, and slid open the doors. All the other women pressed against each other just enough to allow Catherine to squeeze in.

The last sight she had of P. J. Willington was of his silver head as he bent over to inspect the contents of his shopping bag.

Now that she was ascending to the safety

of the sixth floor, she could feel her heart racketing away in her chest so rapidly that she was surprised it didn't shake the elevator. Greedily she squeezed the shopping bag. It certainly felt bulky. What if the old fox had cut up newspapers and filled an envelope with them, or put in Monopoly money? She coughed and struggled to breathe. She couldn't afford to faint.

The elevator stopped at each floor. Women pushed on and off elbowing past Catherine. Finally she was at the sixth floor. She shuffled as fast as she could into the ladies' room and down the long row of stalls until she found an empty one.

She locked the door and collapsed onto a toilet, dropping the cane and her carpetbag to the floor. Inside her shiny dress, she was totally soaked with sweat. Even her hands were slippery.

She pawed through the Macy's shopping bag and ripped open the white envelope inside. She blinked. Her head felt as if it were exploding with blossoms of white fire. Her entire body went tingly and light. Inside the Macy's bag was a thick pack of one-thousand-dollar bills. She started to count them, but her hands were sweating and shaking so hard, she couldn't separate the bills from each other.

She felt wrenchingly nauseated. At the same

time, the white stars of fire were turning black and spinning toward her. She had never fainted before, but she knew she was going to faint now. Clutching her envelope against her chest, she leaned forward and put her head between her knees. She tried to take deep breaths. She forced herself to concentrate on the ordinary sounds outside her stall: toilets flushing, water running, the roller towel flub-dubbing, women chattering in their New York accents.

She opened her eyes. She looked at the porcelain base of the toilet bowl between her legs. It seemed as white and spotless as an angel's soul.

She lifted her head. She was slightly dizzy, but no more stars appeared. She stood up. She bent and took her alligator purse out of the carpetbag. She put the envelope of money inside. She took off the felt hat, the gray wig, the shiny black dress, the support bandages, the orthopedic shoes. Underneath the dress she was wearing a loose cotton dress. She took high heels from the carpetbag and stuffed the old-lady costume into it, along with the Macy's shopping bag. Grabbing up fists of toilet paper, she wiped at the lipstick, rouge, powder, and Pan-Cake makeup until her face burned. She dropped the paper in the john and flushed it.

She picked up the carpetbag in one hand and her purse in the other. The only problem was the cane. She leaned it at the back of the stall, between the toilet and the wall. She opened the stall door.

The room was full of women. Head high, she pushed past them to a sink. She scrubbed at her face. She looked in the mirror. Her hair, which had been flattened by the wig, was already rising and curling, expanding in the humidity. She took a green headband from her purse and put it on, holding her hair away from her face. She put on her gold shell earrings. If anyone looked closely, they might see traces of makeup around her hairline, but other than that her face was clean and tanned.

In the outer lounge, she sat down and toyed with her lipstick and compact for a while. Her hands had finally stopped shaking. When she stood up to leave, she left the carpetbag sitting next to the chair. She strode from the room, shoulders back, head high.

She took the elevator to the first floor. Women were still beavering away, pawing through the scarves and handbags. There were few men in sight. As she walked out of the door onto Eighth Avenue, with her alligator purse full of thousand-dollar bills, she didn't see P. J. Willington or anyone who resembled him.

From Port Authority she took a bus to Newark and met Helen Norton in the bus station waiting room. They walked out together to the old blue Ford Helen had borrowed from a friend and sat in the parking lot, with the windows rolled down because of the heat, counting the bills. There were one hundred of them. Helen took one-third of the money, and Catherine took the rest to divide between herself and Piet.

"Listen, kid, I'm going to Vegas," Helen said. She was wearing a pink-checked sundress with white cuffs and collar. She looked like a Boy Scout's mother, taking a break from making cookies. "I figure if old P. J. ever decides he's angry at me, even New Jersey's too close and too small. Anyway, I've got friends in Vegas. I'll have a good time."

"Well, good luck," Catherine said.

"Do you know, honey," Helen said, "we've been through all this together and I don't even know your last name?"

Catherine was silent a moment, thinking. Then she smiled. "That's right," she said in what she hoped was an inoffensive tone.

Helen looked at her. She whistled. "Kid, you've got brass balls."

Assuming that was a compliment, Catherine

smiled and said, "Helen, so do you."

Then she got out of the blue Ford and went back into the bus station and bought a ticket to New York. Helen Norton didn't come in to see her off. Catherine didn't stand at the window watching the blue Ford pull away. They didn't wave good-bye. They had changed each other's lives completely, and they never saw one another again.

That night Catherine couldn't sleep. She paced the floor, drank warm milk, tried listening to music. Nothing calmed her. Now that the blackmail was successfully completed, the dread and excitement of action had evaporated, leaving an aftertaste of guilt that filled her mouth and stomach with nausea. She had deliberately chosen to commit a crime; by the laws of man she had made herself guilty. Yet she also felt triumphant — victorious. P. J. Willington was guilty of physically abusing Helen Norton, and in their own outlaw way, they had extracted a reparation from him that could never have come from any court.

She forced herself to lie in bed, but the air was stifling. She went into the living room and curled up on the sofa. She was exhausted, but she couldn't sleep. Tossing and turning, she thought of herself now as a female Robin Hood, and now as a criminal.

The next morning Catherine found Piet in the shop basement. It was early September, but as sultry as the hottest August day. Piet was on a ladder, stretching to replace a light bulb. Because of the heat, Piet had already removed his shirt, and now she could see the long undulations of muscles beneath his smooth skin, the sweat beading along his shoulders and sliding down his back so that the beltline of his jeans was darkened by the moisture.

She'd seen Piet without a shirt before, but there was something about his body, an urgency just under his skin, that shocked her each time she looked at him. It was not just the black hair on his chest and the way it grew swirling around his nipples, or the way his jeans hung low on his narrow hips, threatening with each movement to succumb to gravity. Sometimes she saw bruises on his neck or the inside of his arm. Then she'd be overcome by a sudden image of a woman lying with Piet, clutching, kissing, biting his arm, while he did to the woman the things that made her bruise him in return.

Piet came down the ladder. Catherine caught her breath. Her presence never seemed to interfere with his breathing. They were standing very close, but still she whispered.

"Here's your share — a little over thirty thousand dollars." She handed him a manila envelope. "Helen's already left for Las Vegas."

"Great," Piet said. He folded the envelope and stuffed it inside the work shirt he'd thrown on a chair. "Thanks. Here." He put a box of containers in her arms. "Would you take these up? We'll need them today."

Arms weighted, Catherine stood staring at him. "Don't you want to talk about it at all?"

"I think the less we discuss it, the better for all of us."

"But — Piet. I'm still in shock — I guess I can't believe we really did what we did. And you're the only one I can talk to about it."

"You think talking about it will make you feel better?"

"I guess I do think that."

"All right. Listen. You and I both know that old Willington got his money from a father who did much worse things than we did, and who did it every day. You and I know Willington's not going to miss the money. And we can be pretty certain no one will find out."

"I know all that. But I still can't believe I did it. A girl like me, coming from the background I've come from. Can you believe I did it? Aren't you even a little surprised?"

Piet grinned. "I don't know about your background. What about it? Are you the child of a pair of nuns?" Before Catherine could reply, he reached forward in a surge of energy and swooped up several boxes of containers. "The shop's got a busy day ahead. What's done is done. Talking about it won't change anything." He went up the stairs, leaving Catherine in the basement, her arms aching from the heavy containers. There was nothing for her to do but follow Piet up and, once on the main floor, obey Mr. Vanderveld's frantic orders, which drove other thoughts out of her mind.

And she had to admit, it was a relief to have so much money. She knew her father was in the city, meeting with realtors and appraisers, so when she was through with work that day, she ran down to her parents' Park Avenue apartment. In her father's dark den, she handed him enough cash to pay for Shelly's last year at prep school and for another year for Ann at Miss Brill's and stood at her father's side while he wrote tuition checks and signed the late forms. She took them from her father, addressed and stamped the envelopes, and told her father she'd mail them herself that evening. Her father tried to smile graciously and act as if this weren't a humiliating experience for him.

"Where did you get so much money, Pudding?" her father asked.

"I borrowed it from a friend."

Her father smiled wistfully. "That's the perfect way to lose a friend, you know." He hesitated, then said, "I don't suppose you could loan me a few thousand more? Just for a month. I'm about to sell some paintings your grandmother brought over from England as a bride. When I get that money, we'll be able to keep this apartment."

"All right, Dad. I'll lend it to you, but it's only a loan. I have plans for my money. I'll need it back in a month."

"You'll have it." Her father clapped his hands together and rose with his old take-charge, let's-lead-the-teams-onto-the-field sort of air.

"Well, time for a drink, don't you think? To celebrate."

CHAPTER 6

New York, 1964

"Piet," Catherine said one afternoon in late September, "come have coffee with me."

She studied Piet as they settled into a booth and ordered coffee. She had worked with this man for three years. She had committed a crime with him! But she knew nothing about him. What did he want in life? What did he care about?

He was invaluable to the shop, that much was certain. He was strong and energetic, and he dealt with the flower wholesalers down on Sixth Avenue and Twenty-eighth better than she ever could. All those delicate feminine blooms being handled by tough, gruff, callused bruisers always seemed ironic to her. It took brute strength to haul ice-weighted boxes of hundreds of fresh blooms shipped in from Long Island or New Jersey or Florida. These men who brought the cartons of flowers from truck to wholesale house had to be strong. Often they were men new to this country, working at manual jobs until they perfected their English. Catherine, who spoke only English and French, couldn't understand most of them.

But Piet could talk to them, in Portuguese or Italian, complete with universal male gestures. If he tried to bargain with them for better prices, they laughed and joked and hit his arm. When Catherine tried to bargain for a lower price, they only chewed on their toothpicks or cigars and let their eyelids droop down over their eyes, their lips curling upward in that age-old superior smile of the stronger sex. Piet, on the other hand, was always polite to Catherine. Sometimes maddeningly polite.

Their coffee, in thick white mugs, was set before them. Piet looked at Catherine, waiting.

"Piet. I want to buy the shop."

His expression did not change.

"I've been thinking about it constantly since we — got — the money. Your aunt and uncle are tired. They need to rest. They're running the shop into the ground. But you and I could do wonders with it. Piet, do you want to buy the shop with me? Be my partner, at any percentage?"

"Thank you, Catherine, but no," Piet said unhesitatingly, as if he were refusing a piece of pie. He met her eyes. "I have other plans for my money."

"What?"

Piet shrugged.

"Jesus, Piet, we've known each other for three years now! Think what we've done together! Can't we at least talk to each other?"

Piet remained silent, unruffled. She might as well talk to a tree.

"All right. At least tell me this much. If I do manage to buy the shop, would you stay on? You know I'd need you."

"Yes. I'd stay on. For a while."

"Oh, Piet, I have so many ideas! If this all works out . . . well, there's so much I want to do, and — " She stopped. "I'm forgetting it is your aunt and uncle involved here. No matter what sorts of changes I make, they will be hurt. Offended." She held her hands out, palms up. "Piet, I don't know what to do."

"Look, Catherine," Piet said. "My aunt and uncle are decent, hardworking people. I love them. They have been wonderful to me. But I can still see their errors. They *are* running this shop into the ground. They're afraid to try anything new. They're old. Not in years, but in mind. You *should* buy the shop. It would be best for everyone."

Catherine stared at Piet. His words were

so sensible. That they had come from such a sensual mouth was amazing. She would have thrown her arms around him and kissed him in gratitude if he had been anyone else.

Instead, "Thanks, Piet," she said quietly. "Well, we'll see what I can do."

Catherine had often overheard the Vandervelds discuss selling the shop with each other, and from time to time Mrs. Vanderveld confided her worries to Catherine. They were only barely making a profit. Now that they were older, the work was becoming more difficult and tiring. It took a good amount of physical energy and stamina to create even the most ethereal floral display. Piet and Catherine did all the heavy work, but even so the Vandervelds were exhausted at the end of the day.

Every night in September Catherine sat in her room making lists. Planning. On Wednesday, her day off, she called carpenters and painters, getting estimates. She kept an appointment she had made with a lawyer, a man who knew her father well enough to appreciate her background, but not so well that he was aware of the financial difficulties her father had gotten himself into. Not so well that he would ask her where on earth she had managed to find enough money to buy the flower shop.

The lawyer, Mr. Giles, did express a gentle skepticism at her abilities to run a business. He was an older man, portly, white-haired, restrained. It was with exquisite politeness that he pointed out to her that she had little experience in business and no education in accounting.

Catherine bristled. Seated before him in her green linen suit and high heels, her legs primly crossed at the ankles as she had been taught at school, she was aware of how young she appeared. She wanted to toss her head and stalk dramatically from the room, offended, but as Mr. Giles continued to speak, softly, logically, she realized he was trying to be helpful, not patronizing.

"Bookkeeping is an art in itself," he said. "No matter how successful the rest of the enterprise is, the bookkeeping can make or break it."

"Perhaps I should hire someone to do that," Catherine said. "I admit it's not my strong point. I intend to do the design work and the marketing, the selling."

"Of course. And of course you should hire a bookkeeper. But may I suggest that you take a course in accounting yourself? As soon as possible. You must learn to read the books. You must be able to check the figures. You must be prepared to understand this part of your business. Unless you have a partner in mind whom you trust completely, not only with your finances, but also to live a long life and to work for you forever and to keep all information to himself."

Catherine stared at Mr. Giles. "This is more complicated than I thought," she said. "Very well. I'll take a course in accounting. The fall semester hasn't started yet. I'll be able to get in somewhere."

Mr. Giles smiled. "Good for you, young lady," he said. "I know how hard it is to take advice. I was young once myself. I think you just might manage to be as successful as you'd like, since you can obviously summon up some cool-headed reason to balance out your passion for this business."

"Your passion for this business." An odd phrase from such a temperate man. Not until Catherine had met Mr. Giles would she have thought to put the words *passion* and *business* in the same sentence. She did not think she had a "passion" for this business. She had had a passion for Kit. She still did. What she had for this business was something less fiery. But perhaps better: what she felt for this business was certainty.

One day in late September, Mr. Vanderveld

fell on the wooden stairs to the basement and broke his ankle. Catherine and Piet, one on each side, carried him to the shop van. Piet drove him to the hospital. The old man had been white-faced with pain and embarrassment.

During the three years Catherine had worked in the shop, Mrs. V and Catherine had been friendly, but it was with Mr. Vanderveld that Catherine felt a real bond. He was her teacher, her mentor, her elder. He was also a man from the old world, and along with his charming Dutch accent, he retained a fierce old-world masculine pride. He was the owner. He was the artist. He was, above all, the man. He might have been proud when Catherine learned quickly and well, but he was also perversely vexed, perhaps threatened. Catherine would have preferred a closer relationship, one in which they could touch, or joke, or praise each other. If Jan Vanderveld ever wished the same, he never indicated it. Certainly he hated having Catherine and Piet see him in the humbling dependence forced by pain.

Catherine knew that it was Mrs. Vanderveld she had to approach about buying the store. Only Mrs. V could make her husband listen. And now was the time. The next day, when Mr. Vanderveld was home with his ankle in a cast, she told Mrs. Vanderveld she would like to buy the shop from them.

Mrs. Vanderveld stared at her, speechless with shock.

"Oh," she said. "Oh."

Catherine could almost hear the other woman's thoughts arranging themselves: "I forgot, this little errand girl and help is from a moneyed background. Well, well."

"I think this could be a possibility, Catherine," Mrs. Vanderveld responded at last, speaking as slowly as if learning a new language. "It would be lovely to have you instead of a stranger taking over our shop. I've always regretted that we have no children of our own to pass it on to. But you are almost like our child to us. Oh, this is interesting! Let me talk it over with Jan tonight. We'll talk more in the morning."

The next morning, eyes shining with happiness, Mrs. Vanderveld made her proposal: Catherine wouldn't have to buy the shop. The Vandervelds would let her become a partner. That way Catherine would be assured of Mr. Vanderveld's artistic abilities and Mrs. Vanderveld's accounting skills. Catherine's money could give the business the shot in the arm it needed while they continued to provide the skill.

Catherine hurried back to Mr. Giles. But his blunt words echoed her own doubts: under Mrs. V's proposal, Catherine would be contributing much needed capital to the Vandervelds without receiving any power or control in exchange. Did Catherine think the Vandervelds would accept her as an equal? That they would let her implement any changes or let her decide any policies? Could she make any of the improvements she'd been planning with Mr. and Mrs. Vanderveld scrutinizing and approving every move?

Catherine went back to the Vandervelds. Mr. V was seated on a stool, his bandaged ankle resting on a box, furiously arranging mums and carnations into a fall bouquet. Mrs. V was making bows from ribbons; she stopped working when Catherine entered.

"I've been thinking," Catherine said without preamble, "I want to buy the shop. I don't want a partnership — I want to be the sole owner." She had trouble keeping her voice even as she spoke, knowing this would upset them.

Mr. V tried to act as if he hadn't heard her, but his mouth compressed so completely that his chin and cheeks bulged out around it and his face went red.

Mrs. V twisted her hands in front of her. Her hair began to slip from its bun. "Oh, dear, oh, dear," she blithered, turning toward the ribbons as if for help, then back toward Catherine. "This does present a problem. We don't really want to sell the shop entirely. We just need a little financial boost — "

"Well, think about it," Catherine said. "I'd better get back to work."

It was a wonder that all the flowers in the shop didn't die that week, wilt from the troubled air that hung in the shop like a plague. Mr. Vanderveld was insulted (as Mrs. Vanderveld told Catherine privately, when he was at home one afternoon resting his ankle) that Catherine did not jump at the opportunity to be partners with him. After all, he had the talent. She had only the money. Mrs. Vanderveld approached Catherine as a friend, almost a loving relative. Catherine should not forget that they had taken her in untrained and taught her everything.

"If Jan were freed up from financial worries, he could really let his creative energies flourish!" Mrs. Vanderveld said. "He would make arrangements that would be wonders! He would be famous. The shop would make more money!"

"Then let me buy the shop. You'll have lots of money, and I'll pay Mr. Vanderveld to work as my main floral designer," Catherine said.

Mrs. Vanderveld shook her head. "No, you do not understand. Jan could not work for you. A young lady for his boss? No."

Catherine held fast. On her lunch breaks she raced to the coffee shop to call Mr. Giles from a pay phone for moral support, like a boxer turning to the coach. With each hour that she steadfastly refused to become a partner, the atmosphere of the shop darkened proportionately.

"After all, Jan is sixty," Mrs. Vanderveld said one morning. "A talented man, who should not be thrown on the dustbin. You must know, Catherine, that when older people retire, they lose their reason for living, and die, poof, for no reason at all. Statistics prove this. What would Jan do without his shop? He would have no reason to live."

"The two of you have worked so hard all your lives," Catherine countered sweetly. "Isn't it time you enjoyed yourselves? Just think, with the money you'd get, you could take cruises together. You could visit your relatives in Amsterdam. Mr. Vanderveld shouldn't have to work so hard. At your age, neither should you. Isn't it time to be selfish and take some pleasure from life after all these years of working?"

"Humph!" Mrs. V replied, bustling off.

Now Catherine dreaded coming to work,

because the Vandervelds no longer greeted her cheerfully but merely nodded tersely. There were no more gossip sessions about the latest celebrity scandal over coffee. There was no more joking around. Orders were barked, replies bitten off. It was dreary. If she had not wanted to buy the shop, she would have quit.

Catherine's refuge and pleasure came when she sat over her desk at night, planning, sketching, figuring. She enrolled in the book-keeping course at Hunter College. She studied hard. If she was tempted to think of Kit — or even of Ned — she pushed those thoughts of love away. She forced herself to concentrate on the business she wanted to have. Her mind clicked and spun like an efficient machine. Her heart dangled inside her like a crystal, transparent, empty, cold.

Catherine was cleaning fresh, bud-tight, long-stemmed roses and putting their stems into water tubes for a casket piece. Florists almost always filled out funeral wreaths and arrangements with their old dying flowers that couldn't last another day. It was a waste to put fresh, tightly budded flowers on a grave. The Vandervelds spoke of florists they knew who, if forced to provide fresh flowers in top condition for a funeral, often went to the graveyard that night and stole the flowers back in order to sell them again. But this particular casket piece was for an important man whose casket would be on view in a funeral home for three days. The flowers had to last.

The front door bell tinkled. Mrs. Vanderveld came through the curtain with two sinister-looking smarmy little men.

The taller man, chewing on a toothpick, slouched down the aisle between the tables, eyeing the shop, eyeing Catherine. He grinned.

"She come with the shop, too?" he said nastily, jerking his head toward Catherine as if she were a thing that could not see or hear.

His cohort laughed vulgarly.

"Miss Eliot works for us, yes," Mrs. Vanderveld said. "Whether she stayed on to work for you would depend on whatever agreement you worked out with her, I suppose. She does have three years of training with us."

Catherine dropped the flowers on the table. She looked at the two men — slimy hoods, they wouldn't know a pansy from a peony! She looked at Mrs. Vanderveld. Mrs. Vanderveld raised her trembling chin in defiance and stared back.

Catherine walked to the back of the shop. She washed her hands, took off her smock, and hung it on a hook. She took her purse in her hand, and without a word she walked past Mrs. Vanderveld and the two oily men to the front of the shop.

"Catherine!" Mrs. Vanderveld said sharply. "Where are you going?"

"To find another job," Catherine said. "I quit."

She walked through the curtain one last time, out the door with the tinkling bell, and onto the street, which was brilliant with early fall sunlight.

Catherine walked. Stopping only to buy a hot dog and soda from a street stand, she walked for hours around the Upper East Side. There were other flower shops dotted throughout the neighborhood. She knew some of the florists. Maybe one of them would want a partner. Or she could find a vacant storefront in the area and start completely new. In many ways it would be easier than trying to rehabilitate the Vandervelds' aging shop. She stopped to write down phone numbers when she saw "For Rent" signs.

When she entered Leslie's apartment that evening, with blisters on her feet and a bag of groceries in her arms, the phone was ringing. As she put away the milk, the apples, the wedge of cheese, she listened to Mrs. Vanderveld's newest proposal: They would sell the shop to Catherine if she would agree not to change the name from Vanderveld Flowers and to keep Mr. Vanderveld on as head florist.

Catherine said, "No. I want my shop to be my own. I *will* change the name."

"If you change the name, it's as if you erase our lives!"

"I'm sorry."

Mrs. Vanderveld was crying into the telephone. "We loved you, we helped you, we taught you, you were like a daughter to us, and now you want to change everything, to take everything from us."

"No," Catherine said. "I want to *buy* everything from you."

"Jan will die," Mrs. Vanderveld sobbed.

"No, he won't," Catherine said. Her bright crystal heart glittered inside her, throwing off inspiration. "He'll be happy. You'll both be well off and free from financial worries. I'll name him as head floral designer on all our ads."

"I don't know, I don't know," Mrs. Vanderveld cried.

On October 21, 1964, Catherine Eliot sat

221

in Mr. Giles's office with Mr. and Mrs. Vanderveld and their lawyer. They signed the papers, and the flower shop became hers.

On October 22 the carpenters arrived.

By then, Catherine had already been at work.

Her first act as the new owner was to return to the shop that evening after dark. With her own hands she pulled down the hideous dusty curtain that had hung between the front and back of the shop. The material was so old, it shredded in her hands.

"Ha!" she laughed when the curtain was down.

Then she walked up and down the length of the shop, rethinking all her plans. Had she calculated every inch of space correctly? Was this right? And this? In her mind the new shop took shape. The city grew dark around her while she remained in her cube of light, walking up and down, planning. She didn't go home that night, but toward morning she turned off the lights and lay down on a work table at the back of the store. She slept a few hours until Piet, coming in the back door with the day's flowers from the wholesale market, woke her.

"Good morning, boss lady," he said, bending over her.

He was close enough to kiss. Catherine

felt the strangest impulse to do just that but held back, feeling rumpled and sour-mouthed and off-guard, caught asleep on the table. She sat up and pulled her skirt back down over her knees.

"Piet," she said cautiously, "would you go down to Nini's and buy me a cup of coffee? Buy yourself one, too."

"Sure thing, boss lady," Piet said.

For the first morning in three years, Catherine didn't make the coffee on the little hot plate at the back of the store. She wondered when she'd get the courage to tell someone else to make it.

She told the Vandervelds to take two weeks' vacation. They argued: it wouldn't be right, they didn't want to desert her on her first few days as owner. Catherine insisted. The Vandervelds hadn't had a vacation together for years. They needed it. They deserved it.

Besides, not much work could be done during the renovations.

"Renovations!" Mrs. Vanderveld gasped. She placed her hand over her startled heart. She stared at Catherine as if Catherine had turned into a monster.

"Renovations!" Mr. Vanderveld roared. "How long do you plan for these 'renovations' to take?"

"Two weeks," Catherine said.

"Ha!" Mr. Vanderveld replied triumphantly. "Two weeks, it will be at least a month. You'll see. It always takes longer. You'll be into Thanksgiving and we won't be able to fill our Thanksgiving orders, all those centerpieces, one of the busiest times of the year. You've made a terrible mistake, young lady!"

When the Vandervelds returned in early November, they were stunned.

"Oh, *God,* what have you *done!*" Mrs. Vanderveld cried when she entered the shop. She burst into tears.

Before, on entering Vanderveld Flowers, one had immediately encountered the high scarred wooden counter with beady-eyed Mrs. Vanderveld perched on a stool behind it. The walls and floor had been dark with old paint, old dirt. The "reception" area had been cramped.

Now one entered a long bright space with tiered display brackets on the walls, freshly painted in milky white. Tiered tables for potted plants were set around the room. The old wooden floor had been covered with a washable vinyl in a marbleized pattern of greenish white with pale green veins.

In front of one of the refrigerators, in the

middle of the room, was Catherine's grandfather's magnificent desk, which Kathryn had sent from Everly. The burled mahogany and shining brass drawer handles gleamed. Also from Everly had come the two Queen Anne chairs, upholstered in pink-and-white-striped silk, which sat on each side of the desk, one for Mrs. Vanderveld, one for the customer.

The glass-doored refrigerator that had been at the back of the shop in the work area had been brought forward to the middle of the room. The other wide refrigerator was moved back so that both refrigerators acted as dividers between front and back as well as displays. Between the two refrigerators there was no door. No hanging curtain. Only open space.

"People will be able to look back here and see me working!" Mr. Vanderveld exclaimed.

"Yes, absolutely. That's the point. You're an artist. It will intrigue them."

"Humph," he replied, slightly conciliated by this new vision of himself. "Well, look, now I will have to walk all the way to the front to get flowers from the cooler."

"Before, you had to walk to the back. It's the same number of steps. Just a different direction. This way the flowers are all on display. People can see what we have, and they might want to buy what they see."

"You've spent a lot of money," Mrs. Vanderveld said wistfully.

"Yes, and I'm not done yet, but I think it will pay off," Catherine replied.

With Piet and the Vandervelds managing the regular business, Catherine continued at her frantic pace to get ready for the opening of her new shop. She rose every day at five-thirty to get down to the flower district to consult with container wholesalers, flower wholesalers, ribbon and cardboard box suppliers. She spent a few hours helping clean and arrange the flowers. At night she went to her bookkeeping class. After class she sat in her apartment, copying selected names and addresses from her Miss Brill's alumnae book, from her mother's address books, which she'd secretly borrowed from her parents' apartment, from the directories of yacht clubs and garden clubs and charitable organizations to which her parents and her grandmother belonged.

In early December the sign painter arrived to paint in gold, high on the plate-glass window, the name of Catherine's store:

BLOOMS

" 'Blooms'!" Mr. Vanderveld said. "What

kind of foolish name is that!"

Blooms' colors were foam white with a hint of green, like the underside of certain leaves in a storm, and gold. The new cardboard boxes were white, the ribbon gold, the stationery, billing materials, and gift cards all read in discreet gold letters: BLOOMS.

Catherine told Mrs. Vanderveld she should answer the telephone by saying, "Blooms." Mrs. Vanderveld walked off, muttering in a low voice.

Catherine set wicker baskets of everlasting arrangements, buckets of fresh flowers, and porcelain or terra-cotta containers of houseplants and trailing ivy on the tiered tables and wall display shelves. Now people who entered stopped several times before they got to the counter, and inevitably they were delighted by something that had caught their eye and that they realized they had to have.

But Catherine was not counting much on walk-in trade. She had spent the money renovating the front of the shop because she wanted it to look elegant. All her training at school and her parents' homes had taught her that it was elegance people paid money for.

In early December a truck pulled up in the alley and two men delivered the five hundred custom-made containers Catherine had ordered.

"What's happening!" the Vandervelds exclaimed in horror. "What's all this?"

"Wait a minute," Catherine said, too excited now to be calm herself. "Let me show you."

She raced down the stairs and tore open the boxes. She took out one of the containers, which she had designed herself and had specially made. It was a small, open treasure chest, made of copper-alloyed tin that looked gold. She grabbed up a handful of sphagnum moss and molded it into a rectangle, then stuffed it inside the treasure chest. She filled the container with water. She anchored a large, luminous, amethyst orchid in the moss. She opened the small box of cards she'd had printed up. The cards all read, in gold letters on pale white:

For the pleasure of treasures,
Order flowers from Blooms.
Catherine Eliot, Owner
Jan Vanderveld, Floral Designer
Telephone 555-5343
73rd Street at Park

She raced back upstairs to show the Vandervelds.

"Humph," Mr. Vanderveld said.

"What will you do with this?" Mrs.

Vanderveld asked.

"Announce the opening of my shop," Catherine said. "I'm sending out five hundred of these to people I know who can afford flowers and who don't know this shop exists."

"You're mad! That will cost you a fortune!" Mr. Vanderveld said. "The orchids alone — "

"I know. It's expensive. But to make a lot of money, you have to spend a lot of money."

"Where did you hear that?" Mrs. Vanderveld said. "Some ivory-towered philosophical economics course, I suppose."

"Actually, I thought of it myself," Catherine said. "But I'm sure someone said it before I did. Now, let's get to work."

She had asked Piet if he could find some inexpensive temporary help, with the understanding that they were on trial and that if things went well, they would be hired full-time. Later that day Piet showed up with two men named Jesus and Manuel, who worked along happily in the basement, singing songs in Spanish while shaping the moss into bricks, which they put into the containers.

Mrs. Vanderveld addressed the envelopes while Catherine wrote personal messages on the backs of all the cards:

"Dear Robin [or Anne or Melonie and every other girl she had known at Miss

Brill's], When you get married, let me do your flowers! Love, Catherine."

"Dear Mrs. Evans, I know Grandmother would want you to know that I've carried on her love of flowers. Respectfully, Catherine Eliot."

"Dear Mr. and Mrs. Collier, I hope I'll see you and George at Everly this Christmas. Shelly loves school. I love my shop! Come visit me. Affectionately, Catherine."

"Dear Mrs. Stone, When Debbie has her coming-out party this spring, I'd love to be of some help. Best wishes, Catherine Eliot (Miss Brill's '61, with your daughter Mary)."

"Dear Mr. and Mrs. Jones [or Hyde-White, or Slate, and so on for two hundred names], I know Mother and Father would want you to know I've started my own business. Best, Catherine Eliot."

"Dear Mother and Father, See? I've started my own business. Maybe I'm not a total loss after all. See you at Everly at Christmas? Love, Catherine."

Finally all the cards were handwritten and all the envelopes addressed. Piet had to make two trips to the wholesalers to pick up the orchids Catherine had special-ordered. With the help of Jesus and Manuel, they slipped an orchid into the moss and a white card into five hundred treasure chests. Catherine had spent hours the night before making a chart of addresses and blocks so the deliveries would be organized to take the least amount of time. Almost all the addresses were on the Upper East Side.

Mr. Vanderveld grumbled about all the fuss as he continued to make his standard Christmas wreaths and decorations.

"What a waste of money," he said to himself sotto voce, but loud enough so that Catherine could hear.

The next morning the phone began to ring.

"Catherine! How did you know? I *am* getting married! In January! To Linden Douglas! I'd love to have you do my flowers!"

"Robin, I'm thrilled for you. He's a dream. Congratulations! Let me come see you on the twenty-sixth, when all the Christmas fuss has died down."

"Catherine? This is Mrs. Evans, dear. I love the little treasure chest. I'm giving a formal dinner party for eighteen on New Year's Day. Do you think you could help me come up with something original? Refreshing? I do get tired of the same old thing, don't you?"

"I know just what you mean, and I'd love

to try, Mrs. Evans. Perhaps I could stop by on the twenty-seventh to see your dining room colors and the table service you plan to use, and so on. Then I'd have a better idea of what would coordinate with your decor."

"What a lovely idea, dear. I'll see you then. I hope you'll stay for tea."

The phone kept ringing. No sooner did Catherine put it down than it rang again. By noon she was getting complaints from people that they were having trouble getting through. After she finished a call, Catherine kept the receiver off for a moment so the phone wouldn't ring.

"Mrs. Vanderveld," she said, "would you please run down to the coffee shop and phone the telephone company? Tell them we need another line put in right away."

"Oh, no, my dear, that's not necessary!" Mrs. Vanderveld said. "I'm sure all this will die down. You don't want to go to the expense of another line just because of one day's excitement."

"Mrs. Vanderveld — "

"Really, Catherine, you mustn't — "

"*Henny.* Do what I asked, now, please!"

It was a toss-up as to who was more startled at her sharp words, Mrs. Vanderveld or Catherine. But Catherine put the receiver back on the hook, and the phone rang again, and

Catherine began to write down another order. Henny Vanderveld, head high, sniffing, gathered up her purse and went off to do as she was told.

Catherine didn't go to Everly that Christmas. She intended to, to make more contacts. But she was so exhausted that she spent the day in bed, sleeping. Christmas night she sat looking out the window of the apartment just as she had only a few weeks before. Tonight she was sitting in her robe, drinking champagne and eating stuffed olives straight out of the jar with a fork. She had opened the window in spite of the cold to hear the street sounds of people calling out, "Merry Christmas," and singing carols as they hurried through the dark to dressy parties. Occasionally a new idea popped into her head, and she wrote it down on one of her notepads. She was glad she wasn't stuffed into a proper dress, sitting at a proper dinner, eating turkey. She decided this was the happiest Christmas she had ever had in her life.

Catherine sat in the shining expanse of the Terrys' living room sipping tea with Robin Terry and her mother. Catherine was wearing a killingly expensive, terribly plain black wool dress, which she had stolen from her mother's back closet, and her pearls. She didn't think Mrs. Terry would remember her from Miss Brill's — there had been so many girls there — and Catherine had a black mark against her for not attending any college. But Mrs. Terry took one look at Catherine's dress and was reassured. Catherine was one of them.

". . . so good of you to come to us," Mrs. Terry was saying. "We're in such a rush, with the wedding happening so soon."

"Oh, it's just not fair!" Robin wailed. "I've dreamed all my life of having a spring wedding out at our place in Southampton. We have a rose trellis there. I wanted to wear a summer gown and take my vows under the rose trellis. Apple blossoms in bloom, you know, a romantic wedding. January is such a boring, ugly time to get married!"

"Well, why don't you wait?" Catherine asked. "April's only a few more months away."

Mrs. Terry cleared her throat.

"Oh, Mother, really, everyone is doing it these days!" Robin said. She shot Catherine a look of exasperation.

Mrs. Terry rose. "I'll just tell Cook we'd like some biscuits with our tea," she said, and click-clacked out the room on her high heels.

Catherine leaned forward. "Robin, you're pregnant!"

"Of course. How do you think I got the fool to marry me?" Robin laughed. "Oh, he would have eventually, this just helps speed things along. We're both delighted about the baby, really. Of course Mother's acting like I've escaped from a reform school, but Daddy's amazing, he's great about it. The only thing I really *hate* about it all is that I had my heart set on a spring wedding. Apple blossoms and a tent and all that. And I have a great collarbone. I wanted to show it off in a summery gown. God knows I can't show off anything else for a while."

Catherine looked at the Corot above the marble fireplace, the Fabergé egg in its stand on the mantel, the Staffordshire hounds by the hearth, the heavy silk drapes at the French doors.

"You could have a spring wedding if you really wanted it," she said. "Indoors, with a rose trellis and trees in blossom and all that."

"You're kidding!" Robin said. "How?"

"It would take some work. It would be like setting a stage. Illusion. Of course it would cost the earth — "

"Oh, who cares what it costs, I'm their only daughter — Mum! Come here! Catherine's had the best idea!"

It was spitting sleet the late January afternoon when Catherine and Piet drove out to East Hampton in the florist van with a U-Haul trailer weaving drunkenly behind. At Everly, they discovered, the wind was even wilder, sweeping across the water and land in a frenzy.

Catherine was fairly frenzied herself. She had a clear idea in her head of what she wanted to do. She had made sketches and discussed it with Piet and Mr. Vanderveld, but the wedding was tomorrow evening. With these wedding flowers it was a do-or-die situation. There was no dress rehearsal for the flowers. She felt like a diver about to attempt her first triple somersault from a ten-meter board. If she did it perfectly, she'd be famous. If she made a mistake . . . the results could be disastrous, and there was no second chance.

Earlier she had called her grandmother and received permission and directions to the part of her land where Catherine could cut some saplings. Piet parked the van on the edge of the forest. In boots and heavy jackets and gloves, they tromped around searching, yelling at each other over the wind. They found eight bare deciduous trees with trunks about three inches thick, about ten feet tall.

Piet used a hatchet to cut them close to the ground.

Catherine helped Piet get them out of the forest and into the van and trailer. The wind tore the trees from their grips and flipped the small branches into their eyes. It was like wrestling witches.

But finally the trees were in the van, clattering against the metal walls. Catherine and Piet returned to a more protected part of the forest where the ivy had not been discolored by winter and carefully tore the vines away from the trees. Catherine had bought some from the wholesaler — but had she bought enough? She ripped at the vines, the wind shrieking, carrying the vines away from her like a kite's tail, until Piet gently led her away.

"Enough!" he said. "We have enough."

The drive back to the city was terrifying. The roads were covered with ice, and visibility was limited to a curtain of blowing sleet.

"It was a mistake to rent the U-Haul," Catherine said after they had skidded several times. "It's so high and light, it catches the wind."

"We'll make it," Piet said.

"I don't know, I don't know," Catherine said. "I wish we had done this yesterday. I was a *fool* to wait until now."

"We'll only lose about an hour's time," Piet said.

"We don't have an hour to lose," Catherine said grimly. "Oh, God! Watch out!"

Piet steadied the van, which seemed more to be floating above the road than actually touching it. With the trailer teetering behind, the van rocked back and forth like a sinking ship on a tossing sea.

"Oh, God," Catherine moaned.

"Close your eyes, Catherine," Piet said. "You have a busy day ahead. Save your energies. Rest."

"Oh, sure," Catherine snapped. "The one event that could make my fame and fortune, and I'm supposed to sleep."

Piet reached across the cab and put his hand on Catherine's neck. She jumped.

"Lie down," he said. "Use my leg as a pillow. Don't watch the road, it will only make you anxious. Rest."

She didn't resist the gentle force of his hand as he pulled her so that she lay on the seat, her head on his thigh. His leg was as hard as iron. How could he possibly think she could use it as a pillow? The heater was blowing, the air of the cab was warm, and Piet had unbuttoned his navy pea coat, which was bunched up behind her head. She could feel the muscles of his body as he downshifted or turned. She could smell him — clove gum, fresh air, the hot denim smell of his jeans. She could not help but think of what her face would be nestling against if she were turned in the other direction, facing against the seat, and his body, and the fork of his legs.

Before she knew it, they were pulling up in front of the Waldorf-Astoria. She hadn't slept, but she certainly had stopped worrying.

The Vandervelds were already there, along with Jesus and Manuel. Thousands of flowers had been brought in and were standing in buckets. Robin's wedding would take place in a small formal room used for cocktails and meetings, then the wall, which was really two accordion partitions, would be pushed back to open onto the main ballroom for the reception and dinner dance. Earlier Catherine had over-seen the setting up of the trellised arbor where the vows would take place and the draping of the pink-and-white-striped tent top across the ceiling of the ballroom.

Now her workers anchored the eight trees in buckets of sand, which had been placed around the ballroom. Standing on light metal ladders, they began to fasten pink-rimmed white carnations to the bare limbs of the trees with precut snippets of florist wire. At Catherine's request, Jesus and Manuel had brought their girlfriends to help. The girls cut the carnation stems short and handed them up to the men, who tied them. There were buckets and buckets of carnations — over a thousand, a little over one hundred for each tree.

Catherine and Piet drove the van back to the flower shop to get the pedestal stands she had sprayed white, the pots of azaleas and gardenias, the small wicker picnic baskets, the bows, the roses, the tuberoses, the stephanotis, and the forced white lilacs.

"My *Gott!*" Henny Vanderveld had shrieked on seeing the white lilacs. "What have you done! How much did these cost? Too much!"

"Henny, the Terrys will pay for them," Catherine had said, controlling her temper.

"Foolish girl, spendthrift, you'll be the ruin of yourself and the shop, you'll see," Henny had muttered under her breath.

"Oh, disappear, you old witch," Catherine had muttered under hers.

Now the Vandervelds had gone home to sleep, thank God. Piet, Jesus, Manuel, and their girlfriends worked tirelessly. Catherine played the radio full volume on a rock and roll station. At three in the morning she sent out for hot pastrami sandwiches, coffee, and sweet rolls.

The tables had already been set up in the ballroom by the hotel. Catherine covered them in the pink-and-white-striped cotton that matched the tented ceiling. She placed a wicker basket with a pale green bow on the handle as the centerpiece on each table. Later, just before the wedding, she would bring around the lush pink roses and white daisy mums to place in the baskets.

The trees were finished earlier than Catherine had thought, about nine o'clock the morning of the wedding. Never having done such a thing before, she had thought it wiser to allow more than enough time to wire a thousand carnations to eight trees. Everyone went home for a quick nap, promising to return at four that afternoon for the final touches. The wedding was called for seven-thirty.

Catherine didn't nap. She showered and fixed her hair and packed a dress bag and suitcase. As Robin's friend, she was invited to the wedding, but she could hardly wear her evening dress to finish the flowers in. She forced herself to lie down on her bed, but her mind would not turn off in spite of the night without sleep. She kept going over details. Had they remembered . . . had they done . . .

She was back at the Waldorf-Astoria before

anyone else. Good thing, for the Neanderthals bringing in the two fountains she had rented were there early. She had to tell them where to put them, at one end of the ballroom on each side of the bandstand. She draped the fountains and the area around them with ivy, then set buckets of azaleas here and there, so people would not trip on the electric cord that made the water cascade with a lovely summer splashing sound from tier to tier. Once the fountains were running, she took the water lilies that had been waiting in buckets and floated them in the lowest pool.

Then she started on the trellised arbor in the smaller room where the actual ceremony would take place. First she draped it all with variegated ivy. Then Mr. Vanderveld arrived to help her wire white and pink roses, gardenias, daisy mums, carnations, and the sinfully expensive lilacs to the trellis. Catherine rested for a few moments, sitting on a folding chair, sipping coffee, admiring Mr. Vanderveld. He was so assured of his skill that his movements with the flowers looked abrupt, even brutal. He didn't waste a twist of the wrist. His hands flew. Secretly Catherine despaired of ever learning his secrets — one swift motion, and a rose or a heavy spray of lilacs was anchored in the trellis, curving and pointing as naturally as if it had grown there, instead of hanging down stupidly the way it often did for Catherine.

Other workers from the hotel were in the room now, setting up the chairs for the guests at the ceremony and around the tables in the ballroom. The band members arrived and tuned up. Piet, Jesus, Manuel, and the two girls arrived. They put the pink roses and white daisy mums in the picnic baskets on the tables. Catherine had placed long, tapered pink candles on each side of the wicker baskets. Tiny, twining vinca minor vines were tied around the candlesticks and trailed down and over the sides of the table. The air was spicy with the clove fragrance of the thousand carnations, the white lilacs, and the old-fashioned grandmotherly scent of the tuberoses.

At six Robin's mother and father arrived, chattering nervously. By then Catherine had shut all the accordion partitions to the ballroom. The Terrys were pleased with the flowered arbor and the potted azaleas set around the room, but when Catherine had the partitions opened, revealing a ballroom with trees in full blossom, Robin's mother burst into tears.

"It's beautiful!" she cried. "It's magic!"

"It should be," Mr. Terry said gruffly. "I could have bought a house with the money

I spent on the flowers."

"It's worth it!" Mrs. Terry said. "For Robin."

Mr. Vanderveld brought in Robin's bouquet, the bouquets for her matron and maids of honor, and the wicker basket full of rose petals for the flower girl. These were delivered to the rooms the Terrys had rented at the hotel for Robin and her party to dress in. Everyone took one last look to see that each flower was in place, each detail perfect. Then Mr. and Mrs. Vanderveld and the others went home.

"It's brilliant, Catherine," Piet said just before leaving.

"Thanks. Oh, Piet, I hope everyone else thinks so!"

"They will."

"Oh, Piet!" she said again, and impulsively hugged him to her. He responded by kissing her full on her mouth.

"That was for luck," he said, grinning, then grabbed up his coat and left.

Catherine went into the ladies' lounge off the ballroom and changed into the evening dress she would wear for the wedding and dance afterward. She was so tired by then, her vision was blurring, but she was still so anxious that her palms were sweating. The Terrys had been pleased with the way the

for that evening. Last night might have been the climax of Catherine Eliot's twenty-one years, but this was New York City, and a new day.

Robin Terry's wedding made Catherine moderately famous and her shop more successful than her wildest dreams. There were photographs and write-ups about it in *The New York Times, Daily News,* and *Women's Wear Daily* and, later, in *Vogue* and *Glamour.* The New York Metropolitan Bank hired Catherine to provide their lobbies and executive offices with weekly fresh flowers using terra-cotta molds of the treasure chest flower container she had designed. Dozens of engaged women who lived in New York or Connecticut wanted her to do their wedding flowers. Restaurants called her, corporations called her, wealthy fans infatuated with actresses pleaded with her for something original and magnificent to send their adored ones on opening nights. She was called months ahead of time so that the chairwomen of charity galas would be certain of her services.

Jesus and Manuel and their girlfriends, Lina and Maria, came to work full-time for Catherine. She rented the second floor for office space for Mrs. Vanderveld, a consulting room for clients that doubled as a lounge for employees, and a private office for herself. She had her grandfather's mahogany desk moved up into her office.

Along the walls of her private office, filing cabinets grew as if self-propagating because every night Catherine sat making meticulous notes about her clients. She wrote down everything: their address, the period of their decor, the subject and colors of the art on the walls, the amount of money they had been willing to spend in the past, any private observations she had about what they might want in the future. Later, when she was finished with her notes, she turned on the lights in Mrs. Vanderveld's office and checked over the daily accounts.

Catherine was obsessed with Blooms. She lived for it. She thought of nothing else. Kit was a star twinkling at the back of her mind, but Blooms was sunlight, fresh air, real life. She never cooked for herself but grabbed sandwiches from the deli or pints of ice cream or Sara Lee cheesecakes. Occasionally she had dinner with her family at her parents' Park Avenue apartment, if Shelly or Ann were home from school.

Her parents couldn't seem to decide how to react to Blooms. Marjorie seemed more irritated than pleased by Catherine's success. It was as if Catherine had become successful only to spite Marjorie. Marjorie was wary around her daughter, as if all her life Catherine had been hiding secrets. But her father treated Catherine with a new respect. Certainly he should have. Both parents knew Catherine was giving them the money for Shelly and Ann's schooling, but Drew was the one who actually took the checks from her. In the privacy of his den, he told Catherine how grateful he was. This year Shelly was applying to colleges. All his test scores and even his teachers indicated that Shelly was bright but undisciplined. "The boy needs a firm hand," Drew Eliot said, clutching his whiskey glass in his own trembling hand.

In her own way, Marjorie at last became helpful to her daughter when she agreed to let Catherine pick and choose what she liked from her back closets. Marjorie changed weight so often that she had suits and gowns and dresses in all sizes, and one entire bedroom had been changed into a dressing room/storage room for anything from the previous seasons. Marjorie had beautiful taste, and every year there were times when she dieted so strenuously, she was able to buy small sizes. Of course in each year she also gained back huge amounts of weight, leaving the smaller sizes almost unworn.

"Would you mind if I borrowed something

from the back closet, Mother?" Catherine asked one day.

"Oh, go ahead," her mother replied.

"Actually, I have borrowed some of your things before," Catherine confessed. "I didn't know if you'd noticed. You weren't home when I needed to ask you about them."

"If it's from the back closet, you can borrow it any time. I've got more to do than keep track of old clothes," Marjorie said.

So Catherine left her parents' apartment each time with a dress bag full of clothes. For consultations with her wealthy clients, the right clothes were essential, and all the clothes Catherine wore were simple, expensive material cut and sewn well. There was a navy Chanel suit with gold chains that was especially successful. A deep green wool dress with a high neck and long sleeves. A clean white-and-brown wool checked dress that fell straight to the knees, then flounced out in pleats when she walked, and a matching coat that fell to the flounce. A pale blue knit with a matching coat. Catherine spent her clothing money on expensive shoes and handbags and gloves.

Most of the time she was in work clothes, covered with a smock, up to her arms in leaves or paperwork. But as the year progressed, she decided she needed to attend more of the parties she was invited to. She had achieved a minor celebrity in the city. The more people she met personally, the more orders Blooms received. She didn't enjoy the parties, because by the evening she was dreadfully exhausted, and there was always something else in the shop that needed to be done. Besides, most of her male escorts, men her own age or even slightly older, seemed frivolous to her. Puppies. And too often they were pleasant but patronizing. "You work with flowers? That's nice. My grandmother likes flowers." Or, "A florist, hm? Do you think you'd like to be an interior decorator someday?"

One night she went to a charity ball at the Plaza with the brother of a classmate at Miss Brill's. It was March. She had been so busy, she hadn't had time to buy a serious evening gown, and as healed as she had thought her heart was, she still could not bear to put on the turquoise gown she had worn when she met Kit. Just looking at it made a sob rise in her throat. Just touching it made her want to sink to her knees, bury her head in the foamy hem, and weep like an abandoned child.

The only other real evening gown she had in her closet was the low-cut green work of art Helen Norton had given her not even a year ago. Catherine slipped into it. She had lost weight the past few months, worrying and working, but the gown fit all right, even if it did reveal more than she would have chosen. To cover the plunge between her breasts, she fastened in an orchid, then pinned a matching one in her hair. She looked fine, she didn't care, she really only wanted to sleep.

It was amazing to her how little she had to say or do at a dance in order to seem even conscious. For many of the guests, these events were the high point of the week. Many of the women had stayed in bed all afternoon, resting for the party that night, or had spent the day having their hair and nails and faces done.

So that night at the dance, while the flower-decked, bejeweled, beribboned, adorned and spangled, frosted and iced, painted and garnished women whirled and laughed and called, "Darling, divine!" Catherine just drifted, nodding, smiling in reply to the compliments. She was bone-tired from hard work and deeply contented. She was really half-asleep even as she walked and talked and danced.

But she found herself jerked out of her lazy daze, like a fish caught on a hook and pulled to the surface of a frightening reality, when she found herself face to face with P. J. Willington. Her date was introducing them.

The old man stood before her, tall and respectable, his white starched tuxedo shirt as stiff and pure as truth itself.

"Mr. Willington, sir, I'd like you to meet Catherine Eliot. She's the owner of Blooms, the flower shop on — "

"The shop that provided the flowers for this evening," Catherine interrupted breathlessly. Mr. Willington would make no associations with the name Blooms, but the address of the shop where he'd gone so often to send flowers and baubles to the woman who eventually blackmailed him might ring an unwelcome bell.

"Oh, yes. I believe I recognize you from somewhere," the old man said, scrutinizing Catherine.

Recognize the dress? Catherine wanted to say hysterically. *I got it from an old friend of yours.*

But she didn't speak. She couldn't. Her breath was stuck, frozen inside her throat. How could he fail to connect her, a woman whose face he had seen dozens of times before when she wrote down his order for flowers for Helen Norton, with this gown, the very gown that Helen Norton had worn with him? Christ, P. J. Willington had paid for this gown!

"Yes," P. J. Willington was saying. "Of course. I know your grandmother, Kathryn Eliot. She owns Everly. My wife and I spent a very pleasant Christmas night there a few years ago. Charming woman, charming. No wonder you're a florist. She's a real gardener, the real thing. Knew your grandfather, too. He was quite the rakehell in his day, you know. Would you care to dance?"

Catherine swallowed. What she really wanted to do was toss her champagne and canapes on P. J. Willington's snowy shirt-front. What she did was to nod, smile, and slide into the old goat's arms.

He whirled her onto the dance floor. The emerald gown swirled around her. Blooms flowers glittered from every table and pedestal stand and niche like jewels. It had been six months since P. J. Willington had been blackmailed, and here he was, hale and happy. The old pirate liked her looks, she could tell. Catherine relaxed. She waltzed in P. J. Willington's arms.

CHAPTER 7

New York, 1968

April in New York. Catherine in blossom.

A wealthy Texan whose wife wanted to be part of the New York art scene hired Catherine to do the flowers for an extravagant cocktail party they were giving at their new home on Washington Square. Their interior decorator had painted the walls of the huge room that served both as living and dining areas chalk white. The furniture was either teak or polished black enamel. The Texans wanted something "futuristic." They said they had invited "everyone who was anyone."

The husband had taken Catherine aside to tell her that this was the most important event in his wife's life.

The wife had taken Catherine aside to tell her that this was the most important event in her life.

Catherine told them she would deliver something original and spectacular. She asked only that she and her crew work without interruption.

It was two hours before the party. The caterers were setting up their tables. Catherine was surveying her work.

She had bought eight mannequins, four of each sex, removed their heads, and painted them eight striking colors: magenta, chartreuse, acid yellow, carmine, ink black, raw umber, peacock blue, and emerald. She had shaped sphagnum moss into heads and wired them onto the torsos. Ivy trailed like pre-Raphaelite tresses over some heads, some were bald, some had dark or daisy or grass hair. Different flowers — carnations, mums, roses, bachelor buttons — had been stuck into the moss faces as eyes, noses, mouths, and ears. The result was humorously eerie.

Catherine knocked on the door leading to the hall, bedrooms, and den. Mr. and Mrs. Simon appeared in a flash. They hurried into the middle of their living area, stood still, and looked around. They approached each of the mannequins and inspected them closely.

"Oh," the wife said in her high little drawl. "These are certainly . . . unusual."

"Yes," echoed her husband in his great big drawl. "They are definitely . . . unusual."

Catherine took a gulp of Scotch to keep herself from screaming: "Okay, let's *have* it! Do you like them? Hate them? *What?*"

The husband looked at the wife.

The wife looked at the husband.

"Well, we'd better get dressed, darlin'," the wife said.

Mr. Simon turned to Catherine. "Thank you, Miss Eliot," he said formally. "If you'll excuse us, we'd better get dressed."

"Thank you, Miss Eliot," the wife called from the hall doorway. She fluttered her hand good-bye.

They don't know if they like the arrangements or not! Catherine realized. She had seen this happen before. Not until the guests came and either were enraptured or disgusted would the hosts know what to think.

The next morning the phone rang at Blooms.

"Miss Eliot, I just want to thank you again," Mrs. Simon cooed. "Everyone just went wild about those flower people. Some photographers took some shots, and one man told me he's putting a story in *Chic* about the flowers and us. You are just so clever. Oh! My husband wants you to know he's sending an extra little something to you — all in gratitude."

Now the paralysis that had frozen Catherine's lungs evaporated. She hung up the phone and took a deep breath. She was alone in her office, trying to hide her fear from her employees. At times like this she remembered she was only twenty-five. At times like this she remembered she was only pretending to know what she was doing.

Fortunately everyone else seemed to think she knew exactly what she was doing. In three short years she had made Blooms a prosperous company and herself a moderately wealthy and well-known young woman.

Accordingly, she had changed her look. These days she could afford to have her hair done. Her hairdresser scissored it short in a gamine cut. Her make up consultant praised Catherine's vivid coloring instead of despairing of it as Marjorie had. Now Catherine smugly wore the brilliant tones that paler women couldn't carry.

Catherine lined her dark eyes with deep seal brown liner. She painted her lips scarlet. She had her ears pierced in spite of the fact that her mother insisted only whores and gypsies had holes in their ears, and she bought herself half-carat diamond ear studs. More and more she spent money on clothes for herself, because her mother's expensive outfits were too simple and restrained for the look Catherine liked. The boldest women wore pantsuits these days. Catherine looked wonderful in slacks.

With the help of Mr. Giles and a money

manager he recommended, she invested most of her money. Her major investment had been buying herself an apartment, the second floor of a dove gray stone building on Seventy-fifth Street just off Park. It had a fireplace in the living room, a balcony off the bedroom overlooking a tiny walled-in garden, high ceilings, ornate moldings, shining dark wood floors. Best of all, it was near Blooms.

She didn't spend much time furnishing the apartment. She chose everything one afternoon in Bloomingdale's. It was all good-quality, comfortable, dark mahogany contrasting with bright floral prints. It was satisfactory, and she was in a hurry.

Besides, she seldom had anyone in her home. If she entertained, she took people out for dinner or drinks or held small cocktail parties in the lusciously decorated consulting room at Blooms. She concerned herself with every detail of Blooms and with her own person as an adjunct of Blooms. Her own apartment was merely a convenience and a retreat.

It wasn't only that she wanted to spend every waking moment and every ounce of her energy on Blooms. It was now also that she had to.

With each passing day, Mr. and Mrs. Vanderveld grew less helpful and more troublesome. With Mr. Vanderveld it was the sad fact of aging that caused him to slow down, but Catherine was not sure whether Mrs. V was losing her mind or employing a cunningly destructive one.

Catherine had to spend all day helping Mr. V with the flower arrangements; he was still an artist, but a weak and trembling one. Upstairs in the business office, Mrs. V, who had never been very efficient at her best, was now turning muddle into chaos.

Every night Catherine went over the account books as Mr. Giles had advised her, and she was glad she'd learned bookkeeping because more and more, Mrs. V was making disastrous mistakes. Her addition and subtraction were wrong. She entered credits in the debit column. She forgot to mark accounts paid and billed important customers several times even after their checks had cleared.

What was worse was that whenever Catherine confronted Mrs. V with her mistakes, Mrs. V reacted with vehement denial.

"You silly girl! How can you say such a thing! I would never do such a thing!"

"Mrs. Vanderveld — "

"Shame on you! You should be ashamed of yourself!"

One night Catherine went into Mrs. V's office to find that the account books had disappeared. The next morning when Mr.

and Mrs. V arrived for work, Catherine saw them in Mrs. V's arms, clutched to her breast.

"I'm taking them home with me every night from now on. You go into my office at night and mess them up. You write mistakes in them. Now you don't get the chance to."

"Mrs. V, I cannot allow you to take the books home," Catherine began calmly.

"Who are *you* to tell me what I can and cannot do!"

Mrs. V's voice was shrill. Her hair, now almost totally white, exploded from her bun as she shook her head in anger. Catherine was both angry at the woman and frightened for her.

"I've been keeping books for more years that you are being alive! I — "

"Henny." The one word in Mr. V's iron voice brought his wife's shrieking to a dead stop. "You forget Miss Eliot is our employer. You must do what she says."

Mrs. V's face went crimson. She turned abruptly and hurried up the stairs.

Mr. V gave Catherine a look that said clearly, "See what you have done?" then turned away, shoulders bent, and went back to his work.

Catherine was torn. She wanted to fire both the V's and start over with young, willing, pleasant employees. Yet did she not have some kind of duty to this aging pair? At the least she wanted to prevent their relationship, which had once been affectionate, from ending in bitter antagonism.

Before she could decide what to do, another element entered the brew — Jason LaFleur.

Even in New York in the sixties, Jason LaFleur was an unusual sight. An extremely tall, handsome, affected young black man, he arrived at Blooms one afternoon wearing a pink suit with a lavender cravat. Nervously smoking pastel cigarettes in a long holder, he displayed his portfolio for Catherine: photographs of flower arrangements he had done and sketches of designs he would like to do. Catherine was immediately enchanted with his work. It was modern, fresh, fanciful. She hired him on the spot.

For one horrifying moment, when she introduced him to Mr. V, it looked as if Mr. V were going to have a heart attack and die. His face turned as red as the roses he was arranging.

"We do not need another florist!" Mr. V shouted.

"Mr. Vanderveld, he is here to help you. He is here to make things easier for you. He'll assist you. He — "

But Mr. Vanderveld turned his back on Catherine before she could finish her sentence. Puffing so heavily he sounded like a radiator exploding, he hurried up the stairs to his wife's office.

Jason and Catherine were left alone at the back of the shop. Explosive phrases in Dutch filtered down to their ears.

Catherine ran to the top of the basement stairs.

"Piet!" she called. "Please come up and help!"

Piet came at once and listened while Catherine explained. He hurried up the stairs to calm his uncle and aunt.

But when Piet returned, alone, he said, "They are packing their things. They are leaving for good."

"Oh, no. Piet — "

Mr. and Mrs. Vanderveld came clumping heavily down the stairs.

"We are leaving. If we find we have left something personal here, our nephew Piet will bring it to us." Mr. Vanderveld did not look at Catherine as he spoke.

"Mr. Vanderveld. Mrs. Vanderveld. Don't leave this way. There's no need for — "

But the older couple ignored her. They bustled, heads high, toward the door. Catherine was shaken. It was as if yet one more set of parents were saying: Enough. We've had enough of you.

"Please," Catherine begged. "Don't let our relationship end like this. Piet — what can I do?"

"Let them go," Piet said softly. "It's time."

"Time, perhaps, but surely not the right way for them to go."

"Catherine. For them there may be no other way."

"What about a retirement party? Gold watches, champagne, words of thanks — "

"I don't think they want to admit they are old enough to retire. They don't want to admit that they've slowed down or lost their capacity for work. This way they are leaving not because they are old, but because you are so difficult to work with."

"But that's not fair! I'm *not* too difficult to work with!"

"Catherine. If you care for them, let them have their pride."

"Yes, but — don't they care for me? What are they giving me?"

"The shop."

"I *bought* the shop! It's legally mine. Rightfully mine."

"Now it is totally yours."

Then the phone rang, breaking the tension. Piet went back to the basement while Catherine showed Jason around the workroom. Only when she was alone at home did she let herself dissolve in tears of self-pity. It would have meant so much to her if the Vandervelds had passed their shop on to her with love and respect, knowing they were leaving it in capable hands. She had thought they were all a sort of family; but she had been wrong.

She spent the next few days interviewing prospective bookkeepers; she settled finally on Sandra Klein. Sandra, in her late thirties, was plump, pleasant, and sane. She told Catherine that she "enjoyed working with numbers," and she meant it. She had two daughters in high school and was married to an accountant who dropped her off at Blooms every morning and picked her up every night. During her lunch hour she read paperback romance novels, which she kept in her desk drawer. What she lacked in humor or style she made up for in reliability, and Jason had enough style for the entire workforce.

Jason had hands like Mr. V's; they flew among the flowers with utter certainty. At first he angered the tough young men who did the heavy work in the shop by casually calling all of them "sweetie." "Hey, sweetie, bring that bucket of glads over here to me, would ya, darlin'?" They'd obey, but not without muttering under their breath.

He called Piet "gorgeous." Yet once the

workers saw that this didn't annoy Piet, that he even teased Jason back, they relaxed.

Jason called Catherine "boss baby" and "queen honey."

"Boss baby," Jason would say with his hands on his hips, "why don't you just let me try it my way for once? I guarantee your little ladies will be enchanted!"

These were the first endearments lavished on Catherine in years, and Jason was the first person who had been nurturing and maternal toward her. She loved it.

Before long, Blooms became Catherine's real home. Jason teased and flattered her. Sandra organized the books and helped make the office into a place of comfort and simplicity. Once, when Catherine came down with the flu, Sandra sent her home and showed up after work with chicken soup, 7-Up, aspirin, and one of her romantic novels. After Maria fainted one day, then threw up all over the minicarnations the next afternoon, Catherine called Manuel into her office for a little talk. Soon after that, she was a guest at Maria and Manuel's wedding, and she promised Maria that when their baby was old enough to leave with a sitter, Maria could have her job back. At last, in a way, Catherine had a family.

Catherine got into the habit of eating out

with Jason at least once a week. They always had plans and fresh ideas to discuss, and they enjoyed discovering new restaurants and nightclubs. They needed to keep up with whatever was hot to keep one step ahead of their clientele.

They loved making an entrance together. *Guess Who's Coming to Dinner* had just been nominated for an Oscar, but a white woman with a black escort was not yet a common sight even in New York. Jason and Catherine played it for all it was worth. Jason would drop his foppish mannerisms and act like an amorous Cary Grant. Catherine wore Katharine Hepburn–ish pants. Both tall, they strode behind the maître d' with bored looks on their faces as all eyes turned to stare. Once seated they leaned against each other, making kissy mouths, eyes laughing.

For the first time in her grown-up life, Catherine had someone to have fun with. As different as they were from each other, Catherine and Jason shared a common bond: they were both outsiders in their world. But rather than being cowed by this, Jason gave her the courage to play it to the hilt.

Piet remained a puzzle and a stranger. He was always there when Catherine needed him, always willing to do anything she asked. But he never needed anything in return. He took his paycheck and the raises and bonuses she gave him and asked for nothing more. It was as if he were willing to befriend her without desiring her friendship in return, which in a way was an insult.

Certainly he had plenty of friends of his own. One day a perplexed delivery man, after walking back and forth in front of the shop several times, entered to deliver a box of a dozen red roses from another florist's shop to Piet.

"You got a Piet Vanderveld here? I feel like I'm delivering sand to a beach," the man said, winding his way through the flower-filled shop.

"Piet, why would someone send you flowers?" Catherine asked. The smile on his face embarrassed her. "I *mean,* it seems odd to send flowers to a florist."

"She doesn't know what kind of work I do."

"My, my, gorgeous, aren't you a prize!" Jason giggled.

Sometimes women came by the shop looking for Piet. Usually they were blond. Often they spoke only broken English. Always they were stunningly beautiful. Piet handled them all with delicate aloofness, steering them out of the shop and down to Nini's to talk.

Catherine envied the women. They knew

more than she did about Piet. Piet kept his private life so hidden from Catherine that it was as if he always came and went into darkness. That frightened her . . . and aroused her. Many nights she dreamed of Piet, and every day his presence incited a confusing pleasure deep within her.

One bright spring morning, Catherine opened *The New York Times* to the society page. She read:

Mr. and Mrs. Bruce Hilton of New York and Palm Beach announced the engagement of their daughter Haley to Mr. Christopher Bemish II, son of Mr. and Mrs. Christopher Bemish of Boston and Camden, Maine. The wedding will take place June 7 at St. James Episcopal Church in New York. The bride is a graduate of Ethel Walker's School for Girls and Smith College. The groom is a graduate of . . .

Catherine put down the paper. She was alone in her office. She rose and locked her door. But when she returned to her seat to give way to tears, nothing happened. She could only feel that same old ice-cold prism heart of hers, hard and chilled, impervious to sorrow. She put her hand over her breast, which felt warm. How could so much cold exist within a living body?

She wished she could talk to someone. Leslie was still her closest friend. They wrote each other every month, telling all, and they'd always vowed to be there in a time of need.

But this was not a crisis. Not really. Catherine had always known this was going to happen. Yet every day now for almost four years she had thought of Kit, and not without some small seed of hope in her heart. She couldn't believe that what had been between them wasn't lasting.

What a fool she'd been. Savagely she stuffed the newspaper in the wastebasket. She unlocked the door, straightened her shoulders, and went down to the main floor of her shop to work.

Easter weekend Catherine was invited to her parents' Park Avenue home for Sunday dinner. Ann came down from her senior year at Miss Brill's, Shelly was on spring break from Chapel Hill. Catherine had driven out to Everly in the Blooms van to pick up her grandmother; she'd spend the night there when she took Kathryn home. She brought a sumptuous arrangement of iris, tulips, daisies, and hyacinths for her parents' dining room table. Her mother's eyes flicked over it when she sat down, but she said nothing.

"Pretty flowers, Cath," Ann said.

"Nicely arranged," Kathryn added, and Catherine smiled.

Marjorie and Drew were in unusually fine moods. They'd just returned from three weeks as guests at a friend's home in St. Lucia, so they were relaxed, tanned, full of good gossip. Shelly was exuberant.

"I can't wait till school gets out," he said, slathering mint jelly on his lamb. "Todd's got a VW camper, and he and Matthew and I are going to spend the summer driving across the country."

"How nice," Drew said, sipping his wine. "Will you see the Grand Canyon? Mt. Rushmore?"

"Well, maybe, but mainly we're aiming for San Francisco. We've got it all mapped out. Between the three of us, we've got a friend in every state, all along the way. That means plenty of hot food and hot showers, not to mention a little party time with the local girls."

"How are your grades this semester?" Catherine asked.

"What's it to you?" Shelly asked, his voice rich not with anger, but with amusement. At nineteen he was a golden boy, big, handsome, charming, happy, accustomed to adoration.

I'm paying for your damned tuition, that's what it is to me! Catherine retorted silently. Some instinct kept her from saying this to her brother: the knowledge that it would disgrace her father and bring Catherine no praise.

"I'm just concerned, Shelly. If your grades are as bad as they were your freshman year, you should go to summer school, or you'll never graduate."

"You're one to talk!" Shelly laughed. "You didn't even apply to college!"

"I may not go to college, either," Ann said so enthusiastically that wild rice flipped from her fork and rained down on the tablecloth. As she blithely picked up the tiny grains, one by one, and nibbled them, she continued, "Probably I'll get married." She sighed.

"Are those the sort of table manners you're learning at Miss Brill's?" Marjorie asked, and Catherine was surprised to hear the chill in her mother's voice. Usually Marjorie dripped honey when talking to Ann.

Drew shoved back his chair with unusual force. He crossed to the sideboard and poured himself a large glass of Scotch. Obviously his wine was not enough for him.

"I had a letter from Madeline," Kathryn said. "You girls remember Elizabeth. She's getting married. To a very nice man named

Tom. He's an accountant, so he can help with the books, as well as taking over various other chores — chauffeuring, general handyman work, I suppose."

"How's Ned?" Ann and Catherine spoke at the same time.

"He's well. He's working on a book."

"A book!" Catherine said, astonished.

"Is he married yet?" Ann asked.

"Oh, no. He's only twenty-five. He won't marry young. It will have to be the right woman for him."

"Mm, I can imagine," Catherine said. "Someone with money."

"That's not very nice!" Ann snapped.

"Catherine's right," Kathryn said. "Ned will need to marry someone with money. It would be best. It might even be necessary. Madeline told me they make enough running Everly as a guest house to keep them all in food and clothes, but not enough for major repairs on such an old enormous place. It's a real problem — I do hope they won't have to sell it."

"Sell it!" Catherine and Ann cried out simultaneously, then sat staring at each other in dismay. Although they'd seldom discussed it, they felt quite possessive about the British Everly. It was a refuge and wonderland for them, and they both liked knowing they could return to it one day.

Ann put her elbows on the table and sighed. Musing aloud, she said, "Then I guess it's just as well I'm in love with someone else. I'd be no help to Ned — I don't have any money."

"That's why you should marry someone with money," Marjorie said.

"Your mother's right, you know, Pudding," Drew said.

To Catherine's surprise, Ann's eyes filled with tears. "You don't understand!" she said, and rushed out of the dining room.

"Would you pour me another Scotch, dear?" Marjorie asked Drew, holding out her glass.

"May I have some more lamb?" Shelly asked.

"Excuse me," Catherine said, and rose to go after Ann.

Ann was in her frilly bedroom, sprawled on her stomach across her canopied bed, oblivious of the way she was wrinkling her silk polka-dot dress. Hearing the door open, she looked over her shoulder and, seeing Catherine, said, "Oh. It's just you."

"Whom did you expect it to be?" Catherine asked, sitting next to her sister.

"Dad. I wanted it to be Dad. Coming in to tell me he's sorry and that I can date Troy."

"Who's Troy?"

Ann sat up in one quick burst of movement, grabbing Catherine's hands. "Oh, Catherine, Troy is the most wonderful man in the world! I'm in love with him! Really in love. And Dad and Mom are being pigs about it."

"Why?"

"Because Troy's poor. He's a car mechanic. But he's soooo handsome, Catherine, and he's soooo . . ." In spite of her little-girl looks, Ann's voice held a newly adult resonance.

"How did you meet him?"

"He works in Fairington. One day Molly took a bunch of us from school into town, and her car broke down, and that's how we met him. Actually we'd all noticed him a million times before when we went into town to the drugstore or post office. Oh, Catherine! It makes me feel all melty just thinking about him!"

Catherine had to smile. Ann's happiness made her glow, and Ann was undoubtedly a smashingly beautiful girl. Her eyelashes, wet with tears, glittered around blue eyes as variegated as the depths of an iris flower.

"And Mom and Dad don't want you to date him?"

"They don't want me to marry him."

"Marry! Ann, you're too young to get married."

"I'm almost eighteen! I'm so bored with school. The thought of college and more tests and classes makes me barf. I want to start my life."

"Which would mean living in a rented apartment in Fairington and working as a waitress?"

"Why do you say that? I wouldn't have to be a waitress. What an awful thing to say."

"I don't think car mechanics make enough money to keep you in the style you're used to."

"Well, I thought Mommy and Daddy could give us the money they were going to give me for college. Then Troy could buy his own gas station."

"Oh. I see. Does Troy like this plan?"

"I haven't even mentioned it to him! Oh, you just think he wants to marry me for my money! That's not true! There are plenty of other girls at Miss Brill's richer than I, and you know it. Troy's lived in Fairington for years. He's twenty-six, so if he were just a fortune hunter, he would have snatched someone else up before now. He could have anyone, he's so handsome! It's me he loves, Catherine, not my money, and I love him. Oh, Catherine, if only you could see him. If only you could see us together! It's not just sex, it's — We have so much fun together. I can be so silly with him. We're always laughing. He — "

Catherine kicked off her high heels, curled up against the footboard, and let Ann rave on. Troy rode a Harley-Davidson and wore a black leather jacket. He looked like James Dean, like Elvis Presley. He had a tattoo. He'd served some time in a boys' reform school when he was younger, but underneath the tough front he was as sweet as sugar, as helpless as a baby. He *needed* Ann. Ann knew he did. With her help, he would become the man he should be.

The more Catherine heard, the more guarded she became. She would have preferred to disagree with her parents and side with Ann, but Troy sounded like trouble. Still, listening to her sister made her remember how she had felt with Kit. She had been so alive. So complete. So vivid, like a flower flaring up from its sheath.

She had been happy then.

Catherine pulled herself back to the present. Kit was marrying someone else. Her life was in the shop. *Happiness* . . . well, that didn't matter to her now.

"Look, Ann, I'll make a pact with you. I think you'll like college. Try it for just one year. If you still want to marry Troy after a year, I'll be on your side against Mother and Dad."

"But that means waiting for so long!" Ann wailed. "Besides, Mom and Dad will make me go to the Vineyard with them this summer! I won't get to see Troy for almost three months!"

"Perhaps he could come visit you."

"Oh, I'm so sure. Dad and Mom would be thrilled to have him as a house guest, right? Can you see them taking him to dinner at the yacht club?"

"All right, you won't see him all summer. You'll survive. He can work hard — and you can get a job and save some money for your married life."

Ann's eyes narrowed in suspicion.

"Ann, if you marry Troy, Mom and Dad won't give you much money. You know that. In the first place, they'll be mad. In the second place, you know they don't have much money to give. They're just muddling along as it is. Before you get married, I think you ought to go out and take a good hard look in an appliance store. Do you know how much a washing machine costs? A stove? A refrigerator? Do you know how much a house costs? How are you going to get groceries to cook your love god dinner? Ride on the back of his motorcycle? Do you — "

"Oh, stop it!" Ann cried, throwing herself back down, stomach first, and burying her head under a pillow. "You're just ruining it all!"

"I'm just trying to help you see the practical side," Catherine said.

"Who cares about the practical side! I'm in *love*. I love Troy and he loves me! Don't you know about love? When you're in love, everything works out. When you're in love, nothing else matters!"

Catherine waited a few moments for her sister's tantrum to subside, but Ann was weeping greedily now, enjoying her martyrdom. Catherine rose, slipped back into her shoes, and went out, closing the door behind her. She intended to join the others at the dining room table but was waylaid by her father, who was waiting in the hall for her.

"Catherine. Could I speak to you? Privately? Just a moment, before dessert and coffee."

They went into his den. He paced the floor, obviously gathering his thoughts. "You've turned out to be the level-headed one in the family," he said finally, without preamble. "So perhaps you can come up with something to do to take Ann's mind off this Troy character."

"If we can only get her to try one year

of college . . . "

"That might be too late. What if he . . . gets her pregnant? So that she'll have to marry him? You know that's exactly what's on this boy's mind. He's a fortune hunter. Ann's an innocent. She doesn't have a clue about men like this. She — "

Catherine listened stoically as her father talked on and on. Ann was her father's darling, his little girl.

"I'll do what I can, Dad," she said when he had quieted.

Drew sighed, then said, as if the words were pulled from him, "Catherine, you know I'm grateful for the assistance you've given us in sending Shelly and Ann to school."

Anger flared inside Catherine. Assistance! I paid for their entire tuition, she thought. She didn't speak, but her expression said it all.

"It's not just a matter of tuition, you know," Drew said, catching her look. "We have to buy them the right clothes, and pay for all their trips to and from school during holidays. . . . But I'm getting off the point. Catherine, you've already been so generous in helping your sister toward the right kind of life. Surely you'd hate to see all your money — not to mention your sister's life — go to waste on someone like Troy."

That was true. The thought of Ann with a

fortune-hunting Romeo made Catherine sick.

"I'll think of something, Dad." She had an inspiration. "Maybe I'll take her to Everly this summer. The British Everly. She'd like that, I know."

"Great. I knew you'd come up with something." Drew looked at Catherine, an honest, studying look. "You've turned into a capable young woman." Clearly this baffled him. "Well, let's go have dessert and a little drink."

Clara, Kathryn's live-in housekeeper, had hot chocolate and pastries waiting for Kathryn and her granddaughter when they arrived back at Everly that night.

"You're a lifesaver, Clara," Kathryn said as they settled themselves in the living room. To Catherine she said, "Your father always gives me too much alcohol to drink, too much wine. I feel dreadful."

Kathryn had slept during the long drive home, but now she was awake and wanted to watch her favorite Sunday night television shows. Catherine joined her in dutiful silence. Her sister's conversation had left her restless. All that talk of love. And it was spring, that juicy, skittish time when one's nerves were stirred by perfumed breezes.

Clara went to her room after serving them their late night snack; she would clear up in the morning. Kathryn went to bed at ten and told her granddaughter she'd see her early in the morning. Kathryn always rose early, around five, and Catherine would, too. She'd have breakfast with her grandmother, then drive back to the city for the start of a new week.

Clara had prepared one of the second-floor bedrooms for Catherine tonight. Perhaps her grandmother felt she had graduated from the nursery floor, an adult in her own right. It was a nice big bedroom with a fireplace and a high, deeply comfortable bed, but Catherine couldn't fall asleep. Oh, she was just in a strange and irritable mood.

She needed to move, to walk. Pulling on her light wrapper, she let herself out of her bedroom and padded down the hall and down the stairs. Her grandmother slept at the other end of the house; she wouldn't waken.

Catherine moved through the dark house without turning on any lamps. Silvery light from the full moon slanted through the windows, illuminating the rooms, which were warm, dusty, and slightly stuffy, having been closed all winter. Living room, dining room, library, conservatory, butler's pantry, maid's pantry, kitchen; the kitchen belonged to Clara. She'd never invited the children to be her friends, never showed them how to cook a soufflé or called them in to lick the icing bowl. Her rooms were off the kitchen, and Catherine didn't want to wake her, but she stood for a moment in the kitchen, enjoying a perverse sensation of invading the other woman's domain. A mud room and potting shed led off the back door. If Catherine had her way, she'd have those slapdash structures rebuilt with a glass roof, turn them into a decent greenhouse.

Not for the first time, Catherine wondered who would inherit Everly. No doubt her father; he was the proper heir. And if he managed to keep it, he would pass it on to Shelly. But probably he'd sell it immediately. God knows they needed the money. Besides, Marjorie hated Everly, hated gardening, found it boring and dirty.

And Drew would do what Marjorie wanted, Catherine thought, leaving the kitchen and wandering back down the long passageway to the wide front hall, because he lived to please Marjorie. Catherine hated to admit it, but she knew that Kathryn was somehow at fault here. Kathryn had never loved Drew, not completely, unreservedly, the way children needed to be loved; his mother had left him damaged. Her father was like a tree, Catherine thought, that had had a limb lopped off and to keep its balance, to survive, had grown twisted in another direction, searching for its life.

Marjorie had grown up in Baltimore, the only child of wealthy parents who placed great importance on beauty. No doubt she'd suffered when she'd presented her parents with her first child, a squalling creature with curly dark hair and hazel eyes. Catherine was happy with her looks these days, but she could understand what not having a perfectly beautiful, blond, blue-eyed baby had cost her mother. Marjorie's parents were dead now. She and Drew clung to each other like two orphans united against the world. With a whiskey bottle as their mascot, Catherine thought wryly, entering the library.

There was brandy in the cut-glass decanter, and Catherine poured herself some. She seldom drank, but a little brandy seemed appropriate in this dark room in the middle of the night. She stretched out on a leather sofa, reaching down to pull her wrapper over her bare feet, and looked out through the glass French doors at the silver gardens.

Who would inherit Everly? It would be a neat irony if her father inherited and passed it on to Shelly, who would most certainly sell it in order to play away the profits, just as his great-uncle Clifford had done with the British Everly.

Or was Catherine being too harsh? Certain characteristics were inherited, she believed, certain propensities and qualities and abilities, just as much as the color of eyes or hair. She could quite easily believe she'd inherited Kathryn's inability to love people; look at her, she was twenty-five, unmarried, not in love, not even seeing anyone. Her letters to Leslie were always about Blooms, with side notes about her family. Leslie's letters to her were about her love affairs, and in the past five years Leslie had had more than she could remember. And they were really *love* affairs. Every time Leslie wrote of a new man, she wrote about him in tender, exalted language, emotions Catherine had felt only once, with Kit.

Sexual desire was something else. Certainly she'd felt that, strongly, for Piet, but that was not love, and the craving was so physical, from such a depth, that she often felt it was shameful. Shame. Funny, Catherine was not ashamed of the blackmail she had committed. The blackmail had two sides, like the moon. She had blackmailed in order to help her family — so from whom had she inherited the crushing responsibility to help her amazingly frustrating family? Not from her father, or mother, or even Kathryn. Hers had seemed a glorious sort of crime, justified by cause and mitigated by the victim's own sins. But she *was* ashamed of what it said about her. She was capable of vice; Piet knew this, and furthermore, so was Piet. Desiring him had a darkness to it, a taint of corruption, because of what they'd done together.

Agitated by her thoughts, Catherine set aside the untouched brandy glass and flung herself from the sofa. She paced the room. She was only twenty-five! Why did her father expect her to save Ann? Well, because she had allowed him to grow accustomed to her help, of course. But why had she become responsible for any of her family at all?

Her irritation with Shelly's terrible grades was not simply born from concern about his life, she knew that. She was jealous of him. His darling choirboy looks let him get away with everything, and this summer he'd been driving across the continent, laughing and singing with friends. Catherine would be slaving away at Blooms, except for the time she'd probably take off to take her sister to Everly and out of Troy's clutches. A part of her would like nothing better than to be laughing and singing and driving across the continent in a convertible. She'd meet strange men with western accents and rough hands and make irresponsible love with them.

No. She'd work at Blooms, because without

her there it would lose its edge of success. Shelly would drive across the country, and Ann would float on oceans of love, and when Drew inherited Everly, he'd likely leave it to those two impractical, lovable children. Catherine could just hear his sensible reasoning now: "Well, Catherine, you have Blooms, after all. You have money and a livelihood. Shelly and Ann are the ones who need my help."

Catherine found her brandy snifter in the dark room and took a large drink. Immediately her stomach burned and her face flushed with heat. She crossed the room and leaned against the French doors. Outside in the moonlight, the apple trees, swollen with white blossoms, hung lush and luminous in the night. Daffodils shivered in the light breeze. Oh, her sister was a flower, her brother was a tree, and what was she, only the damned peasant gardener, hunched over a wheelbarrow, unloved but useful.

She was tired now. The brandy had finally made her sleepy. Catherine went quietly through the dark house, up the stairs to her adult room, and fell asleep at once.

During the next few weeks, Catherine couldn't sleep. She broke into tears for no reason at odd times, even at work in front of her employees. She was exhausted half the time, manic half the time, irritable all the time.

"I think you've got spring fever," Jason told her.

"Catherine, when was the last time you had a medical checkup?" asked Sandra.

Piet said nothing. But he looked at her.

She started walking over to Central Park for her lunch breaks. The air was sweet, the grass and trees that surprising tender green of springtime, and the apple blossoms hung in snowy clusters, bursting from the branches. She longed for Everly. She longed to be little again, running through her grandmother's gardens or lying on a brick path looking up at the way sun shone down through the flowers, making the petals expand and shimmer into clouds of color.

One morning she and Jason were together when Piet and Jesus brought in the first shipment of iris of the spring. They all crowded around the flowers, touching the delicate petals. It was like dipping their fingers into rainbows, for there were irises of every color ranging from deep violet to swan white.

"I've always identified with the iris," Jason said, his voice serious for once. "It's the perfect flower. Complete. I mean sexually. The sword-shaped leaves surrounding the curved flower. The three upright, erect, masculine petals, inside the three opened, falling, surrendering feminine petals. Male and female combined. See what I mean?"

Catherine didn't reply. She was lightly running her fingers over the sweetly tickling fur of the beard of a dark iris. Jason's words and the sticky silk in the throat of the flower made her shiver with desire. Jason went quiet. She could feel Piet watching her.

"I've got work to do," she said brusquely, and hurried to the refuge of her office. Slamming the door shut, she leaned against it and surrendered to memory: Kit's body, Ned's breath, her own heat and ecstasy. The luxuriance of love — would it ever be hers again?

A knock sounded behind her; gathering herself, she opened the door.

"Yes?" she said, all business.

Piet stood there, holding two dozen luscious iris in his arms.

"I bought these. For you."

"Piet — "

He thrust the bundle into her arms. She felt the chill of the flowers, the heat of his hands.

"You wanted them. You should have them," Piet said.

Catherine stared at him, almost crushing the flowers against her breasts.

"Piet," Sandra called. "Telephone!"

"Coming," Piet yelled back, and went off,

but not before nodding at Catherine, as if to confirm an agreement they had silently just now made.

Such self-indulgent moments were rare for her. Blooms was busy, which was good, but Catherine was overworked, restless, irritable. There were no more moments alone with Piet. The thought of England refreshed her, and in May she told Ann she wanted to take her to Everly as a graduation present.

"Oh, Catherine, that's fabulous!" Ann cried, hugging her sister. Then her face fell. "But it means being away from Troy."

"We'll only be gone twelve days, Ann. I can't leave Blooms for longer than that."

Ann looked conflicted, but she smiled in spite of herself. "I know I'll miss Troy — but I want to go! Oh, thank you, Catherine!"

Being with her sister was a pure pleasure that spring, and Catherine often spent Sunday driving in the Blooms van up to Fairington, where she'd pick Ann up and take her out to dinner at the local inn or to a movie.

One Sunday in May as they were driving through Fairington, Catherine met Troy.

"There's Troy!" Ann squealed. "Stop, Catherine, oh, stop, just let me say hello. *Hello!*"

Catherine pulled the van over to the curb

next to Troy's motorcycle. Troy stuck his head in the window on Ann's side, nodding abruptly at Catherine as Ann introduced them. He was certainly handsome. He wore his sexuality like a second skin; it was almost as visible as the spots on a dalmatian or long hair on a Himalayan cat. His dark, blatant, intense attractiveness was much like Piet's, and like Piet's it held a hint, a hue the eye could almost see, of danger.

They drove away. Ann was flushed and animated, yet at the same time serene; she licked her lips slowly and smiled to herself. Which of us is the wiser? Catherine wondered. Ann, who was so completely lost in perilous love, who would someday weep in anguish at her loss, or Catherine, gripping the steering wheel, fighting to remain in some kind of control?

By the time the end of June came, Catherine was exhausted. Blooms seemed to have been chosen to do the flowers for every June wedding in New York City, and while she was of course pleased by that, she had gone into a state of overdrive that kept her from feeling pleasure, from tasting the food she ate or resting while she slept.

Piet would be in charge of Blooms while she was gone.

"Don't you worry about this shop while you're in jolly ol' England," Jason told her. "You just have yourself a jolly ol' time."

"I'll probably be bored to tears," Catherine replied, slamming desk drawers open and shut, trying to discover anything she'd forgotten. "I'm only going because I have to take my sister. It'll probably rain the entire time, and I'll come back with pneumonia."

During the flight Catherine was wretchedly uncomfortable. When she finally fell asleep, she was awakened after a few minutes by a stewardess offering breakfast just two hours after they'd had dinner.

Ned met them at Heathrow. Beautiful, dazzling Ned. In the past four years he'd taken on a firmness, an adult solidity; beneath his gray tweed jacket his shoulders were broader, and his movements as he greeted them and handed them into the old Bentley were polished and assured.

"My God! You both look gorgeous! Wait till you see Hortense, she's turned out rather nicely, too. The old house is packed, and Hortense is slaving away in the gardens like crazy today so she'll be able to have some free time to spend with you. How are you? How's your grandmother?"

His eyes were the color of violets. He'd let his black hair grow romantically long, curling down over his shirt collar. He looked like a poet. Catherine looked sideways at Ann's face. Her eyes were shining. Catherine got in the back of the car and let Ann sit next to Ned. Suddenly she was overcome with drowsiness. She slept all the way to Everly, and when she arrived she excused herself after greeting everyone and went up to her room, where she fell asleep the moment her head touched the pillow. Ann couldn't get her to wake up for tea or for supper, and she slept on, coma-deep, until late the next afternoon.

"Where have you been? I thought you'd died!" Ann cried, leaping up from the garden path. She was wearing a blue shirt and white shorts. Her knees were crisscrossed from kneeling on the white pebbles next to Hortense.

"I had the most marvelous sleep! I couldn't wake up!" Catherine said, stretching, yawning.

"You missed breakfast!" Ann scolded. *"And* lunch."

Hortense rose, pulling off her gardening gloves and dropping them in the basket. She'd been working on the roses, inspecting, spraying, feeding. She hugged Catherine and kissed her.

"We'll find some tea for you. And biscuits. Or would you rather have coffee? Proper tea's only about an hour away."

"Are you okay? I couldn't get you to wake up last night. It was scary!" Ann said.

"Jet lag, that's all. And I'm very tired, Ann, I've told you that. My shop was so busy recently, I haven't had time to scratch my nose. It's lovely to be lazy. Tea would be fine, Hortense, but don't go to any trouble. I can find something — "

"Nonsense. Go sit on that bench and smell the roses. Come on, Ann, you can help."

Hortense had become a beauty, Catherine thought as she followed the path to a marble bench next to the brick wall almost hidden by tumbling wisteria. The air was sweet and hot as honey. Catherine put her feet up on the bench, tossed the skirt of her sundress over her legs, and wrapped her arms around her knees. She leaned her head back, throat exposed to the heat of the sun. Closing her eyes, she inhaled the perfume of hundreds of roses.

"Tea, ducks," Hortense said.

"Did you fall asleep again?" Ann asked.

"I'm just relaxing. It's heaven here."

"Come on, Ann. Help me with the watering. Let your sister have some peace."

Hortense set a tray on the bench next to

Catherine, then the girls went chattering off together. Catherine smiled. Hortense didn't seem to realize how lovely she'd become. She must have gotten contact lenses, for she no longer wore glasses. But her glossy dark hair was pulled back in one lopsided unruly braid, she wore no makeup, and her clothes were disheveled. It was not just that she was working, for Catherine remembered Hortense looking much the same the previous night when she'd briefly said hello to everyone. She'd met everyone again last night, she'd even met Elizabeth's fiancé, Tom. But she had been so exhausted that now they blurred in her memory.

The tea was hot and smoky, the cream thick, the crumbly biscuit topped with sweet jam. She licked her fingers. Birds chirped from trees and bushes. The girls must have gone to a completely different part of the garden, for she couldn't hear their voices anymore. Bees droned. Catherine felt the pace of her heart slow inside her. She set the tray on the ground and stretched her legs out on the bench. The marble arm behind her was not soft, but it was strong, and she leaned against it. There was something to be said for having an ocean between you and your business, she thought. Between you and your real life. If she were at Kathryn's

Everly, her mind wouldn't rest; she'd be mentally listing all the things that needed doing, all the improvements that could be made. Here none of it was her responsibility, and there was something reassuring, even optimistic, in knowing that a young woman like Hortense, energetic, serene, capable, was in charge of the gardens.

I think like a woman one hundred years old, Catherine thought. She nestled her head and shoulder against the back of the bench. From a distance the wisteria looked lavender, but now as she studied the long drooping clusters nearly touching her nose, she saw how the blossoms subtly slipped through shades of white, lilac, amethyst. Some of the pod-shaped blossoms were closed like lockets, some opened like wings. It was so quiet, she thought she could hear the tight buds of the roses unfurling in the sun.

Later, she heard distant laughter from the other side of the brick wall. Hortense and Ann.

Later still, the girls swooped down to bring her inside for tea.

The days slipped past Catherine like flowered silk. She rediscovered the pleasures of leisure. Now she ate slowly, savoring flavors, and sat for long quiet hours in the gardens, without a thought in her head. Whenever Ned suggested they all see a movie, she couldn't be bothered. She let Ann go off with Elizabeth and Tom and Hortense and Ned while she stayed at Everly, in their small music room, listening to their library of classical records. Beethoven, Brahms, Schubert, Schumann. When had she had time to sit so calmly, listening to music, letting it lift and sweep her into pure peace? Never before in her life. Every night she went to bed feeling physically enriched, as if she'd eaten jewels.

She spent some few hours of the day talking with the various Boxworthys. Elizabeth especially claimed her attention, wanting to tell her about Tom and their wedding plans. They sat on the third floor, in Elizabeth's room, fingering the buttery satin she was using to make her wedding gown.

"Tom's so good," Elizabeth confided, enraptured, "so kind, so intelligent! He's not like Ned, all fast and quick and brittle. He's deep. And so wondrously handsome. I never dreamed I'd marry such a handsome man."

Catherine smiled, amused and touched. Actually, at his best Tom could be called pleasant-looking. He had brown hair, brown eyes, pointed ears, and a nose that was rather too large for his face, and he was slender, but not muscular. Catherine thought he looked soft and would be pudgy by forty. The most attractive thing about him was how happy he looked when he talked to Elizabeth. Sometimes when they were all together having tea, Catherine would see the two lovers glance at each other across the room, smile their conspirators' smile, and then Tom would blush, a rosy hue spreading from his collar up and out to his glowing ears.

Elizabeth at twenty-three was still soft and gentle, her light brown hair waving around her face to her shoulders, her gray-blue eyes bright; she looked like one of God's milder angels. Her body was full, gracefully curving and sloping. Undoubtedly the lucky Tom found her voluptuous.

For Elizabeth and Tom were already lovers, and clearly that made everything in life worthwhile. Catherine listened while Elizabeth spoke of love, of feeling that profound certainty that this person was the right, the only, person, that the world had been created solely for the purpose of their meeting and loving.

This was how Catherine had felt with Kit. She was flushed with memory. She dreamed of him. When Elizabeth spoke of love, there was nothing in her voice to suggest the obscene or extreme, no danger, no terror, no challenge. Their love was as safe as cream in a pitcher.

But Kit was marrying — had married, by now — Haley Hilton. Yet here in England, Catherine did not feel the pain as piercingly. Here she felt protected.

They were to stay at Everly for ten days, and by the seventh Catherine began to sense her body filling up with energy, strength, renewed desire, as if she were a wilting plant placed in a bowl of water, drawing nourishment up through her roots. One night it rained, and Ned entertained the guests and his family by reading poetry in the library, where a fire burned, warming the chilly room. Catherine had seen little of Ned during her stay. He was not around during the day; busy working in the office on the accounts, she supposed. At night he always took a group into town for a movie or to visit the most picturesque pubs, but she'd never gone along. Her experiment with Ann appeared to be working; Ann was nearly drooling as she watched Ned read, and whenever Ned looked at her, Ann's cheeks flamed.

" 'Though nothing can bring back the hour/Of splendor in the grass, of glory in the flower;/We will grieve not, rather find/ Strength in what remains behind . . .' "

As Ned read Wordsworth's words, Catherine pondered them. Surely she had not had her hour of splendor in the grass. The time with Kit had been so brief — and in the end, so false! She was only twenty-five and not ready to live the rest of her life muddling on with only strength.

The next morning, after breakfast, when Ann had gone off with Hortense to the gardens, Catherine was surprised to have Ned gently take her by the arm as she was leaving the dining room.

"I haven't had a chance to talk to you during this visit," he said, "and you're here only for two more days. Have you been purposely avoiding me? Be honest."

"Oh, no, Ned. I've just been very tired. I spend so much of my life surrounded by people, it's been a luxury to be by myself."

"Ah. I thought perhaps there was a man in your life, a jealous man, who might not appreciate any attentions you'd pay to your old friend."

"No. There's no man in my life, jealous or otherwise."

"Then spend the day with me. I thought we could take a picnic lunch and walk up the back hill. You can see all over the world from up there, and it's a glorious day."

"That sounds wonderful. I'll put on my walking shoes."

"I'll get a picnic ready and meet you here in thirty minutes."

They walked through Everly's formal gardens, which ended with a wall of green boxwood, passed through the arched doorway cut into the hedge and out into open fields. The land rolled gradually down to a stream, then gently ascended again. It was a nice knobby hill, undulating, fallow, the young grass only ankle-high. Catherine and Ned walked companionably, matching their strides in an easy cadence, taking their time, huffing slightly, for the hill was higher and steeper than it looked. Ned carried a wicker basket with him, Catherine the blanket he'd given her.

"We're lucky in the weather this year," Catherine said.

"You've changed since you were here last," Ned told her.

"I'm older. We're both older."

"Yes, but I don't think I've changed as drastically as you have. Do you?"

Catherine smiled at him. "No. You're the same. Happy Ned. Well, I bought a business. When I came last time I was only a little shop girl, and now I'm the owner of a very successful flower shop. I wish you could see it, Ned. Blooms is a marvelous place. I have four full-time employees and hire others seasonally, I've made enough money to buy my own apartment in New York . . ."

As she talked about Blooms, strange shoots of sensation pierced Catherine, and she realized with a smile that what she was feeling was homesickness. She was so utterly engrossed in her thoughts of the flower shop that she was surprised when Ned said, "But what about men? True love? No marriage in sight? No Prince Charmings in hot pursuit?"

Catherine laughed. What if she were to tell Ned she hadn't slept with any man since she'd slept with him here at Everly? He'd probably faint with fear, thinking she'd placed too much importance on their little amorous episode.

"No men. I've been too busy. I see some men, of course, but really, Ned, I work so hard, and believe it or not, it's possible for a woman to be happy without a man in her life."

They had reached the top of the hill now. Together they spread the blanket over the soft grass, then stretched out on it.

"What a wonderful view! You can see all over the world from here!" Catherine said, looking down at the fields of jade and emerald, which unfurled like banners in all directions. Everly was a spot of chimneys hidden behind trees. In the distance a ribbon of road wound past, dotted with an occasional bright spot of car.

Ned set out the picnic things: watercress sandwiches, ham and tomato and cheese sandwiches, hard-boiled eggs, pears, chocolate bars. From thick white linen napkins, he unrolled champagne and two crystal glasses.

"How lovely! How elegant!" Catherine cried. After they'd toasted and sipped, she asked, "And what about you? And women, I mean. You're my age, twenty-five, and I don't see any sweet young thing wearing your engagement ring."

"I imagine it will be a long time before I find the perfect girl," Ned said, leaning back on his elbows. "I believe in love, of course, but it would be nice to fall in love with a girl with money. To help out poor Everly."

"What if you fall in love with a girl with an Everly of her own? Her own estate to keep up?"

"That wouldn't work at all. The woman I marry must be willing to spend her life here, to devote her life to Everly. I'm the oldest son, I'll inherit, this is my home, and it's up to me to live here and take care of the place, and, eventually, my mother."

"You mean you couldn't ever leave Everly to live somewhere else if you wanted to?"

"Why would I want to?"

"That's not the point. I mean, don't you feel a little imprisoned by all this? A bit like a sacrificial lamb?"

"God, no! I feel incredibly lucky. As for love and marriage, what woman wouldn't be proud and honored to live here? I'm glad I have such a home and such a family to support. I only wish I did it better. I'd like to take some of the burden off Mother. She's almost sixty now and shouldn't have to work so hard."

Men and their families, Catherine thought, thinking of Kit. Some men, some families. Her father didn't feel that way about the American Everly, and Shelly certainly felt no responsibility toward his parents.

They continued talking as they ate their lunch, then lay back drowsily on the blanket in the heat of the sun. It was a good thing she didn't love Ned, Catherine thought. As much as she loved the British Everly, she'd never want to give up Blooms, and she'd never be able to submit her life to the needs of Ned's family and his family's house.

Closing her eyes, she stretched languorously. The champagne and the sun's heat made her feel as if she were melting. Then Ned rolled close to her and kissed her full on the mouth. At first it was a friendly kiss, then it became more serious.

"Ned!" she said, opening her eyes, pushing him away. "We can't! Not up here, not out in the open!"

"Why not? Who in the world could see us? No one! Look, we're on top of the world. It would take anyone half an hour to climb up here, and I can see all the way around, no one's in sight."

"Ned — "

But she was too aroused to protest further. Fully clothed, he lay on top of her, kissing her, moving against her, and then he shoved her skirt up around her hips and gently pulled off her underpants.

"Unbutton your dress, Catherine. Let me see your breasts."

She unbuttoned her dress. He unbuttoned his shirt and undid his trousers. The ground was hard and unyielding beneath Catherine's back, and a pebble dug uncomfortably into her shoulder. It had been so long since she'd made love with a man that at first it was unpleasant, almost painful. But Ned was beautiful and sweet and gentle in his love-making. She loved having her arms and legs wrapped around this hard man, loved the rush of breath against her cheek, on her neck, in her ear, loved the heat and push of his body. The smell of his clean hair and skin mingled with the fragrance of the sweet grass they were crushing. Above Ned's shoulders, high in the blue sky, swallows wheeled and soared. Closing her eyes, Catherine was lost to the birds' shrill cries and Ned's deep, gruff, gasping pleasure. Then he collapsed against her, nuzzling her neck, telling her how lovely she was, and there on top of a hill in England, in the hot quiet bright light of the summer sun, Catherine did feel completely lovely.

Walking back down to the house, Ned said, "Come to my room tonight. And tomorrow night. We've got only two nights before you leave."

"I'd love to, but Ann . . . Not that she'd be shocked if she thought I were sleeping with a man, not that. I think Ann's got a crush on you, Ned."

Ned grinned. "You could be right. I like Ann, too. Oh, don't be alarmed. She's only seventeen. I'm not going to seduce her. She's too young. Yes, I see the problem. I'd hate to hurt her feelings. You're right. You're a good sister, Catherine." He put his arm around her and patted her shoulder in a comradely way. "We're good to our families, you and I."

But after they'd passed through the arched hedge into the formal garden, Ned said, "Still. Perhaps if you wait until she's asleep? We'll get her to drink a little brandy, maybe she'll pass out — in a nice healthy way."

"You're awful, Ned," Catherine said, but returned his smile. Secretly she was quite pleased to know that it was she Ned was interested in, not her golden-haired princess-faced sister.

And in spite of her virtue, she managed to slip away to his room and make love with him both nights before they left. She never thought she loved Ned, but she liked him a lot, and he had rekindled within her a desire for sexual pleasure that she'd completely forgotten. She felt alive again, renewed, ready for anything.

On their flight back to New York, Ann said, "Catherine, guess what! Hortense suggested I spend next summer at Everly. I could work there, and they might pay me, at least they'd give me room and board. Wouldn't that be heavenly?"

"What about Troy?"

"Oh, come on, Catherine. How can you even ask? Troy just seems so — one-sided — after everyone at Everly. I mean, he's handsome, but Ned's handsomer, and he's much more interesting than Troy. But anyway, Hortense says she's not ready to give up her life to drool around after some man, and I'm not either. Maybe college won't be so bad. I'm going to work really hard. I want to learn everything! I feel so stupid around the Boxworthys!"

Catherine leaned back against the headrest, relaxing, listening to Ann chatter on. She felt smug, clever, proud of herself. She'd taken Ann to Everly to make her forget about Troy, and she had succeeded.

More important, Catherine had been reminded of what she needed to make her own life full, and she was conjuring up a new scheme for getting it.

CHAPTER 8

New York, 1968-1970

Catherine had forgotten the noise of the city.

Standing on 72nd Street at eight-thirty on an early July morning, she took a deep breath and looked around. No solitude, no serenity here. The subway and the passing traffic made the sidewalk vibrate beneath her feet. Horns blared. Windows opened, doors slammed. A woman with harlequin sunglasses and an Hermès scarf trotted by with a poodle in a rhinestone collar. A delivery boy on a bike cut in front of a taxi driver, who leaned out of his window shaking his fist and swearing in Greek. Gray-suited men with bulging briefcases in their hands slid into their sleek limousines. On the corner a grizzled old man sold hot pretzels, across the street from another who ran a ramshackle newsstand that had been there for years. Wind tugged at the pretzel stand's striped umbrella. The city hummed with hurry.

Catherine loved it. Here was the pace that

matched hers. Her visit to England had refreshed her, dipped her in a well of peace, but she knew that too much peace would drown her. She liked action, work, accomplishment. But also, she thought as she walked toward Blooms, she liked sex.

Jason and Sandra rushed to greet Catherine when she entered. She'd been gone less than two weeks, yet they hugged and kissed her, talking so fast that their words tumbled on top of one another. Catherine had brought them presents: for Sandra, she'd bought a beautiful silk scarf covered with flowers; for Jason, another silk scarf, also covered with flowers, but in a slightly different design and color. She'd brought Piet a present, too, but she planned to give it to him alone: it was an English paisley silk robe from Liberty's, an invitation.

But now Piet was down in the basement, supervising the men who washed the containers, unpacked the deliveries, and cleaned and conditioned the flowers he had bought downtown in the flower district earlier that morning. She merely called hello to him from the top of the stairs, and he answered that he'd have coffee with her later.

Up in her office, Catherine shut her door; then, stretching her arms wide, she turned around slowly, savoring being back in the room she loved best. Her enormous mahogany desk was piled with mail, trade magazines, and folders Sandra had pulled from the files of clients who had called recently. The summer was usually quiet, but there were still weddings and parties. Business didn't really flatten out until August.

Catherine sat at her desk, kicked off her shoes, and began to dig in.

"Hi, kid."

She was so engrossed in her work, she hadn't even heard the door open. The voice startled her.

"Leslie!" She raced across the room and hugged her friend tightly. "My God, what a surprise! Come in! Sit down. What are you doing here?" She studied her friend's face. Leslie looked artistically bizarre, like a vampire, or rather as if a vampire had been at her. Even on this hot July day, Leslie was wearing a long-sleeved turtleneck black miniskirted tunic, no jewelry except heavy dangling silver earrings. Her hair was short, her skin was white as paper, and she was pencil thin.

"I've been here for days, I've been calling you constantly. It never occurred to me that you wouldn't be here. From your letters I got the impression you were chained to your shop. It's great, by the way, really marvelous.

I came down a few days ago and talked with one of your staff — Jason. He told me you were off in England."

"I sent you a postcard."

"I didn't get it — it will probably be waiting for me when I get back to Paris. So how are you? Is this a good time for me to be here?"

"When are you going back to Paris? I mean, if you're leaving tomorrow, I'll stop work now, but if you'll be here a few days more, I'd like to get some things out of the way. . . . Let's have dinner tonight."

"I don't know when I'm going back. I'll be here at least a week. Daddy's not here, but he's coming in a few days. All right, let's have dinner tonight. I have a lot to tell you."

"I have a lot to tell you — "

Leslie had left the office door open when she entered, and now Piet was standing in the doorway. Catherine's heart jumped. His white cotton shirt, damp with sweat, clung to his chest. His sleek black hair was long, and for a moment, in the dim light of the hallway, his face looked as beautiful as a woman's. Then he stepped inside, and the light illuminated the hard line of his jaw where his beard was already showing stubble so black it was almost violet.

"You must be Piet."

Catherine looked at Leslie, stunned. Lust had lowered Leslie's voice several notes. Leslie rose from her chair, crossed the room, and shook Piet's hand. All perfectly friendly, but full of innuendo. "I'm Catherine's old school friend, Leslie Dunham. Catherine's told me so much about you. Actually" — Leslie laughed — "what am I saying? Catherine's hardly told me anything about you at all."

Piet leaned against the doorjamb, smiling. "Yes, our Catherine can be secretive," he said.

"Well, hey," Leslie said, "Catherine and I are going out to dinner tonight. Why don't you join us?"

Piet looked over at Catherine. His dark eyes seemed to hold amusement, but then they often did.

Catherine felt that in a few brief seconds she'd lost control of her life and her plans. "Yes, Piet, do join us," she said. "We'll dress up and show Leslie a great time in her old town!"

Piet nodded, his eyes betraying nothing of his reaction, then he excused himself. "See you later, Leslie. Catherine — it's nice to have you home."

The moment he'd turned to go down the stairs, Leslie pushed the door shut and shot across the room. She bent over Catherine, who was still seated on her desk chair. "Jesus," Leslie whispered. "He's sublime! I've never seen anyone like him. Don't tell me that after all these years you still aren't sleeping with him."

"Sit down, Leslie, and cool off. Look, we work together."

Leslie sat down. Pulling out a pack of cigarettes, she said, "I sleep with a lot of people I work with."

"What? I didn't know you worked."

"I model. And sleep with the artists. And guys model for me, and I sleep with them. God, Catherine, I've written you. How's your family? Now where have you been?"

Relieved that Leslie had changed the subject, Catherine relaxed. She told Leslie about going to Everly with Ann and asked about Mr. Dunham. But Leslie was restless. Catherine could see her mind was elsewhere, probably in the basement of Blooms, she thought dryly. "I'll let you get back to work. See you tonight."

They met at six at Blooms. Leslie wanted to try a new French restaurant she'd heard about in Paris, and Piet drove them there in the van. Catherine was a little embarrassed: a van seemed so déclassé. But the air of the van was marvelously perfumed from a crush of elaborate pedestal arrangements of summer roses Blooms had done for a summer wedding. The van's front seat was actually a long bench, so all three of them could fit comfortably. Leslie snaked her way into the van first so that she was the one squeezed against Piet as he drove.

Catherine was wearing the sleeveless black dress with the gold chain belt around her hips that she'd started her day's work in; in the end she'd been too busy catching up to go home and change. Leslie was wearing a shapeless, shimmering batik Indian dress made of gauze, hung with beads and fringe. Ornate earrings, intricate and vaguely sexual, like carvings from a primitive temple, hung from her ears. But Piet was the surprise. For once, he was wearing a summer navy blazer with white linen trousers. He looked like a crown prince of the raj dressed for an English tea.

At the restaurant, to celebrate, they ordered champagne, and then escargots with baguettes to soak up the garlic butter, and tournedos and *pommes frites*. Almost at once Leslie and Piet began chattering to each other in French. Catherine was miffed: she hadn't known Piet could speak fluent French, and her own facility had faded considerably. Imposing what she hoped was a pleasant expression on her face, she watched and listened, trying to understand the lilting conversation that lopped back and forth between Leslie and Piet. She was distracted. She was restless and unhappy. She wanted to be alone with her old friend, she wanted to be alone with Piet. She could hardly tell Leslie about making love to Ned with Piet sitting there — especially when she was hoping to seduce Piet.

Leslie wasn't doing a bad job of seducing Piet herself. She met his eyes, leaned close, laughed, and touched his arm as she spoke. She was flirtatious, fluid, feminine.

Piet appeared to be charmed. Certainly he was charming. Catherine had never seen him like this, at ease, sophisticated, even courtly. She let the conversation slide past her — Piet and Leslie could have been discussing art or astronauts for all Catherine could comprehend. Stop that! Catherine wanted to shout at Piet. Stop acting so cosmopolitan, I know what you're really like! But of course, she didn't know what he was like at all.

"You're so quiet, Catherine," Leslie said in English. "Is something wrong?"

"I think I'm just tired. I was in England only yesterday morning. I'm — disoriented. And I have to admit, despite Miss Brill's I can't keep up with you two in French."

"Oh, darling! Then we'll talk in English."
Leslie smiled at Catherine, then immediately
looked back at Piet. "I'd love to paint you. I
mean, I would really love to paint you. I don't
suppose I could get you to pose for me."

"I thought you were going back to Paris,"
Catherine said.

Leslie shot Catherine a smile, but from
her eyes glinted — what? a warning? a
challenge? Catherine's breath caught in her
throat. She'd never competed with Leslie
for a man's attentions before.

" — no rush to get back," Leslie was
saying. She took out a cigarette. Piet leaned
forward to light it. She put her hand on his
to steady it and let her hand linger there
just a few seconds longer than necessary.

Leslie had to go back to Paris sometime,
Catherine thought glumly as Leslie babbled
on. Leslie had to go back to Paris, and Piet
would remain here, but she didn't want Piet
later, and she didn't want Piet after Leslie
had been his lover, and she also didn't want
Piet now if it meant engaging in some kind
of seductive contest for him. I'm doomed,
Catherine thought, drinking her champagne,
toying with her steak, doomed never to have
him. She'd had such fantasies on the flight
home! No. More than that. She'd had *fantasies*
for years now. On the plane she'd made

plans, imagined how to arouse him. When she'd arrived back in New York yesterday afternoon, she'd purposely, and with great difficulty, kept away from the shop to sleep off her exhaustion before she saw him. The silk paisley robe was in its purple box in her living room. She'd planned to invite him to her apartment for a drink tonight. She'd planned to give him the gift . . . and she'd imagined the rest would follow. Damn Leslie!

"Why are you so twitchy?" Leslie asked, suddenly focusing on Catherine.

"Oh, I'm sure it's just jet lag," Catherine lied.

"Well, perhaps you ought to go home and get some more sleep."

And it would be fine with you if I left now, wouldn't it! a wicked voice in Catherine's head taunted. Aloud, she said slowly, "You're probably right, Leslie. I should just go home — "

"Unfortunately, I have to go, too," Piet said.

"You do? Why?" Catherine asked, shocked.

Piet smiled directly at her. "You don't know why?"

"Well, no — "

Catherine stared at Piet. She knew her cheeks were flaming. She could see Leslie looking at her with a mixture of envy and curiosity on her face. Catherine couldn't speak. She looked at Piet, and their gaze was a kind of touching, a stream of heat flaring between the two of them.

"Catherine." Leslie's voice was sharp. "What's gotten into you?"

Catherine tore her gaze away from Piet's eyes.

"Why do you have to go now?" Leslie asked Piet, her voice sweet. "It's so early."

"I apologize, Leslie, I should have warned you. I thought Catherine would understand — but perhaps she thinks I never sleep. I buy the flowers for the shop at the flower district every morning. I have to be there between five and six — and if I don't turn in around ten o'clock, I'm useless."

"God, how dreadful for you!" Leslie said. "I usually don't go to bed until four in the morning, and I sleep till noon."

Leslie and Piet chattered easily as they paid the check. Catherine was still quiet. If Piet hadn't known how she felt about him before, he'd know now. She wandered out of the restaurant after her friends like an amnesiac.

She didn't bother to listen to Piet and Leslie as they talked on the drive back across to the East Side. She leaned her head against the back of the seat.

319

"Oh! Well! Here we are! I didn't realize — "

Leslie's shrill cheerfulness startled Catherine.

"Would you like to come up for a drink? Both of you? Either of you? Oh, no, I forgot, early days tomorrow. Well, it's been lovely, and Piet, I hope I see you again. Catherine, I'll come to the shop in the afternoon. Kiss kiss." Leslie pecked the air on both sides of Catherine's face.

Catherine watched Piet walk Leslie to the door and kiss her on both cheeks. Then he was back in the van with her. Alone.

"I'll take the van home with me," Piet said. "That way I can drive it back to the shop in the morning, take out the pedestals, then go for the new flowers."

"Fine. That's fine, Piet," she said tonelessly. She didn't look at him.

Minutes later he was pulling the hand brake. Catherine blinked, disoriented.

"Piet. You've parked in the alley behind Blooms — I thought you were going to drive the van to your place."

"I am. In a while."

She turned to look at him. From a lamppost at the end of the alley a light burned, casting their faces in a silvery glow. As if they were on the moon, or in a dream.

"There's something I want to show you."

"What?" Piet's voice was so casual, she forgot her embarrassment.

"Let me show you."

Piet slid out of the driver's seat, came around to help Catherine down from the high step of the van, they slid open the side door. The small overhead light beamed on but was diffused by the crush of petals against the ceiling of the van. Eight sturdy but graceful white iron stands, used to raise flower arrangements to eye level, supported white baskets holding hundreds of creamy pink roses, some still fully in bloom, their petals spread open, arched backward as if in surrender; the floor of the van lay inches deep in rose petals. The sweetness of the roses swept out at Catherine like a drug.

"Ah," she said, breathing deeply.

"Come inside," Piet said. In one swift movement he was up inside the van, and before she could speak, he had put his hands on her waist and lifted her up. He pulled the sliding door shut. She heard the click of the lock. The overhead light went out.

Catherine leaned back against the front seat of the van, her arm touching Piet's as he leaned beside her. The rose petals slipped like pieces of silk against the bare skin of Catherine's legs. As her eyes accustomed themselves to the darkness, the tiny room that the back of the van made came clear to her, and it looked like a cave of roses. Roses above her, branching, curving, spreading, roses beneath her, soft, slithery rose petals dropping in silence, slowly, a feathery brush of flower against her face, her arm, her ankle.

"This is delicious," she said at last.

"Yes."

It was a warm summer night, but the heat Catherine felt was the flare of heat from Piet's body next to hers. He was like a dark sun, making the flowers bloom in the darkness of night.

He moved slightly, covered her hand with his. After a moment he moved his hand up her arm, slowly, as if tracing a line, his fingertips light against the vein that throbbed in her arm. He moved his hand up her arm, to her shoulder, her neck, and then he lifted her hair and moved to kiss her lightly, on her neck.

"Piet. How did you know?"

"I've been watching."

She turned to him, wrapping her arms around him, pulling him to her with such urgency that they toppled over, sprawling against each other among the roses.

"For a long time," Piet said again, kissing

her, his knee pushing her legs apart, "I've been waiting."

It was quickly so hot inside the van, so moist from their breath and sweat, that their skin grew slippery, and as they moved together they were covered with an aromatic film, as sweet and slick as attar, the oil of roses.

They slept in the van until the first light awakened Piet. He drove Catherine back to her apartment.

"Come to my place tonight," Catherine said. "I'll fix something for dinner."

"It will have to be early," Piet replied, stifling a yawn.

Catherine laughed and nuzzled him. "Piet, I think I've worn you out! Look, take the day off after you buy the flowers. Sleep all day."

"All right," Piet said, kissing her softly. "Good night."

It was odd to be in her apartment, awake and dressed, at five-thirty. Her head felt light and buzzing. She walked from window to window of her apartment, looking out at the New York City streets as if her building were a ship newly landed in a foreign port. Now the streets appeared to be paved with silver, and window boxes blazed with geraniums and petunias like jewels. In her bedroom, she stripped off her clothes and crawled naked between white sheets.

In the early afternoon, Catherine awoke, clear-headed and lighthearted. She sang as she showered and dressed, hummed as she hurried into her office. She worked steadily until late that afternoon, when Leslie knocked on Catherine's office door.

"Is this a good time?"

"Yes. Come in," Catherine said. "We're really slow today." She kicked off her heels and curled up on the opposite end of the sofa from Leslie.

"You look like the cat that got the cream," Leslie said.

"I am the cat that got the cream."

"Well, it's about time. So, how was it?"

Catherine grinned. "Absolutely perfect."

"Lucky you. I can't believe you waited all these years. I wasn't even sure you were interested in him until I saw you with him last night."

Catherine told Leslie about Ned in England and, in a different tone of voice, about Piet the night before. "I'd better make an appointment to see a gynecologist."

"Do it right away. Believe me, it's not something you want to wait on."

Something in Leslie's voice made Catherine ask, "Leslie. Are you pregnant?"

"Not now I'm not!" she answered, standing

up with a surge of energy. "Let's go for a walk. I hate just sitting. Can you leave for a while?"

"Sure. I'll just tell Jason to take over."

They walked out into the afternoon sunshine, heading for Central Park. Perhaps it was the motion that freed Leslie, or the way walking kept them from meeting each other's eyes, or perhaps it was the bustle of the city around them that put everything in its proper perspective. But finally Leslie was able to tell Catherine why she had come to New York.

"I love Paris. It's my place. I feel more at home there than I do here. But I had to get away for a while."

"Why?"

"I had an abortion. Just three weeks ago. Oh, I'm fine — I've never felt better, it was done in a doctor's office and I wasn't very far along. I didn't want to marry the father, and I don't think he would have married me. Well, we'd only just met. It was all a mistake. It shouldn't have happened. I don't feel guilty, and I'd have an abortion again, but I do feel just — sorry. Sorry it all happened."

"I'm sorry, too, Leslie. Sorry you had to go through all that."

"Well, it comes down to choosing your

life, doesn't it?" Leslie said. They'd entered the park now and slowed their stride as they walked along a sidewalk dappled with sun and lacy shadows from the trees overhead. "I'm serious about painting, Catherine. I always have been. You know that. Part of the reason I came back to New York was to remind myself what I'm escaping. I've visited Robin and Terry the past few days, and they're happy and sweet as always, but Catherine — they're just like we knew they'd be. Paper-doll husband, home, and children. Textbook life. It gives me the creeps. Just seeing them makes me want to run screaming back to Paris."

Catherine laughed. "Oh, Leslie, you're too hard on them."

"You don't understand!" Leslie stopped on the pavement and grabbed Catherine by the arm, turning Catherine to face her. "I want to choose my life," she said hotly.

"I do understand, Leslie. Let go. I'll tell you about something I did."

Sitting in the sun on a bench in Central Park, she told Leslie about blackmailing P. J. Willington. Somehow, she was not surprised by Leslie's whoop of laughter.

"How wonderful! How brave! I've always wanted to do something like that."

"It's illegal, Leslie. It's wrong."

"What does illegal mean? Laws are made by men."

"Still — "

"We're mavericks, you and I, Catherine. And that sometimes means making our own rules."

Listening to Leslie, Catherine felt something inside her relax. It was as if she'd been offered absolution, sufficient for her own needs. As they walked back to the shop, Catherine linked arms with her friend.

"Oh, God, Leslie, I wish you lived in New York! I miss talking with you! It's so hard to sort things out."

"I think you're doing beautifully," Leslie said as they entered Blooms, where Piet stood, relaxed and idle, waiting for Catherine.

Catherine lay naked on her bed, facedown, legs spread, hands grasping at the sheets. It was late, after midnight, and hot and dark in her bedroom. She was covered with sweat. Behind and above her, Piet moved. They'd been making love for hours. Several times she had stopped him from doing certain things. "Don't," she'd said. "I can't." And he had stopped at once. Now he was only touching her back, her waist, her hips, lightly, but she knew what he was doing. Piet had a way of slowly making love that was like gently tracing lines all over her body. Yet when he chose, he could touch that one spot in her that made her plunge, blinded, deafened, crying, into a dark realm of such extreme pleasure that she cried out in terror. Now he flattened his body on top of hers so she could feel the scratch of his hairy chest, the rod of his penis against her skin. She was wet, shuddering against him. He took her too far, too deep, he made her feel too much, yet she knew she would want him over and over again.

In early August Leslie went back to Paris. Piet always took two weeks off in late August to visit his family in Amsterdam, and when he told Catherine he was going this year as usual, she was both disappointed and relieved. Disappointed, because she knew she'd miss him ferociously. Relieved, because his absence meant she could rest, sleep, see Ann on the Vineyard, recover herself.

At first, after they became lovers, she couldn't help but worry what working together now would be like. He was still her employee. And with all her employees, Jesus and Manuel and Lina, even with Sandra and Jason, Catherine knew that she had to maintain just the slightest distance. She felt like the captain of a ship who at times had to be obeyed or they'd all go down, yet because of her youth and femininity it was hard work. She could laugh and joke with her employees, she could even fall apart occasionally, but she had to recover quickly. Her clothes, her Miss Brill's voice, above all her competence, earned her her workers' respect. But she knew that would be weakened if they sensed her lust for Piet.

But a day went by, then two days, then a week, and she realized that Piet hadn't changed toward her at work at all. In the shop he was completely natural and unassuming with her, cool and deferential as he always had been. She was grateful, yet she also wondered at his composure after the nights they spent together.

During the two weeks Piet was in Amsterdam, Catherine was struck anew at how essential he was to the smooth running of her business. Now she had to rise at four-thirty and get to the flower district to buy the flowers for the day. It took knowledge, skill, and rapport with the wholesalers to do the job well. Some flower wholesalers offered better prices on their flowers if the transaction was paid in cash rather than charged to the house account. Catherine had to compare flowers at various wholesalers, judging by touch and instinct which were tight and fresh, keeping in mind the orders for the day and which arrangements called for closed or open flowers. Back at her shop, she missed Piet in the basement. He managed the workers with a mixture of good humor and fierce authority that Catherine could never hope to imitate. Even in August, Blooms required one man who did nothing but wash containers, unpack nonperishables, and keep the shelves clean and stocked, one man to clean and condition the flowers that came into the shop from the market, and one or two delivery men who could set up Jason's often intricate, fragile arrangements in hotel lobbies and meeting rooms without destroying them. The delivery men had to know how to get around New York quickly, how to speak politely and intelligently with hotel managers, yet they had to be strong enough to carry all the heavy containers. And these men didn't always find it easy to take a young female boss seriously.

After giving them their orders for the day, she had to talk with Jason about the day's arrangements, touch base with Sandra about which clients were expected. By midafternoon she was exhausted, and by evening all she wanted to do was sleep. She couldn't wait for Piet to return.

Late in August she met his plane and drove

him back to her apartment. They made love quickly and greedily, then slept. When they awoke, Piet presented her with an unusual necklace of bronze and beads and little bells, which she kissed him for but secretly didn't like. Over scrambled eggs, she screwed up her courage and asked, "Piet? Now that we are . . . involved . . . is there anything you'd like to change about work?"

He seemed surprised. "No. What would I want to change? I'm happy."

"But I know you have a lot of money. Why are you working for me when you have so much money? You could start your own store. You could become partners with me."

"I'm planning, Catherine."

"Well, don't be so secretive! Tell me!"

"I will when things are worked out. Right now everything is vague. Don't worry. I'll let you know if I foresee any changes in my life."

Piet was able to keep his private life utterly separate from his working life, and that both frustrated and pleased Catherine. He continued to rise early to buy the flowers and to leave the shop early in the afternoon while she worked into the evening. As the autumn unfolded, they saw each other several times a week. Piet would come to her apartment, they would eat dinner, make love, fall asleep.

They had little time for small talk or evenings out; they were both so busy with work and so eager to spend what time they had making love.

In September New York's social season began. Catherine's desk was piled high with engraved invitations on creamy vellum and carbon-smeared invoices on onionskin. She had to meet with prospective clients, usually for tea at their offices or homes, where she could look at the room to be decorated. This year, she found herself full of energy, bright ideas, charm, patience, and tact. In response, her clients recommended her to friends, and she began getting more calls, more business. She loved it. She worked hard.

Ann called Catherine from Boston often that fall to tell her how much she loved college. Shelly had returned from his camping trip to start his junior year, then dropped out after a month. He told his father college was too much of a drag. Shelly's friend Todd had dropped out, too, and they were heading back to California in Todd's van. Catherine's father called her to complain.

"Dad, there's nothing I can do. Shelly's on his own now."

"But, Catherine, we're afraid he's smoking pot."

"All the kids are smoking pot! Come on,

Dad — " Catherine drummed her fingers with impatience.

"But San Francisco. Hippies. Who knows what Shelly might do? You know he's always been hard to handle."

"Yes, and he's a grown man now. He's responsible for himself. There's nothing we can do." Catherine softened her voice. "Let him go. You know, I heard from Ann last night. She got an A on her history exam." Talking about Ann always cheered their father up.

Blooms did a staggering amount of business over Christmas and New Year's. People who never bought flowers wanted flowers now, and those who always bought flowers wanted something special. People who didn't know what to buy for presents, or had forgotten a gift, came rushing desperately into the shop and went out smiling, laden with an unusual plant or a sheaf of fresh-cut flowers. Women too busy with shopping and parties and Christmas balls and charity dinners and celebrations had Catherine come in to decorate their homes for Christmas.

"Now this is wealthy!" Catherine whispered to Piet as they set up a fourteen-foot Christmas tree in the marble-floored foyer of an apartment that looked out over Central Park. In the four niches of the semicircular foyer were four marble busts representing the virtues of the women of the British empire. Catherine attached a sprig of red-berried holly jauntily over the ear of each marble lady. That was the sort of touch the clients liked; it made them seem witty.

Once Catherine asked Piet if he would attend a holiday ball with her.

"Sorry. I know I'd be too tired. Besides, I don't have a tux."

"Well, buy one, Piet. You can afford it!"

"Look, Catherine. Don't tell me what to do with my money, and I won't tell you what to do with yours."

"Oh, Piet! You drive me crazy!"

"I know. It's good for you," he replied, and began kissing the back of her neck.

It was true. Piet was good for her. Catherine was grateful for his odd way of loving her, if love was what it was. They had never said "I love you." Not once. They never spoke about a future together. They didn't trade intimate stories about their families and their past. They made love, and they talked shop. They lived in an infinite present, concerned only with each day's work, each night's pleasure. However odd it seemed, Catherine was very happy. She was free to give her life over to her ambitions for the store, knowing that she could have companionship without complications. Piet brought her pleasure, took pleasure from her, and asked for nothing more.

There were moments when she was drifting up from sleep, or relaxing in a scented bath, when thoughts of Kit would rise within her like a spell, and she remembered how with Kit she had felt like one-half of a whole. When she and Kit had made love, she had felt that they were working together toward the same thing. It was different with Piet. He did things to her. She liked what he did, and she enjoyed doing things to him, but she never felt more separate from him than when they were in bed.

So, Catherine told herself, the body lies, our deepest instincts lie. Kit was married to someone else. She shook her head sharply, snapping herself out of memory into real life.

In the spring of 1969, a national women's magazine did a profile on Catherine as one of the new young female millionaires. Catherine wondered if Kit would see the article, especially the picture where Piet stood at her side in front of one of Blooms' opulent displays. She was surprised at herself: when would she ever stop thinking of Kit?

"Spring bulbs will be plentiful," Kathryn said. It was late March, a windy, rainy, bleak day, but cozy by the fire in the library, where the two women sat looking at the sketch pad on which Kathryn had drawn up her diagrams and lists.

Catherine was now in the habit of visiting her grandmother once a week, on Mondays, her day off. The drive out to East Hampton and back provided her with valuable quiet time, and her grandmother's house and gardens always gave her new ideas. And she knew her grandmother liked having her around, although it was always on Kathryn's terms.

Kathryn was obsessed. She was seventy-three, and before she died, she wanted to plan and plant a white-and-purple garden at Everly. Years ago she'd chosen the spot, a peaceful, flat space of ground that she could see out of her bedroom window. Back then she'd had Japanese lilac trees, lilac bushes, and rhododendrons planted. Now, in the spring of 1969, these bloomed lavishly, enclosing the chosen space in dense, plumy, fragrant walls of blossoms.

Now she was making diagrams and lists of what she would plant that summer. "White: snowflowers, paperwhite narcissus, crocuses, and lily of the valley. I must write to Holland for some white tulip bulbs. Purple: crocus again, and a multitude of hyacinths. I want to have the walkways paved in a swirling design, with white paving stones. The heather and heath will grow wonderfully with that sandy soil. Late in spring, an army of iris. Then violets, although they need the shade. In the summer, larkspur, snapdragons, and sweet pansies. I've always loved pansies."

"If you had a greenhouse, Grandmother, you could start the pansies, and many of the others, in the house in the winter."

Kathryn brushed at the air as if at an irritating gnat. "I've always thought greenhouses looked vulgar. Like factories. No, there's no need for a greenhouse. I can start what I want in the windows of the pantries and sheds."

Catherine didn't argue. She didn't want to offend her grandmother by presuming to tell her how to run Everly. Still, with Blooms, it was such a temptation, all this open space here, so close to New York; if she could have only an acre of ground to plant. . . . The floral trade was such a competitive business, especially in New York. Yet while Kathryn encouraged Catherine to talk about her latest, most clever arrangements, she grew impatient with any real shop talk, to say nothing of discussing finances. Catherine supposed one of the prerogatives of old age was that of choosing to listen only to what was pleasant.

★ ★ ★

Catherine worked hard, and she was getting rich. Twice a month she had dinner with her financial adviser, Mr. Giles, who adored her for making so much money at such a young age. Following his advice when she was offered the chance of buying the apartment beneath hers, she grabbed it and turned her apartment into a spacious duplex. Now she had a living room, dining room, and guest room on the first floor and a huge bedroom with a fireplace, a dressing room, and an office on the second. She furnished the apartment with European antiques that Mr. Giles considered shrewd investments she bought at Christie's or one of the smaller auction houses like Tepper.

She did not suggest to Piet that he move in with her, for whenever she even approached the subject, he shied away. The more she tried to learn about him, the more mysterious he became. If she tried, however subtly, to pry, he closed up, a creature with a shell. She knew everything about his body, but almost nothing about his private thoughts. The few times she got angry, he remained fatally cool; the more she stormed, the thicker his invisible shield became. Frustrated, she now and then threatened to break things off. But this always led to Piet smiling and touching her, drawing her near him, kissing her, embracing her, and then they were making love and she forgot about leaving him.

That summer she took Ann to France to spend a week touring the castles in the Loire Valley. Then Ann flew to England to work with Hortense for the summer, and Catherine spent a week in Paris with Leslie. Leslie's Left Bank loft was full of vivid abstract paintings that Catherine found rather alarming; and Leslie herself seemed a bit alarming, too. She still wore black constantly, with heavy black eye shadow and white lipstick, and she worried constantly, neurotically, about her paintings. "I didn't get this one quite right," she said over and over again to Catherine, biting her nails, intense. Catherine met Leslie's current lover, another artist named Paul, a skeletal, nervous, vaguely sadistic man who gave Catherine the creeps.

"Don't you ever think about getting married? Having children?" Catherine asked Leslie. They were sitting under an umbrella at a sidewalk cafe, drinking Pernod.

"God, no. The very thought horrifies me. Don't tell me you're thinking of that kind of life! Catherine, you're a closet bourgeois."

"Perhaps. At least I'm beginning to wish whatever it is I have with Piet were a little more definite. Do you know, we've been lovers for a year now, and he hasn't ever said he loves me!"

"What about you?"

"Of course I have — " Catherine grinned. "But now that I think about it, I've always said it when we've been . . . in bed. I've never said it when we've been, oh, walking down the street. As a matter of fact, when we're not in bed, we're rarely together, unless we're working. And then it's as if we're completely different people. He never touches me at work — and I'm grateful, but still, Leslie, don't you think that's weird? After a year of being lovers?"

"Mmm?" Leslie's attention had wandered. A handsome young man in blue jeans had sat down at a table near theirs and was eyeing Leslie over his beer.

"Leslie," Catherine whispered, "he's too young! I'll bet he hasn't even graduated from college!"

"They're the best kind. They can go on all night."

"You're a hopeless degenerate."

"I'm working at it. You should work at it, too, Catherine. You don't want to end up married and dead." Leslie lowered her eyelids and smiled invitingly at the young man. "I'd die if I didn't get a look like this at least once a week," she said.

When Catherine returned from her vacation, Piet was gone to Amsterdam. She had to work twice as hard to make up for his absence, and what free time she had she spent at Everly with her grandmother. Almost every Sunday Catherine spent weeding and watering the white-and-purple garden, which was taking nicely; then she'd sit with Kathryn and Clara, drinking tea and admiring the results of their labor.

One Sunday afternoon Catherine spotted a postcard on the front hall table, message face up. She recognized the handwriting.

Dear Grandmother, I've got blisters on my hands from the secateurs and spades, aches in my back, dirt under my nails, and I've never been so happy. The next time you come to this Everly, you can see what I've done. I think I'll become a horticulturist.
Love, Ann.

Well, Catherine thought, good for Ann. At last. She, too, had found her vocation among flowers.

Yet beneath her pleasure for her sister, Catherine felt a vein of fear streak through her heart, a greedy faultline of possessiveness. What was Ann up to? Would Kathryn leave her Everly to the grandchild who planted flowers rather than to the one who sold them?

Such thoughts, Catherine knew, were ugly and destructive; they blackened her heart. She had never counted on her family to give her anything. She must remember to remain that way.

She was glad when the rushing routine of fall returned. She was too busy for jealous fancies, and anyway, Ann was safely back at college. The Arthritis Foundation wanted Blooms to do the flowers for their charity ball at the Waldorf. The New York Insurance Company was working on a new publicity scheme and wanted to change the containers of the flowers she delivered each week. They wanted their image to look more "natural," more "healthy," so she designed an arrangement of ferns, begonias, and African violets in plain green ceramic containers. Deep inside the containers were moss balls to hold the fresh flowers Blooms would add on special occasions.

A container wholesaler called Catherine with a scoop: he had in a new line of containers in plastic, a novelty and luxury in 1969. The vases were dark orange, dark green, dark blue, strikingly modern. A well-known artist in the Village wanted something distinctive for his opening and called Catherine. She knew the dark plastic containers were perfect — a stark arrangement of five cattails cut at different lengths, a large white lily arching to the right, and an arum leaf branching to the left. The effect was as haunting and original as the artist's own work. And so Blooms became the favorite of the Warhol crowd as well as high society.

It wasn't until the second day of 1970, after the holiday rush, that Catherine and Piet were finally able to relax together in her apartment. Catherine had cooked a homey meal of roast chicken and wild rice, which tasted exotic and delicious after all the takeout food they'd consumed standing up while rushing through work during Christmas. She had even attempted a homemade chocolate cake, and now they lingered over it with freshly brewed coffee. It was by far the most elaborate meal she'd ever made for Piet — and she hoped he was as impressed as she was.

"Catherine," Piet said, "I need to go to Amsterdam for a while."

"Oh? Is something wrong? Is someone ill?"

"No, no. Nothing like that. Just some things I want to attend to. I should be gone only a month. I'm sure you can get along without me for a while. I'll be back in time for the Valentine's Day rush."

"You've never had to go over at this time of year before." Catherine waited for Piet to explain, but he only sipped his coffee and took another bite of cake. "What's over there now?"

"Just some business. Something I want to look into."

"Jesus Christ, Piet!" Catherine threw her napkin on the table and leaned toward him, clutching the table's edge. "Why must you make your life such a mystery? What are you, a spy? A criminal? You never share anything with me. I've known you for years — we've been lovers for years — why can't you confide in me?"

"Catherine, don't be so upset. There's nothing to confide."

"Then why are you going — "

"Look. I have an idea about something, and I need to explore a few things. If they work out, I'll tell you about them. If not, then I haven't wasted any of your time."

"Wasted my time! Piet, why won't you talk to me? You never talk, you never tell me what you want out of life, what's hurt you or made you happy. For all I know, you have a wife and children in Holland!"

"I don't have a wife and children in Holland."

"Don't you trust me?" Catherine felt wild, desperate.

"My dear Catherine, I trust you completely." Piet reached across the table and held her hands in his. "You are the only woman in my life. You are the only woman I want. Be patient with me. I need to take this time in Amsterdam, and then, when I come back, I'll share everything with you."

CHAPTER 9

New York, 1970

By the end of January Catherine was exhausted. With Piet in Amsterdam, everyone suffered. Sandra's husband liked to pick her up at six o'clock sharp, when he'd finished his work at the accounting firm. With Catherine's crowded schedule, she was often late, and Sandra was rattled, knowing that while she explained necessary information to Catherine, her husband was driving around the noisy streets, tired and impatient. Jason was unhappy, too, for Catherine usually helped with the flower arrangements, bantering and teasing and complimenting him. He felt neglected. He sighed a lot. His shoulders drooped.

"Only a few more days, troops," Catherine told them. "Then Piet will be home and we'll be back on schedule."

In late January Catherine had returned from a client's apartment and was in her office, dictating her notes from the meeting into a recorder. She liked to get her thoughts down while the imprint of the room, the preferences of her client, and her instinctive reactions were fresh in her mind. Jason would listen to the tapes, then discuss his own ideas with her before they settled on a definite theme.

Now her intercom buzzed. "Boss baby," Jason said, "your daddy's here to see you. He's on his way up."

Great, Catherine thought, what does he want now? But when he entered, he looked so drawn and troubled that she felt ashamed of herself.

"Sit down, Dad. It's nice to see you. Would you like a cup of coffee?" She took his overcoat and hung it in the closet.

"That would be very nice, thank you."

She poured fresh coffee into the Limoges cups she'd found in an East Hampton antiques shop. He was so handsome, such a gentleman, with his hair gone silver, he looked like a worried diplomat, and she felt a wave of affection for him.

"Now. What's up?"

"Your brother's come home. He's in rather bad shape. Actually, I had to go get him. Over in the western part of the state. In a hospital. The detox section."

"Oh, Daddy!"

"It's a mystery." Drew Eliot smiled his

charming smile. "Your mother and I have always said we have a tolerance for alcohol, and alcohol is tolerant of us. We drink too much, I'll admit that, but it's never affected our lives, not the way this drug business has Shelly's."

"What kinds of drugs was he using?"

"What wasn't he? Everything. Even heroin. When he was admitted to the hospital, he had no identification on him, and he was so incoherent they couldn't even find out his name. He was there for three weeks. Then he could tell them who he was, and how to reach us. Now he's apparently 'detoxified.' But Catherine, he looks terrible. It breaks my heart."

"He'll recover. He's young, Dad." But Catherine felt a rush of concern for her brother.

"I don't know. It's not just his looks, it's his state of mind. He just sits. Sometimes . . . sometimes he cries." Drew steadied himself with a long sip of coffee. Then he looked at Catherine. "I wish you'd come talk to him."

"Well, of course I'll come see him, but what can I say that will help him? I'd do anything for him — you know that — but — "

"He's always admired you."

"Come on, Dad, he's always thought I was a drone."

"I don't think it's asking so much for you just to come see him. Talk to him. Let him know you care."

"All right, Dad. I will. Not for a few days — I'm swamped with work. But as soon as I can."

"Good girl. Thank you, Catherine." Drew sighed and rose. "Do you know, it's a terrible thing, but I hate going into my own home. He's just sitting there. Like some wax statue. Probably a memorial to the sort of father I've been."

"Oh, Daddy, don't be so hard on yourself. Look, Ann and I are doing fine."

"But Shelly's my son."

"Well, Shelly will come out of this. I'm sure he will."

As Catherine helped her father shrug back into his expensive wool overcoat, she felt his thin shoulders beneath her hands. He looked brittle, and she imagined his bones were transparent shells, sapped of healthy minerals by years of drinking and neglect. Her father had not come out of the life his drinking had led him into, but he had survived it because of the money his father had left him. Shelly would not have that kind of inheritance. Or that stamina, she suspected. She smiled encouragingly at her father and kissed his cheek, but when he had gone she sat at her desk, musing on families and family traits, all the blessings and blights that bodies passed on through generations.

Friday night, just before closing, the phone rang at Blooms.

"Catherine? Good. You're still there. It's Piet. I'm back. I want to see you. Can you wait for me there?"

Lust warmed Catherine's body at the sound of Piet's dark voice. "Piet. You're home! I'm so glad. I've missed you. Listen, don't come here. Meet me at the apartment. I'll make you dinner."

"No. I'd rather meet you at Blooms. There are some things I need to pick up."

"Well, all right. God knows I've got plenty to do here while I wait."

"See you soon."

Catherine hurried to the mirror. She was wearing a red wool suit with black trim and her enormous diamond earrings. The red made her lips and cheeks glow and made her hair look jet black against her skin. Pleased, she hurried down to be sure everyone had left for the day and the shop was locked up. Piet had his own key. They had never before made love in Blooms, but there was a sofa in her office.

Back in her office, she forced herself to concentrate on her accounts until she heard the back door open and then the sound of Piet's footsteps on the stairs. Then he was there, in the doorway. He wore his sleek black overcoat around his shoulders, European style, and he looked at once both tired and excited. She hurried across the room to kiss him.

She was astonished at the coolness of his response.

"Catherine. We have to talk."

"Well. That certainly sounds ominous." She spoke lightly, knowing from experience that the harder she pushed with Piet, the more closed he became. He really was like a clam. If she pried, he clamped himself shut. She had to be still, sly, cunning, had to pretend to look in the other direction, and then sometimes he would relax his vigilance.

"Would you like a drink?" she asked, moving away from him. He smiled, and she poured them each a Scotch. He sat on the sofa, and Catherine on her chair behind the desk. She kicked off her heels and put her stockinged feet on her desktop. "So. Talk."

"Catherine, I have to leave Blooms."

"*What?*" She felt the panic rising in her voice.

"Wait. Please. I'm leaving the States for a while. I have to live in Amsterdam for a few months, perhaps even a year, and after that, I'll have to live there for at least six months every year."

"For God's sake, why?"

"I can't tell you. I can tell you that I have an idea that I think will make me, and you, rich, but I don't have everything worked out yet."

"You have an idea that includes me? Then, by God, why can't you share it with me? You *have* to!"

"Let's just say I'm paranoid. I don't want anyone else getting to this first. I've been working on it like a dog, and I'm very close to implementing it. I've got to go back to Amsterdam. When things are ready, I'll contact you."

"Piet, that's not fair. I have no idea what you're talking about!" There were times when she thought it was the fact that English was Piet's second, or third, or fourth language that made him seem so distant. But right now, it was far more than language that separated them.

"I know. I'm sorry. It's the best I can do."

"Piet. Tell me the truth. Is another woman involved in all this?"

"Catherine, I've told you — please believe me. It's nothing like that."

His words were kind, but Catherine caught the tang of condescension in his voice.

"Well, there'll be another man in my life, you can count on that, if you go away and leave me like this!" Catherine wrenched her legs off the desk and slipped back into her shoes, glad he couldn't see her face. She was close to tears.

"Yes. I know that's a risk I run. You are a beautiful woman."

He sounded as if he meant it. When she looked at him, she couldn't help the tears that rolled down her cheeks.

"Piet, what in the hell are you doing? We've been lovers for more than two years now. You've got to know what you mean to me. You've got to know how I care for you. I'm not trying to trap you or lay claim to you, but don't you owe me something?"

"I owe you a lot, Catherine. And I want to give you a lot, but first I have to make certain that I can."

"You're talking in riddles."

"I'm sorry."

"If you were sorry, you'd try to talk to me honestly."

"It's business, Catherine, why can't you believe that? It's strictly business, and important, significant business. If it works, it could change my life, and make a huge difference in yours."

"But you won't tell me what it is."

"No."

"And you're just going to leave me and my shop, without even a promise about returning."

"Yes. Although I do promise to try to return."

Catherine was sobbing, her shoulders shaking. How could Piet watch her so coolly, without crossing the room to embrace her, to comfort her? He rose.

"Piet, you can't go! I won't let you! Don't you love me? Don't you need me?"

He hesitated before speaking — and that hesitation enraged her, told her more than anything he'd said all night.

"I love you," Piet said at last. "I love you. I thought you knew that. I would like you to believe it, even though I know I make it hard. But to answer your other question, no, I don't need you."

"Then God damn you!" Catherine wanted to run and hold him back. She wanted to hurl her glass paperweight at his back. "Get out of here. Don't come back. I never want to see you again."

Even then, she thought he would stay. She sank onto her chair and buried her face in her hands and waited for him to cross the room. She waited for the weight of his hands on her shoulders. Instead, when she looked up, she saw that he was gone. He had left her office door open. Holding her breath, she listened and heard the downstairs back door open, then click closed.

Catherine locked up and walked through the winter streets to her apartment. The curbs were banked with dirty snow that glittered vilely in the streetlights, and the wind buffeted and shoved at her. She was crying as she walked, oblivious of the people who were rushing by her, their heads down against the wind. At home she shed her suit and sat in her dark bedroom wrapped in her thick terry robe, a glass of Scotch in her hand. But by midnight she was exhausted. She woke at three in the morning to find that she'd fallen asleep on top of her bed. She took a long, hot, cleansing shower, then walked through her apartment with a glass of milk. She turned on all the lights in each room. This antique mahogany sideboard, these silver candlesticks — what had they not witnessed in the hundred years they'd existed — perhaps other abandoned women. She was not the first. She had never, ever, desired the role of weak woman, victim. And she had been left before, by a better man.

She hated her pain. She would not tolerate it. She would not let herself think of Piet again.

The next morning Catherine held a brief conference with her employees. "Piet has left the company," she told them. "He's gone to Amsterdam." Holding up her hands, she forestalled their questions. "No, I have no address for him. I don't know his plans. His absence will call for some adjustments on all our parts." She lowered her eyes to avoid meeting their collective gazes. After the meeting, she called a dozen employment agencies; by the end of the day she'd hired Carla Shaw to act as receptionist at the front desk, answer the phone, and run errands for herself, Sandra, and Jason. Carla was only nineteen and a bit rough around the edges. She lived on the Lower East Side and hadn't had the money or grades to go to college, but she was cheerful, energetic, quick, eager to please, and eager to make something of herself. As the days passed, she learned how to be prim with motherly Sandra and flirtatiously complimentary with sensitive Jason. With Carla on board, Catherine could relax just a little. And with Piet gone, perhaps forever, she went back to her routine of buying the flowers early in the morning and catching a nap in the early afternoon on the sofa in her office. She was tired, and she was determined, and she could fall asleep in an instant and in an instant be awake and ready to get back to work.

Sunday afternoon Catherine walked over to her parents' apartment. It was about one o'clock, early by their standards, when she arrived, and as she expected, her mother wasn't yet out of bed. Her father answered the door in his robe.

"Hi, Dad. I've come to see Shelly."

"Come in, Catherine. Christ, I feel like a truck hit me. Shelly's in the living room. I'm going back to bed."

She found Shelly sitting alone by a window. He was dressed for the day in khakis, a buttoned-down shirt, and red crewneck sweater, but the clothes hung loosely on him. Catherine was glad to have a few seconds to catch her breath before he saw her. He sat hunched over like an old man. He was twenty-one years old, and he sat looking out the window at nothing.

"Shelly!" She crossed the room and bent over to kiss his cheek. "Don't get up." She put her hands on his shoulders.

"I can stand up!"

"Go ahead, then. But I'm sitting down."

Catherine ignored his bad humor, pulled a chair close to him.

"How are you, Shelly?"

"Just great, can't you tell by looking?"

Catherine had leaned forward, but she could tell that her scrutiny made Shelly nervous; he was trembling, like someone with palsy.

"I mean, *really*, how are you?"

"I'm okay now. I'm clean. This has not been the best time I've ever had. But I'm clean now. I'm tired, though, man. I'm beat."

To Catherine's horror, Shelly's face crumbled and he began to cry. He covered his face with his hands.

"I know you think you're being nice to come see me, but I wish you'd go away. I hate this charity shit."

"Shelly. I'm not here out of charity."

"Yeah, you're here because I'm such fun. Because we're so close."

"Shelly, you're my brother. I love you."

"I don't know why. I'm such a fuck-up."

"No, you're not."

"Give me a break. You've turned into Miss Moneybags and even dippy little Ann's going to graduate from college. I've just wasted my life. Shit, Dad's an alcoholic, but people only think he's charming. I'm not even charming."

"I think you're charming." But she didn't think Shelly heard her. Catherine was surprised at how much it hurt to see Shelly like this — her handsome brother, once so full of energy and mischief. When he had wiped his eyes, she said, "I do think you're charming. I think you're smart. I *know* you're smart. Remember how you always used to win at Monopoly? God, it always made me crazy, Shelly. You're six years younger than I, and you still always beat me at Monopoly, every time."

Remembering brought a smile to Shelly's face. "You used to get so mad."

"And at Everly, when we played hide-and-seek. I could never find you. You could always find me."

"You'd get so mad, you'd scream your head off at me when you found me."

"You were a whiz at poker. You've always been good at tennis, and I've always been a spaz."

"Now you're successful, and I can't do a damned thing."

"That's not true."

"Name one thing — just one thing I could do."

"You could go back to college."

"I doubt it. Besides, all my friends have graduated." Shelly was choking up again. "I just totally fucked up my life. I'm just sitting here, left behind, like some pissy helpless old man."

Catherine took a deep breath. "Then why don't you come work for me?"

Shelly looked shocked. "Work for you? What could I do for you? Don't you understand? I can't do anything." He laughed. "Anyway, can you see me standing around playing with flowers like some fairy?"

"Shelly. Every day, six days a week, my employees have to carry in over a hundred boxes. They're packed with flowers and newspapers and ice, and they weigh about a hundred pounds each. I think that you, brain-dead and pathetic thing that you are, could still lift and carry. I always need another body. I need someone to deliver. Someone who knows the city well enough to get around it fast. Perhaps when you're through feeling sorry for yourself you'll remember that you know that city as well as you know the Monopoly board. Or if you really want to stay at the basket-weaving level, I can stick you in the basement and let you mold sphagnum moss into cubes. I just had a guy quit. Honey, I need help so much I'd hire the Hunchback of Notre Dame."

"Are you serious?"

"Yes."

"What if I don't like it there?"

"Then *you* can always quit. And believe me, if I don't like the way you're working out, I'll fire you in a minute. I'm serious. I didn't get to be successful by being soft-hearted."

Shelly smiled, a real smile. Even his eyes were brighter. "When do you want me to start?"

"The sooner the better."

Walking back to her apartment later that afternoon, Catherine noticed poinsettias in apartment windows and Christmas wreaths still hanging on some front doors. She remembered the Christmas night long ago at Everly when her mother banished her to the third floor. She had been furious then, certain that she did not belong with her family, terrified that she didn't belong anywhere. Now, ten years later, she was surprised at how strong, how lasting, the bonds of family felt. No matter how she chafed at them, hated them, fought them, they would not break. Was it possible that in other families pity, hate, and anger held as fast as comfort, gratitude, and love?

Catherine told both Jason and Sandra that she'd asked her brother to come to work for her, but that he was not being given any special privileges or treatment. To her surprise and relief, Shelly endeared himself to everyone by working hard and eagerly. His only real problem was an amazing ignorance of flowers. "Honey, bring me that bucket of glads, will you?" Jason would call.

"Do you mean the tall things?" Shelly would respond. But he tried hard, and learned fast, and as he grew more comfortable with his duties, the magical charm he'd inherited from his father and grandfather returned, and it became a real pleasure for them all to have him around.

Catherine always received invitations to all the best galas and parties. As Shelly improved, she began to ask him to be her escort. He had always loved good times, and he was wonderful fun. After their harried and often grimy work during the day, Shelly and Catherine would run home and get glamorous. Wherever they entered, heads turned: Catherine, dark and exotic; Shelly, boyishly all-American and blond. They hardly looked alike, yet you couldn't miss the family resemblance. Shelly always met lots of pretty young women and inadvertently picked up new contacts for Blooms in the bargain.

Catherine was moderately famous in New York and was frequently invited to serve on the boards of prestigious artistic and charity organizations. Always, she refused. With Piet gone, it took all her time and energy to keep Blooms running with the perfection she insisted upon. Besides, the competition was always out there, so she was constantly searching for new ideas, new styles, new trends. She worked as ferociously as she had when she'd first bought her shop and took an equally passionate pleasure in its success. Her old school friends Robin, Terry, Melonie, and others openly admired Catherine's achievements, and in the spring of 1970 she was asked by Miss Brill's to be their graduation speaker. With a great warm wash of inner smugness, she agreed with pleasure.

Even her own parents were behaving civilly toward her, and at Easter dinner that year Catherine looked around the table at her parents' house with a sense of triumph and pride. There sat pretty Ann, well on her way to becoming a horticulturist. And Shelly, now handsome and healthy, entertaining his mother with tales about the posh parties he'd been to — all because of Catherine and Blooms. And there sat Kathryn, clearly delighted to be talking with Ann about new techniques in grafting. Drew was openly grateful to Catherine and now never lost an opportunity to hug her tightly in appreciation. Only Marjorie remained wary, as if Catherine's success might suddenly turn out to be a trick or an insult.

Catherine knew her success was real, solid. She felt it in the silk of the dresses she wore, the bite of her custom-blended perfume, the glow of her brother's healthy skin, the laughter shared among her employees, the continual ringing of the telephone at Blooms.

Still, sometimes at night, when she had come home from a party or wakened early to go buy flowers, she would sit in her peach-and-indigo bedroom, staring out her window at the night sky, remembering a richer sweetness: love. In certain ways, the silk-and-velvet texture of the flowers she worked with, their scents and saps, filled her life as a lover might. She did not miss colors or the slide of skin. But to last, flowers had to be kept cool. The moist chill of their stems and leaves made her lonely.

She missed warmth. She missed heat and breath and movement.

She remembered how Kit, after climaxing, had collapsed on top of her, letting his body touch hers all over. She had wrapped her arms around his naked back; he had put his face against her neck. Together their bodies had slowed, readjusted, like ocean divers fathoms deep.

With Piet it had been more like skydiving. He always took her breath away. She had fallen, exhilarated, calling out with terror and joy, pushed to her limits, pushed beyond her limits, frightened and finally triumphant.

With Ned it had been almost a kind of child's play, sharing a candied apple, not frightening, not significant. An easy pleasure.

She missed sex, love, life. Perhaps, Catherine mused, she should go to England this summer.

But before she could make her plans, Kathryn phoned her in June to tell her the Boxworthys were coming to visit. Not all the Boxworthys, unfortunately, and not the one Catherine was hoping to see. Ann was going to fly over to work at the British Everly until the last week in August. Then she'd bring Madeline and Hortense back with her while Ned and Elizabeth and Elizabeth's husband, Tom, ran the bed-and-breakfast back home. Kathryn was hoping Catherine would help spruce up her garden, especially the purple-and-white one.

So the summer unfolded. She worked at Blooms and Everly. When Madeline and Hortense arrived in August, she took pride in showing them around Blooms and pleasure in their company at Everly. Kathryn held a great dinner dance in honor of her British guests, with the garden strung with hundreds of tiny white lights and a band that played old jazz and buffet tables laden with delicacies and champagne. It reminded Catherine of Kimberly Weyland's wedding party so many years ago, which made the night bittersweet for Catherine. She was glad when the summer was over, Ann back at college, the Boxworthys back in England, and a bracing chill back in the air.

All afternoon and into the evening, Catherine had met with clients. It was after seven when she finally got back to Blooms. Everyone else had gone home, and she was glad for the quiet. Walking through her cool, fragrant shop, she breathed deeply, relaxing. As always, Carla had left the important mail and messages on her desk and fresh coffee in the pot. The late September sky shone silver through the windows. Catherine turned on her desk lamp. Bursts of honking horns and laughter from the street below drifted upward as the city slid into night. Catherine took off her suit jacket, kicked off her heels, collapsed onto her desk chair. Yawning, she stretched and picked up the pile of pink memo slips awaiting her. It was an evening like hundreds before.

The name *Kit Bemish,* written in Carla's

firm, rounded script, struck her like a slap. Catherine's heart turned inside out. She pulled the pink slip from the others. It took a few seconds for her to steady her hands, which were trembling so hard that she couldn't read what was written before her.

Carla hadn't written "Kit Bemish." She had written "Mrs. Kit Bemish." Mrs. Kit Bemish wanted an arrangement for a dinner party two weeks away and asked that Catherine call her.

Mr. and Mrs. Kit Bemish lived in a building on East Eighty-sixth. Catherine arrived precisely at four-thirty. She had tried on every outfit in her closet, looking for the one that would give her confidence, would express the real Catherine — the woman who was successful, intelligent, clever, and also madly sought after by men. She'd settled on a red paisley silk suit with a long swinging jacket of solid red lined with the same rich paisley.

She had had two Bloody Marys at lunch, unusual for her, but she still felt nervous, almost manic. She gave her name to the doorman, took the wood-paneled elevator to the tenth floor, and was deposited in a marble foyer, facing the Bemishes' door.

A maid with a white crimped cap opened the door at her knock and led Catherine into Kit Bemish's home.

It was very modern. Leslie's abstracts would have fit right in. Chrome-framed mirrors hung everywhere. The living room sofa was deep grape leather. A bearskin rug stretched across the white carpet in front of the brick fireplace. The coffee table was chrome and glass. A gigantic white tortoise shell sat upside down on the coffee table as an ashtray. A mountain goat with elaborate whirled horns hung above the chrome stereo cabinet. On a chain anchored to the ceiling hung a basket chair woven from cane. So did several baskets of the creepy spider plant, its skinny stalks reaching out like the arms of something starving. A beautiful Kentia palm towered in one corner.

"I hunt."

Catherine turned.

Haley Bemish stood there, unsmiling, perfect. She had the type of body that always unnerved Catherine. Tall, lanky, naturally slender, even bony, Haley Bemish showed off her easy elegance in a khaki jumpsuit. She wore gold flats of alligator skin. Her honey-blond hair swung chin length, Mary Quant style. She wore no makeup. Her skin was smooth and tanned, her eyes aquamarine. Here was the daughter Catherine's mother had wanted. Still wanted. They shook hands.

"Scotch?" Haley asked. When Catherine hesitated, she said, "Or a vodka gimlet. I make a dynamite vodka gimlet."

"A vodka gimlet would be nice."

The glass Haley handed Catherine was thick blue, rough, uneven, full of bubbles.

"From Mexico," Haley said. "Cheers."

They sank onto opposite ends of the grape sofa.

"I've heard you were at Miss Brill's."

"Yes. That was it for me and school, though. The traditional path seemed like too much of a rut."

"God. How true." Haley took a Gauloises from a lacquered box. She offered one to Catherine. "I only did one year of college. At Vassar. I was so bored. So I went off fishing with Daddy. We did some hunting, too. I miss it."

They chatted formally, two civilized women. The fishing had been in Alaska and Scotland. The hunting had been in India and Africa.

Catherine couldn't help it. She admired Haley Hilton Bemish. She was a strong character.

"I've brought my portfolio," Catherine said at last. "Photos of what we've done before, and — "

Haley tossed her head irritably and interrupted Catherine. "Forget it. I don't want to see anything you've done before. I want something completely new. Something you *haven't* done before. This is an important dinner party." Her tone implied that Catherine probably hadn't encountered that level of importance before.

In fact, Catherine had encountered that level of importance many times before. All too often. With relief she stopped liking Haley.

"Perhaps if I could see the dining room . . ."

"Of course."

Haley rose and led Catherine into an enormous room. The walls were orange, covered with African and North American Indian masks. The fireplace mantel, stripped down to bare wood, was covered with wooden fertility gods and goddesses, squat creatures with swollen bellies, funnel-shaped breasts, and exaggerated penises. A sharp-leafed yucca plant stood guard in one corner. A huge rubber plant stood in another. Its flat leaves were well dusted. Clearly Haley liked the bold and unusual. Yet all this prickly harshness made Catherine wonder what it would be like to live with her.

"What table service will you be using?"

Haley crossed to a teak hutch, took out

a wooden plate, handed it to Catherine. The grain was beautifully striped, like a wild animal.

"The plates and bowls are zebrawood. From Africa. The glasses will be Mexican. Blue. Like the one in your hand. The napkins bleached burlap. The silver will be our own pattern from Tiffany's. At least it's plain." Haley sounded as if she wished they could all eat with their fingers.

Catherine watched Haley carefully. She wasn't kidding. Catherine couldn't imagine dear gentle Kit with this Tarzanella.

Catherine turned. She walked up and down the long glass-and-chrome dining room table.

"There will be twenty for dinner," Haley said.

"I see snakes," Catherine said.

"What?" Haley's eyes widened.

"Snakes," Catherine repeated. She stretched out her hands toward the table. "Four terrariums down the length of the table. Live snakes inside. Harmless, of course, and with lids on the terrariums. Moss — no — grasses and straw and bamboo on the lids. Carrot and beet greens wound in and trailing to the table. Orange allium heads, very spiky, sticking out. Pebbles here and there. Ranunculus heads stuck here and there for color, harmonizing, of course, with the color of the snake inside. Or moss roses. Candles scented with Indian jasmine in your pottery holders."

Haley looked at Catherine. Her blue eyes were as pure as truth. Catherine met Haley's gaze.

"Snakes," Haley said.

"I've never done them before. I've always wanted to. So colorful, you know, and then movement is always clever. I've done birds. It would give the table a rather . . . mysterious . . . wilderness . . . atmosphere."

"Um. Yes. I see."

Haley walked around the table, envisioning it as Catherine had described.

"Wonderful," she said at last. "Brilliant. Of course you'll come get the snakes after the party? The next morning?"

"Of course." Catherine waited a beat, then said, "I'm afraid it will be rather expensive. . . ."

Haley shook her shining head. "That doesn't matter."

"Fine, then," Catherine said. She raised the gimlet glass to her lips to hide her irrepressible smile.

Somehow Catherine made it through the next few minutes and back out to the street without exploding with laughter. Hurrying down Park Avenue toward Blooms, she began to giggle. Snakes. Poor Kit. Haley was actually rather wonderful in her own way, but she was also either slightly crazy or stupid. The giggles spiraled wider and wider, so that when she entered Blooms she leaned against the door and burst into such helpless laughter, she ended with tears running down her face.

The next day she went to a pet shop and picked out four snakes, each a little over one loot long. A bull snake of yellow brown with dark geometrical blotches. A slender grass snake of such emerald brilliance, even Catherine enjoyed looking at it. Two king snakes, one black with yellow rings, one with black, yellow, and scarlet rings.

"Want some baby mice or little toads for them to eat?" the pet owner asked.

Catherine declined.

Catherine hoped Kit might be at his apartment when she went to set up the flowers for the dinner party, but the only person she saw was the maid who let her in. "Those things can't get out, now, you're sure?" the woman asked Catherine nervously.

"I'm sure," Catherine said. "Look. The lids are heavily weighted."

"They give me the creeps. I'm afraid to be alone in the room with them, setting the table."

"Try to think of them as living flowers. Moving colors," Catherine said, knowing her words might be repeated to Haley Bemish. Secretly she felt pity for the maid and for Haley's guests. The muscular coiling of the snakes seemed intestinal, repellent, unappetizing.

Catherine never went to collect flower containers anymore. It was the sort of thing the least-experienced, lowest-paid employee could do. But she wanted one more chance to see Kit, so she rose early the morning after Haley's party and presented herself at the Bemishes' apartment at eight-thirty, hoping Kit wouldn't have left for work yet.

The maid with the starched cap admitted Catherine and Danny, one of her men, and led them to the dining room.

"I wouldn't say your 'flowers' were a great success," the maid said in a matter-of-fact voice.

Catherine hid a smile. "Shall I leave the flowers and grasses on the table? Or shall I take them?"

"Mrs. Bemish didn't say. She's not up yet. I'll ask Mr. Bemish." The maid disappeared.

Catherine's heart jumped.

"Danny, take those terrariums down to the van. You can carry two at a time, I think. Don't drop them."

As Danny turned and left the dining room, Kit came in.

He stood just inside the doorway, looking at Catherine. He was in suit pants, a striped shirt, and socks. His tie was draped around his neck but not tied. Obviously he had just shaved, for his face had a ruddy, smooth glow. The image of him bare-chested, shaving, hit Catherine deep in her stomach. He was thirty-two and had a few lines at his eyes and a hardness to his jawline that made him look not older, but more masculine.

"Hello, Kit," she said.

He nodded in reply.

"I asked your maid whether you and Haley wanted us to leave these flowers and grasses or take them with us. I know she wanted me to take the terrariums and snakes."

"Leave the flowers, I suppose."

"How did everyone like the arrangement?"

"Not much, since you ask. It made the meal very tense. One of the women couldn't eat. She was almost paralyzed with fear."

"Oh. I'm sorry."

"I doubt it. I have a feeling you were making fun of Haley. Having a joke at her expense." His eyes were wood catching fire.

"Your wife wanted something I've never done before. Something unusual — "

"She is serious about her interests and tastes — "

"So am I! I didn't get successful by making fun of my clients."

"I'm surprised you have any clients, if this is your idea of something exotic — "

"Excuse me, sir." Danny was back for the second two terrariums. He slipped past Kit, widening his eyes in consternation at Catherine.

Catherine turned her back on Kit and bent over the table. Her shaking hands made the bamboo and grasses rustle loudly against each other.

"Danny, take these on down to the van. I'll rearrange the flowers on the table and be with you in a minute."

Danny hefted the two heavy terrariums and, ducking his head at Kit, headed out.

She felt the heat of Kit's body when he came to stand next to her.

"Catherine. How are you?"

Catherine straightened. She turned to look at him. He was close enough to kiss. After all these years, she knew she still loved him. His heat was like a signal, like the sun.

"I'm fine," she said, smiling. "And I'm still in love with you."

"Jesus Christ, Catherine," Kit said softly.

"I'll let your wife do the rest," Catherine

said coolly, for the maid had entered the room. Catherine moved away from Kit. "I would suggest putting the flowers in shallow bowls of water. They'll float and last quite prettily for a few days. Without water, they'll wilt today. Also, the ranunculus — these — are fragile." She looked at Kit. "I'll be glad to put them in a bowl for you."

"That's all right, Catherine," Kit said. He was in control again, aware the maid was watching them. "I'll tell Haley. Thanks."

"Thank you, Kit. And here's my card, if you and your wife would like to have me work for you again." Catherine went out the door.

He called her at Blooms that evening.

"Look," he said, "I'd like to see you. To talk things over. To hear how you've been."

"Come here now."

"I can't. I'm rushing. I told Haley I was just out for cigarettes."

"Tomorrow. Whenever. Wherever."

The urgency in her voice made him cautious. "This is just to talk. To — renew a friendship. That's all, Catherine."

"Of course," she said, knowing he couldn't see her smile.

She left work early the next afternoon.

So did Kit. They met at the tiny Bemelman's bar at the Carlyle. Catherine was purposely late. She was wearing a minidress of deep red wool, long-sleeved, severely straight. It looked businesslike, but in fact she knew when she walked the lines of her body moving the fabric were more seductive than many more obvious dresses. There was a flower made of white handkerchief linen on the shoulder.

She slid onto a chair across from him. He ordered martinis for both of them.

"Kit, I have a confession to make. I didn't think of the snakes to make fun of Haley. But I did think of them because I was angry at her. For being married to you."

Kit smiled. "Haley loved the snakes. She prefers almost any animal to humans. She grew up with her father, who's a naturalist. Spent most of her life outdoors. In many ways she's very innocent."

"Unlike others we could name," Catherine said, sipping her martini.

"What does that mean?"

"I'll tell you sometime — if we 'renew our friendship' enough."

"Catherine — "

Catherine erased the mischief from her eyes. "All right, Kit, I'll be good. Tell me. What are you doing in New York?"

"Working for Woodrow and Spiegel. I'm just another corporate lawyer now, Cathy. No politics for me. These aren't especially idealistic times we live in."

"You've given up on the idea of entering politics?"

"Cathy, I don't even know where I stand on Vietnam. My father's a Republican. He fought in World War Two. I admire him. I can never believe his beliefs are wrong. On the other hand, I hate this war. If I can't decide in my own heart how I stand on such matters, how would I dare try to lead other people?"

"You're still so idealistic."

"I don't think so. At any rate, I got tired." Kit leaned back in his chair and sighed. "Haley prefers New York to Boston. It was easy enough to get hooked up with a firm here."

"Do you like the work you're doing?"

"Not much. It's cut and dried. Boring. But I don't think about it when I try to sleep at night."

"What do you think about?"

Kit grinned. "I suppose you think I'll say 'you.' "

"Only if it's true. God knows I've spent a few nights thinking about you." She wanted him too much to save her pride. She reached over and put her hand on his. The touch was electric.

Kit shook his head. "No, Cathy."

"Do you love her?" She didn't move her hand. He didn't take his hand away.

"Catherine — "

"Do you?"

"She's my wife."

"Because if you love her, you should leave right now. But if there's any chance you want to go to bed with me, then please, Kit, go to bed with me. I'm not asking for anything more than that. Just come home with me tonight. Or any night."

Kit took his hand away from hers. He rose.

"I'm sorry, Catherine," he said, walking away.

She knew he would call her. That one touch of her hand on his told her more than his words ever could. She knew, had always known, instinctively, what Kit needed, and it wasn't the crisp, brittle life Haley was giving him. Her memories and dreams were strong enough to carry her for an entire week. Kit lasted that long. Then he called her again.

This time he came to her apartment in the afternoon. This time he didn't stop to talk. He came in the door and took her in his arms.

They went into her bedroom. Catherine was crying. Kit kissed her mouth, her neck, her breasts, her tears. He had the face of a Puritan, but he had the eyes of an idolater. She pulled him down on top of her. Their bodies closed together, and all the years they'd lost vanished. It was a coming home for both of them, and for a long while they did not move but simply lay together, Kit hard and large inside her, Catherine's legs twined around his, her hands stroking the lovely stretch of his back, their eyes closed, their breathing warm and steady against each other's cheeks.

Catherine was crying quietly. Kit raised himself up on his arms, and looking down at her, he began to move slowly inside her. She raised her head and looked down where their bodies joined and parted. Kit watched the rising blood flush her throat and breasts; they permitted each other to hide nothing. They looked at each other until they came, when sensation united them in shuddering elation. When he fell against her, she sank her teeth into his shoulder.

Afterward, Kit held Catherine against him, not speaking, until it was time for him to go. He told her he would be back, and she knew he would.

When he returned two nights later, he

told her that Haley had gone down to Virginia to see a friend's new thoroughbred. He could spend three whole nights with her. But after that, he had to break it off with Catherine. He shouldn't have let all this get started in the first place. He hated himself.

"Hate yourself later. Come to bed now," Catherine said.

They both had Sunday off. They spent the day making love, sleeping, and eating. He brought her breakfast in bed. She brought him champagne. The next two days they had to work, so they met after work at a French restaurant tucked away on East Eighty-third. It was almost a relief to be in public. They were forced to keep their hands off each other. Catherine could tell how Kit enjoyed her company. She made him laugh. Catherine told him about Blooms, about putting Ann through Miss Brill's and college, and about her grandmother and the British Everly. Kit told her about his work, his new sailboat up in Maine, where he and Haley were building a summer house on a piece of land his parents had given them.

The third night together, they made love, then lay curled against each other. Catherine's back was pressed against Kit's stomach. When he spoke, she felt his warm breath in her hair.

"I thought you'd be married by now."

"I've met some interesting men, but they all want the same thing — a nice wife, mommy, and social secretary all rolled into one. I'd go mad. But you know the real reason — I've never stopped loving you."

She felt his muscles tense. "Don't say that. It's not true."

"It is true."

Now he moved away from her, to sit on the side of the bed.

"I shouldn't have come here. It was wrong."

"No." Catherine's voice was strong with certainty. "Your marriage to Haley is wrong. You married her for your parents, for your career, and not for yourself. You don't love her. You love me. You should be with me."

"Catherine, stop."

"No, Kit, I won't." She turned to face him. She didn't touch him. "You know it's right between us. You *know* it is. Have you and Haley always been faithful to one another?"

"Of course."

"But now you're here with me. And you're happy here. That's the truth, Kit, and you know it."

"Catherine — Christ!" He rose and dressed with abrupt, angry movements. "I've got to leave," he said, "and I can't come back."

"I'll wait for you," Catherine said. She was sad when she heard the front door close behind him, but not afraid. She knew he would return.

It was a good season for waiting. There was the Thanksgiving rush to prepare for, and the social season was in full swing.

Catherine filled the ballroom at the Plaza with red geraniums, mauve begonias, and orange chrysanthemums, all growing in pots so the guests at the brunch for Mrs. Wilder's guests from Florence could take the plants home as party favors. Mrs. Wilder liked party favors. She also liked tax deductions. She instructed Catherine to have the plants that weren't taken home by guests taken to a nursing home the day after the brunch. This gave Mrs. Wilder a tax deduction as a charitable donation — which helped offset the cost of the flowers in the first place.

Catherine and Jason designed and built enormous arrangements of pheasant feathers, ostrich plumes, silver birch, gold alstroemerias, snapdragons, and gladioli for the wedding of a Moroccan man to a Peruvian woman. Their guests were invited to take home the gold place settings from the dinner party. They didn't care about tax deductions.

With her brother as her escort, Catherine

went to the parties where she expected to make the most contacts. She prepared her makeup and clothes very carefully, in case Kit and Haley were there. But she never saw them.

She waited. She didn't give up hope.

On Christmas Eve day, a delivery boy arrived at Blooms with an enormous ribboned box of champagne, cheese, nuts, caviar, smoked fish, and exotic fruits. The card read: "Merry Christmas to everyone at BLOOMS, from Piet in Amsterdam."

Catherine had also received a private note from Piet that day. "Catherine. This is taking longer than I thought. There have been some minor problems. But I'll see you soon with good news. Love, Piet."

She was too rushed with the pressures of the day to do more than read the note before she crumpled it tightly and tossed it in the wastebasket.

She spent Christmas Day sleeping, then joined her family for a holiday dinner at her parents'. When Shelly left early to go to a party, Catherine left with him, but she went home to spend the rest of the night in solitude, waiting for the phone to ring.

It was almost midnight on New Year's

Eve when Catherine and Shelly staggered from Blooms to Catherine's apartment. They each carried an open bottle of champagne, and from time to time they stopped to lean their heads back for a giant swig. They were exhausted. With Jason, they had decorated four hotels and eight private homes that day for New Year's Eve parties. Catherine's hands were stinging from the multitude of tiny scratches and slices she got from the flowers and twine and florist wire; whenever she was rushed, she got sloppy. Her arms were actually shaking from exhaustion. Muscles jumped in her legs.

Catherine was wearing a mink coat that fell to her ankles, high-heeled custom-made black boots, and a green silk minidress with a wide black leather belt clasped loosely around her hips. The mink was her Christmas present to herself. The dress she'd worn because she always ran into her clients when she was working, and she needed to look ready at any moment to join their party, which often they begged her to do. She had had four personal invitations from acceptable, presentable, even desirable men for New Year's Eve and invitations to more parties than she could keep track of. She had turned everyone down. She wanted only the comfort and routine of work and waiting for Kit.

"When I get home, I'm going to crawl into bed and sleep for two weeks straight," Shelly said.

"No, you're not. We've got two buffets and four dinners to set up for tomorrow."

Shelly groaned, but Catherine knew it was only an act. Shelly was making himself indispensable to the shop, and he liked the feeling it gave him.

Turning onto Seventy-fifth Street, they saw a man sitting on the steps to Catherine's front door. It wasn't snowing now, but it had snowed most of the day, and the sidewalk, streets, and steps were covered in glistening white. The stranger had his coat collar turned up and his hat pulled low over his head. Obviously, he had had too much to drink and was sleeping it off on Catherine's doorstep.

"Oh, man," Catherine groaned. "I can't deal with this. I have no charity left in my heart."

"We'll get his address and call a taxi for him," Shelly said.

Hearing their voices, the man turned his head. He stood up. When he rose, Catherine recognized the grace of his movements, the size of his shoulders. She stopped dead in her tracks.

"Kit!"

She dropped the champagne bottle and ran. Champagne geysered out of the bottle, which fell into a snowdrift.

"Don't waste this stuff, it's expensive!" Shelly called, stopping to pick it up.

But Catherine was already there. She looked up at Kit.

"What are you doing here?" she asked. But a smile as large as the world was spreading across her face.

"Catherine," he said. "I've been calling. Your shop. Your home, your parents' home — "

"We were at the Plaza. Decorating for their New Year's Eve ball. Last-minute stuff. You look like you're freezing."

Shelly approached. Kit looked startled. Catherine realized that the two men had never met. She'd never told Shelly about Kit.

"This," she said firmly, "is my brother. Shelly. He works with me, and he was walking me home before going on to our parents' apartment. Shelly, this is a friend of mine. Bye, darling."

Shelly grinned and kissed her cheek. "Happy New Year, sis," he said, then headed off into the night.

Catherine opened the door, and they went inside.

Kit looked awful. His slacks and sweater

hung on him; he had lost weight since she'd last seen him. He had dark circles under his eyes; he looked as if he hadn't slept in days. He had a suitcase in his hand.

"You look terrible, Kit. Sit down. I'll make coffee."

"No, Catherine. Wait. You sit down. I want to talk to you. Please."

Catherine sat on one end of the sofa. Kit sat next to her, not quite touching.

"All my life I wanted to be a good man. I never wanted to hurt anyone." He stopped. "I'm going at this backwards. Let me start over. Catherine, I love you. I've always loved you. I've been in hell since I saw you. I told Haley about you. I told Haley I want a divorce. Catherine, I want to marry you. If you'll marry me. I want to have a life with you."

"Oh, Kit!" Catherine said.

"I feel like a monster. I feel like I've destroyed Haley."

"Nonsense!" Catherine said. "Haley will be happier without you. You're too civilized for her. She needs — an anthropologist, an archaeologist or something. You know that's true. She'll be fine, Kit. You know she will. Kit, *I'm* the one who needs you."

Kit looked at Catherine. He seemed exhausted and weak, but his eyes burned with hope. He looked like someone shipwrecked who finally sights land.

"And I need you."

"Kit. Before we say anything else, there's something I have to tell you, about something I did."

"Tell me."

"Let me make some coffee first. It's a long story, and I want you to hear it all." Catherine rose from the sofa and went into the kitchen. She returned with two mugs of creamy sweet coffee in her hand, handed him one, and sat on a chair across from him.

"Kit. You need to know this. I blackmailed someone. Years ago. My family needed money badly, and I didn't know what else to do. And I don't regret it."

She told him about Helen Norton and P. J. Willington. About the bruises, and the flowers. About Piet and the dark closet and the camera, her old-lady disguise, and the terror in Macy's. The money.

When she was through, Kit shook his head. In a low voice he said, "Christ, Catherine. I don't know what to say."

"Tell me this. Do you think I'm evil?"

"Evil? No, not evil. But wrong — "

"No one suffered. Not even P. J. Willington."

"Still — no matter what good you've done . . . Where is Piet, anyway?"

"I don't know. I think he's in Amsterdam. I haven't seen him since last January. Piet doesn't matter. You matter, Kit. I want a life with you. Can you love me, knowing what I've done?"

He didn't hesitate. He rose and pulled her from her chair to stand against him. She threw her arms around him. "I love you, Catherine. We've both made mistakes. But this is right."

A jubilant trembling jangled the air around them. Catherine's skin went shivery with goose bumps. From outside came noises heralding the new year. In the apartments above and below Catherine's, the televisions reverberated with Guy Lombardo's orchestra playing "Auld Lang Syne." Boats in the rivers and harbor blatted and blared. Every taxi driver in the city honked his horn. The air of the city effervesced as a million bottles of champagne were opened. Clocks chimed. People on the street below blew whistles, rattled noise-makers, shouted, "Happy New Year!"

"Happy New Year," Kit said to Catherine.

Catherine had never been so happy in her life, so she was surprised at how exasperated she felt about Kit's anguish over Haley's heartbreak.

"God, she's so alone," Kit said.

"Give her a dog," Catherine wanted to say, but didn't.

Fortunately, when Haley realized Kit was going to go through with the divorce, she stopped being pathetic and became vindictive and predictable. Kit stopped feeling pity for Haley and started to feel angry, which set off a chain reaction in him, explosive capsules of memories of her coldness, her selfishness, her diffidence toward him. This Catherine could listen to with guilty pleasure. In fact, she was amazed at her own capacity for ill will.

One of the most enjoyable evenings in her life arrived when she and Kit were invited to dinner at the home of a couple who had known Kit and Haley intimately. The wife, Janie, spent the entire evening criticizing Haley. Catherine decided that she and Janie were destined to become great friends.

Still, it was a relief when Haley began to fade from their lives. Kit was eager to start his life over with Catherine. Every evening after work, Kit and Catherine ate in restaurants, planning their future. They were delighted by the similarity of their desires. Because he had been an only child, Kit wanted at least two children, close together. Catherine wanted to have children only if Kit would agree to help raise them, to really be there with her, rather than leaving them to a nanny or governess. Every Sunday they drove to Connecticut looking for houses. Afterward, in candelit restaurants, they held hands and exchanged suggestions: where they would honeymoon, who should come to their wedding, how they should decorate their house, what they would name their children.

Catherine thought she was often happiest in the middle of the night. Then, after Kit had fallen asleep, she could lie next to him, just listening to him breathe. Carefully, with delicacy, she moved her hand or thigh just close enough to feel the heat and hair of his arm or leg. He was really there. She could sleep, and when she awoke he would still be there. She was not thinking as she lay next to him. She was just being happy.

When she wasn't with Kit, she wanted to scurry around preparing things to make each moment she was with him luxurious, sensual. When she had once spent hours sketching designs for a dinner party, she now spent hours at Saks Fifth Avenue, buying rainbows of lacy lingerie. Kit had moved into her apartment, and now Catherine kept the apartment filled with vases of the most exotic, fragrant blooms her shop had in stock. She hung pomanders of jasmine potpourri in the closets and burned jasmine-scented candles to perfume their bedroom with its exotic spell. It suddenly became necessary to find a butcher who would supply her with the thickest, most succulent cuts of steak, a greengrocer who carried the freshest fruits and vegetables, a baker whose bread rivaled France's finest, a wine merchant who truly knew his wares.

She loved making an entrance with Kit. In his happiness, Kit had recovered his healthy good looks, and she knew they looked enviable together. He was so tall, so fair, so handsome, and these days she beamed happiness like the sun. She loved going to dinner with people, meeting his friends, introducing him to hers.

They were to be married in June at Everly. Kit was going to fly to a small Caribbean island for the divorce after his lawyer and Haley's had worked out the terms and settlement. Kit had gone to Boston to tell his parents his plans. They were appalled that he was leaving Haley and refused to give his new union their blessing. They vowed they would not come to the wedding ceremony. Catherine didn't mind. She had worked behind the scenes at too many weddings to believe that the magic of marriage came from all the trimmings. The magic for her was Kit's presence at her side.

* * *

They had agreed that Catherine would continue to run Blooms even after they had children. Catherine couldn't imagine her life without it. She was terrified of being bored and boring, and Kit said she should do whatever made her happy. As time went by and he realized how much his divorce was going to cost him, he admitted he was glad that she had money of her own. He would never be dependent on her, but he wouldn't be able to give her luxuries, at least not for a while.

"Any luxuries." Catherine smiled when he said that. It was a luxury for her to sit with Kit on a Sunday morning, drinking coffee, reading the *Times*, reading snippets aloud and laughing or arguing over them. It was a luxury to hold his hand in the movies. It was a luxury to let down her guard and sob with pleasurable mawkishness at *Love Story*, knowing that her own love story was ending happily. It was a luxury to feel his eyes, his breath, his skin, his weight, his heat, upon her body.

In late June Catherine sat in her office dictating memos to her staff. Shelly would be in charge, but she wanted to leave detailed instructions for everyone so she and Kit wouldn't be interrupted on their honeymoon.

In one week, she and Kit would be married and honeymooning in Venice. When they returned they would move into the white colonial house in Connecticut that they had decided would be their home. The house had a flagstone path leading up to it and flowering bushes growing around it. Huge evergreens sheltered the northern side, and an apple tree grew outside the breakfast room window. It was a storybook house, the house of a million dreams. It came with enough land for riding horses and a six-stalled stable. There was a small orchard and a pond. It was out in the country and yet only a short drive to a charming New England town that had a decent public school system and a fabulous private school.

Flicking off her recorder, Catherine rose, stretched and yawned. On her desk was a photo she and Kit had taken of the house, which she kept there to remind her it was real. On her hand was her flashing engagement ring — not the emerald one that had belonged to Kit's grandmother — Haley got that — but a simple diamond solitaire.

This was only normal life, she told herself. People got married, went on honeymoons, bought houses, every day. People had done it for years. She was not so different from every other human on the planet, after all.

She really could have a husband, a home, a family. Most people accepted that as naturally as their breath.

"Hello, Catherine."

She looked up.

Piet stood at the open door to her office. His white linen suit was exquisitely civilized, but when he smiled, his eyes flashed like a gypsy's.

Catherine surprised herself. For the instant she saw Piet, she wanted to touch him, to run her hands over his face, his hair, his chest, to kiss him. The sight of him made her heart glad.

God. What was wrong with her?

"I'm not going to hurt you," Piet said.

"What?"

Piet nodded at the high-backed swivel desk chair that Catherine had pulled in front of herself, as if for protection. She looked down to see her own hands gripping the back of the chair so tightly, her knuckles were white.

Catherine laughed and released the chair. "Well, this is a shock," she said. "Come in. Sit down."

"How are you?"

"I'm well, thank you." She moved in front of her chair and sat down. She waved Piet onto the chair across from her. She couldn't help the formality, the stiffness, with which she moved. "I'm going to be married next week. To Kit Bemish. A lawyer. We're going to Venice for our honeymoon."

The darkness in Piet's eyes deepened. "Congratulations."

For one brief moment they stared at each other. Then Piet smiled.

"It's a good thing I got here before you left. I've finally gotten all the loose ends tied up, and I now have a serious proposal to make." He waited one wicked beat of time before adding, "A business proposal."

"Oh?"

He leaned forward. Now he was intent, all business. "Catherine, what I'm going to say is just between you and me. I've been working all year on this. It could be very big. In the next few years the flower business is going to change dramatically. Refrigeration and communication technology and air freight will make it possible for a better-quality and a larger variety of flowers to be shipped from Amsterdam than will be available locally. Land on Long Island is becoming more and more valuable for developers, and eventually flower growers there will sell their land. They'll have to. Most of this country will buy their flowers from all over the world, shipped into and out of Holland.

"I have set up my own wholesale company.

I want you as my partner. I will work out of Aalsmeer and Amsterdam. You will call me at, say, nine in the morning your time, to tell me what flowers you need. I will buy them at the flower auction, have them packed and flown to you. Because of the time difference the flowers you order in the morning will arrive that same afternoon. For your shop, for Blooms, you will have the finest quality of flowers, and a huge variety, unusual flowers. In addition, you will cut out the cost of the wholesaler.

"But more than that, I want you to branch out. I want you to wholesale flowers from Holland to the other New York florists. We will start simply working from a truck. Our prices will be competitive, and the flowers will be high quality. We will be the first to offer an enormous variety and such an unusual selection."

Catherine sat, thinking. "Won't the cost of air freight be enormous?"

"Yes. But we will import such a large quantity that I, buying the flowers, will be able to get a price break that will more than make up for the freight cost. I have the figures to show you. With the volume of flowers Blooms uses, if you save even one cent a stem, you will be making good money. In addition to what you'll charge as wholesaler to other florists."

Catherine's brain was already in high gear. "Perhaps it would be wise not to publicize to my competitors that Blooms is importing. Perhaps the wholesale business should be under a different name."

Piet smiled. "So you are interested."

Catherine returned his smile. "You knew I would be."

It was night. Kit was furious. He was pacing the living room.

"I can't believe you're serious about this. How do you think I'll feel, knowing your old lover is around you all the time?"

"I don't love him anymore, Kit." Catherine spoke as honestly as she could, confident that she could keep any fleeting desire for Piet under control. What she felt for Piet was undeniable, but Kit was necessary to her life, and she would never betray him. "Kit. *I love you.* I told you, he was just — a temporary thing. I haven't even seen him for over a year! Isn't that proof that we weren't seriously involved? I shouldn't have told you we were lovers, but I wanted no secrets between us. Look. Piet won't be around me all the time. He won't be around me at all. He'll be in Holland."

"And what about our new life? Our marriage? Why do you want to take on a new time-consuming, ambitious project like this just when we're beginning our life together?"

"That's not fair. I'm not asking you to give up practicing law in order to give all your time to me."

"Women's lib."

"No. I've never been part of a herd, and you know it. Look, Kit, you have to understand what Blooms means to me."

"I do understand. I've never suggested that you give it up, or sell it, or even stop managing it. What I don't understand is your desire to take on more. Importing and wholesaling flowers is a major undertaking, Catherine. You'll need more employees, accountants, truckers — it's like starting a whole new business. I'm not asking you to give up what you have. I'm only asking you not to take on more at this point in your life. In our lives."

"I promise you I won't spend any more time at Blooms than I already do. I'll delegate more. I've got Jason, Carla, Sandra, and now Shelly, all of whom are completely reliable and who can run Blooms without me. I'll give them new positions, more responsibility, larger salaries, and they'll be motivated to work harder. Kit, I really want to do this."

"Why? Is it money?"

"Partly," she admitted. "I like having

money. I want to make more money, for us, for our children. So they never have to go through what I went through — that feeling of the bottom of the earth falling out from beneath their feet."

"You can't trust me to provide for that?"

"Kit, be realistic. Haley is getting everything you have in the divorce settlement."

Catherine was silent then, but her thoughts lay unspoken between them. It was Catherine's money from Blooms that they'd used for the down payment on the Connecticut house. When Kit's parents died, he would inherit the Maine house, the Boston house, and a great deal of money. Until then, in all likelihood, Catherine would have more money from Blooms than he did from his legal practice. Catherine had been proud of him for not letting money come between them. It was a potentially more sensitive and more destructive matter than anything else.

"Kit. I've loved you ever since I met you. I've never stopped loving you. I never want to hurt you or make you unhappy. But I need you to understand how I feel about Blooms. It's like — like a child to me, in a way. I love it. It's mine. It's not enough for me to let it just remain as it is. The business world is always changing. If you remain the same in business, you fall behind.

If I didn't do this for Blooms, it would be, oh, like not sending a child to college. Or not getting it proper medical care. Or not feeding it. It needs to grow."

Kit didn't reply. He stood at the window, looking out at the night. His back was tense.

Catherine went up and wrapped her arms around him. "I wish you knew how much I love you. How much I've always loved you. I've never been happier in my life."

Still Kit remained tense, silent.

She nuzzled her head into his back. "Do you mean you'll be happy only if I don't go into the importing business with Piet? Is that what you want?"

She felt Kit's muscles loosen.

"No," he said. "I wouldn't ask that much of you."

Kit turned to face Catherine. He looked at her, then pulled her against him. Holding her tightly, he kissed the top of her head.

"I know you love me. I love you. I want you to be happy. I want you to be the way you are. So — go ahead. Do it."

"With your blessing?"

"With my blessing."

Catherine sighed and leaned against him. She had just taken a terrifying risk. If Kit had wanted her to, she really would have given up the idea of importing flowers with

Piet. She loved Kit enough to do that for him. But *God* how glad she was not to have to make that choice!

In June Catherine and Kit were married in the garden at Everly.

It was not a fairy-tale wedding. The best that could be said for it was that it made their union public and official.

They were married in the garden at Everly, by the lily pond. The weather was perfect. A flawless blue sky blazed with light. The air was warm but not yet heavy with the humidity that would come in late summer. Kathryn's garden was a lush rainbow of roses, lilies, iris, peonies, foxglove, mock orange, and lilacs.

Catherine wore a dress of ivory peau de soie that fell from pleats at the shoulders and a floppy brimmed hat with the band trimmed in maiden blush roses. The wedding bouquet, which Jason had designed especially for her, was a mass of tiny pink roses, white roses, and gardenias and slipped with ivory ribbons onto her grandmother Kathryn's white leather prayer book. Ann was Catherine's only bridesmaid. She had flown back from the British Everly, where she was working, just for the wedding. Kathryn acknowledged the importance of the occasion by wearing her valuable diamond necklace with a silk dress; at the last moment she popped on her floppy straw gardening hat to protect her face from the sun. Catherine's father, looking marvelously handsome — for this was the sort of occasion he excelled at — gave Catherine away. While the minister led Catherine and Kit through the vows, Marjorie Eliot squirmed, fanning away, exasperated, at nonexistent bugs.

Jason wore a lavender silk suit that probably cost more than Catherine's wedding dress, and when Catherine said, "I do," he cried more than anyone else at the ceremony. Catherine's mother didn't cry at all. Sandra and her husband had brought Carla out for the wedding. Shelly was there, of course, and Catherine's beloved Mr. Giles. Kit's parents had steadfastly refused to attend, but his friend Don and his perceptive wife, Janie, were there, and the law partners, Mr. Woodrow and Mr. Spiegel, were there with their wives.

When the ceremony was over, a champagne dinner was served in the dining room, with the doors thrown open to the gardens. It was a beautiful, elegant day, but not what Catherine had thought it would be like. She did not feel swept away on clouds of love. She had come out to Everly the night before with Ann. And all through the wedding Catherine couldn't stop noticing how run-down Everly was. It needed painting. It needed another full-time gardener. Catherine made a mental note to see if she could convince her grandmother to let her help out, but still she could not dismiss the foreboding she felt.

Also, she didn't feel well. For several days she'd vomited every morning. Nerves, perhaps, though she'd never been the nervous type. It was more likely, since her period was three weeks late, that she was pregnant.

CHAPTER 10

New York, 1976

The January 1976 issue of *Vogue* ran a photoarticle about Catherine Eliot Bemish in their series "Women We Admire." The largest picture was of Catherine holding her son, Drew, three years old, and her daughter, Lily, nine months old. Catherine was wearing a voluptuous crimson, lavender, and gold silk caftan. Gypsyish gold hoops hung at her ears. Drew was wearing a blue plaid bathrobe. Baby Lily was naked except for a pink bow in her blond whale spout, but the billowing sleeves of Catherine's caftan covered much of Lily's tiny body, leaving only her legs, arms, and shoulder exposed in their rosy plumpness.

Supposedly Catherine had just finished bathing her children, but in fact it had taken them three hours to get this casual-seeming setup ready. And certainly Catherine could never have worn the caftan to bathe her babies. The winged sleeves would have drooped in the tub and become waterlogged and heavy, the silk ruined. Catherine really wore jeans and a sweatshirt to bathe her babies, or sometimes even got into the tub with them. Afterward she would put on a comfortable, often washed terrycloth bathrobe that she wore for the rest of the evening. But for the photo, she wore the caftan. She sat where the photographer posed her, on her dressing room sofa, where the rich chintz flowers gleamed against the apple green wall of Catherine's dressing room at her White River home, instead of in the children's bedrooms, which were always littered with toys.

Another photograph showed Catherine seated behind her desk at Blooms, talking on the phone, pen in hand. She was wearing a designer suit in a navy wool pinstripe, a mock man's suit complete with white shirt and English rep striped tie. In another shot, Catherine and Kit were caught in a camera flash at a charity ball at the Met. Kit was in his tux, Catherine in a full-skirted emerald evening gown. Behind them towered a massive arrangement of flowers, done for the gala, of course, by Blooms.

"My secret?" Catherine was quoted. "Organization. A superb staff both at work and at home. I learned the hard way, by trial and error, in my business, to structure, delegate, and categorize. I just apply the same principles to my home life."

"What a pack of lies," Catherine said, reading the article. "But I'm the modern woman, I couldn't say I owe it all to my delicious husband."

"That would be a lie," Kit said. "You are organized. You do delegate. You do have a good staff."

"But if I didn't have you, and time alone with you, I'd lose my mind," Catherine said. "Oh, Kit, sometimes I feel like one of those poor criminals tied to four different horses, being pulled bodily in four different directions."

"Roll over. I'll give you a back rub," Kit said.

It was a cold January Sunday. Before their children were born, Catherine and Kit had agreed that they would bring up their children themselves and not leave them solely to the care of governesses and nannies and maids. Sundays would be family time, they decided, but after Lily was born they changed their minds. Sunday mornings would be family time. Sunday afternoons would be reserved for the two of them to be alone, a luxury they sorely needed.

This morning they had been awakened by

Andrew, who raced into their room and crawled into bed with them for tickles and hugs. Catherine had gotten Lily from her crib and changed her, and the four had gone down to the kitchen for a leisurely breakfast of pancakes and bacon. Then they'd all dressed and gone out to play in the snow. Kit and Catherine pushed the children on sleds down the slight incline at the side of the house. Kit and Andrew built a fort while Catherine watched Lily eat snow. The pony Santa had given Andrew for Christmas had whinnied and pranced back and forth in the ring, begging for attention. Kit and Catherine brought their children back into the house, gave them hot baths and warm lunches, then settled them into their rooms for quiet time.

Now it was early afternoon, and their nanny, Mary, who loved having Sunday mornings to sleep late, was on duty with the children, and Kit and Catherine were secluded together in their bedroom. The lay together, looking at the article about Catherine in *Vogue*.

Catherine rose to slip off her clothes, then stretched out naked on the bed. She was still nursing Lily, but Lily was also getting solid food, so her long large breasts were not uncomfortably full. She raised herself up on a pillow to keep from crushing her breasts, which were sensitive. She was so very tired. A back rub was just what she needed. As Kit moved his hands over her shoulders and back, she took deep breaths, relaxing, trying with each exhalation to breathe away thoughts of the world outside this bedroom.

Deep breath: first, their children. Lily was over her cold, and the antibiotics had cured the ear infection that had caused the little girl to wake screaming a few nights ago. As Catherine rocked Lily, she'd remembered the nurse who had been with her during her labor with Andrew. It had been a long hard labor. When the doctors and Kit had gone out into the hall to discuss whether to give Catherine a spinal or a C-section, Catherine had cried to the nurse, "It's really not the pain I mind. It's the lack of control. I *hate* not being in control." The nurse had smoothed Catherine's wet hair off her forehead and smiled down at her. "Oh, honey," she'd said, "this is the easy part."

Catherine had thought the nurse was nuts. Now she understood. Here at their White River home, she and Kit had a full staff: a housekeeper/cook and caretaker, Mr. and Mrs. Bunt, who lived in a suite on the first floor off the kitchen, and Mary, the nanny, who lived on the third floor. They'd hired a maid, Angela, to run the apartment in the city. Kit had told Woodrow and Spiegel that although he'd accept a partnership, he didn't want the toughest cases, because he wanted time for his family, and Catherine had delegated more and more work at Blooms to Shelly, Sandra, Jason, and Carla.

But still every day was crowded, rushed, sometimes nerve-racking, always exhausting. Children were such mysteries, so fragile and dependent on the adults in their lives, and their health went through such dramatic changes: croup, colds, rashes, sudden pains, and even when they were in perfect health, Mary wanted to put Andrew on his pony, or Kit wanted to teach the children to swim. Suddenly to Catherine the world seemed a maze of dangers: ponies could kick, water could drown, on the most peaceful summer day a bee could sting. . . . Since Andrew's birth, Catherine often felt she'd never been at rest except at night, when she knew both children were tucked away in bed, healthy, asleep.

But now they were safe and healthy. Vaguely, through the walls, she could hear their shrill laughter and thumps: they were building a house of blocks with Mary. They were safe.

Deep breath: Blooms. There had been all

kinds of snags setting up GardenAir, the wholesale flower importing business, but now after three years most of the problems had been worked out and the profits were finally beginning to roll in and promised to increase dramatically in the coming months. Piet was always in Amsterdam, except for the executive meetings twice a year, so Kit had no reason to be jealous, and Catherine had no reason to feel guilty. She was too busy, too much in love with her children and her husband, to even remember how she had once felt for Piet.

Also, Kit was becoming increasingly involved with Blooms and GardenAir. At first she had only talked over specific problems and plans with him as they sat at dinner or during the drive from White River to New York for a play or an opera. He'd responded with such a fresh point of view, such sound and logical advice, that they were now in the habit of spending one night a week at the Blooms office together. Kit's involvement with the inner workings of her company as they worked alone in the darkened building deepened the intimate connection between them, drew them even closer together.

But Catherine did feel guilty about the others at Blooms. The family atmosphere there had dissolved. It was her fault, she knew. She no longer had time for giddy dinners with Jason, and the attention she gave to Sandra or Carla's personal gossip was all too brief. Sandra, who had grown daughters, understood and went her own calm way, but Carla had often complained of feeling left out. The entire staff had pointed out that Blooms, while holding its own in the competitive floral trade, was no longer the hottest shop in New York, and in response to their grumblings, Catherine had agreed to do the *Vogue* article. The publicity would boost sales and status for a while and keep her employees too busy to complain.

Shelly was a more serious problem. He worked hard as always, but in the past three years he had started to play hard, too. More nights than not he was out drinking, dancing, partying, always with the "right" people, always insisting when Catherine questioned him that it was all good for business. Just before Lily's birth, Catherine, swollen, restless, unable to sleep, had gone in to Blooms at dawn, something she hadn't done for months, to discover that Carla was off buying the flowers. Charming Shelly, often too drunk or too tired, had persuaded her to take over this early morning task so he could go home to sleep. Catherine had reproached Shelly, but he'd responded with accusations of his own. He'd told Catherine she was ignoring her business, and Catherine knew he was right — with poor Carla, weeping and martyred, trying to take all the blame herself. Catherine had settled it all by hiring a new florist, a quiet man named Leonard, who didn't have the flair for arranging that Jason did but knew how to judge the quality and freshness of flowers and was willing to make the early morning runs. Shelly was now free to sleep late, and accordingly, he gave more time to the importing business. It was working out. Shelly was a grown man. He'd be all right. Eventually he'd get married and settle down.

Deep breath: finally, Everly. Kathryn was seventy-nine and becoming more reclusive and eccentric with each passing year. She'd refused to fly to England the past few years to visit the Boxworthys and Ann, who had graduated from college and was working full-time at the British Everly. The international travel was too difficult for her, Kathryn claimed, and her family understood. But in the past few months she'd refused to leave her house even for day trips. She'd declined to come in to the city for Thanksgiving or Christmas dinner at the Eliots'. When they'd said, very well, they'd come out to see her, she'd said flatly, "No. Don't come. It's too much bother. I don't want any presents, I don't want to give any presents, and the day means nothing to me. Don't clutter up my life."

Worst of all, Kathryn wouldn't see a doctor. Clara, her maid, who was almost as old as Kathryn, assured Catherine and Drew and Marjorie that Kathryn was in good health and, in her idiosyncratic way, in good spirits. She just preferred to be alone with her house, her plants, her books.

During the past summer, Kathryn had agreed to let Catherine sow an unused field at Everly with wildflowers for Blooms, but she'd refused to enter into any contractual or written agreement. "If you'll let me lease space from you, Grandmother, I can write off certain expenses," Catherine said. "We could hire more gardeners. Perhaps even have some work done on the house."

"It's my house, my garden," Kathryn had said testily. "I'm happy with it as it is."

Catherine worried that her grandmother might forget their agreement, might suddenly snap and tell her she couldn't use the field or pick the wildflowers. More than that, she worried about what would happen to Everly if someone didn't start attending to it soon. Deep down, of course, she worried about who would inherit Everly — but that was a subject she didn't dare broach with her cantankerous grandmother. She didn't want to offend her. Even more, she didn't want to hurt her. When they worked together on a sunny day among the flowers and the weeds, she loved her grandmother more than ever. During those moments, the rest of the world, even Andrew and Lily and Kit, faded, and the brown spots on Kathryn's hands blended with the freckles on the lilies and the dots on the back of the jolly ladybugs, until Catherine felt she was part of something blurred and timeless.

Deep breath: Kit. Here he was, rubbing her shoulders and back so that she was warm and relaxed. Outside, the fierce wind howled and frosted the windows white. Inside, on their wide warm bed, she felt like spring, like summer, blooming with fragrance and beauty and hope. All that they had first guessed from touching had come true: they were right for each other. She was speed, passion, color, light; he was stability, endurance, depth, safety.

Now she rolled over to face him. She'd gained weight after having the children, and her body was silvered here and there with stretch marks, yet she felt completely lovely and unabashed.

"I'm so happy," she said. "I wish this

could last forever."

In August Catherine received a note from Ann, who was in England, living and working at Everly.

Dearest Catherine,
Excuse this scribbled mess, but I never have time to write a proper letter, we're all so busy. I just wanted to tell you I'm thinking of you a lot these days. The gardens are flourishing and so many wonderful things are happening, I wish you were here to share them. Will you ever come over again?

Love, Ann

Catherine sat holding the note, thinking. With Andrew's birth, Kit's parents had at last let go of their anger and welcomed Catherine and their grandson into their home and lives. Every summer of their marriage, Catherine and Kit had gone, first with baby Andrew, then with Andrew and Lily, to Maine, to spend two weeks of August at the Bemishes' summer home. For Kit, this was heaven. He sailed around the familiar islands and coves, played tennis with old friends, and showed his children the tree house where he had played as a child.

For Catherine, these visits were tedious and dull. She hated sailing, especially with the children on board, even if they did have life jackets on. She couldn't understand why anyone would go to so much work to have fun. She hated tennis, she hated trying to swim in the frigid water, she hated being dutifully civil to her in-laws. No matter what she did, it seemed Joan Bemish always reproached her in her gentle Puritan voice: if Catherine fed Andrew carrots, was she sure she was giving him enough protein; if she fed him hamburgers, was she giving him enough roughage? She knew Joan meant well, and she surely loved her grandchildren. Her own parents wouldn't notice or complain if she gave her children gin and tonics. And really, Catherine didn't mind letting Joan nurture her only grandchildren, she only minded having to stand aside politely while Joan did it.

At the beginning of this summer, she summoned up her courage to tell Kit how she felt about going to Maine. Kit was baffled. "Well, Catherine, I don't want to force you to do anything you don't like, but . . . if you don't like to sail, or play tennis, or sunbathe — well, what do you like to do?"

What Catherine liked to do, she realized,

was to sit by herself at the British Everly, looking at flowers and waiting for cream tea. It had been years since she'd had that luxury, and as she told Kit about it, she realized it all would be changed, destroyed, even, if Kit and Andrew and Lily were there, pulling on her, needing her attention. Drew would run down the hedgerow screaming like an Indian. Lily would eat the dirt and probably the flowers. Kit would be bored to tears.

"Why not go over by yourself?" Kit suggested, breaking into Catherine's maudlin reverie.

"Oh, I couldn't."

"Why not? Mother would love to have the kids to herself, and Mary can take over whenever necessary."

"Well . . . I haven't really seen Ann for years now. It would be lovely to see her there, and to see Everly again."

"Then go. Really, Catherine, go."

"It just seems so — wicked! To leave my little children!"

"Think of yourself. Think how tired you are, how much time you've spent with the children, how refreshed you'll be, and more energetic with them after a break."

"You mean it, don't you? Oh, Kit, I'd be so grateful! If you're sure . . . I think I'll go."

Of course she didn't tell him that Ned would be there. Or rather, though Kit knew that Ned Boxworthy lived at Everly, he certainly didn't know Ned had once been Catherine's lover. And of course she didn't intend to sleep with Ned ever again, she'd always be faithful to darling Kit — but . . .

But it would be part of the pleasure of visiting Everly to see Ned, to enter his particular electromagnetic field and experience those old sexual sparks. Her body had belonged to her children for over three years now, in pregnancy and birth and nursing; it would be fun to see if it could, this old stretched and wearied body of hers, still incite Ned to desire.

In August Kit took the children to Maine, and Catherine boarded a plane for London. The flight was rough, due to a summer storm, and then the plane circled above Heathrow for over an hour. The customs lines were crowded, and when the driver met her and handed her into the Everly car, it was pouring rain. An American couple was also going to Everly, and the wife talked at Catherine incessantly for the entire hour's drive.

When she finally arrived, Catherine hoped she could retreat to a room for a nap before saying hello to anyone. She was jet-lagged and suddenly in that state of surrender to exhaustion that, for Catherine, only happened when someone else was taking care of the children and the business. But Ann was waiting. She greeted Catherine with a warm hug.

"Catherine, I've got so much to tell you!"

"I want to hear everything, Annie, but please let me catch a nap first. I'm too tired to think straight."

Ann showed her to her room. Catherine promised she'd be down for tea, but to her amazement she awoke to find she'd slept the day and night through. She threw back her covers, pulled on a bright cotton dress and sandals, splashed her face with water, and hurried down to the dining room.

"Catherine! At last!" Madeline Boxworthy was seated at the long table. She held out her arms, and Catherine bent to hug the older woman. "I didn't know whether to wake you or not. But now here you are. You look marvelous. Tell me everything. Did you bring pictures of your children? Oh, but I'm being selfish. I know you want to see Ann. She's already out in the gardens with Hortense. Do you want to go on out?"

"Not until I've had a nice big breakfast!" Catherine said, laughing. She rose and helped herself at the buffet, heaping her plate high. "I looked at the gardens from my window.

They look wonderful."

"Well, it helps to have Ann with us. And Tom, you know, is such a good worker. Elizabeth is pregnant again, and I shouldn't tell you, because Hortense wanted to, but Hortense is getting married!"

"When? What's he like?"

Madeline clapped her hands. "Perfection! He's an architect! He loves Everly, and wants to renovate it himself, put everything in tip-top shape!"

"Mother! You promised you'd let *me* tell! Hello, Catherine. *God,* it's good to see you. Don't mind the dirt, it's clean." Hortense entered the dining room, a basket of roses over her arm, and embraced Catherine with her arms, holding her dirty hands away.

"Catherine! You're up!" Ann rushed over like a child, grabbing Catherine in a big, greedy hug.

Catherine put her hands on Ann's shoulders and held her away to study her. The past few years had changed Ann. Her hair was still golden, her face still sweet, dominated by her large, expressive blue eyes, but sun and weather had worn Ann's face, which was finely lined now and covered with freckles. Yet in spite of these imperfections, and rather because of them, Ann's face looked interesting. It had a quality of experience behind it, of laughter and sun. Ann's long blond hair was carelessly tied back with a string. Catherine touched the string and laughed.

"Oh, I'm just a poor working girl!" Ann said, her eyes shining. "I can't be bothered with makeup and frills. But Catherine, you look gorgeous! Motherhood must agree with you. Did you bring pictures of my nephew and niece?"

Catherine was happily caught up in the heat and chatter of the moment. Before the morning had ended, Elizabeth and her two-year-old son came in, kissed Catherine, and sat down to trade news. Tom passed through with some papers for Madeline to sign and greeted Catherine with a peck and a smile. Before Catherine noticed her coffee cup was empty, someone jumped up to refill it. When the telephone rang, it was never for her. Hortense wanted to show Catherine her wedding gown, Elizabeth wanted to talk about babies, Madeline wanted to hear about Kathryn, Ann wanted to hear about Drew and Marjorie.

Then Ned came in. He was wearing only a white shirt and blue jeans, and his black hair was mussed as if he'd been dragging his hands through it, but his entrance caused all the women to go quiet, each in her own way satisfied at the presence of this handsome male.

"Catherine," he said. "You're back."

He just stopped inside the doorway, so Catherine rose and crossed the room to hug him. She kissed him on the cheek, which was stubbly. He smelled like ink and electricity, dark and sharp and vivid. She took his hand and pulled him to the table.

"It's so late. What have you been doing?"

He sat down next to Catherine. Ann put a cup of coffee in front of him.

"I, my lazy dear, have been working. Since before dawn. I've just about finished revising a book, the first in a series, I'll have you know, and a series that a publisher is seriously interested in!"

"My God, Ned, how marvelous!" Catherine said. "Tell me about it."

"Yes, Ned, do tell her about it," Hortense said, her voice tinged with mischief.

"Oh, he won't tell anyone anything," Madeline said. "He's a wretched tease. No one will publish his awful books, he isn't even writing anything, he's just pretending so we'll all wait on him hand and foot. How I've spoiled the child."

Catherine laughed and listened to the family banter. As she watched, Ann said, "Madeline, your tag's sticking out," and rose to tuck in a tag in the neck of Madeline's shirt.

Ann's hands on the older woman were gentle, but casual, possessive, relaxed, as if this sort of touching were a common thing. And Catherine remembered how, so long ago — twelve years ago! — Catherine had fallen in love with this family and wished her own were like it. Now little Ann, her baby sister, had done her one better and made this family her own. She was living here, working here, one of them.

As Catherine watched, Hortense said, "Well, all, we've got to get back to work. See you at tea, Catherine."

"Are you sitting in the garden today?" Ann asked Catherine, rising with Hortense. "Don't worry. I'll find you. I want to have a nice long lovely private talk." She kissed Catherine on the cheek, then, before going out the door, bent to kiss Ned's cheek, a more lingering kiss.

Well! Catherine thought. What is innocent little Ann up to?

But Ned excused himself before she could ask, and soon everyone had gone off on their various errands. Catherine was left alone, stuffed with food and new thoughts.

After she bathed and unpacked, Catherine wandered out in the early afternoon to survey Everly's gardens. It was a hot, clear August day. The flower beds made her jealous. Ann and Hortense had been working hard over the past few years, and it showed. The house rose above the gardens in its grand stone solidity, scorning wood and its submission to time and weather.

Catherine found a corner to herself on a stone bench by a brick wall so covered with lustrous ivy, it seemed quilted. Above her the apple, pear, and plum trees hung down their tight green or purple-blue fruits. She had purposely found the wilder part of the garden, where the flowers blazed untidily, abundant and boisterous, greedily unkempt. Fat, prickly globe thistle, as silvery blue and swollen as a pigeon's breast, mingled with golden rudbeckia, white Shasta daisies, and pink trumpeting Crinum, exiled here because although their fragrance was heavenly, their long, flopping, slender swords of leaves made them unwelcome in a more well groomed section.

She could hear Madeline's secateurs click-clacking away nearby. Birds chattered and chirped, bees hummed. She closed her eyes and was almost asleep again when a fresh rush of cool air passed over her. Ann slid onto the bench next to her.

"Didn't I arrange a smashing day for you?"

Catherine laughed. "I can't get over how

British you sound!"

"I love it here! Listen, Hortense said to take all the time I want, but we've got buckets of work to do, so I don't want to leave her alone for long. Tell me, how is everyone back home? Anything you can tell me out here that you couldn't tell me at the table?"

"No, not really. Mother and Dad are just like always. How their bodies continue to function, I don't know. I think they miss you, Ann. They see very little of Drew and Lily. You know Mother, she's afraid the children might mess up her clothing, and she does have a point. Children are so messy! But God, Ann, how I love them! And Kit is — " Catherine smiled, out of breath, out of words. "Wonderful."

"You have a perfect life."

"Perfect? Oh, I don't know. Nothing on earth is perfect. But I know I'm very lucky."

"And rich. And happy."

"Yes. And rich. And happy."

"How's Kathryn?"

"Stranger and stranger. Very reclusive. But physically in good health. I suppose we all should be glad she has that big place to ramble around in. Her own private institution. We don't have to worry about her. Anyway, she's fine. Now tell me all about you. I can't believe you haven't been home in four years."

"This is my home, now, Catherine."

"Oh, Ann, really — "

"Listen." Ann turned on the bench to face Catherine more fully. "Catherine, Ned's asked me to marry him." Her eyes were shining.

Catherine was surprised at the jealous little kick in the stomach Ann's words gave her. Where did that come from? she wondered.

"Annie. How lovely. But — "

"It is lovely. Catherine, I've had a crush on him since I first saw him. When I was just fourteen! I've held every man I've met up to him, and no one compares. I love him, Catherine. And he loves me."

"Oh, Annie, how wonderful."

"We haven't told anyone else yet. This should be Hortense's summer. She works so hard, she deserves her time of celebration. We'll probably make an announcement after her wedding."

"I'm so happy for you, Annie."

"I knew you would be — oh, and Catherine, I need to ask you something. I need your help. Ned wanted to marry someone with money, for Everly. But he loves me, Catherine, and he's been so frustrated by this money business — Catherine, please help us. I've thought of a plan. You could sign over your rights to Kathryn's Everly to me."

Catherine flinched as if she'd been slapped. "What are you talking about? I don't have any 'rights' to Everly!"

"Oh, come on, Grandmother must have — "

"She hasn't ever said a thing about her will or to whom she's leaving Everly!"

"Well, we all know she'll probably leave it to you. Won't you just hear me out? I've thought it all through. You've got your home, your children, your husband, you've got your apartment in New York, and your White River house, and I know when Kit's parents die you'll have their place in Maine. You can't possibly want to be saddled with Everly. It's falling apart. It will need tons of money to get it back in shape. But it's worth a lot. The land alone is worth a fortune. Grandmother's old. When you sell Everly, you'll have more money than you'll know what to do with."

Catherine sat silent, stunned, staring at her younger sister. "Ann. Listen. We don't know who will inherit Everly. Perhaps I will. If I do inherit Everly, I won't want to sell it. But it's just as likely that Kathryn will leave it to you, or to Mother and Father, and then part of it will eventually come to you — "

"Exactly!" Ann snapped, triumphant. "All right, then. I'll sign over *my* rights to Everly to you. Now. And you give me money in return."

Catherine laughed, astonished. "Annie, I can't just 'give you money'! Well, of course, I can give you something, and I will, gladly, but I can't possibly give you enough to make any difference to this place. You're going to need pots of money to restore this Everly."

"You've got pots of money."

"I've worked for it! It's *my* money from *my* business! I certainly don't have enough money to restore this Everly and keep my business going. I don't think you understand. A lot of my 'wealth' is tied up in the business — "

"Oh, you're so selfish!" Ann burst out, pounding her knees with her fists in frustration.

"That's not true."

"Yes, it is. You're selfish, and you always have been. Oh, just go away. Leave me alone. If you won't help me, then just leave me alone!"

Ann was in tears. She rushed off from Catherine, down the white stone path, around the corner of a boxwood hedge, and out of sight. Catherine was left sitting on the stone bench, breathless. What could she do now? The silence that before had spread around her in sunny innocence now seemed to hold a quality of waiting, listening — it was as still as if the garden were holding its breath. Who had heard their words? Catherine no longer heard the gentle clicking of Madeline's secateurs. How close was Hortense? And even if no one had overheard, how many of the Boxworthys were aware of Ann's plan? Undoubtedly Ned knew, and Ann and Hortense were best friends, and if Hortense knew, it was a good guess that she had told her mother.

Catherine shuddered. It was completely unrealistic of Ann, and completely self-centered, to expect Catherine simply to hand over a fortune, for a fortune was what it would take to bring this Everly back into first-class shape. But Ann had never had to deal with money before, and it was true that Catherine was wealthy.

But if all the Boxworthys were waiting for Catherine to share her wealth, and if they would sit in judgment of her, think ill of her, even hate her if she didn't — Oh, it was so unfair! This Everly had been her haven, at least in her mind, the place where she could retreat from the cares of the world. Now it could never be the same. Ann had brought the cares of Everly and dumped them all in her lap.

At that, Catherine rose, as if brushing them off her skirt. Quickly she retraced her steps along the garden path to the house. What could she do, track down each of the Box-worthys and explain her position, her finances? Damn Ann! But now it was done, and although Madeline and the others would no doubt remain kind, even understanding, they were bound to be disappointed. And would Ned marry Ann now if she had no money and no chance of ever having real money? That was not her responsibility, Catherine thought.

Through an open window at the side of the house, Catherine saw Elizabeth and one of the local girls washing up after breakfast and measuring flour into a large bowl in preparation for tea. She could hear Elizabeth's two-year-old yammering from the kitchen playpen. Hard work, yes, but Elizabeth seemed happy enough. As she looked, Catherine also saw how the wood framing the kitchen scene was chipped and warped. It needed painting. More, it needed rebuilding. It had cracked in the middle, and the wood was splintering. Above it, a rusty gutter pipe hung down, unhinged. Ivy climbed up the wall and wrapped around the pipe on its way to the second and third stories. Cosmetically, Everly was charming. Underneath, it was falling apart.

But Catherine knew that if she was lucky enough to inherit Kathryn's Everly, it would take all her money and more to restore that house. She couldn't be responsible for this Everly, too, and it was wrong of Ann to expect it of her.

Still, Catherine felt she'd been tossed out of the Garden of Eden. She walked through the long shadowy hallway and up to her room. She sat for a while, thinking, and then she began to pack.

Madeline appeared to be genuinely distressed when Catherine found her in the library and told her she was leaving.

"But, my dear," she said, her hand going to the brooch at her throat.

"It's just that I miss my children. I've never been away from them before, and little Lily is only a year old, I've only just stopped nursing her."

"Oh, well, I do understand. I felt that way about my little ones, too. In fact, I never took a trip away from them until they were all in their teens. So I do understand. Still, it's a pity that you can't stay."

The chauffeur had just returned from Heathrow with two couples arriving as guests at the bed-and-breakfast, but he was cheerful enough about driving Catherine back to the airport. Catherine left him to load her luggage and went out into the garden to find Ann.

Ann was pushing a wheelbarrow of compost down to the far end of the kitchen garden, hidden from the public garden by a brick wall. Her forehead was streaked with dirt, and she looked tired.

"I'm leaving, Ann," Catherine said. "I thought I'd say good-bye."

"Good-bye. I think you're selfish and mean."

"Well, I'm not, Ann, and someday I'll tell you some things that I've done that have helped you — "

"Helped me!"

"Yes. But I won't tell you now. I'm going home. But I do want to say that I hope it works out somehow, for you and Ned."

"I'll just bet you do."

"Oh, Ann." Catherine sighed and waited, wishing for a sign of softening on her sister's part, but Ann only stabbed at the compost with a pitchfork and angrily dragged it onto the pile.

Catherine was so angry, so frustrated, and over all, so wretchedly tired from the two transatlantic trips that when she phoned Kit from Logan to tell him she was back in the States, and why, she broke down on the phone and began to cry.

"I'll rent a car and drive up. God. It's

so embarrassing. People are looking at me as if I'm a lunatic." She crunched the receiver between her head and shoulder and used both hands to dig into her purse for a handkerchief.

"Catherine, listen. Do what I say." Kit's voice was firm, even harsh. "Go to the Ritz-Carlton. When we hang up, I'll call and make a reservation for you there. I'll drive down today. I should be there by this evening."

"The children — "

"The children are being spoiled rotten by my parents. You'd have a heart attack if you saw the amount of sugar they're consuming. You need a break. You wanted to relax and look at some goddamned flowers, and that's exactly what you're going to do. I'll be there tonight to take care of you. All right?"

"All right," Catherine said.

She followed the porter to a taxi and gave directions. The Boston day was so hot that it took her breath away, but she was already breathless and as giddy as a teenager in love for the first time. Kit was going to come down and take care of her. She'd been feeling so soiled, so shabby, because of Ann, like a second-rate sister, not worthy of being loved, and here was Kit, shining, sterling, coming to her rescue, and in the light of his love she was renewed.

* * *

She spent a week with Kit, the first week they'd had alone together since the children were born. Since she'd spent so many summers in Maine, he thought she deserved equal time, and he drove her to western Massachusetts. They went to concerts at Tanglewood and plays at Stockbridge and Williamstown. They toured the vast mansions, former summer "cottages" of the very wealthy at the turn of the century. Some of the estates had been made into public gardens. There were bridges arching over meandering streams where willows bent and trailed their leaves like a maiden's tresses; clever gates and stairways in the midst of nowhere, built simply as a setting for birches and bushes and plants; fountains, mirror pools, waterfalls, gazebos, pagodas and temples, sunken gardens, terraced hills, mazes, cul-de-sac rooms hiding statues with blind eyes and smiling mouths. Catherine studied it all, wishing she could copy this or that at Everly someday. When she confessed her secret fantasies to Kit, he said calmly, "Well, if Kathryn doesn't leave you Everly, perhaps we can arrange to buy it." Catherine was overwhelmed by the way Kit championed her. She couldn't tell him enough how much she loved him.

In September she returned to work, rested

and refreshed, and glad of it, for Shelly overwhelmed her with his newest plan: he wanted to computerize Blooms. At first the very thought terrified her. She was still able to spend a few moments in each section of her business and understand what was going on, what shape things were in. She prided herself on the fact that in an emergency she could take over any job at any level in her business and do it well. But computers! It was a technological outer space she wasn't sure she was prepared to enter.

Once again, Kit reassured her. Of course she could understand how to use computers. She'd only have to take a course or two, and what Shelly was proposing was really very simple, just a faster way of ordering, invoicing, paying out. Catherine finally agreed to the computer plan and then, in the process of going over their bookkeeping needs, realized what an octopus her company had become now that they were wholesaling. No wonder Sandra had sprouted gray hairs! She took over the tenth floor of their building for the business offices, gave Sandra and Shelly each a posh office at the front of the building, and moved her office up to the back. Jason and his assistant, Leonard, were moved to the second floor, and a freight elevator was put in to streamline the scurry from the storage and cleaning space in the basement to the second floor. Carla ran the first floor, taking care of walk-in customers, receiving and checking the flower shipments against invoices, and answering the phone and opening the mail before sending it on up to Catherine or Shelly or Sandra. Some days Catherine felt like the mayor of an efficient and very fragrant city.

Catherine remained so angry at Ann that at Christmas she sent the Boxworthy family a huge box of gourmet fruits, chocolates, and liqueurs but did not send her usual private gift and card to her sister. In return, she didn't receive a card or present from Ann, nor did her children. Very well, I don't care, Catherine thought.

But one January Sunday when she and Kit were alone in their bedroom, reading the paper by the fire and enjoying their private time, Mary knocked on the door to tell them that the phone call was for them, long distance from England, and urgent. Catherine's heart plunged with fear. Ann. But her news was good: Ned's book was a great success, and they were getting married in June at Everly, and Ann wanted Catherine and Kit and everyone to come.

Ned's books, it turned out, were mysteries

starring a sardonic, attractive, rather mischievous chief inspector who lived in a home much like Everly. His first novel was already on the best-seller list, a television company had optioned the series and was in the process of having the novel made into a television screenplay, and he'd just delivered his second book to his publisher. The TV series money alone would cover the major work needed at Everly.

In the face of such great amazing good luck, Catherine knew she couldn't stay angry, or at least she could not stay away from the wedding. So in June she and her family flew to Everly, along with Drew and Marjorie and Shelly. Everyone had tried to convince Kathryn to go, but she remained adamant and stayed home.

The Boxworthys had shut down the bed-and-breakfast for the summer and scheduled the renovations on Everly to start after the wedding, so there was plenty of room for all of Ann's relatives. Ned had also insisted on hiring a housekeeper and two live-in maids so that his mother and sisters could have a week of idle luxury, enjoying their guests and eating meals and drinking tea they didn't have to prepare. It was a week of indolent, often spicy, companionship as everyone got to know everyone else. Groups lingered over the enormous breakfasts or strolled together in the gardens, little boys chased each other from the grand front door through the long hallway and the swinging door to the servants' quarters, out the open back door from the kitchen to the back stoop, then around the house and back through again. Individuals flashed and regrouped and fit together like chips in a kaleidoscope: Madeline Boxworthy, Elizabeth, Tom, their six-year-old son, Maddy, their three-year-old son, Stephen, pregnant Hortense and her husband, John, Ned and Ann, Drew and Marjorie and Shelly, Kit and Catherine, and four-year-old Andrew and two-year-old Lily. It was for just such occasions that these houses had been built, Catherine thought, and remembered how much larger families used to be a century ago, with more children, fey old spinster aunties, and daft bachelor uncles all crowded together under the same roof. She tried to envision growing up at Everly with her parents and Kathryn, and the thought made her shudder. It was still the people, not the house, that made a family.

But the Eliots and the Boxworthys and the Bemishes all blended together for the week at Everly in surprising harmony. Ann greeted Catherine and Kit with perfunctory kisses and the obligatory cries of delight at seeing Andrew and Lily, but once they'd gotten over their initial wariness, she surrendered herself to the pleasures of being her parents' blue-eyed angel child. And she *was* their angel child; she had done what no one else could do, she had brought the original Everly back into the family. Marjorie and Drew had brought trunks of presents, and Marjorie had already sent over her wedding gown for Ann to wear. Marjorie hadn't offered the gown to Catherine for her wedding, Catherine remembered, then swallowed her jealousy. She had been afraid of this, that childish old envies and shallow petty wounds would revive in this celebration of her sister's marriage, and as the week passed she had to fight off crimson devils of temper that continued to prick at her. Marjorie and Drew practically ignored Andrew and Lily, who were as adorable and cherubic as children could be, in order to concentrate their adoration on Ann. Watching them, Catherine resolved to be much nicer to Kit's parents, to be grateful to them because they loved their grandchildren.

Fortunately Elizabeth and Tom and their children were there, and Catherine was able to sit in Everly's gardens, watching all the children play, talking with friends. She had been right about her children at Everly: Andrew did run, with Elizabeth's son, whooping like a maddened Indian through the gardens, and Lily did eat not only the dirt, but some of the flowers as well. Tom took Kit off several afternoons to play golf, and in the light of their husbands' friendship, Elizabeth and Catherine grew closer. Catherine almost felt at home at Everly again.

One late afternoon Catherine managed to get off by herself for a private ramble through the gardens. She'd just sat down on her favorite marble bench when she heard footsteps and saw Ned approaching.

"Hello, gorgeous," he said, sitting next to her, close to her. "I hoped I'd steal some time alone with you."

"Ned," Catherine said fondly. "Lucky Ned."

"God, yes, isn't it the truth! I do love it, you know, writing these mysteries, and I love every minute of the fuss and glory from my publishers and fans."

"And you love Ann."

"I love Ann. I do, Catherine, don't you worry about that. And I won't be the first famous Brit to be involved with a woman, then marry her younger sister!"

Catherine laughed with him. "You *are* pleased with yourself these days! Tell me.

Does Ann know that you and I — "

"*I* haven't told her. Can't see what good it would do."

"I never told her about us, either. I suppose you're right. There's no reason for her to know. It would only make her unhappy."

"No reason at all, gorgeous Catherine!" Ned said, and leaning forward, he drew her against him for a long, deep, provocative kiss.

Finally they pulled away from one another.

"Ned!" Catherine said happily, terribly pleased. "You're a cad!"

"I know. Can't help it. I do love Ann, and God knows I'll be faithful to her, but I'll always be fascinated by you. Good thing we've got the ocean between us."

"And I love Kit."

"Of course. He's perfect for you, too. Gives you stability, I can see that."

"Oh, Ned, Kit is a rock. But privately, between the two of us" — Catherine smiled, unable to find the right words — "it's *heaven,*" she finished.

"Then you're lucky, too," Ned said. He grabbed her hand and pulled her from the bench. "Come on. Let's go grace the others with our marvelous presences."

The night before the wedding the entire group gathered for a formal dinner after the rehearsal at the small village church. Everyone dressed gorgeously, and local girls were brought in to baby-sit. Champagne was served throughout the elaborate meal of trout, pheasant, roast beef with Yorkshire pudding, and fresh raspberries, vivid as jewels, with clotted cream. During dessert, countless toasts were exchanged, and since by then almost everyone was at least tipsy if not smashed, the toasts were fervent, exalted, romantic, even sappy.

Catherine's father was the last to rise. He spoke for several minutes about the glories of marriage, extolling his own happily married life, and went on to praise his youngest daughter and her superlative taste in men. He finished by saying, "Marjorie and I regret that our wedding present at this point isn't equal in richness to our joy. But we would like to announce here, now, publicly, that when we inherit the American Everly from my mother, we will give it to you, Ann, our darling daughter, and Ned, our new son, as a wedding gift. Then both Everlys will belong to one family."

"Oh, Daddy, Mummy, thank you!" Ann cried, bursting clumsily up from her place at the table to hug and kiss her parents.

Ned led the others in jolly shouts of goodwill and clapping. Kit clapped with the others while at the same time meeting Catherine's astonished eyes.

"Jesus Christ, Dad, thanks a lot!"

Catherine turned to see her brother pushing back his chair, rising. His face was red and white, blotched with anger.

Marjorie put a restraining hand on his arm. In a low voice she said, "Shelly, dear. We plan to leave the Park Avenue apartment and the Vineyard house to you. They're much more your style than that old white elephant on Long Island."

Shelly sat back down, placated. "You could have told me before I made a fool of myself," he grumbled.

"Darling, there just wasn't time." Marjorie patted his arm, then looked at Catherine, who was glaring, enraged. "Catherine, don't make a scene," she said in a low, silky voice. "You don't need anything from us. You have everything."

Before Catherine could speak, Kit leaned forward. "Yes, Marjorie, that's right. Catherine does have everything," he said.

Catherine flashed an angry look at Kit, then let her eyes fall to her plate. Voices and laughter rose around her. She worked at staying calm. She sipped her champagne and tasted bile. Stop this, she told herself. You *do* have everything. Kit's right. Grow up!

For the rest of the evening and the next day, Ann's wedding day, Catherine behaved perfectly. All the saints in heaven could have monitored her thoughts and found nothing wrong. But the next day, just before she and her family left Everly to fly back to the States, Ann hugged Catherine warmly. She whispered in Catherine's ear, "I'm so happy. I forgive you for everything!"

Catherine, smiling sweetly so the others wouldn't suspect, whispered back in the shell-shaped ear beneath Ann's golden hair, "You're a spoiled little pig, and someday I'll prove it to you!"

Ann drew back, surprised. Catherine stooped to pick up Lily, then turned to walk toward the car. She waved at the Boxworthys, at all of them, including Ann Boxworthy, Ned's wife and the next mistress of Everly.

Catherine ranted and railed about her family to Kit for months after Ann's wedding. Kit responded with patience and good humor, as well as with an almost analytic curiosity. He was an only child, and the ways of sibling rivalry were as bizarre to him as those of some aboriginal tribe. Intellectually, he could understand her sense of being wounded and abandoned, but he could not really comprehend the pain. Still, it hurt him that Catherine felt hurt, and he doubled his efforts to make her happy. Thoughtfully, he instituted a new tradition: each August they left the children with his parents in Maine and went on a trip to study a famous garden, which brought Catherine much solace and delight. The year of Ann's marriage, Kit softened Catherine's exile from the British Everly by treating her to a long stay at the Empress Hotel in Victoria and many visits to the Buchart Gardens. The year after that, they went south to see the magnolia gardens in South Carolina. The next year, to Koloa, Kauai, Hawaii. He was increasingly indispensable to Blooms, advising Catherine on legal matters and keeping her informed about current tax twists and international commerce changes that would affect her business.

Buoyed by Kit's love, busy with Blooms, and overwhelmed by her ceaseless fascination with her growing children, Catherine gradually forgot her feud with Ann. She saw little of Drew and Marjorie, and when she did see them the visits only spurred her to spend more time with Andrew and Lily. She had an office set up in her White River home so that she could work from there while her children were at play school and kindergarten. That worked so well that she spent more and more time at home. Every day that she drove her children to school and picked them up again she considered a triumph of management on her part, a solid expression of her love. She was there for them — to kiss a scraped knee or praise a finger painting or share a joke. They were such golden children, so good, so happy, and as they grew it was as if she were growing all over again herself, this time growing with love.

In the spring of 1978, Ann sent the news that she was pregnant. That Saturday it rained, and Kit had both children with him at the Museum of Natural History so Catherine could spend the afternoon at Blooms. Catherine sat with Shelly in his office, going over orders and accounts, and when they'd finished with the business she leaned back in her chair and studied her brother.

He was twenty-nine and looked younger, but Sandra had apologetically reported that he was showing up at Blooms drunk more often, that he seemed bored with his work, that he wasn't keeping up with it. He seemed increasingly dissatisfied and restless; he wouldn't inherit his parents' property for years, so he got no immediate joy from that. He was not essential to anyone or anything. He needs *connection*, Catherine thought.

"Shelly," she said now, "do you think you'll ever get married?"

Shelly looked startled, then let out a burst of laughter.

"You've got to be kidding." He rose from his chair, crossed to open a secretary, and poured himself a Scotch. "Want one?"

"No, thanks. I'm serious. Don't you ever think about settling down?"

"Never. And you'd better thank your lucky stars I don't. Your business would go under if I ever singled one woman out."

Catherine swallowed her immediate rush of anger. "Do you think so?" she asked, keeping her voice pleasant.

"Yes, 'I think so,' " Shelly said, mimicking her tone, prissing it up a little. This, Catherine knew, was how he got when he'd been drinking, but so far he'd had only a sip of Scotch — although she didn't know what he'd had for lunch. "Look, Catherine, at least half the contacts Blooms has are ones I've made for you. I'm at every party, every dance, every gallery opening — "

"It's really a sacrifice for you, I know." Catherine couldn't resist the dig.

"No, it's *not* a sacrifice, hell, did I say *sacrifice?* But you should know that I bring in a lot of business for you. Every time some newspaper or magazine runs a photo of me with some society broad at a fancy party, it's like a free ad for you. Not to mention that I keep your employees happy for you, now that you've deserted them all. Especially Carla."

"I hope you're not leading little Carla to think you're serious about her!"

"Give me a break, Catherine." Shelly rose to pour himself more Scotch.

"Oh, Shelly. I don't know. This seems wrong, somehow. I never get bored with my business because it's mine. Also, I really love working with flowers, coming up with new ideas. But what you're doing — don't you get bored?"

"Sometimes."

"Shelly, I have an idea. I've often worried about the fact that we don't have a liaison in Amsterdam. Not that I don't trust Piet — I'm not saying that at all. But since this importing business started up just when I was having the children, I haven't been able to set it up to my satisfaction. I haven't even been there. I mean, if Piet dropped dead tomorrow, I wouldn't know whom to contact over there, or how to check the books. How would you like to go to Amsterdam for a while?"

Shelly grinned. "I'd like that. I'd like that a lot."

In the late seventies wildflowers became the

rage, and Catherine was ready. From Everly's overflowing gardens she picked goldenrod, Queen Anne's lace, maidenhair ferns, honeysuckle, blue globe thistle, and luscious overblown climbing roses, which she gathered in opulent drooping bouquets, stuck in buckets of water in the Blooms van, and drove into the city to sell for hundreds of dollars. The only problem was that she was the one who had to do the actual picking, because she didn't want to offend Kathryn by sending out one of her employees. Kathryn didn't mind Catherine planting and plucking in her gardens, but she steadily refused to enter into any routine agreement with Blooms. The one time Catherine had been bold enough to bring Manuel with her to help her lift and carry, Kathryn had refused to come out of the house to meet him, had refused that day to come out even to see Catherine.

Catherine was often frustrated by Kathryn's peculiarities, and at the same time she was ashamed of herself for wanting to use her grandmother's home for her own profit. As the months and years went by, it became increasingly difficult to talk with Kathryn. Probably she was not as deaf as she pretended old age had made her, but it was a mask she could hide behind whenever she chose, and she often chose to hide.

On this October afternoon, however, Kathryn was outside, lying on her wicker chaise in the sun, dressed in sweaters and scarves, covered with a plaid wool blanket. Clara was napping in the house. Tea sat cooling on the nearby table, but there were plenty of cakes left for the children. Andrew and Lily were sailing a twig-and-leaf boat back and forth to each other across the lily pond. Catherine sat on a lawn chair, enjoying this moment of peace.

She had come out to Everly to pick great burlap bags of autumn leaves for some Blooms arrangements. Andrew was six now, Lily four, old enough to understand that they had to behave with a modicum of good manners around their ancient great-grandmother. Kathryn seemed to enjoy seeing them. "My dears," she said. "Come here. Let me hold you. Goodness, your face is as smooth as a rose petal." She said this to Andrew, who smiled politely enough at Kathryn, then turned away and rolled his eyes and grimaced at Catherine, who winked at him in reply. "You have fairy-tale hair," Kathryn said to Lily. "Princess hair. You were appropriately named."

Catherine had taken the children with her into the forest and fields to gather up the leaves. It was a rare autumn day, with warm yet dry air and the sun so low and glowing that light seemed to flare from inside the earth, the trees, the flowers. Grasses burned amber, berries shone like amethysts. I would like to be buried here, Catherine thought. She could imagine her body stretched out under these expansive maples; her spirit would soar up their trunks and out over their outstretched arms into the sky with the ease of smoke up a chimney. Forest creatures would feast on her eyes and entrails, smacking their lips over her, gnawing at her bones with tiny pointed teeth — somehow the image filled her with pleasure.

She thought a lot about death these days, but not morbidly. Anyone with children was forced to face the idea of their own mortality in planning for their children's future, and of course there was Kathryn, practically dissolving back into the universe before their eyes. Kathryn didn't seem afraid of death. But then Kathryn remained a mystery. Once Catherine had tried to raise the topic of death: "I've thought it would be nice to be cremated and my ashes sprinkled over these gardens," she said, hoping that Kathryn would tell her what she herself desired. But Kathryn had said only, "That would probably be good for the flowers."

Several times Kit had suggested to Catherine that she plan an elaborate garden at their White River home, but Catherine found the thought unappealing, though she couldn't say quite why. Perhaps it was that she didn't want to impose her own obsession on her children. There were some flowers there, of course, the easy spring and summer bulbs, the democratic phlox and chrysanthemums, and many flowering fruit trees. But most of their land was taken up by the barn, the riding ring, and the pasture for the ponies and horses. The children loved riding, and sledding in the winter, simply running like gypsies all times of the year — and Catherine didn't want a garden to interfere with all that.

Really, she knew that her heart belonged to Everly, and Kit knew that as well. If Kathryn did leave it to Drew and Marjorie, and thus to Ann, then perhaps Catherine would turn to their White River home, to begin the mammoth undertaking of gardens there. But if Kathryn willed Everly to Catherine . . . Catherine shifted on her chair. She wouldn't think ahead. She wouldn't sit here like a vulture, waiting for her grandmother to die.

"All right, children," she said, pushing out of her chair and going down to the lily pond. "Let's get back to work. We need to gather some grasses for my window."

CHAPTER 11

New York
November 1988

"Since they're so expensive, why don't we put spring flowers in the guest rooms . . . and in all the rooms!"

Catherine smiled at the beautiful young woman seated across from her. Recognizing her youth and her eagerness to please, Catherine behaved charitably toward her. She would never forget what it was like to be young, confused, needing advice and direction.

But it was not kindness alone that motivated Catherine; it was also good business sense. Wide-eyed, doll-sweet Melody Dewey was the new, second wife of Braden Dewey, president of the Metropolitan Bank of New York, and a long-standing, important customer of Blooms. Braden had been one of Catherine's first major clients twenty-three years ago when she was just starting out. Now they ran in the same social set. Braden would count on her subtly to educate his new wife — who was a good two decades younger than he — in the ways of dignity and protocol. Any girl named Melody in the Dewey social set would need help, and this girl, as fully pulchritudinous and smooth-skinned as a rubber doll, needed all the help she could get.

"Melody, I think spring flowers in *all* the rooms would be . . ." Catherine paused. The words *tacky* and *ostentatious* sprang to her lips, but she bit them back. Melody was a nice young woman. Also she now had access to enormous amounts of money, and she was innately smart. Braden wouldn't have married her otherwise. When she realized how Catherine had helped her, she would come back to Blooms again and again.

Catherine could have made several thousand dollars on this one order for the upcoming visit of Braden Dewey's former school chum, now the president of a prestigious Ivy League college, and his wife. Instead she steered Melody toward a more moderate course.

"*Unnecessary.* If you have them on the table for your dinner party, they'll be a delightful surprise. A sort of *event*. For the rest of the time, it's usually best to use seasonal flowers. Flowers provide the appropriate mood and embellishment for each time of the year. This is especially important in the city, where we're deprived of nature. People like having chrysanthemums and dahlias, or bittersweet berries and wild grape vines around them in the fall, just as we enjoy a wood fire or paisley velvets in the fall more than we would in July."

Melody listened carefully, soaking it all in. She was so pleasant a pupil that when Catherine finally showed her to the door, she thought about saying, "And Melody, a bit less jewelry would be more effective than flashing it all at once."

But it was too soon for that suggestion. As an established society florist, Catherine acted as interior decorator, party organizer, trendsetter, educator, therapist, and counselor. When invited to comment, from time to time she also played the role of fashion consultant, but she needed to know Melody better before offering such personal advice.

Besides, this session had already gone far beyond the hour budgeted in her schedule. It was seven o'clock; everyone else had gone home. Kit would be here in only a few minutes; when he'd called from his office earlier today he'd said he had something serious to discuss with her.

Now Catherine said good-bye to Melody and gratefully shut the door. She took a deep breath, kicked off her high heels, and paused to appreciate these few moments of peace.

Just looking at her office refreshed her. She had made it as much like a summer garden as any room on the tenth floor of a gray-stone Park Avenue building could be. The thick carpet was pale grass green. The heavy drapes were patterned in pink roses, lilies as orange as melons, amethyst irises, which swirled together on dark green stems against a creamy chintz background. This material had also been used to cover the long deep sofa and a wing chair where she and Melody had sat together in the far corner of the room, looking at the photographs and sketches and Blooms brochures that were arranged on the square glass coffee table.

A hollowed-out pumpkin, lacquered and filled with a loose arrangement of enormous yellow sunflowers, cattails, and bittersweet, was centered on the coffee table. Near it was the silver tray with the Limoges tea service. Catherine had served Melody China tea and tiny cakes and, later, a small glass of dry sherry. The small utility kitchen, complete with stove, microwave, and a refrigerator stocked with champagne, chocolate, fruit, and pastries, was hidden behind one wall of her office.

That wall, paneled in carved, beveled mahogany, also hid an enormous television set,

VCR, and compact disc system, all state-of-the-art. Catherine had chosen mahogany for that wall because it matched the massive Empire desk her grandmother had given her twenty-four years ago, when Catherine had bought Blooms. Catherine's grandfather had used that desk, and Catherine thought it brought good luck.

Not easy luck, but good luck.

All those years ago, when she had bought this flower shop, she had not had the money to buy an apartment or a car or even the right kinds of clothes.

Now she could buy anything she wanted, and the paintings on the walls of her office were testimony to that. Above her desk hung a Georgia O'Keeffe of white lilies. On the wall above the sitting area hung a seventeenth-century Dutch oil of a massive bouquet of flowers, and a small Renoir of lush glowing pink roses hung next to a smaller Impressionist oil of flowers in a spotted pitcher painted by Vanessa Bell at Charleston.

Success, she thought, and remembered Kit. Too often it seemed she forgot that Kit was not only her children's father and, since Mr. Giles's death, Blooms' lawyer, but also her husband and lover as well. Now she slipped into her private bathroom, brushed her hair, freshened her lipstick, and carefully drew a stripe of dark brown just above her eyelashes.

Like everything else these days, the sight of her own face and body was bittersweet. Sweet because finally she had learned to accept herself and because it was a face and body that had been used. She had given birth to children, she had made love, she had laughed and cried and fought and cheered; she had seduced men with this body, and with this body she had surrendered everything. And that too was sweet; her life on earth had been full, as this body and face attested.

But she was no longer young, and all the face creams and exercises and aerobics and fresh-fruit diets in the world could not change that fact — and that was bitter.

She knew that she could still be stunning. Because she had made herself rich, she could afford certain helpful luxuries: weekly massages, manicures and pedicures, shampoos and expensive cuts for her wild curly dark hair, fabulous clothes. Her body, always curvaceous, was now voluptuous, and she had her own designer and dressmaker, who garbed her in outfits like the one she was wearing. Under a suit of heathery silk-and-wool tweed, a white silk shirt parted just above the curving cleavage of her breasts, so that the severe and businesslike cut of the suit was softened by the hint of creamy lace and creamier skin. She wore real pearls at her ears. Her only other jewels today were her wedding ring and diamond engagement ring, her watch, and, on her suit, between her breast and shoulder, her trademark jewel, an outrageously expensive bouquet of flowers, suitable for the woman who owned Blooms, of rubies, emeralds, sapphires, diamonds, and pearls. She had chosen and paid for this piece herself. An extravagance, perhaps, and yet in its way therapeutic. Over the years she had come to rely so much on Kit's opinions and judgment that now and then she got frightened, nervous — couldn't she think for herself? She'd never meant to be so dependent on any man, and the brooch reminded her that she didn't need to be.

Kit's knock on her office door broke her reverie. She hurried to let him in. They kissed briefly, and she could tell at once that it didn't matter what she looked like today. He was worried.

"Would you like some coffee, Kit? A drink?"

"I'll take a Scotch. And you'd better get one for yourself. Catherine, I think you've got a problem on your hands. With Shelly. Or, perhaps, Piet."

"All right," Catherine said calmly, pouring

their drinks. Kit never could understand the emotional responses her brother and sister aroused in her — how she could criticize them bitterly at one moment, only to jump to a feline defense of them whenever anyone else dared attack them. Catherine couldn't understand this herself, but over the years Kit had pointed out her often illogical explosiveness, and now Catherine tried to monitor her reactions.

"Sit down, Catherine. Just listen to me a minute. Sandra came to see me today. She's upset. She thinks Blooms is being cheated out of a great deal of money. She — "

"Wait a minute! Why did Sandra come to you? She's my employee!"

"First of all, I suppose, because I've been Blooms' lawyer ever since Mr. Giles died. More important, because she knew this would upset you, so she thought I should be the one to tell you."

"That's ridiculous!"

"Maybe so. But Sandra said that she's noticed for quite a while that our profits are down. She's checked and rechecked the books and records. She was certain that something was wrong, and then about two weeks ago Carla called in sick. Carla's the one who receives the shipments of flowers from Amsterdam and checks them against the invoice.

Carla initials the invoice if it's correct or marks it if a change is needed, then sends the paperwork on up to Sandra, who pays the invoices."

"I know all that. Why are you telling me — "

"Wait. The day Carla was sick, Amsterdam invoiced us for twenty boxes more than we received. When Sandra mentioned this to Carla, she said casually, 'Oh, that happens sometimes. I usually catch it.' But it bothered Sandra, especially since our profits have been down. So she asked Jason — "

"I don't believe this. I don't believe she didn't come to me right away!"

" — to try to count the boxes when they're delivered, without letting Carla know he was doing it. Three times he's done it during the past two weeks, and each time Carla's count was almost exactly twenty boxes higher."

"Perhaps the truckers — "

"Sandra's husband rode with the truckers the last three days. He counted the boxes that Amsterdam shipped to Blooms as they were loaded on the truck at the airport and unloaded at the shop's back door. Then he called Sandra with the count. Each day Carla initialed invoices stating that we got twenty boxes more than were delivered."

"Sandra talked to her husband about this

before coming to me!"

"Catherine, Sandra was worried. This is a major accusation. She didn't want to come to you until she had reasonable proof. She knows how you feel about your employees — she was afraid this would devastate you. She's more worried about your emotional state than the state of Blooms' finances. And of course, she's worried about Carla."

"Good old Sandra," Catherine said with a sigh. "I mean it. Good for her for noticing all this." She ran her hands over her neck to ease the tension. "Well. So it looks like Carla is a little snake."

"She's not doing this alone. Someone in Holland has to be doing this with her. Amsterdam's billing us for more than they're sending us. Carla's covering, and they split the profit."

"When you say 'Amsterdam,' you mean Shelly or Piet."

Kit nodded uncomfortably. "You can see why Sandra was reluctant to talk to you. To accuse your own brother of stealing from your company — that takes a lot of nerve."

"It may not be Shelly or Piet. It could be some other employee over there, someone who's talked regularly with Carla."

"That's a possibility."

"I have to go to Amsterdam."

As she spoke the words, pleasure flowed through her, warming her heart, setting her fingertips tingling. She would see Piet again, after all these years, walk the streets of a city she'd never seen, hear a language she didn't speak; she would be a woman alone and free.

She looked at Kit, suddenly guilty. Had he read her mind? Had she given herself away, had she smiled?

"I could go," Kit said.

"No. I need to be the one. I'll go tonight. I want to surprise him — whoever it is. I'll say I've come to see the *Bloemenveiling*, which will be the truth. I've never seen it. I'll call Piet after I've gotten there, and tell him I want to see the auction, then I'll ask him to let me see his offices — then the books."

"You're going to just come right out and ask Piet to show you his books?"

"What else can I do? I can't very well just show up at the offices and start searching through desk drawers. I have to bet on someone, and my bet is that it isn't Piet. His company is too large for a swindle this small. I'm sure he has someone else doing the invoicing. Besides, I just don't think Piet would be stupid enough to jeopardize our business relationship. Carla and her accomplice can't be making the kind of money that would interest him."

"All right," Kit agreed. "I see your point. And I agree someone should go now, before Carla realizes there's any suspicion on our parts. Let's go to the apartment. I'll get a plane reservation for you while you pack. I'll drive you to the airport."

"And you'll hold down the fort at home," Catherine said. She crossed the room and wrapped her arms around him. "I don't know what I'd do without you."

"I don't know what I'd do without you. Be careful over there."

Kit booked a first-class seat for her on a nine o'clock KLM flight. Catherine tossed clothes and papers in a suitcase. As Kit drove her to Kennedy, they went over the details of their plan. Both Andrew and Lily were at boarding school this year and so happy there that they seldom called home. Catherine would probably be back in the States before they even knew she'd left. She intended to stay in Amsterdam only two or three days at the most. Kit would call Sandra in the morning; he'd tell her that Catherine was in bed with a bad flu. Sandra could pass the word along so Carla wouldn't suspect that Catherine had gone to Amsterdam. And Catherine promised to call Kit as soon as she had any news.

In spite of her excitement, Catherine managed to sleep a bit on the flight over, but by the time she'd gone through customs and checked into the Amsterdam Hilton, she was exhausted. It was noon in Amsterdam, dawn in New York. The auction and packaging of flowers would already be over for today. So she showered, left a wake-up call, and collapsed into a deep sleep.

At four-thirty the phone woke her. Immediately, she was alert, her brain clear. She dialed the GardenAir office number, and in only seconds a secretary had put her through to Piet.

"Piet. This is Catherine. I have a surprise for you. I'm in Amsterdam. I've come over to see the *Bloemenveiling*."

"You're here now?"

"Yes. I arrived this morning. I've already caught up on my sleep."

"This is a surprise. Well. Shall we have dinner tonight?"

"That would be lovely."

"Shall I call Shelly and ask him to join us?"

"No. As a matter of fact, Piet, I'd like you to do me a favor. Don't tell Shelly I've called. Don't tell him I'm here. Not yet."

"Ah. So you are here not just for the auction."

"I'd rather discuss this with you in person, Piet."

"Very well. I'll pick you up at seven."

Catherine showered and dressed carefully. She and Kit had been married for sixteen years now. There were times when she thought she would happily have murdered him for his obsession with *The New York Times* crossword puzzle or some other daily ritual. When Kit was engrossed with that damned crossword puzzle, she knew she could crawl across the carpet naked and bleeding, and he wouldn't look down until he'd finished the last word. There were also times, she knew, when Kit wanted to murder her, usually for being too impetuous, too neurotic. In the middle of a peaceful Sunday afternoon she might decide she needed to visit her grandmother at Everly. Or she'd have a great idea for a new flower arrangement, and she'd want to rush into her office to work. Often she made major decisions about their house or children without first discussing it with him. It was the children they fought about most of all: Kit was more of a disciplinarian, while Catherine was quick to give and forgive.

But over the years they had tempered each other. They knew this, and it pleased them.

Catherine had learned to share more with Kit, because she had learned to trust him. Most and best of all, never in all the times of anger or bitter disagreement had she stopped wanting him. Even now there were moments at business meetings in the Blooms conference room when Catherine would look down the length of the table to see her husband speaking in his utterly calm, rational, reasonable way, and she would flash on how different he was in bed, how passionate, demanding, abandoned, ardent. She would be flushed, flustered, and as happy as a young girl in love for the first time. She had never been unfaithful to him, and he had never been unfaithful to her.

And she did not want to go to bed with Piet. But she couldn't help but think that it would be nice if he wanted to go to bed with her. He had never married. He hadn't been back to the States for several years. He and Catherine spoke often about business, but for the past few years Shelly had been their main contact. The international life had been good for Shelly, Catherine had thought, had given her brother a sufficient taste of an exotic, challenging world in which Shelly had seemed to thrive.

Catherine looked at herself one last time in the mirror. She had put on an Escada suit whose stained-glass hues set off her coloring. She couldn't help it. She wanted Piet to find her ravishing.

And she could not help it when she saw him in the lobby and her heart leapt like a bird, exploding from its cage, flaring and soaring and swooping. He still frightened and excited her at the same time.

Piet was wearing a beautifully cut custom-made suit complete with vest and Italian shoes of leather as supple as silk. From the neck down he looked like a prosperous, respectable, even bourgeois businessman. But his sleek black hair was pulled straight back and tied with a black velvet ribbon into a short, low ponytail, emphasizing the angles and arches of his face and eyebrows. He looked as diabolically seductive as dark wine.

They kissed lightly, European style. As the hot perfume of his cloved breath brushed her cheek, Catherine swayed. She had to put her hand on his arm to steady herself. Jet lag, perhaps, but she felt giddy.

Piet was a gentleman as always and said nothing about her brief weakness. He spoke about Amsterdam and the world news as he escorted her into his car and to the d'Viff Vlieghen restaurant. Not until they were seated almost in secrecy in one of the dark, museum-like rooms and had ordered their dinner did he ask her why she had come.

Catherine looked across the table at Piet. Old lover, old friend, she thought.

"You say you've come to see the *Bloemenveiling*," Piet said, smiling.

"I do want to see the auction. But there's something else. Piet, I'm taking a chance by telling you this. I'm assuming you'll be truthful with me."

Piet shrugged but smiled at the same time, and the smile was also in his eyes.

Catherine took a deep breath. "We have reason to believe, at home, that you — no, wait. That *someone* in your company is billing us for more flowers than we're receiving." She told him all that Kit had told her, watching to see if she could read any reaction in his face.

He seemed displeased, but not anxious.

"I'm sorry to hear this. Twenty boxes a day can amount to quite a considerable sum over time. How long has this been going on?"

"We have no idea. It would be impossible to judge by our records. Our profits have been dropping for some time, but of course there are all sorts of variables to consider."

"Carla still receives the shipments and checks the invoices at your end. Correct?"

"Yes."

Piet sighed. "Well, my dearest Catherine,

472

I have no choice but to tell you. Shelly is the one who oversees the packaging and the invoicing. Tomorrow morning I'll take you through the auction from start to finish so you can see how it's done."

"But then he'll know I'm here."

"Tonight, after our meal, I'll take you out to my offices. We'll check his desks."

"Does he have a private office?"

"Oh, yes. With a lock and key. But your brother is a charming man, don't forget. He has many admirers at my offices. One of them keeps a key to his office in her desk drawer, and I have access to that desk."

"I'm sorry to ask you for this. I'll be very sorry if it's Shelly who's colluding with Carla. Perhaps I was wrong to send him over here, but I needed someone from New York to know how this side works. Shelly was bored. He wanted more responsibility in the company."

"I don't think you made a mistake. Shelly works hard. And he has learned to speak excellent Dutch. He is respected and very much liked."

"In New York he ran with a rather fast crowd. He still does, when he's home. Lots of parties. Lots of drinking. Just like my father."

"Yes, he's that way here, too. And more

473

than drinking, Catherine. Although I don't want to be what you Americans call a rat on your brother."

"What do you mean, more than drinking? What can be more than drinking? Is he gambling?"

"No, no — "

"Prostitutes?"

"Your brother does not need to resort to prostitutes — "

"Well, what are you saying?"

"Catherine, you're so naive. What I'm saying is that Shelly, like most young men of his social level, tends to indulge now and then in drugs. Specifically, cocaine."

"Oh, Piet, no. Are you certain?"

"I've never actually witnessed him using it, no. But I've heard things recently. And if he's developed a habit, it would explain why he's started ripping you off. God! What a stupid thing to do!" Piet finally sounded angry.

"We don't know that it's Shelly. It could be someone else."

"I don't think so. When we go over the books, we'll have a clearer idea. But don't look so miserable, Catherine. Forget about that for now. Enjoy your meal. The food is delicious. Tell me about your life."

Catherine relaxed. She sipped her wine,

which was delicious, a ruby Burgundy that swirled through her body, releasing memories, tight buds, large blossoms, velvet petals of remembrance. For just a few moments she held herself back from her usual rush through life. She let herself look at Piet. She let the memories stain her body from inside.

"I'm very happy, Piet. Kit is a wonderful husband, and my children are healthy and as happy as adolescents can be." Suddenly, the wine made her bold. "Piet, I've always wondered. If I hadn't been engaged to Kit when you returned — what would have happened?"

Piet studied Catherine, his eyes serious. She had forgotten how dark his eyes were, not black, but the deepest purple.

"I loved you," he said. He said it as easily, as simply, as saying hello, and Catherine was shocked. "I think you loved me. And I still care for you, I always will. But you and I are strong individuals, ruthless in our ways. I am very powerfully drawn and connected to Amsterdam. I worked in the States to get established, but I am only at home here. I think the same is true for you. You are at home in New York, and perhaps at your grandmother's. Oh, I suppose that long ago, when I was young and full of foolish dreams, I intended to present you with a fait accompli, the wholesale business, a partnership, and marriage. But it wouldn't have worked. You would have been unhappy here. I would have been unhappy there. Besides, you're too bossy."

He had taken her through a range of emotions in the few moments he spoke, and his final words made her burst into laughter of appreciation and relief.

"Oh, dear Piet," she said, reaching across the table for his hand. "I did love you so much at one time. You're right, I still care for you. I wish someone loved you madly."

Piet smiled. "Don't worry. Someone does."

"Tell me about her!"

"I think we'd better turn back to business instead. It's getting late. It will take about an hour to drive out to Aalsmeer. Have you finished your coffee?"

"Damn you, Piet! You like keeping yourself secret from me, don't you? Why?"

Piet shrugged. "It's just my way, I suppose. Just my nature."

It was pitch black when she and Piet slid into his small dark Peugeot. As Catherine shut her door, she realized how intimate European cars were compared with American ones. She could hardly avoid touching him as they sat side by side. She could not help but breathe in his clear spice scent.

476

"We are going south and a little west, back toward Schiphol airport, and past it to Aalsmeer," Piet said. "Did you know that Schiphol lies thirteen feet below sea level? All this area is a polder, hollow land claimed from water. In fact, we are driving along the top of the dike that keeps the polder dry. If you had come in the spring or summer, I could treat you to a beautiful sight — seventy miles of bulb fields in bloom. However, in November the fields are not such a pretty sight. I'll show you the hothouses instead. All the flowers are grown in about eight hundred acres of land and nurseries all around Aalsmeer, so there is no time lost in getting the flowers to the auction fresh. Tomorrow we'll see the *Bloemenveiling*. Tonight, my offices.

"You know, when I first started wholesaling by air, I was only working with you. GardenAir. That is still the only wholesale business I have with the U.S. Shelly came to Amsterdam about the time I was expanding, so it worked nicely for me to put him in charge of the GardenAir export business. But for various reasons, some to do with my mania for privacy" — in the dark Catherine saw the flash of Piet's smile — "I have kept the U.S., and GardenAir, separate from the rest of my export business — separate offices, separate staffs — though we're all in the same building.

"All the flowers I export to the U.S. go through GardenAir, exclusive with you. But as you know, in the past two years the value of the American dollar has dropped. So America has to pay almost twice what it used to pay for each stem — and as a result, I am exporting to the U.S. perhaps half of the amount of roses, carnations, and mums we did only two or three years ago."

"Yes. I know. We're starting to buy a lot from Colombia now. They fly flowers fresh into Miami each day."

"Well, I export all over Europe, and I'm developing a branch with the Far East. You are welcome to inspect all my books, but I think you will really need only to look in Shelly's office. Here we are."

Piet's company was housed in a modern and rather ugly stone-and-glass building. He led Catherine through a maze of low-ceilinged rooms, switching on lights as he went. He stopped in a warren of desks to fish a key out of a secretary's desk drawer, then unlocked the door to Shelly's private quarters.

Shelly's office was unmistakably his — the domain of a handsome, wealthy man, a man who didn't take his work too seriously. A low comfortable sofa stretched along one wall;

across from it was a long teak table holding a CD player and shelves of cassettes, a television and VCR, and a silver tray with lots of glasses, a selection of alcohol, an ice bucket. The walls were hung with photos of Shelly with family and friends, for here was a picture of Andrew and Lily and Kit and Catherine, and here was a picture of Ann, Ned, and their son, Percy. An exercise bike sat in one corner and next to it a chrome valet covered with clean terrycloth towels. An unobtrusive door led into a small private bathroom.

Almost incidentally, there was also a desk in the room, and Catherine sank down onto the leather chair behind it.

"Would you like me to leave you alone? I could go to my office — "

"No. Stay. Please."

"Of course." Piet poured himself a drink and sat on the sofa.

Catherine flipped through the piles of papers on Shelly's desk, finding only normal forms and letters, some recent memos from her. The middle drawer and the two top side drawers were filled with necessary paraphernalia: pens, pencils, paper clips, boxes of staples, letterhead stationery and envelopes, stamps, Scotch adhesive tape, rubber bands, labels, stickers. In the second drawer she found only a pile of men's magazines.

"I might have to get into the computer," she said.

"I can do that for you."

"Wait a minute." Catherine had opened the bottom drawer, a deep file cabinet. Mixed in between folders of letters were two green account ledgers. Catherine pulled them out. "Piet, come look at these with me." She placed them on top of the desk and opened them. "The arrogant little fool! Couldn't he go to a little more trouble to conceal his stealing!"

Piet bent over Catherine's shoulder, reading, then switched on the computer and punched a few keys. After a few minutes he said, "Look. This book matches with what is printed out on the computer, here in our office, and what is sent on to you with each shipment. It shows exactly twenty less sent every day than what is entered in *this* book."

"I'm taking these books with me," Catherine said. "God damn Shelly! I could kill him!"

"What are you going to do?" Piet's voice was cool, curious, almost amused.

"I'm going to fire him, of course. How dare he steal from Blooms!"

"Catherine. If he has developed a drug habit . . ."

"Yes? What if he has?"

"You might want to do more than fire

480

him. What I'm saying is that he might need help. Getting off it. An addiction — "

"Don't make me responsible for my brother again — I'm not his mother! I've done what I could to make his life work out for him. It's not my duty to take care of my brother for his entire life!"

"All right, Catherine. I'm sorry. Forgive me. Please. Calm down. Here. Have a drink."

"I'm just so angry at him, Piet. That he would betray me — cheat me! Doesn't he have any responsibility for himself?"

"Please. Catherine. Look, let me take you home now. You're tired, and we have to get up early tomorrow."

They rode back to Amsterdam in silence. Catherine cradled the two account ledgers against her chest. She was too tired to think and gave Piet a perfunctory good-night kiss on his cheek when they arrived at the hotel. As soon as she was back in her room, she put through a call to Kit. It was after midnight in Amsterdam, but only evening in New York. Briefly she explained what she and Piet had found. She still wanted to see the *Bloemenveiling*, she told Kit, but she planned to fly home that evening. She was very tired, and sadly, she had accomplished what she'd come for.

Almost. She still wanted to see the flower

auction, so she left a wake-up call for three-thirty and was ready at four-thirty in the morning. Piet had warned her there would be a lot of walking, so she wore a cashmere sweater with jeans and loafers, and her mink coat and scarf. Piet was waiting for her just outside the hotel. It was still dark, and slightly misty.

"Are you tired?" Piet asked as she slid in next to him.

"Tired? I don't even know. I feel the way I did when Drew and Lily were first born — exhausted but functioning."

"Why not lean back and nap? We'll have almost an hour. It will be too dark to see anything, and there's nothing to see in November anyway."

"I doubt if I could fall asleep," Catherine said. "I feel a little crazy. I keep thinking about Shelly, all I've done for him. He's my brother! How could he do this to me!"

"I'm sure he doesn't think of it that way. That he's doing it to you. I think Shelly sees you as being terribly self-sufficient, even invulnerable. And he wasn't taking enough money to really damage Blooms." Piet leaned forward and switched the radio onto a classical station. "Relax. Lean back. Close your eyes."

Catherine obeyed, even though she was certain she wouldn't sleep. And she didn't sleep, but her mind drifted free on the humming of the car's engine and the music.

Piet's voice broke into her daze. "Ah, Catherine, there it is. Wake up — you can see it, the *Centrale Aalsmeerse Bloemenveiling*. It is only two stories high, but in terms of floor space, it is the largest building in the world."

Yawning, Catherine opened her eyes and saw a streak of dawn light illuminating the dark around an enormous building sprawling in the midst of a flat landscape. Piet drove his way past armies of cars, vans, and trucks through a parking lot and around to the side.

"There are many wings in this building. Many different auction rooms. I will take you to the wing that is only for export. The Dutch and local people can't buy here; they have their own wing. There are auction rooms for potted plants, cut flowers, bulbs, roses. Roses are very important always. I will take you to the rose auction. You'll like it."

The bright lights of the corridors and rooms of the auction building jarred Catherine awake as she trailed behind Piet. She was here at last! Most of the flowers she and Jason and Leonard placed in their arrangements began their mornings here, fresh-picked from the acres of hothouses and greenhouses in Aalsmeer. They passed groups of men, most of whom nodded and greeted Piet. She saw few women. She was aware of how foreign she looked.

"Here," Piet said, pushing a door open for her. "The roses."

Inside the echoing, gleaming hall were hundreds of thousands of long-stemmed roses, laid in bunches on dozens of carts. Mostly the roses were the much loved deep red, but there were also white, yellow, and every shade of red ranging from pale pink through coral to vermilion.

"Everything here has been inspected by the auction commissioners and the price negotiated and established with the grower," Piet said. "Also the buyers, like me, must inspect the roses and compare what is available with what we need. The roses are sold in bundles of twenty-five or fifty. Depending on what Blooms and GardenAir needs for any given day, I buy around a thousand or more lots each day. Now follow me. I will introduce you to Harrie Brouwer, my main buyer. He inspects the flowers on each cart and makes note of which carts have the flowers we want."

Catherine looked around cautiously. "Will Shelly be here?"

"Probably not. Not in this room. He comes in at the other end of all this. He supervises the packing and attaching the appropriate invoices and loading. He'll be in another room. We'll go there after the auction." He turned. "Harrie, I want you to meet Catherine Bemish. The owner of Blooms. She's finally come to see our auction."

"I hope you enjoy it, Mrs. Bemish," Harrie said formally.

Then a Dutch voice over a loudspeaker announced that the auction was about to begin. Piet led Catherine up the banked seating arena to their seats. At each desk, each wholesaler had in front of him a microphone and a computerized button linked electronically to a gigantic clocklike machine on the wall. Piet explained to Catherine that the numbers at the rim of the clock were the price, in Dutch guilders, of each lot of roses, beginning with the top price agreed upon beforehand by the grower and descending as the clock hand moved clockwise. Television screens set on walls displayed the quantity of roses, the length, the precise color, the name, and the set bottom price the roses had to bring in order to be sold.

The room buzzed with activity. It was always a gamble, Piet told Catherine, for the buyers to get the amount and quality of roses they needed at the lowest-possible price, but before another broker had bought them. Overpayment of even a few cents each day could eventually bankrupt a company, while buying carefully could make the company wealthy.

Today, for example, Harrie Brouwer needed to buy five hundred lots of red roses for export. The Dutch guilder, like the American dollar, was divided into 100 cents, and the clock started ticking at 100 cents per rose, which was approximately 50 American cents per rose. Harrie watched breathlessly as the clock hand ticked down to 99 cents, 98 cents, and at 88 cents he pressed his button, stopping the clock. He then spoke into the microphone in Dutch, and immediately the television screens recorded that he had bought five hundred lots of twenty-five red roses for 88 cents a rose. The remaining amount of roses would now be sold for less than 88 cents, but Harrie had gotten the quantity and quality of roses he needed.

Several lots of roses were not bid on at the price the grower had demanded, and as Catherine watched, those roses moved along a conveyor belt through a glass wall to a chopping machine. Mechanized knife blades rapidly sliced through hundreds of luscious blood-red blooms.

"Oh, Piet, look! What a waste! All those lovely roses!" Catherine whispered, not wanting to disturb Harrie's concentration.

"It's necessary," Piet said. "To keep the market up and stable. So that these roses don't go out through the back door to be sold on a black market. The only way they can be sold is in this building. It protects the market."

"It's bizarre," Catherine said. "Like the American government paying farmers not to grow wheat to protect the American market, while millions of people are starving for bread all over the world."

"If you want to change it, you have a lot of work in front of you," Piet said, smiling.

When the auction ended, Piet led Catherine to the shed where the flowers Harrie had bought were being speedily bundled into special air freight boxes, all bearing the GardenAir or Blooms label. The room was cool. Rough-looking men, much like the men on 28th Street in New York, were handling the fragile long-stemmed flowers with practiced efficiency.

And there, in the midst of the work tables and carts, clipboard in hand, was Shelly.

Catherine clutched Piet's arm, signaling him silently. They watched as Shelly supervised another man bundling flowers into the boxes. Shelly wrote something on his clipboard. The air was full of laughter and the guttural grace of the Dutch language.

Catherine had decided not to confront Shelly yet; she didn't want him to call Carla. So now she smiled, trying to look happy to see him.

"Little sister!" he called out, startled but easy with it. "What a surprise! What are you doing here? Hello, Piet."

"I decided it was time to see it all," Catherine said. "Business is quiet in New York, and I just had the urge to come."

"You always do things impetuously," Shelly said. He pulled Catherine to him in a bear hug and kissed her cheek.

Catherine returned his hug. As she did she looked down into the box of flowers he had overseen being packed. Next to the bundle of long-stemmed red roses lay a plastic container of blue chemical ice to keep the flowers cool and fresh. Caught in a red rubber band around the dark green thorny stems of the flowers was a small plastic packet of white powder — cut-flower preservative, according to the label.

Of course, it could actually be flower preservative. Or it could be cocaine.

Shelly caught Catherine's look. So did the worker.

"I didn't know we packed the flower preservative at this end," Catherine said.

"We don't for Blooms," Shelly told her

smoothly. He was completely relaxed. "But for GardenAir it makes it all much easier. Much quicker. Our clients can buy the flowers the moment they're unloaded from the truck. We don't have to hold them up putting on the packets, and they don't have to hold up their customers. It's just another service we offer."

"Good idea," Catherine said. "Look, do you have to stay here? Or can you come have breakfast — or lunch — or whatever you eat at this ungodly hour — with Piet and me?"

"We're shorthanded today. One of the packers is sick. You and Piet go on without me. But let's have dinner tonight. Somewhere interesting. There's a great Turkish restaurant — "

"Shelly, I'm sorry. I'm flying back today."

"What? Why? You just got here."

"It was just an impulse trip. A spur-of-the-moment thing."

"Well, damn," Shelly said. "I guess I could leave these guys — "

"No. Don't. It's not as if we never see each other anymore. Look, when will you be back in the States again?"

"I don't know. Christmas, I guess."

"That's fine. I'll see you then!" Catherine gave her brother a hug, and as she did, she was overwhelmed with a melancholy love.

Touching her brother, she thought, My brother, and she felt his broad shoulders, strong arms, she smelled the maleness and the health of him. She wanted to weep with anguish and anger, she wanted to pound her fists against his chest.

She pulled away, her expression serene. Piet and Shelly exchanged a few notes on the day's work, then Piet led Catherine back through the enormous building to his car.

"Are you sure you want to go home today? You haven't seen anything of Amsterdam. You should at least see the Rijksmuseum."

"No, I need to get back. For one thing, I've got to talk to Carla. Until I've done that, I won't be able to concentrate on anything else. I'll be back sometime, Piet. I'll bring the children, and we'll all see Amsterdam together."

Piet helped her get her luggage from the hotel and stayed with her through the bore of checking her bags and getting through security at the airport. She would be leaving about the same time the flowers Blooms had ordered this morning would leave Amsterdam, and she and the flowers would both be in New York around nine in the morning. Amazing.

At the gate, Piet put his hands on Catherine's shoulders.

"You're a powerful woman, I hope you know that. You've always been a powerful woman, and now that you're older you haven't changed. Your birthday's in December; you're a fire sign."

"That's right," Catherine said, charmed. "What are you?"

"I'm air, my darling. So you see, it wouldn't have worked. I was attracted to you, but you would have consumed me."

"No, I couldn't have, Piet. You've always been like air, you've kept yourself invisible to me."

They smiled at each other. Then Piet kissed her good-bye, a long kiss full on the mouth, and she was gone.

The flight home was interminable. She could not sleep. She had thought her life was as orderly as life could possibly get. Perhaps she should have known, or at least *anticipated* — for look how Shelly had been as a boy, as a student. He had loved drugs and fun then; how could she have forgotten what he was really like?

Yet he was her brother, part of her. She loved him, and the thought of tearing him from her life tugged at the cords of her heart.

She had phoned Kit from Schiphol airport to tell him what flight she was on. When her beloved lawyer Mr. Giles had died several years before, she had asked Kit if he would take over Blooms' and GardenAir's legal affairs, and he had agreed. This meant he'd had to ask for a reduction in his workload at Woodrow and Spiegel, and they had not been pleased. Yet he did such an excellent job on the cases he took that they couldn't do without him. Recently Kit and Catherine had been discussing Kit's leaving the firm to work full-time for Blooms and GardenAir. If that happened, Catherine would want Kit to be a full partner in the business — only fair, since Kit already contributed so much. Still, she held back. She was so used to being the one in charge. She and Kit already had to compromise with each other on disagreements about the children. What would the business do to their marriage? What would their marriage do to their business?

Kit met her flight. Riding into the city, he told her Lily had just called from school to say she was invited to a friend's home in Vermont over Christmas break. She wanted to go, because she loved to ski. Both children loved sports, but Lily was the jock.

"Skiing," Catherine said. "Immediately I think of broken legs."

"Lily's strong. She's coordinated. She'll have a great time. And Andrew called to say he got an A on his history exam."

"Good for him." The thought of Andrew was like sunshine to Catherine. She loved Lily, but like all mothers and daughters, they fought. Andrew was Catherine's golden boy. Oh, both children were wonderful and complicated. Sometimes she wondered if either one of them would want to work for Blooms, take it over someday.

She still hadn't talked about Shelly.

"Where are we headed?" Kit asked as he pulled onto the FDR Drive.

"I'd like to go right to Blooms. I want to talk to Carla. I'll have to fire her — today. After that, I assume it won't be long before we hear from Shelly."

"We could also start legal proceedings against them."

"I know. I thought of that during the flight. But Kit," she said unhappily, "I just don't think I could go through with it. I don't think I could take my brother to court."

"I understand. It's just as well. If we did prosecute him, the newspapers would have a field day, and that kind of publicity wouldn't do Blooms any good."

Kit parked in the alley behind Blooms.

"Unless Shelly is a total idiot," Catherine said, "he sent over correct invoices today. I was there when he was watching the flowers being packed. I saw him writing up the invoices. Oh, Kit," she said, suddenly sick at her stomach. "The thought of confronting Carla — stay with me."

"I will."

"Hey, boss lady. Hey, Kit," Jason greeted them. He was sticking orange mums into chicken wire shaped like a pumpkin.

They said hello to Jason, then took the elevator to the tenth floor.

"Oh, you're back — feeling better?" Sandra said, seeing Catherine. "You don't look very good, though, Catherine. Are you sure you should be at work today?"

"I'm just tired. Look, go down and take over the shop, will you? Hold all calls. And send Carla up."

"Of course," Sandra said, her face white.

"We're grateful to you," Catherine said, "but let's talk later."

She touched the older woman on the arm, a gesture meant to comfort both of them. Then Catherine and Kit went into her office. She tossed her mink coat over the back of her chair. Kit hung his coat in the closet.

"Coffee?" she asked Kit.

"Please."

She poured it and stirred in cream and sugar, the actions seeming exaggerated and clumsy as she moved, waiting with each second for Carla to appear. As she handed the cup to Kit, her hands shook.

"You wanted to see me?"

Carla stood in the doorway then, a perky look on her face. As she registered Kit's and Catherine's expressions, her face fell, and her hands flew together in front of her, fingers locking nervously.

"Yes, Carla. I think you know why. Come in — sit down. Carla, I've just come back from Amsterdam. I brought these back with me." Catherine took the two account ledgers from her satchel. "You and Shelly have been cheating Blooms. You've been cheating me. We know how you've worked it from beginning to end."

During her flight home, Catherine had imagined this scene over and over again, and each time she had envisioned Carla indignant, raging, insulted. Carla surprised her by simply bursting into tears.

"Oh, God, now you've gone and ruined everything," she sobbed.

"*I* have ruined everything?" Catherine said sarcastically, but Kit flashed her a warning look. Catherine stopped. In response, Carla, who had flinched and frozen at Catherine's bitter tone, began sobbing again.

"Tell me how I've ruined everything," Catherine said in as sympathetic a tone as she could manage.

"We were only going to do this a while. Until we had enough money to start our own company." Carla collapsed in despair, covering her tearstained face with her hands.

Catherine handed Carla a wad of tissue. "Your own flower company?"

"Oh, *no!* Of course not! We'd never compete with you, Catherine. Actually" — Carla faltered a moment — "I don't know what kind of company. We never got that far. Shelly just said that if we did this, we could save up enough money to start our own company. And it didn't really hurt Blooms. Shelly said —"

Catherine listened, wanting to weep along with Carla. Shelly said. Shelly did. Shelly. Shelly. Charming, endearing, gorgeous, adorable Shelly. Of course Carla would be in love with him, had been in love with him for years. In the years she'd worked for Catherine, she'd learned how to dress. She had her hair cut stylishly; she'd made herself a pretty woman. But she'd never be the sort of woman Shelly would love. She didn't have the flair, the elegance — the money.

"I'm disappointed in you, Carla. You have to know that. You've worked for me for eighteen years now. I would have thought —"

"Yes, eighteen years, and for most of them

I've been nothing to you!"

"What? I've never mistreated you!"

"Mistreated, no, you've just ignored me. When I first came to work here, it was like a family. Everyone cared for everyone else. We spent time together. We joked together. We ate together on holidays after breaking our butts over last-minute jobs. Then you got married and had your babies and everything changed. You just cruise in and out like some queen, never bothering to spend any time with us. I'm not the only one who's unhappy here. Just ask Jason! Just ask Leonard! Even Sandra admits you're too wrapped up in your precious children to pay any attention to us!"

"Carla, you should have come to me. You should have told me — "

"Oh, right. I don't want to have to ask to be treated nicely! Shelly always treated me like someone special, like someone he cares for, like a sister! More than a sister! Shelly loves me. Oh, don't look that way, I don't imagine for one minute that he would marry me, but he does care for me. He always stops and talks to me, asks how I am, sends me silly cards, takes me out to dinner now and then. He's the only thing that has made working here worthwhile!"

Her anger had dried up her tears, and

now Carla sat facing Catherine dry-eyed, quivering, bold.

"Blooms is a business, Carla, not a social organization — " Catherine began.

"You can say that again," Carla interrupted.

" — and you're fired, Carla. As of this moment. The fact that I ignored you doesn't give you the right to cheat me. No — " Catherine put up her hand. "Don't start again. You're lucky Kit and I aren't taking you to court. You've committed a serious crime. You could be fined, you could be sent to jail. But we'd decided not to press charges. I don't want to have to see you ever again. I want you out of here. I want you out of my sight."

Carla stood up. There she was, thirty-seven years old, an integral piece in the puzzle of Catherine's life, and with her chin high, she said in a steady voice, "I hate you."

Catherine just looked at Carla. She could have said: I don't feel your hate, how you feel about me hardly interests me. What I do feel is the misery approaching you like a stormcloud, the despair that I know is about to sweep through your life when Shelly returns and you realize he's played you false. He won't set up a business with you. Now that you're of no use to him, he won't even see you again. You poor, wretched fool.

Something in Catherine's eyes made Carla turn away. Woodenly, she walked to the elevator. Kit and Catherine sat in silence until they heard the rubbery *shoosh* of the doors opening and closing, then silence.

"Who is that poor woman going to turn to now?" Catherine said to Kit. "She says Blooms isn't her family, but I'm afraid we're as much family as she's got."

"Her personal life isn't your concern, Catherine."

"Well, I'll ask Sandra. Or Jason. They must know more about her than I do."

"Catherine! Don't waste your pity on her! She's been stealing from you."

Catherine looked at Kit. "It all just seems so bleak," she said, suddenly drained. "So hopeless."

"You're just exhausted," Kit said. "You need a good night's sleep. It's almost midnight your time. Come on. Let's go to the apartment. You need to go to bed and rest up. If my guess is right, your brother will be in the country tomorrow."

"Oh, God, Kit. That reminds me. We have one more stop to make before we go home. We've got to go down to GardenAir."

Kit drove. On the way to their wholesale store in the flower district, Catherine talked.

She had not wanted to tell him over the phone Piet's theory about why Shelly needed extra money, and she hadn't had time to tell him about the flower packets she'd seen him attaching to the roses in Aalsmeer this morning. As far as she knew, they were only packets of flower preservative. But she wanted to be sure.

GardenAir was a long narrow shop on Twenty-eighth Street, tucked between a container wholesaler and a shop that specialized in South American exotic plants. She was glad Kit was with her when she entered GardenAir. She was the owner of the business, and the men were officially her employees, but she hadn't been down here for a long time, for months, maybe even a year, and she realized she didn't even know each man's name. But Manuel, the head man, had been with her company since it started. She had always been good to him and his family, and she had to believe he was loyal to her in return.

Manuel and Kit and Catherine greeted each other warmly. The other workers only nodded. It was early afternoon now, and some of the men had left. The majority of the business for the day was over. A handsome dark-haired man Catherine didn't know was sweeping the floor.

"Manuel, do you have any roses left from today's shipments?" Catherine asked. "I'd like to take a bunch with me."

"Sure. We've got some. Here. This is a good bunch. How many you want?"

They moved to a table where the long boxes lay propped up, lids off, displaying the roses and other flowers.

"These are from Amsterdam?" Catherine asked. "Fresh today?"

"From Amsterdam," Manuel said. "Fresh today."

"Where are the packets of flower preservative?" Catherine asked.

"What flower preservative?"

Catherine noticed the switchblade glance of the boy sweeping as she spoke, and that Manuel, who managed to keep his face straight and his voice calm, inadvertently stepped backward, as if she'd hit him.

"Let's go in your office," Kit said.

The office was a tiny cubicle at the back of the store, closed in by glass and particleboard. A splintered old desk covered with invoices and bills and dirt, a wooden chair, and a metal filing cabinet were the only furniture in the room.

"I was in Amsterdam this morning," Catherine said. "I saw Shelly putting packets on the roses. He told me he only does that on the wholesale flowers. I can see there are no packets on the roses out there. Tell me the truth right now, or I'll fire you and everyone else in this shop before you can turn around."

"We'll bring in the police and the DEA if we have to," Kit said.

"Jesus, man, cool down!" Manuel said, waving his hands at them. "Look, there's nothing major going on here. Catherine, we're not involved in anything illegal, if that's what you're thinking. You think we're bringing in drugs?"

"I think Shelly is."

The man studied Catherine's face, considering.

Catherine spoke softly. "I don't want to get him in trouble. I know he's my brother, Manuel. That's why I don't want to get the DEA involved. If I don't have to. I just want to know exactly what he's doing, and I want to put a stop to it."

"You might feel better knowing that today, as soon as we can get in touch with Shelly, we're going to fire him," Kit said. "He's already involved himself in other things you don't even know about. So he won't be in Amsterdam anymore. At least he won't be working for Blooms or GardenAir. He won't have any authority over you here."

"Yeah, yeah, all right." Manuel sighed and turned. He bent over, fiddled with a key, and pulled open the bottom drawer of the filing cabinet.

Catherine stepped back instinctively. For all she knew he would pull out a gun.

Instead he merely stepped aside and waved down at the open drawer with his hand. There were no files in the drawer, only glistening plastic packages of white powder.

"This is all Shelly's," Manuel said. "I mean, his personal stuff. He doesn't sell it. He's not dealing. He just sends it over, and we keep it for him to use when he's in the States. For him and his friends."

"Manuel. You should have told me. You should have come to me."

"Hey, between you and your brother, it's a hard call."

"I'm taking this with me," Catherine said. "Manuel, get me a box, any box big enough to hold this stuff."

"Hey, this stuff is Shelly's."

"Now it's mine," Catherine said coldly.

Manuel stepped out of his office and was quickly back with a box. Catherine and Kit took out the bottom file drawer and dumped the contents into the cardboard box and closed the lid.

"This won't be happening anymore, Manuel," Catherine said. "Or if it does happen, I expect you to come to me."

They threw the box in the trunk of Kit's Mercedes and drove back uptown to their apartment. Now they could only wait for Shelly. Catherine bathed, showered, and sat in bed, eating the scrambled eggs and buttered muffins that her maid, Angela, always prepared for her after a long trip. The food was nursery food, soothing, and finally, after so many hours of coming and going, Catherine fell into a deep sleep.

She awoke to darkness. Her head was filled with clouds, her ears were ringing, and anxiety was making her heart clatter inside her like a pair of castanets.

"What?" she mumbled, sitting up. "Where?"

"Catherine, it's all right. I'm sorry. I didn't mean to wake you." It was Kit, just coming to bed.

"What time is it?"

"Just after midnight." He put his arms around her and pulled her down next to him. "Everything's all right."

"I feel so disoriented."

"Everything's all right." Kit stroked her arm and held her against him. He kissed her hair, then her cheeks, then her mouth.

He pressed against her, warm, solid, as strong as a tree in a summer storm. Catherine pressed against him, grateful for his steadfastness in her unsteady world. They made love, and she fell asleep again and slept without dreaming until morning.

It wasn't until three days later that Shelly appeared. Kit and Catherine knew he was coming, for Piet had called several times. He had told Shelly that Catherine had taken the two sets of account books and that as far as he was concerned he didn't want to see Shelly on his premises again. Piet had also fired some of the men working in the loading sheds at the auction. Piet was planning to fly over to meet with Catherine and Kit as soon as they'd seen Shelly.

When at last Shelly called Catherine, she said, "Meet me at my apartment. I don't want to talk to you here." She called Kit and then rang her house, to tell Angela to have coffee and drinks ready for them in the living room. Then she left her shop and walked home.

Catherine had imagined this confrontation with her brother a dozen different times in a dozen different ways. She'd imagined Shelly furious, embarrassed, apologetic, in tears. He came in smiling. He was dressed in a navy blazer and gray flannels, he was clean-shaven, combed, and natty, not wrinkled and gray and exhausted as she'd thought he'd look.

"Hey, babe," Shelly said cheerfully.

"Shelly, you goddamned asshole, I could kill you!" Catherine replied.

"Catherine," Kit said in a warning tone.

"No, I won't calm down," Catherine said to Kit without turning to look at him. "Shelly, *you idiot!* How could you do this!"

Shelly sank onto a sofa and busied himself at the coffee table fixing a glass of Scotch. "It was easy, actually. I mean the setup was all in place, just waiting to happen. I don't know why you're so upset. I didn't take that much."

"Never mind the money, how could you involve poor Carla in the scheme?"

"It was the only way it worked. She was the one who received the flowers at this end."

"But didn't you even once consider what you were doing to her? That you were drawing her into criminal activities? That — "

"Oh, come on, sis. 'Criminal activities.' "

"Shelly," Kit intervened. "I know you'll find this hard to believe, but even though Catherine is your own flesh and blood, it's still illegal to juggle the books."

"How could you do this to me!" Catherine burst out. "How could you use poor Carla that way! She said you were going to set up a business with her."

Shelly shrugged. "Who says I wasn't going to?"

"What kind of business? Dealing drugs?" Catherine had been sitting down, but at the look on Shelly's face she jumped from her chair. Grabbing him by his blazer lapels, she shook him hard. "You stupid jerk! You were going to deal drugs, weren't you! Using GardenAir to bring them in. Shelly, you make me sick."

The smile left Shelly's eyes. Kit rose from his chair and pulled Catherine away, led her back to her chair, his hands on her shoulders.

"He's so cool," Catherine said to Kit as if Shelly couldn't hear her. "How can he be so damned cool?"

"Drink this," Kit said, handing her a Scotch. He turned to Shelly. "Have you talked to Manuel?"

"Yeah, he called. What'd you do with the stuff? I need it."

"You need it? Too bad. We got rid of it," Kit said.

Now Shelly did not look amused in the slightest. The muscles in his jaw jumped. "You got rid of it," he repeated in a monotone.

"Shelly, you're not involved with a mob

or something, are you?" Catherine asked quickly.

"No. Hell, no. I promise. Just for me and my friends. I wasn't dealing at all. It was just an easy way for me to get it into the country."

"That's good to know," Kit said. "Now we don't have to worry that some thug will come gun you down on the street. Because it's gone, Shelly. We threw it out."

Shelly took a deep breath. "I've got a habit," he said.

"You'll have to lose it," Kit said.

Now Catherine was torn again, between anger at her brother and that old protective love. Here he sat in her living room in his blazer, a golden man in his thirties, and she still could see within him, as if she were looking at a double exposure, the bold little boy who had run on the highest brick walls at Everly without any fear of falling, who had built dream castles in the air from blocks, who had run screaming through the hedges chasing make-believe Indians. Shelly had never wanted to be a businessman in a blazer. He should have been a sailor, an explorer, a stunt pilot. He didn't belong here, in the city, where the best excitement he could find lay in a fickle white powder.

"Shelly," Kit said, "I'm sure this won't

surprise you, but you're fired. I'm sure you know Carla's been fired, too. Catherine and I don't intend to prosecute."

"That's right, Shelly," Catherine said, feeling queer. "Just think, if you haven't spent all the money you stole from us on drugs, you could start up that little business you were talking about with Carla."

"I'm fired, the cocaine's been dumped, and fuck you, right? Is that it?" Shelly finally looked angry.

"Shelly, don't look at me that way. You aren't the injured one. *I* am."

"God, I hate you, Catherine," Shelly said. "You are so stupid. You don't have a clue about anything. Haven't you ever, just once in your life, done anything wrong?"

"Yes, Shelly, as a matter of fact I have. As wrong as what you've done. Maybe it's because of that that I'm letting you off so easily."

"So easily!"

"Shelly, weren't you listening to Kit? We could put you in jail. If we wanted to stick to the letter of the law, we could have kept the drugs and thrown that at you, too. Then you'd really be in trouble. But we've decided not to do that. We just want you out of the shop, out of our lives."

"Fine. You've got it." Shelly rose and

stalked across the living room toward the door.

At the door he turned. "Kit, are you sure? I mean, that you dumped it all? Because man, I could use a little right now."

"It's all gone, Shelly. Down the toilet. Where it belongs."

Shelly smiled. "Oh, those lucky rats."

Catherine waited until the front door closed. Then she said, "My God, what a good exit line. He's still got my father's charm. But Kit, what will he do now? How will he get any money? What — "

"Catherine, stop. Shelly is your brother, not your son. Your parents will take care of him. They always have."

"I suppose you're right," Catherine said. "But oh, God, Kit, Shelly just breaks my heart."

CHAPTER 12

New York, 1988

Catherine had intended to go straight back to Blooms after confronting Shelly, but she discovered that she was oddly weak. Instead, she indulged in the rituals that usually refreshed her: a long perfumed bath, a lazy meal eaten in her robe, and phone calls to Andrew and Lily, who were happy and so busy with their own lives that they couldn't stay long on the phone. Still she felt bone tired. She fell asleep at once, grateful for oblivion.

She was not surprised to be awakened by the ringing of the phone while the windows were still black with night. It was as if all along she had been expecting this call, and she thought: Shelly. Something has happened to Shelly, and the police are calling to tell me.

"Catherine?"

The old woman's voice was so weak and whispery that for a moment Catherine couldn't hear her grandmother speaking.

"Grandmother! Are you all right?"

"Come to Everly. I need to talk to you."

"Grandmother, do you need a doctor? Is Clara there?"

"Don't make me waste my breath. Tell me you will come here now."

"I'll dress and leave at once."

Next to her, Kit struggled up from his own deep sleep. "Your grandmother?"

"She wants me there now. She sounded so far away — I think she's dying, Kit. I've got to go." She was already pushing back the covers.

"I'll drive you."

They dressed quickly, efficiently, without speaking. Catherine pulled on her most comfortable clothes, jeans and a sweater, perhaps not perfect for the occasion, but what clothes were perfect for the occasion of death? While Kit walked to the garage to get the car, she made a Thermos of strong coffee. Once they were on the road, she poured coffee for Kit, then took his advice and put the seat back and closed her eyes.

"Catherine? We're here." She awoke to see that day was dawning. The dark fall sky was streaked with gold.

Two strange cars were already in the drive: a navy blue Mercedes and a police car.

She raced from the car almost before Kit could bring it to a full stop and tore into

512

the house. The front hall lights were blazing, and so were the lights up the winding staircase to her grandmother's bedroom.

"Good. You got here in time," Kathryn said.

The old woman was seated in her vast four-poster bed, propped up on pillows, a shawl over her shoulders, her fine white hair pulled back with a ribbon. Standing next to the bed was a man Catherine had met before, Kathryn's doctor, George Holdgarten, and a young man in police uniform. Clara sat on a rocking chair in the corner of the room.

"Grandmother, how are you?" Catherine sat carefully on the bed and bent over the wizened old lady. Kathryn's fingers were as bony and her eyes as beady-bright as a chicken's. But her breath was labored.

"I'm dying. Oh, don't puddle up on me. It's about time, and I'm ready. Reach under the bed."

"What?"

"Catherine. Do you think I have the energy to repeat everything twice?"

Catherine knelt by the bed and raised the dust ruffle. After her eyes had adjusted to the darkness, she saw what she at first thought were boxes but quickly realized were large books. Three of them. Old and magnificent. She pulled them out.

"Those are my botanicals," Kathryn said.

Dr. Holdgarten bent to help Catherine lift the heaviest book from the floor.

"Dr. Robert Thornton. *Temple of Flora.* Extremely rare," Kathryn said.

Catherine opened the cover of the huge book. Inside were colored engravings of plants and flowers against a background of landscapes.

"A copy of Basilius Besler's *Hortus Eystettensis.* Seventeenth-century. And a Redouté. These are yours, now. I'm giving them to you."

"Thank you, Grandmother."

"You should thank me. They're worth a fortune. A fortune, Catherine."

"Thank you."

"Hello, Kathryn." Kit entered the room.

"Hello, Kit. You brought Catherine out, I see. Clara will be down to fix you some breakfast in a few minutes."

"Thanks. I'll wait for her in the library. I brought my briefcase," Kit said to Catherine. "I'll catch up on some work. Don't worry about me."

Catherine smiled, then turned back to Kathryn, who was already speaking again.

"Look, I've asked these kind gentlemen to come here, and I don't want to keep them waiting. Clara."

At her name, the old servant rose and crossed the room with a sheaf of papers and a pen in her hands. She handed them to Kathryn.

"I've made out my will seven or eight times. Always, I've written the same thing. I'm leaving Everly, and everything in it, to you. You sell those florilegia books and you'll have enough money to do some restoration on Everly." Kathryn paused for breath. "Now, doctor, officer, if you will be so good as to witness my signature — you do think I'm in sound mind, don't you? Reasonably sane? Would you like me to give you the names of some state capitals or discuss current events?"

"That won't be necessary, Mrs. Eliot," Dr. Holdgarten said. He watched the old woman sign her name on the will, then he took the document and signed his own as witness. He passed it to the young policeman, who also signed.

"There. That's done, thank heavens," Kathryn said. "Thank you for coming, gentlemen." They were dismissed.

Dr. Holdgarten touched Catherine's arm. "I'll wait for you downstairs. I'd like to speak with you."

"Clara, would you please fix Dr. Holdgarten some coffee, and a nice full breakfast for Catherine's husband?"

Soon, Catherine and her grandmother were alone. Catherine sat on the bed holding the older woman's hand.

"Shelly gets the Jaguar. It hasn't been out of the garage in decades, but it's in beautiful shape. I hope that makes him happy. Ann gets the Audubons. They're worth a lot. Be sure she's aware of that. Your parents will get the family silver. The rest is yours. Your parents will be angry about this. Probably they'll try to fight it, but my will should hold. It should hold."

"Thank you, Grandmother."

"Don't worry about Lily and Drew." Kathryn was breathing hastily now, almost panting, in her hurry to say it all to Catherine. "Be patient. These things often skip generations. If your children don't love flowers and Everly the way you do, you're bound to have a grandchild who will."

"Grandmother — how can I say thank you properly? I promise I'll restore Everly."

"I know you will. I would have if I'd sold my books, but I wanted them near me. And I didn't want the mess of strangers in the house." She closed her eyes and caught her breath. Just when Catherine thought the old lady had fallen asleep, she opened her eyes and glared at Catherine. "I've always loved you best."

"I know. And it's made all the difference."

"You're the one who inherited my love for flowers. From the beginning you took after my side. You think like me, and you look like your grandfather."

"I look like Grandfather Eliot?"

"Certain traits are everlasting, you know. Genetic. Like flowers."

"I wish I had known that when I was a child."

"Why? To have something to lean on? It's good that you're so independent. You know that."

Catherine opened her mouth to argue, but Kathryn closed her eyes and swallowed painfully, exhausted. She rested against the pillow, catching her breath. When she could speak again, she said, "Stay here. This won't be a picnic for you, but you're strong enough. It will be a big help for me."

"Grandmother, you'll be up and around in a few days."

"I haven't been up and around for months. Don't be a fool. I'm dying."

Clara came into the room. "Would you like me to stay with her a while so you can go down and have a cup of coffee and a chat with Dr. Holdgarten?"

"No," Catherine said. "I think I'll stay here. I can talk to the doctor later."

"She knows what he's going to tell her anyway," Kathryn said, laughing wryly, then choking on her laughter.

Catherine sat with her grandmother. She held her hand. Now it was her turn to talk, and Catherine spoke of what she knew her grandmother loved best. Flowers, gardens, their time together at the British Everly. Mazes, walks, arbors. Shrubs, trees, bushes. Annuals, perennials, everlastings.

What is everlasting? Catherine mused as she sat in silence, holding her sleeping grandmother's hand. The everlasting flowers, sea lavender, immortelle, passionflower, and feverfew, kept their color as they dried but lost their softness, moistness, and flexibility. The swamp cypress tree growing in the southeastern United States was so unusually resistant to decay that it had earned from the lumber trade the name "wood everlasting." Its cousin, *Cypress funebris,* or mourning cypress, was a symbol in Mediterranean cultures of death and immortality.

An interesting combination, that: of death and immortality, Catherine thought, watching her grandmother.

But although Kathryn opened her eyes now and then, she said only, "Still here? Good girl," before falling instantly back into a deep sleep.

Dr. Holdgarten came into the room to listen to the old woman's chest and check her pulse. "I'll be back later on."

"Wait," Catherine whispered. She pulled the doctor out of the room into the hallway and in a low voice asked, "Why does she think she's dying now?"

"She's been ill for a long time. She's had a series of small heart attacks. The Lord only knows what else ails her because she won't come into the hospital or even into my office for a decent checkup."

"If we made her go to a hospital — "

"Then you'd probably make her die in a hospital. She's old, Catherine. Her body's tired and worn out. It's shutting down on her. She can't breathe. Her lungs are filling with water. She's got congestive heart failure. If you'd like, I could give her a shot to make her more comfortable, but she's not complaining about any pain. The shot would also make her less clearheaded. I think she'd hate that."

"Is there anything I can do?"

"Only what she asked. Be with her."

"How long — "

"I can't say. But old people often know when the time has come for them to die. It might be a day. It might not be that long."

"She doesn't seem to be afraid of dying."

"She's much too tired to be afraid."

Catherine sat with Kathryn. Her own body was tired, her own spirit weary and strained. But she was not too tired to be afraid, and she was not too tired to be greedy for all the pleasures she knew life could still hold for her.

By early afternoon Catherine was stiff from sitting. Her grandmother was fast asleep. Catherine rose and hurried downstairs. Old Clara slept on a recliner in the same room, snoring loudly.

Kit was in the library, reading legal briefs. He rose when she entered and held her against him.

"How is she?"

"Asleep. Fading. But not in pain."

"How are you?"

"She's leaving me Everly. Kit, so much has happened, and now this. I can't take it all in."

"Have you eaten anything?"

"I'm not hungry. She wants me near her. I can hardly sit there chewing, dropping crumbs on the sheets." Catherine giggled giddily.

"You need something. Wait here."

Catherine sank onto a chair and simply stared into space, not even thinking, until Kit returned with some coffee, juice, and toast covered with jam.

"I'll go up and sit with her while you eat," he said. "If she wakes up, I'll come get you."

"Kit, what would I do without you?" she asked. He touched her hair softly in reply before leaving the room.

Catherine ate quickly, each bite reviving her. Perhaps, she thought as she finished her meal, perhaps Kathryn wouldn't die today after all. Perhaps she would recover. If she did, Catherine would force her to accept some household help. Clara couldn't do anything but look after the two of them and had let the rest of the house fall into disrepair. Dust coated every surface, and cobwebs laced through the chandeliers and curtains. If Kathryn lived, Catherine resolved to spend one day and one night every week out here.

Back in her grandmother's bedroom, Catherine and Kit talked softly. Yes, he had called Blooms to tell them she wouldn't be in today. Yes, he'd called his office. Should he call Catherine's father? Drew Eliot was, after all, Kathryn's son. Still, she had not asked to see him. Better to wait. Catherine would ask her grandmother the next time she awoke.

Kit sat with Catherine for a while, then went back downstairs to his reading. Catherine pulled back one heavy, dusty drape and looked out. It had turned into a glorious autumn day, brilliant with colors. All the gardens, even the purple-and-white one, were a tangle of overgrown grasses and flowers shriveled by frosts. Bumpy apples and pears lay at the base of the neglected fruit trees for the birds and bugs to pick at. Orange, yellow, and wine-hued mums blazed along one wall. The climbing roses were still there, too, blossoming with frilly, summery, pale pink roses.

Catherine opened the window just a little, so that fresh air could sweep into the over-heated, stuffy room. The rush of cool air with its tang of salt braced her. She shut the window and went back to sit with her grandmother.

At some point in the late afternoon, Catherine pulled her chair close to the bed and laid her head down. Gently she rested one hand on her grandmother's so that they were touching, skin to skin. Then she fell asleep. When she awoke, it was almost eleven o'clock at night, and her grandmother's hand was cold.

Kathryn Patterson Paxton Eliot was dead.

Catherine had been expecting this moment for so long that she went through the necessary motions almost as if she'd done them before many times.

She called Dr. Holdgarten first, and when he said he was on his way, she called her father.

"Dad. I'm sorry if I woke you. But I'm out at Everly, and . . . Grandmother just died."

"Are you sure?"

"Yes, Dad. I'm with her now. I've been with her all day. She called me very early this morning and asked me to come out."

"But why did she ask you to come be with her?" Drew asked. "Why didn't she call me? I'm her son!"

"Probably because Kathryn knew if you came out, I'd come out, too," Marjorie said from the extension in their bedroom. "She never did like me."

"Would you like me to take care of the funeral arrangements?" Catherine asked. "Or would you rather do it?"

Drew sighed deeply. "I'll do it."

"Would you also tell Shelly? I don't know when I'll be seeing him again. I don't know if he told you, but — "

"He did," Marjorie broke in. "We're all very disappointed with your attitude."

"I'll call Ann if you'd like, Father," Catherine said, pointedly ignoring her mother's remark.

"I'd appreciate that," Drew said. He sighed

again. "We'll get dressed and be out there as soon as we can."

When Catherine hung up, Kit crossed the room and came to rub Catherine's shoulders.

"That sounded relatively painless," he said.

"I didn't mention the will," Catherine replied.

"All flesh is grass, and all the goodliness thereof is as the flower of the field."

Catherine sat in the front of the church with Kit and Andrew and Lily, whom they'd brought home from school for the funeral. She was aware of the minister's words and of the occasional sob or sniffle from Ann or Clara.

"The grass withereth, the flower fadeth: because the spirit of the Lord bloweth upon it; surely the people is grass."

Drew and Marjorie sat on the first row, with Shelly between them. The past few days had exhausted them all. When Catherine told them about the will, they'd been enraged, then changed tactics and tried with great sweetness to get Catherine to give Everly up, then raged again when she said she wouldn't. Earlier today as they had gathered at Everly in their black garments, preparing for the funeral, they had been civil to Catherine and Kit, but cold. Shelly looked tired and preoccupied.

Ned had flown over from England with Ann, and so had Madeline, but they hadn't taken their two children out of school; after all, they had never known Kathryn. Over the past few years Ann and Catherine had forgotten their enmity in the name of family; once again, they'd taken to sending Christmas and birthday presents, exchanging letters, sharing their lives long-distance. Ann, Ned, and Madeline were staying in the city with Drew and Marjorie, so Catherine assumed Ann had received their version of Shelly and Catherine's quarrel. But the Boxworthys had arrived only the night before, and Catherine had had only a brief moment alone with Ann this morning as they were waiting for the limousines.

"I'd like to talk to you privately sometime before you go back," Catherine had said quietly.

"I'd like that, too," Ann said, and then someone else had entered the room.

Now the Boxworthys sat on their own pew across from the Eliots.

Clara had chosen to sit with Catherine, Kit, and their children.

"The grass withereth, the flower fadeth; but the word of our God shall stand for ever."

Catherine didn't think for a minute her grandmother believed what the minister was saying. If Kathryn thought anything lasted forever, it was not words, but plants, flowers, trees, shrubs. But since Kathryn never went to church, Catherine thought it was thoughtful of the minister to remember Kathryn's particular love. She thanked him afterward, at the quiet reception at Everly.

The burial service had been brief, because it was pouring rain and the wind was blowing off the Sound, driving the rain sideways like needles. A large tent had been erected over the gravesite; nevertheless, those gathered around the casket were quickly soaked. The minister's robes flapped like wet sheets in the wind, and his voice was drowned out by the weather's roar. Yet it was a satisfying ceremony, Catherine thought, dramatic in its own way, as if the elements themselves were mourning, wind and rain, salt and sky, reminding the mortals gathered there that Kathryn had preferred the natural world in all its guises to the human one.

Back at Everly, the local women Drew had hired set out a cold buffet in the dining room. Kathryn had kept to herself so much of recent years, and so many of her oldest friends had already died, that there were few guests other than the immediate family, and they quickly took their leave. Catherine spoke to Dr. Holdgarten, to the minister, and to Clara's grandchildren, who had come to collect her and her things after the funeral. Kathryn had left her friend and servant a generous bequest that would take care of Clara for the rest of her life, whether she spent it on cruise ships or in a first-class rest home, and her grandchildren were grateful. Clara was grateful, too, but in a state of shock: Catherine recognized the look, the wide blank eyes, the bland expression, the slow movements. It was a state much like Catherine's own, her emotions frozen beneath a mask that was vague, polite.

By four o'clock it was dark. The November sky was so black that even the fleet of clouds that rushed across it were hidden. Catherine settled Andrew and Lily in the den with trays of sandwiches, sodas, and cookies and turned them loose with the VCR. They were watching something exceptionally stupid, she realized, taking advantage of the fact that today of all days she wouldn't monitor their choice. For a long moment she stood in the doorway of the den, watching them, listening to them joke and laugh. Her children. They were so healthy, so happy, so relaxed with her. They argued with her, Lily especially, and Catherine always marveled at this. They didn't have a clue how lucky they were, her children, how secure they felt in her love and in Kit's. If she had accomplished one good thing in her life, it was raising these children, who loved themselves and knew they deserved love.

"Catherine, we're leaving now."

Ann appeared at her side. It was stranger for Catherine to recognize Ann in her thirties than it was to see her own face in the mirror. In her mind Ann was forever young, and lovely in her youth. In reality, Ann's golden light had dimmed. Her hair already had strands of gray in it, not shining white, but dull gray, and her face was much more lined than Catherine's — the result, no doubt, of working outside all the time. But then Ann had taken on the Boxworthy women's disdain of cosmetics. And instead of a fashionable cut, Ann simply pulled her hair straight back into an untidy bun. Catherine wondered if Ann ever used face cream at night. Should she suggest it to her? No — Marjorie would do that.

But Ann's blue eyes were bright, and her movements were graceful, the movements of a woman who walked through life being loved and useful. For the few brief seconds that Catherine had been able to see Ned face to face, she had noticed that at forty-five he looked as marvelous as ever. His dark hair was streaked with a silver so bright, it made his entire face seem radiant. And when he and Ann looked at each other, it was abundantly clear they were happy in their marriage.

"Ann, do you think you could come out tomorrow? We could go through the house and see if there are any pieces of furniture or china, whatever, that you'd like to have at your Everly."

"God, Catherine." Ann grinned. "If I have one more precious heirloom to watch over, I think I'll lose my mind. Do you know what I dream of? An A-frame in Colorado, everything white, walls of windows, and a futon on the floor."

Catherine laughed. "I used to have dreams like that, too, especially when the children were little. Well, you can always come back and have your pick here, you know."

"I'll come out anyway tomorrow. Right after lunch. I'd like to talk to you. Without Mother and Dad around. They can show Ned the city. Will you have time for a nice long talk?"

"I'll make time. It's just what I want, Ann."

Her family, coolly civil, left to drive back into the city. Kit made a fire in the library while Catherine brought in sandwiches and coffee. Kit ate, but Catherine was too tired and overwrought to be hungry; she kicked off her shoes and stretched out on the sofa. For a while they simply sat in companionable silence, watching the flames.

"I'm exhausted, Kit," Catherine said finally. "I'm so sad that Kathryn's dead, yet so happy that she left Everly to me — I can't think straight."

Kit moved over from his chair to sit on the sofa. He wrapped his arms around Catherine and held her against him. "You need a good night's sleep."

"I haven't even cried for Grandmother yet — "

"You will, honey." He stroked her hair.

"I have to hire someone to replace Carla and Shelly."

"That can wait."

"And I've been thinking — what would you do if I said I wanted to sell Blooms and the White River house and spend all my time restoring Everly?"

"You can't turn that mind of yours off, can you? That's a radical proposition. If it's what you want, of course we could work it out. I certainly wouldn't mind selling White River now that the children are older. I'd be less inclined to sell Blooms; you'd better give some serious thought to that."

"Oh, I know you're right. I can't imagine life without Blooms. But I'd love to have a long stretch of time to devote to this house and the gardens."

"Then that's what you should do. But you know eventually you'd get bored out here away from the city."

Catherine twisted on the sofa into a tighter embrace around Kit. "Thank God you're here. I couldn't live without you, Kit."

"You won't have to."

"Oh, gross, they're kissing!" Andrew said to Lily as they stood watching from the library door.

"The video's over," Lily said.

"Come sit by the fire," Catherine told them.

It was late. Andrew and Lily talked about the latest school news and what they hoped to do at Christmas vacation, then Catherine and Kit marshaled everyone off to bed. Catherine had had the local help air out and dust the rooms and put on clean sheets. But as she curled next to Kit in an old lumpy double bed that seemed claustrophobically narrow compared with their king-size mattress, she saw cobwebs in the high corners of the room, draped from the elaborate molding. In another corner the wallpaper was rust-stained and peeling from an old water leak. This house needed so much work, and on that thought she fell asleep.

The next day Catherine cooked everyone blueberry pancakes and bacon before Kit drove the children back to their boarding schools.

"The blueberries are from these gardens," she told her children. "We picked them just a few months ago, and froze them, remember? I was just thinking — that entire area has been overgrown with honeysuckle and weeds. If we cleaned it out, we could plant more berries and some fruit trees."

She didn't miss the look of affectionate amusement her children exchanged.

"Don't lose your mind out here all alone, Mom," Andrew said, hugging Catherine good-bye.

"Yeah, keep cool," Lily said.

"I'll call you tonight from White River," Kit said, kissing Catherine good-bye. "Now you'll have a good long stretch of peace and quiet."

"Yes, after Ann comes out. Have a safe trip."

It was delicious being in the large house alone that stormy autumn day. Catherine showered and dressed, washed up the breakfast dishes, and made a fire in the library. She made a proper tea for Ann and kept it warming in a pot under a cozy and put biscuits and cookies from the funeral reception on Kathryn's old floral china. It was a difficult house for one family, Catherine realized as she worked, bringing cups, plates, and tea things in from the kitchen. It was too big. She felt as if she needed roller skates. If a door were put in at the other end of the library, it would be much easier to move from library to kitchen without walking down the long hall.

The library had been dusted, the rugs and carpets vacuumed, some of the brass and silver polished. But the corners of the room were high, dark, and dusty. Paint, soap, new drapes, new everything, Catherine was thinking, and then Ann arrived.

Ann sat by the fire in a pretty pale blue wool dress and her good sensible shoes. Catherine sat across from her in her jeans and white shirt and black cardigan and poured tea.

"Now," she said when they'd settled in, "what first? I'll have the Audubons packed and shipped to you soon."

"There's no hurry!" Ann said. "Honestly, Catherine. I'd just as soon sell them, but we don't need the money. I know I should care about handing on to our children something from my side of the family — and I do care. I just feel so overwhelmed by *things*. But I don't want to talk about that. I want to talk about what a brat I was before I married Ned. I know I owe you an apology. I *was* a selfish little pig, you were right. I was just so desperate to marry him, then, and you seemed so rich. But my actions were inexcusable."

Catherine smiled. "Settle back, Annie, and let me tell you a story. . . ."

Ann tucked her feet under her, curled up on the sofa, and listened with increasing amazement as Catherine told her about the time, years ago, when she had blackmailed P. J. Willington. Because of the cold wind howling outside, shaking the windows, clattering the tree limbs, and the great hearty fire inside, she took her time. She described it, leaving nothing out in detail — Helen Norton, the bruises, the flowers, the photographs, the phone calls, Macy's, the money in a paper bag.

"One thing I did with the money was to buy Blooms," Catherine said. "But I also paid your tuition at Miss Brill's. And Shelly's college tuition, while he was there. And your college tuition. I never told you because . . . well, I thought it would hurt Dad's feelings if you knew he didn't pay your tuition. Ann, the only people I've ever told about this are Kit and Leslie. I never want my children to know."

Ann looked stunned. "That's so awful, Catherine, so awful. I'm so sorry. I don't know what to say. I can't believe you risked so much for me." She sat in silence for a while, staring at the fire. Then she asked, "Why are you telling me now?"

"I don't really know," Catherine said. "I guess because of Shelly, because of what you must have heard from Shelly. I mean, he was stealing money from Blooms in a scheme with one of my employees, *and* he was using GardenAir to ship over his own supply of cocaine. Yet he and Mother and Dad are angry with *me* for firing him. In their eyes I'll always be the guilty one. I had thought, for a long while, that I'd — oh, I don't know. Rescue Shelly. Change Shelly. I even thought I had, for a while. But I was wrong." Catherine began to cry. "I have always, *always,* wanted to help you and Shelly. I have never wanted to hurt you. I did what I could. But now it seems it was never enough."

Ann moved across to sit next to her sister. She put her arm around Catherine's shoulders. "I'm so sorry. It makes me feel even worse about how ungrateful I was — and I'm grateful for what you did."

"Thanks." Catherine sniffed. "I'm glad you said that, but I didn't tell you to make you feel worse. I just needed you to know."

"Here," Ann said, drawing an invisible pie in the air and cutting herself a large piece. "I'm taking this much of the guilt onto myself. Okay?"

Catherine laughed. "Okay. Thanks. I feel better!"

"Oh, I've got my own guilt collection," Ann said. "Nothing as remarkable as yours, but — " And she told Catherine about the times she'd lost her temper with her children or secretly wanted to spit at Elizabeth, about the times she had wickedly manipulated Ned into doing something she wanted but his mother opposed.

"I never imagined your life could be so complicated!" Catherine said. "But of course it would be unrealistic, I suppose, to expect you would all live in Everly in perfect peace."

"Perfect peace!" Ann laughed. "Some months I think we're a family right out of Agatha Christie! Madeline's getting imperious and dotty in her old age and gets upset if any of the routines of the household are changed, no matter how cumbersome they are or how helpful a change would be. God help us if we move a vase one inch on a table! And Hortense and Elizabeth are always squabbling; they can't agree on anything."

"Really! I'm so glad to hear that! It's nice to know other families have their problems living together. Tell me more!" Catherine said greedily.

Ann grinned. "Let's see . . . Ned's doing so well with the mysteries that we don't need to run it as a bed-and-breakfast anymore, but Hortense and Elizabeth and their husbands have devoted their lives to it, so we can hardly kick them out. Madeline's made it clear that when she dies it will pass completely to Ned and to me, but we have a responsibility to the others. There are lots of changes I'd like to make in the gardens, but you know they've always been Hortense's territory, and she gets wild if I suggest a change."

Ann talked about her in-laws, and Catherine responded with anecdotes about hers, and as the sisters sat by the fire in the dark room on that cold day, comparing the complications of family life, they had never been closer, or so happy together, in their lives.

Finally Ann said she had to get back to the city. She helped Catherine carry the tea things down the long hallway, then they went together to the front door.

"One more question," Catherine said as Ann pulled on her coat. "Are you upset that you didn't inherit this Everly, or part of it?"

"God, no! Believe me, one Everly is more than enough for me. Besides, I truly feel at home there. And I know you've always loved this place. What are your plans for it?"

"I'm going to restore it. I promised Grandmother I would. I want to do it right. It will take buckets of time and money, though. How I'm going to juggle Blooms and Everly, I don't know. I've got some serious thinking to do."

"Whatever you do, it'll be right," Ann said. "I've always admired you, you know. The way you just plunge in and make things work. It's helped me have the courage to live my life."

"Oh, Ann, what a wonderful thing for you to say. Thank you." Catherine pulled her sister to her. Then Ann turned her coat collar up against the wind and ran out to her car. A moment later she was gone, and Catherine was alone in the vast rambling house — in *her* house.

She wandered up to the third floor, pausing in each bedroom, looking out the windows at the darkening November sky. It was a source of deep pleasure for her that Andrew and Lily were carelessly, comfortably secure in their family, always inviting friends home from boarding school for long weekends and holidays. If they made a few of the small bedrooms into one large game room, they could put in a Ping-Pong and pool table and one of those computers Andrew and his friends loved so much. For that matter they could have a tennis court built over where the ground was flat and shady; both children would love that. She'd talk to Kit about it; she'd hire a decorator to overlook the renovations and the refurbishing of the old rooms.

For what she really cared about was not the interior of Everly, but the untamed land spreading out from the formal gardens she knew and loved. Almost five acres of luxuriant land, overgrown with weeds, brambles, saplings, woods. Every day she heard about floriculturists coming up with new breeds and strains of bulbs and seeds and flowers; it would be fun to cultivate the land and use it for experimental planting. She wanted a large plot of herbs right away; some of her clients were already getting interested in what could be recycled, and only two weeks ago she'd used potted herbs as table decorations at a luncheon party. That had been wildly successful. And there was Jean-Paul Michette, the chef who had come to her for edible flowers with which he could embellish his newest dishes; so far she had supplied him only with what she knew was safe — violets, pansies, and nasturtiums from Kathryn's gardens, where no chemical pesticides had been used. It would be interesting to see what other clever, delicious delicacies she could discover.

She could use a specialist. Well, Everly was certainly large enough to house a resident floriculturalist or two and a decent working lab. At last she could have her greenhouse. For years she'd been toying with the idea of creating her own potpourri to sell under the Blooms label, something completely original, tangy, and distinctive; out here she could find the room to dry flowers, herbs, and fruits and experiment until she found the perfect fragrance. Last month the owner of an upscale health food store had asked her for something unique and enduring to decorate his walls: she had glazed loaves of breads that were twisted or knotted in appealing ways, entwined them with sprays of wheat and grasses, and sprayed the arrangements with a protective glaze of glossy acrylic. The result had been surprisingly attractive; what other objects could she use as dried-art arrangements for her clients? There wasn't room enough to experiment at Blooms, but there was room here.

Catherine made a pot of coffee, stoked up the fire in the library, and sat for a long time with pen and paper, making lists until the telephone broke into her thoughts. It was Kit, safely back at White River after delivering the children to school.

"How are you?" he asked.

"Actually, I'm disgustingly happy," Catherine said. "I suppose I should be ashamed of myself." She told him about her plans and listened carefully to his response and suggestions. They talked for a long time. Not until he relayed the various phone messages on the answering machine did she feel the weight of the day fall upon her, but when he mentioned the people who had called to extend sympathy about Kathryn's death and the business briefs from Sandra or Jason, exhaustion finally hit.

After they said good night, she rose to pile a triangle of great fat logs on the andirons; that should burn for hours. She had no desire to sleep alone in any of the dusty bedrooms tonight, and the library was warm and fragrant from the maple and applewood that had been burning all day. Its scent was companionable, soothing. The sofa was just as comfortable as the old beds. From the back of the sofa she took a Hudson Bay wool blanket Kathryn had often used as a lap rug, tucked it around her feet, and curled up on the sofa, her head on a needlepointed pillow. Reaching up, she switched off the brass lamp on the end table.

Now shadows leapt on all the walls as the fire flared in the darkened room. She snuggled into the old soft cushions, feeling completely at home, remembering days when she had been very young, before Shelly or Ann had been born, when her grandmother had let her take her nap here by the fire on rainy Sunday afternoons. Someday she'd be a grandmother — and perhaps she'd have a grandchild who'd carry on her work.

Catherine's eyes flickered and closed. For a while her thoughts danced like the flames. Then she entered that blissful state between wakefulness and sleep, when she knew for certain that her dreams would lift off, as light as fiery ashes whirling up the chimney into the dark night, or wildflower seeds spinning off into the air, to drop through the darkness into the sweet welcoming ground, where, if they were strong, they would take root and bloom.